The Skull Gates

P.G. BADZEY

A STONE OWL PRESS BOOK

ISBN-13: 978-1-7328627-1-5

DEDICATION

To my friends in the Orange County Writers Guild Critique Group:
Leigh Mary
Figgy Bottoms
James Topping
Anita Grazier
Candice Baker Yacono
Liz Ray
Summer Salmon
Ris Fleming
without you and your honest, consistent and insightful critiques, I would be a far lesser writer. Thank you for your kindness, friendship, expertise and humor.

Praise for the Grey Riders Series!

<u>Book 1, Whitehorse Peak</u>

"...Whitehorse Peak excels, standing out from the crowd of fantasy adventures...a riveting, emotionally powerful story line...vibrant with realistic action" – D. Donovan, *Midwest Book Review*

"…an excellent balance of worldbuilding and introduction,…fully lavish and exciting, with atmospheric moments of high, epic fantasy that smack of tradition and the old favorites, but then also more modern inclusions and plenty of witty humor… Highly recommended: fantasy fiction at its best." – K.C. Finn for *Readers Favorite* (5-star review)

<u>Book 2, Eye Of Truth</u>

"…a real treasure … Think Dungeons and Dragons or Tolkien, throw in a dash of Patrick Rothfus … recommended for any reader who enjoys high fantasy spiced with a bit of mystery" — D. Donovan, *Midwest Book Review*

"… a charming and rich tale of magic, loyalty, friendship, and secrets, …. I enjoyed the complexities of the plot and characters, and their development and alterations as secrets are uncovered…good world-building…Danger, action, threats, and camaraderie will keep the reader engaged…" – K.J. Simmill for *Readers Favorite* (5-star review)

<u>Book 3, Helm of Shadows</u>

"…wraps its cloak of fantasy around an atmosphere of mystery and intrigue… Impressively vivid…" — D. Donovan, *Midwest Book Reviews*

"…an even bigger and better addition to the Grey Riders series… Helm of Shadows is an excellent addition that once again lifts the series to new heights: a highly recommended read for fantasy fans everywhere." – K.C. Finn for *Readers Favorite* (5-star review)

<u>Book 4, Assassin Prince</u>

"P.G. Badzey has created a complex, absorbing atmosphere …fast-paced and thoroughly engrossing… a compelling saga… satisfying action… whets the reader's appetite for more to come in later sequels." — D. Donovan, *Midwest Book Reviews*

"I am always delighted to return to the works of author P. G. Badzey and the fantastic Grey Riders series, and this new addition is no exception... As always, the worldbuilding and atmosphere are solid, and the closer we get to what is sure to be an epic conclusion, the less I want the series to end." – K.C. Finn for *Readers Favorite* (5-star review)

CONTENTS

ACKNOWLEDGMENTS

The author would like to acknowledge the following individuals for their
superior contributions:
Eugene Badzey and Dora Badzey for their editing prowess,
Veronica Badzey for typesetting
The Orange County Science Fiction/Fantasy Critique group for their
excellent and valuable insights
and, of course, to the superb writers in the Orange County Writers Guild
for their excellent critique and unwavering support.

"As it is, these remain: faith, hope and love, the three of them; and the greatest of them is love."
– 1 Corinthians 13:13

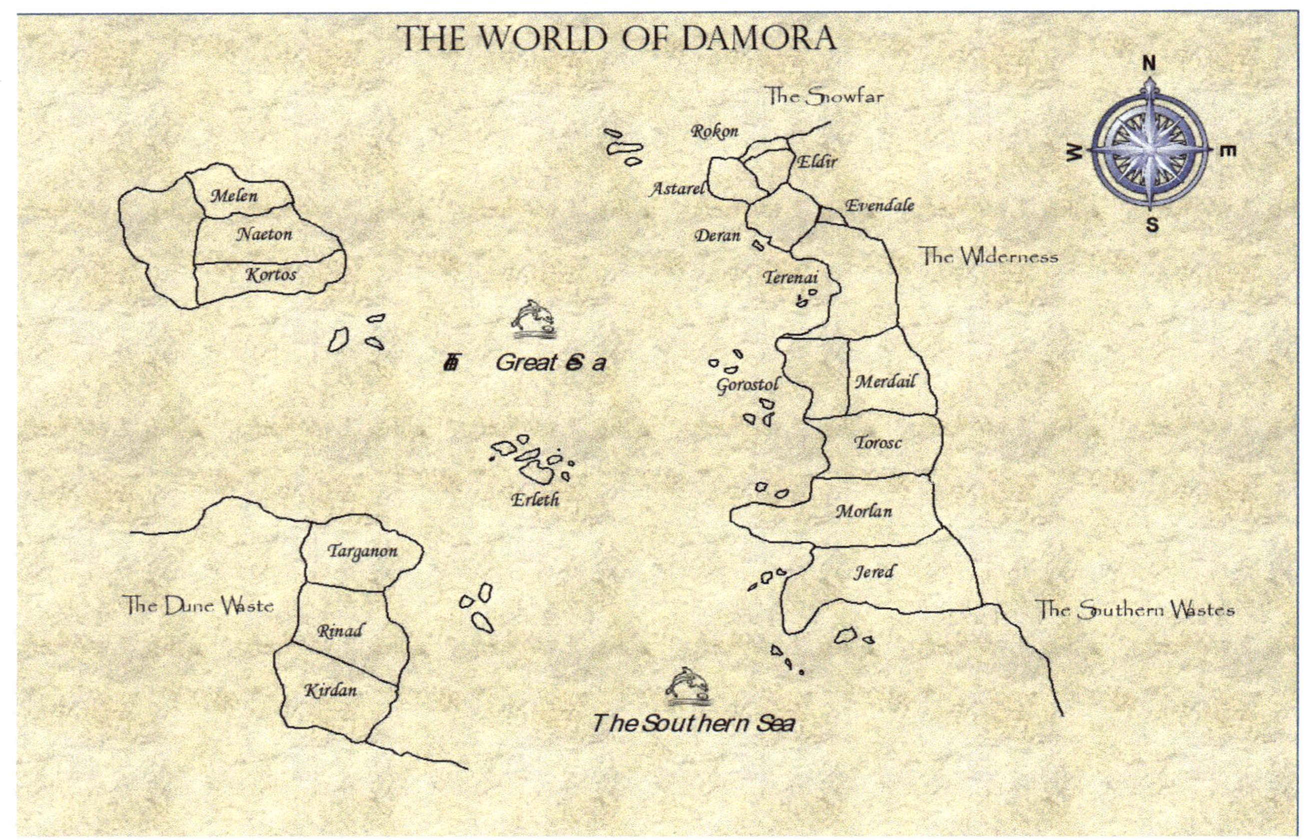
THE WORLD OF DAMORA
N
W
S
E
The Snowfar
Rokon
Eldir
Astarel
Evendale
Deran
The Wilderness
Terenai
Merdail
Gorostol
Torosc
Morlan
Jered
The Southern Wastes
Melen
Naeton
Kortos
The Great Sea
Erleth
The Dune Waste
Targanon
Rinad
Kirdan
The Southern Sea

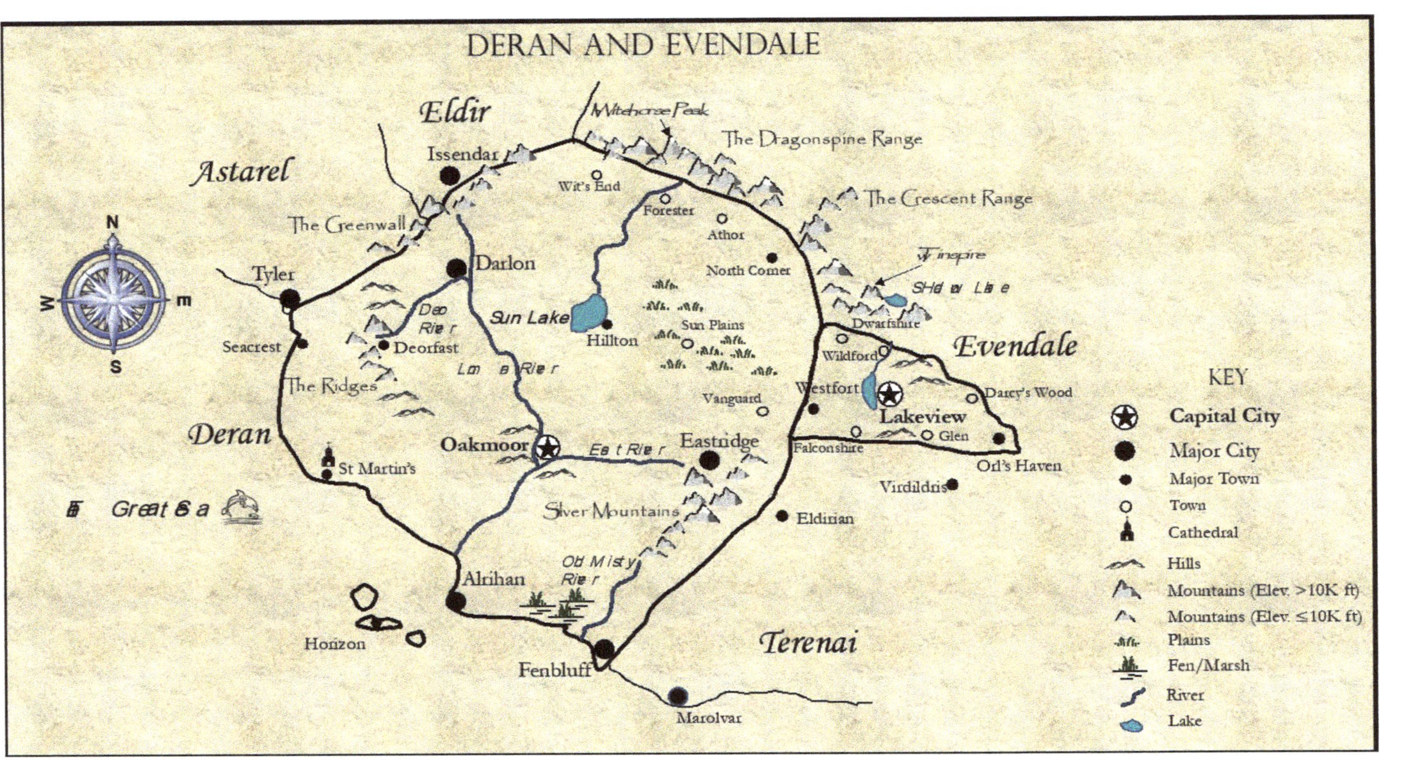

DERAN AND EVENDALE
Astarel
Eldir
Witchorse Peak
The Dragonspine Range
The Crescent Range
Issendar
Wit's End
Forester
Athor
Tyler
The Greenwall
Darlon
Deo River
Sun Lake
North Corner
Spire
Shadow Lake
Dwarfshire
Evendale
Seacrest
Deorfast
Hillton
Sun Plains
Wildford
Westfort
Lakeview
Darcy's Wood
The Ridges
Lone River
Vanguard
Glen
Orl's Haven
Deran
Oakmoor
East River
Eastridge
Falconshire
Virdildris
St Martin's
Silver Mountains
Eldirian
Great Sea
Old Misty River
Alrihan
Terenai
Horizon
Fenbluff
Marolvar
KEY
Capital City
Major City
Major Town
Town
Cathedral
Hills
Mountains (Elev. >10K ft)
Mountains (Elev. ≤10K ft)
Plains
Fen/Marsh
River
Lake
N
S
E
W

THE ELVEN EMPIRE OF TERENAI

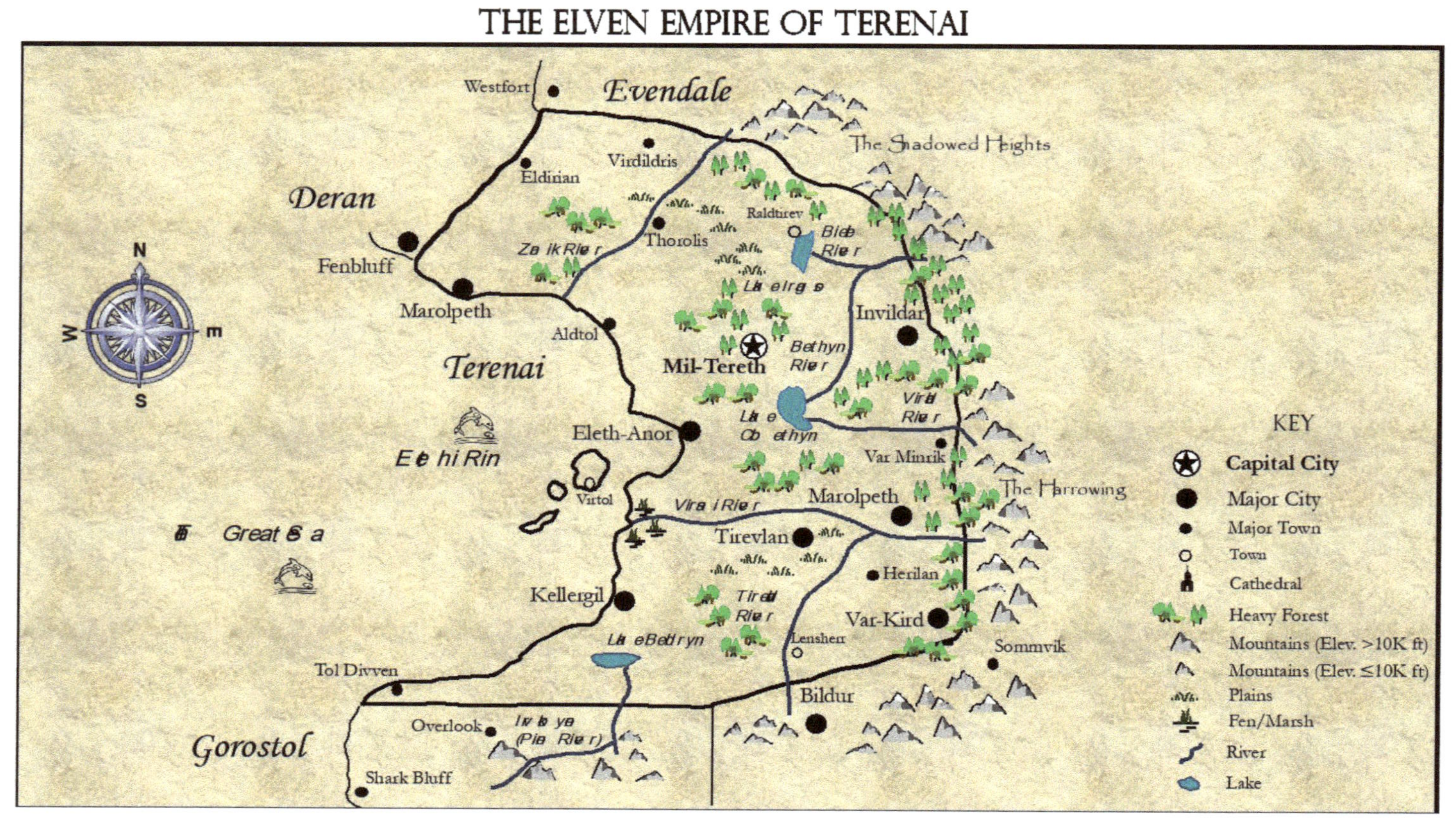

THE REPUBLIC OF GOROSTOL

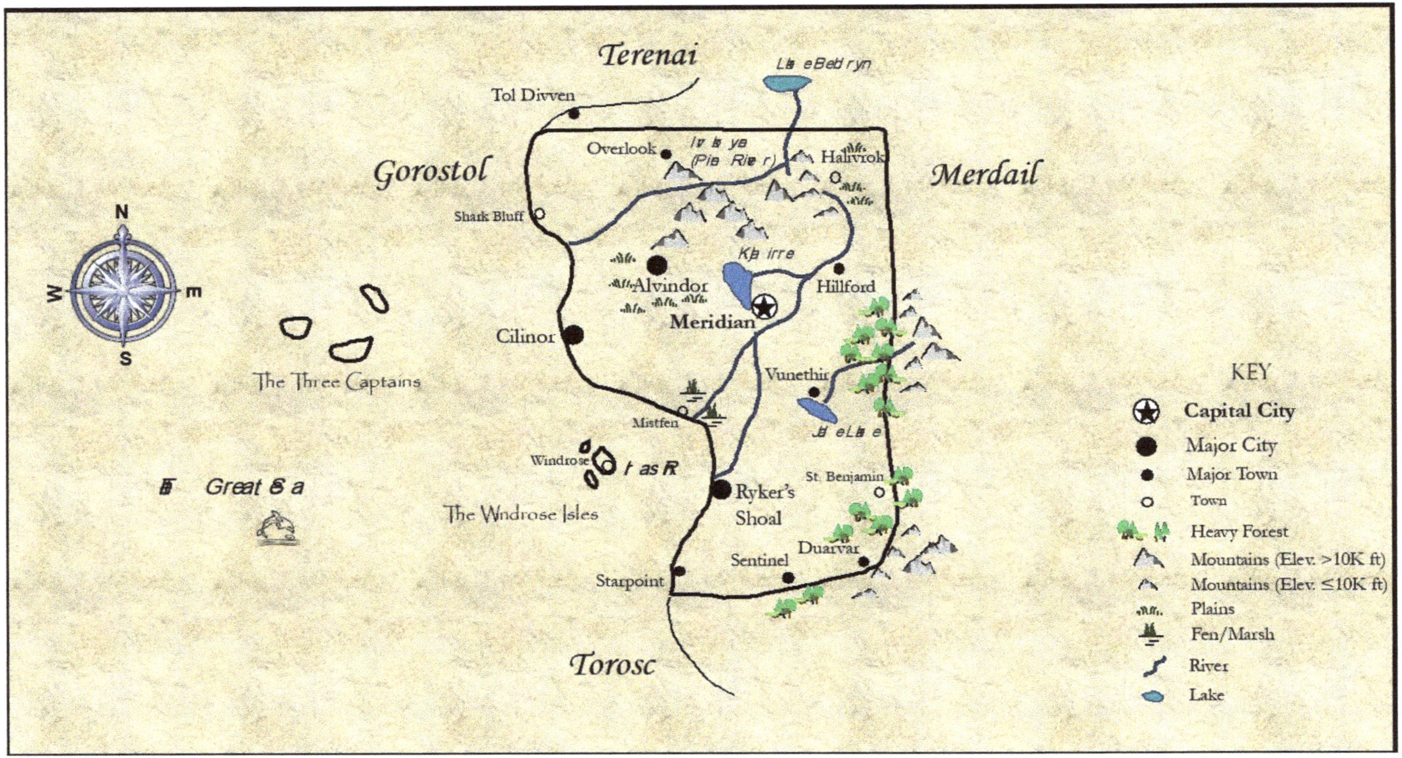

THE REPUBLIC OF TOROSC

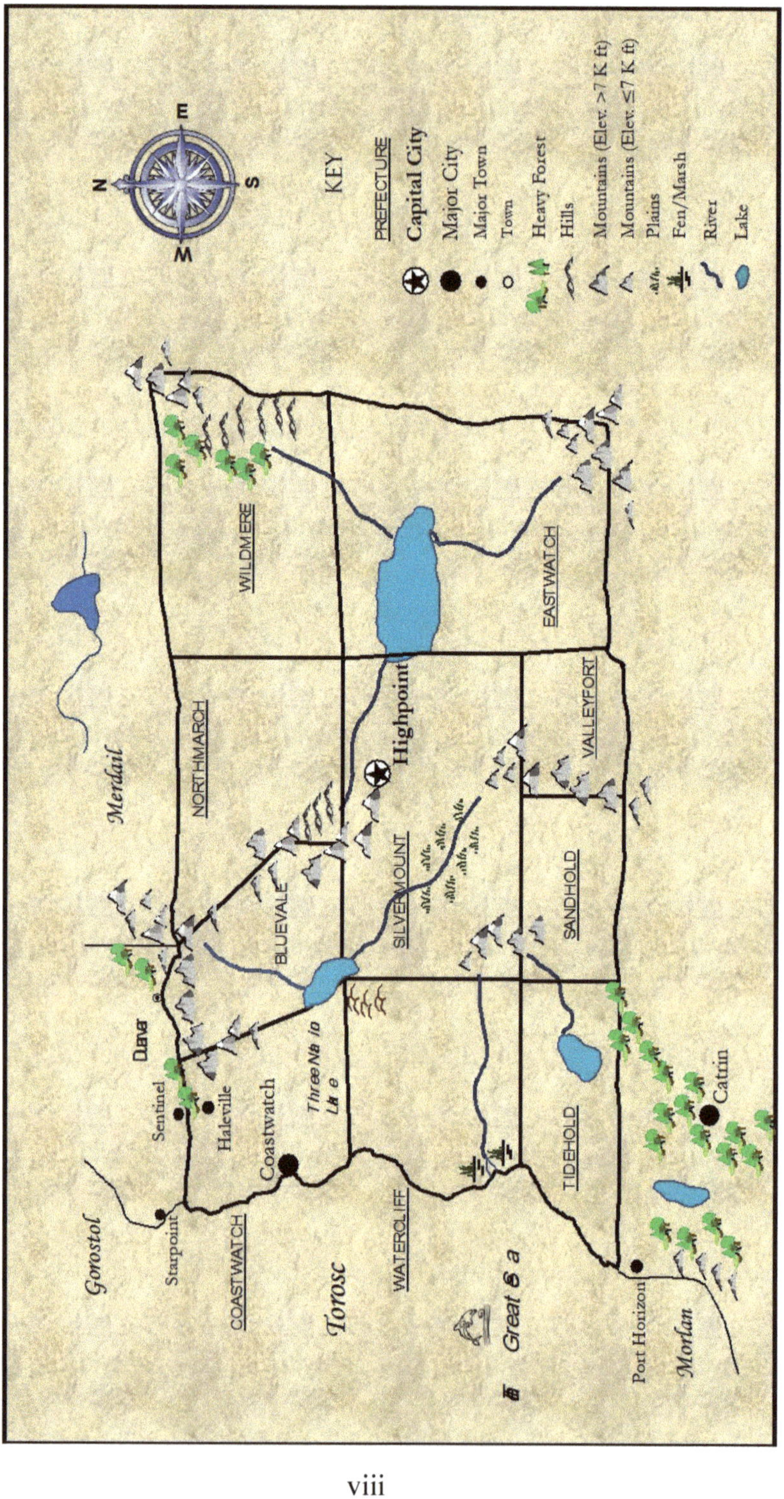

COASTWATCH PREFECTURE, TOROSC

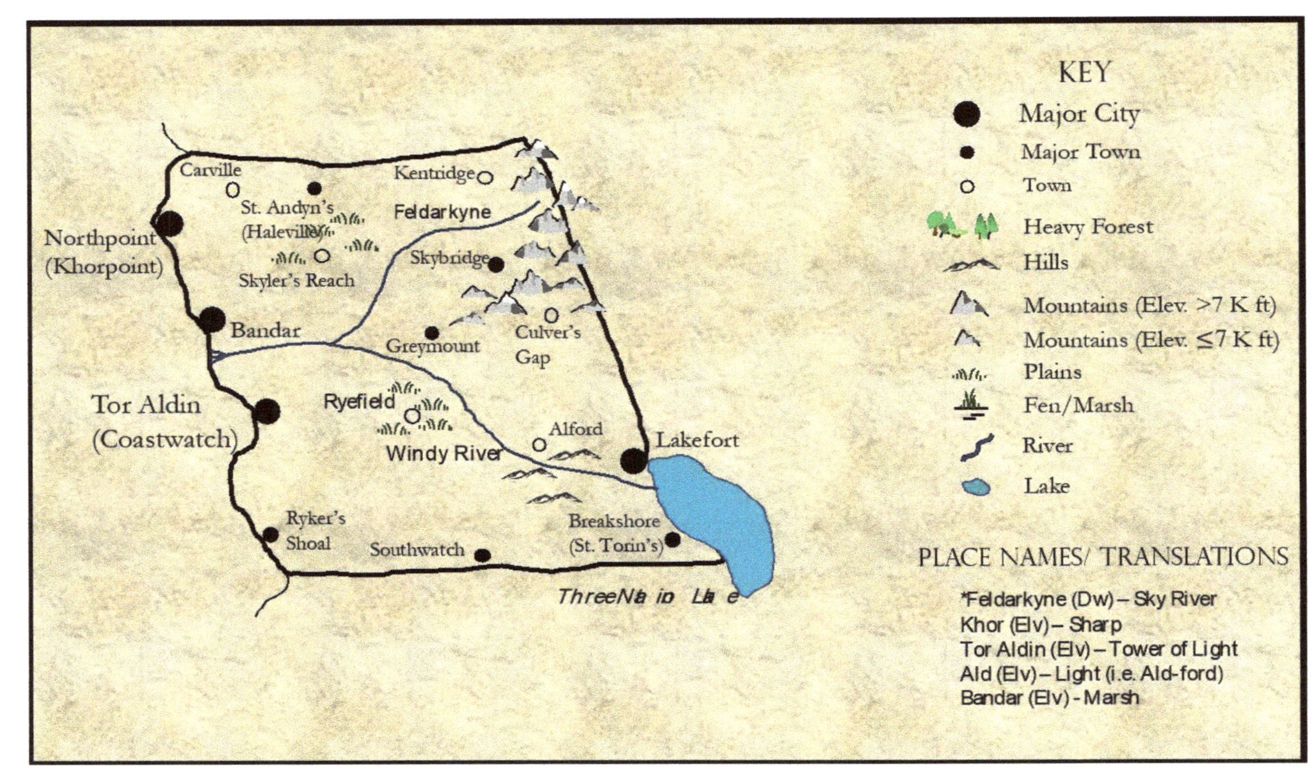

Chapter One - Surprises

"When Nature holds its breath, be watchful," Eric Indidarc murmured.

He crouched against a willow tree behind a screen of shrubs, waiting. The misty forest remained still. The scent of earth, humus and wet leaves hung in the breezeless air.

The arboreal splendor of the woods would have been impressive if Eric could actually see much of it. Now, it just looked like a dark mass of towering trunks, undergrowth, leaves and overarching branches among banks of thick fog. The light of early morning glowed behind the grayness.

Nothing moved. His hand went to a tiny silver crucifix on a chain around his neck.

Many weeks now, and no word, no letters. Where are you, Brandawyn?

If he closed his eyes, he could see her athletic figure and beautiful face, her violet eyes and strawberry blonde hair. He remembered the shape of her ears —just like his, with a slight point at the top—and her pert little nose.

His throat tightened.

Eric shook his head. If he didn't focus, he ran the risk of getting ambushed while worrying about her.

Besides, what would she think of me daydreaming about her?

He knew just what she would say. He could almost hear her voice: *"Snap out of it, Eric. Stop gathering wool, destroy the Skull Gate, and come find me..."*

He reached for a silver, hawk-shaped brooch at the collar of his cloak. It tingled with magic under his fingertips.

He paused for a moment, listening, then brought the brooch to his mouth.

"Stealth," he whispered, holding out his left arm. The silver bauble glowed a soft white, then grew and transformed into a brown hawk with black-tipped feathers. It alighted on his outstretched arm, talons gripping Eric's tooled leather vambrace.

Eric smiled. At first glance, Stealth appeared like a normal hawk. If he inspected it very closely, he could see the thin seams, tiny fasteners, and miniscule hinges. Eyes made of tiger-eye jewels peered at him.

If nothing else, its weight would have told him it wasn't a mere bird.

"Go," he said. The bird-golem launched into the air, soaring between the trees.

Eric took a breath and concentrated. He closed his eyes and reached out with his mind. His vision swirled and shifted and he now saw through Stealth's eyes.

The hawk golem drifted over the fog-shrouded woods. After some time, Eric saw his objective: an overgrown glade with a ruined tower. He guided Stealth to land in a tree about two hundred yards away and waited, watching.

Shapes moved among the crumbling walls and vegetation.

Eight human males in dark-enameled scale mail gathered near the tower. Eric spied the insignia on their shields: a fanged daemon-head in red and white on a black background. The warriors wore helms painted to look like human skulls.

"Skullhead Legionaries," Eric muttered, gritting his teeth.

Four lithe figures of elves joined the Skullheads, carrying longbows. A few moments later, two hulking shapes thumped out from the shadows of the tower.

Bull-satyrs...

The giant creatures stood at least seven feet tall. Their bovine heads swiveled this way and that, beady eyes shining, horns gleaming dully. They stalked among the boulders and shrubs. Like their companions, they wore black scale mail, the lower portions shaped to fit their goat hindquarters and legs.

Eric focused Stealth's eyes at the top of the tower. It looked like it had collapsed or been sheared off, probably by a siege engine shot or magical strike. A remnant of the wall faced him and hid the topmost floor.

He frowned. Stealth allowed him to see with all the acuity of a raptor's eyes. It did not, however, allow him to see through stone.

He considered commanding Stealth to fly closer or to soar above, but one look at the elves and their bows dissuaded him. If they were halfway competent, they could hit Stealth or at least be alerted that someone spied on them. If Stealth were damaged severely, it would be very expensive and time-consuming to get it repaired.

"Well, this just got more tangled," Eric said to himself. He called Stealth to return and shifted his vision back.

Eric and his companions needed to get into that tower without allowing any of the guards to escape and warn others. He considered various possibilities in his head. Judging by their equipment, the Skullheads and their allies weren't just on a raiding mission. They were there specifically to guard something.

With a rush of wings, Stealth alighted on Eric's arm. He whispered another word and the construct became a brooch again.

Eric slipped back through the forest, making for a knoll topped by a stand of oaks. He paused by a particularly large tanrin bush.

A male half-elf in a camouflage cloak slipped out from behind a tree, lowering his composite short bow. He wore dark brigandine and carried a sword and dagger.

"See anything?" Khyron Demaris asked, sea-green eyes scanning the forest.

"Plenty. Where's Andyn?"

"Back at the clearing, sending the pegasi to a safe place. She'll be back in a minute."

Eric nodded. "The others?"

"On a hill about a quarter of a mile back, hidden among a group of boulders. We'll rejoin them as soon as she returns."

Khyron drifted into the foliage. Eric hid behind the veiling branches of a weeping willow.

It wasn't long before Khyron alerted him. "She's back."

Eric drew back deeper into the trees. A trim, golden-haired half-elven woman joined them. Chainmail armor glittered under a green-mottled cloak and she bore two maces at her belt.

"All set," she said in a mellow alto. She reached out her hand and Khyron took it, planting a kiss on the back of her glove. She smiled at him.

"Everything set?" asked Eric.

She nodded. "I saw the direction the pegasi headed. It will be easy to signal them to return."

Something in her demeanor made Eric pause. Khyron measured her with his eyes. "And?"

She opened her mouth, then closed it. After a few heartbeats, she removed a glove and laid her bare hand on a tree trunk. Her lips moved in silent prayer and her fingertips glowed light blue. The air tingled.

"Something evil has come to the woods," she whispered. "I felt it out there when I sent the pegasi away. The animals and plants feel it too."

"Anything specific?" Khyron asked.

She shook her head. "Something menacing. That's all."

Eric and Khyron exchanged a look. Without another word, they slipped into the forest. Khyron led and Andyn and Eric followed.

Eric watched their back trail. Near the base of a hill, Khyron stopped them.

"Someone's coming," he whispered, disappearing between two trees. Andyn scrambled for cover in the nearby bushes. Her hands went to her weapons.

Eric crouched behind a raspberry thicket, bow at the ready. He relaxed when a familiar figure emerged from the woods.

Darius Cabot clambered over a boulder with the barest clink of chainmail armor, a bow in his hand. A human male who stood about as tall as Eric, he had dark hair and a sturdy, lean build. The hilt of a bastard sword poked up over one shoulder and he wore a camouflage cloak just like Eric's. Dark eyes sparked with recognition when he saw them.

Andyn stood, her face showing both relief and petulance. "You know, you rangers are getting as impossible to detect as Connor."

"Damned right. Wait." Dar raised an eyebrow. "Was that a compliment? This early in the morning?"

"Consider yourself blessed," Khyron replied with a wink at Andyn.

"Did you see anything?" Eric asked.

"No," Dar said. "Nothing but more forest and fog. You?"

Khyron jerked his head at Eric. "Eric did, but we'd better get to the others and tell the tale just once."

Dar nodded and joined the group as they headed off once more. Soon, the forest thinned and they clambered uphill to a cluster of boulders.

Two more of Eric's friends stood guard among the massive stones, watching the forest, bows at the ready. Connor Lomin stood next to Buckminster Bydecy. He wore black leather armor under his cloak and carried a heavy broadsword. Though his head barely came up to Buck's waist, he was considered a bit on the tall side, for a halfling. Connor said something to Buck that Eric couldn't make out.

Buck shrugged and replied in a low voice. He adjusted his sword belt. Easily the tallest of the Riders, the sandy-haired human towered over all of them. Lazy brown eyes made him look like he was bored with the proceedings.

His banded armor and helmet gleamed in the dim light. The helmet was unusual: a metal arm curved over one side, terminating just above the crown in a metal fitting with a flat clear gem.

Both of them spun when Khyron ghosted out of the nearby trees, then lowered their bows.

Buck gave them a sidelong look, then lifted his boot onto a nearby rock. "You know," he remarked to no one in particular, "for a famous group of knights and mages who ride winged horses, we sure end up tramping around in the bushes a lot. We're the Grey Riders, not the Grey Hikers."

That got a chuckle from the others.

"Quit your griping, Buck," Eric said. "You just like complaining."

Buck glanced at him and stretched. "You try riding three hundred miles in banded armor, Eric. I'm surprised I still sacrifice for you smaller, weaker people. Maybe I need a bigger percentage of the take."

Andyn rolled her eyes.

"Find anything?" asked Connor.

"Apparently, Eric did," Dar said.

"Good. Let's hear it." The halfling bounded up onto a giant rock and sat with his legs swinging over the edge like a boy.

They all congregated at the center of the boulders. Eric related what he had seen through Stealth's eyes.

Dar frowned, fitting a helmet on his head. "And we're sure this is the right place, Khyron?" He flipped up the hood of his cloak.

"The Blue Mark was adamant," Khyron replied. "His scouts saw figures in dark armor leading some large creatures that carried crates on their backs. It's been going on for weeks, so they said."

"But how do we know they headed here?" Connor asked.

"It fits the pattern of what the scouts said to look for," Khyron answered. "The bull-satyrs are certainly big enough to carry the containers they were talking about. And the tower is in a glade at least forty miles from the nearest town. It's a good hiding place for a Skull Gate."

"If the Ja'al have a Skull Gate here —" Dar began.

"— and we don't know that they do," Andyn interrupted, amber eyes flashing. "But, if they do, we will destroy it."

They stood in silence.

We might be near a Skull Gate, Eric thought. The very idea knotted his stomach and he shuddered. *What if there is one here, already operational? What if they open the gate and bring in daemons? We've never fought them before.*

Tavern tales of nightmares from a hellish, alien world flashed in his brain. He shook himself to clear his thoughts.

"Okay, Khyron," he said, "you're the point this time. What's the plan?"

Khyron held out a hand. "Andyn, do you have an extra parchment?"

She nodded, reaching into a shoulder bag and giving him paper and a charcoal pencil. With Eric feeding him information, Khyron sketched the glade. He pointed at the tower with the pencil.

"That's the key," he said. "If that is the location of a Skull Gate and we threaten it, they will retreat to protect it. It's only about forty feet or so to the tower from the tree line on the far side. Connor, you're with me. We infiltrate the area and hide in the forest."

Connor flipped up his hood. "I'll take the east and you can get the north."

"Agreed," Khyron replied. "Andyn, you have the most magical firepower, so you will need a clear line of sight to the tower if the Ja'al retreat to defend it."

Buck ran a hand over his jaw as he perused the map. "You think they'll retreat if Andyn starts flinging fire bolts and lightning at the tower?" he mused. "I doubt it. Likely as not, they'll stick you with arrows until the bull-satyrs get there to mash you into paste."

Khyron shook his head. "That's where the rest of you come in. Buck, you and Dar and Eric will advance in front of Andyn. Make it look like you're unaware of the location of the tower. Knowing Skullheads, they'll attack on sight. Then Connor and I will strike from hiding."

Dar frowned. "I still don't like that tower. The top is, what, twenty feet in diameter? They could be hiding anything up there. A ballista team, wizards, you name it."

"I'll keep the Eye of Truth handy," Buck said. He rotated the metal arm of his helmet so that the gemstone rested a couple of inches in front of his right eye. The jewel glittered with a rainbow of colors from deep within.

"Just in case they try hiding something from us," he added.

"Great," Khyron announced, giving Andyn's hand a squeeze. "Let's get this done."

She winked at him, then raised her hands, chanting softly. Glimmering nets of blue, green, gold and silver floated down on them in rapid succession and dissipated.

Eric felt a surge of magical energies cover him. He called Stealth from its brooch and sent it skyward, winging back to its previous vantage point. He reached to his belt and unsheathed a dagger with a blade that resembled a spear head.

"Fidelis," he whispered. The dagger's handle lengthened and grew. He now held an infantry spear about six feet long. Elven runes ran along a haft inlaid with silver patterns and the spearhead glittered with orange light.

He drew a short sword from its scabbard with his other hand. "I'll watch for you with Stealth," he told Connor. "What signal this time?"

The halfling pursed his lip. "I'll make a branch wave three times on the east side of the glade."

He and Khyron slipped away into the woods. In the span of a few heart-beats, they vanished as if they had never been there.

"I'm glad they're on our side," muttered Buck.

Despite all their mutual teasing and jokes, Eric knew who were the masters of stealth in their strike team. He grinned. "They *are* on our side. Unless we're playing cards."

Buck smirked.

They waited. Eric used Stealth's superior visual capability to keep an eye on the Ja'al cultists near the tower. As far as he could tell, they kept a watchful eye on the clear space before the structure.

Something bothered Eric. *Why aren't they patrolling near the tower itself?*

He bit his lip, unable to forestall a gnawing worry. Then he saw a branch on the far side of the glade wave three times.

"Let's go."

Buck hefted an ornate longsword etched with dwarven runes on the hilt. He strode forward, shield up.

Dar and Eric marched alongside him, trying to appear alert yet relaxed. Dar shifted his bastard sword to the front and laid a hand on the hilt.

Eric shifted his gaze again. The tall grass in the glade wavered and a slim black ferret scampered towards the Ja'al contingent. It stopped before one of the Skullheads. Eric's mouth set in a grim line and his eyes narrowed.

The enemy warrior made a motion with his hand and the ferret glittered, then vanished in a cloud of sparks. A brooch on the Skullhead's tunic glowed in response.

"They have a Companion Pin like Stealth," he said to the other Riders. "It's a ferret. We've been spotted."

"Well, that's great," Dar muttered.

The Skullhead with the companion pin beckoned to his compatriots. They all gathered together, then split apart, the elves dispersing to the undergrowth on either side of the tower. The humans lifted their shields, drew swords and scurried out to hide behind trees. The bull-satyrs thudded around to the far side of the tower.

Eric related the enemy positioning to the other Riders. "Remember, pretend that we don't know what's going on."

It took a lot for them to play their part, but Eric and his friends managed to act like they didn't know about the ambush until they broke past the treeline outside the glade. Eric's heart pounded in his chest despite their careful planning and his hands grew clammy.

The attack came quickly. With a shout, the humans charged out from their cover, swords held high and shields up. Arrows whined through the air from the hidden elves.

Eric shifted his gaze back from Stealth's vision and dodged an arrow. Buck crouched. Three arrows hit his shield. Dar sidestepped and a pair of shafts sang by harmlessly, but one glanced off his leg armor with a flash of red fire. He drew his sword and a black blade flashed in the dim morning sun.

Andyn drew a mace from her belt and pointed towards one side of the glade. She shouted an arcane word and a ball of fire arced from her hand towards a pair of the elves. The fireball detonated with a thunderous boom, hurling the archers back amid a cloud of flaming wood and leaves. Both elves thumped into nearby trees and crashed to the ground, lifeless.

Connor tumbled out of the bushes near the other two elves, bearing a sword with a fiery edge. He touched something at his left shoulder. A ghostly white sword materialized in front of him, floating in thin air. It slashed at the elves as if wielded by an invisible warrior. The glade rang with curses as the archers drew hand axes. One attacked Connor and the other tried to parry the dancing spectral blade.

The bull-satyrs roared and charged out from behind the ruined tower. Khyron detached from the shadows and followed on their heels, sword and dagger in hand.

The Skullhead Legionaries reached Eric's position and two advanced on him. He forgot everything except his opponents, trusting to his companions to handle their own battles.

Eric feinted to the side, then thrust his sword at one Skullhead's eyes. The other enemy slashed at him. He dodged and deflected the attack with his spear. The Ja'al Legionaries leaped forward with a flurry of cuts and thrusts.

Eric kept his breathing even and his mind focused, dodging when he couldn't block, stabbing and slashing. He always kept one of the warriors behind the other so that they couldn't attack him from two sides at once.

Purple light flared from the Skullheads' black armor each time he scored a hit.

This could be a little harder than I thought.

He leaped backwards, putting distance between them. He thrust his sword into the earth and raised his hand. Faint white light burst from his palm and both Skullheads staggered back, their armor smoking.

They shouted obscene insults and charged anew. This time, Eric's spear punctured scale mail. One of the guards went to a knee, bleeding from his side. The other guard bull-rushed Eric, slamming him back with his shield.

Eric lost his grip on the spear and tumbled backwards, his side aching. The Skullhead continued on, battering and slashing. Eric parried with his sword, then put out his hand.

"Fidelis!"

A glittering shaft of light grew in his palm and he held his spear again. The Skullhead's eyes widened. Eric thrust. His opponent slammed the spear aside with his shield, raising his sword overhead. Eric spun with force of the shield parry, thrusting his sword behind him. With a metallic thunk, he ran the guard through.

He jerked out his blade, looking for his companions.

A sudden motion drew his gaze to the top of the tower.

Damn it! I knew there was something up there.

Then his eyes widened as a horned, reptilian head curved up over the broken wall. Cat-like eyes leered down at him. Scales of reddish-brown gleamed in the wan sunlight and a massive tail lashed the air.

Eric's heart went cold. "Dragon!" he shouted.

The dragon gripped the edge of the tower's surface with taloned fore-claws and unfurled huge bat wings. It was at least thirty feet long. Fiery eyes locked on the Riders with baleful menace. With a roar, it launched itself into the air.

Eric's remaining enemy joined the four surviving Skullheads. They formed a shield wall and marched forward. Dar and Buck gave ground.

"Back to the trees!" Buck ordered. They retreated.

The dragon soared overhead and curved around in a lazy loop, almost as if it didn't really care. Then, it snapped its wings close to its body and dove.

"Khyron! Connor!" Dar shouted. "Pull back to cover!"

Connor had no trouble doing this since he had dropped both his opponents. Khyron spun under an axe swing and leaped up, slashing the throat of the offending bull-satyr. He rolled away as it crashed to the earth. He darted off to join Connor as the remaining satyr snorted and lumbered off in pursuit.

The enemy warriors drew back. The dragon swooped over the glade. Its maw opened and Eric saw raging hellfire. The air reeked of sulfur and acid.

"Together!" Andyn said. Eric jammed his sword into the ground and grasped her hand.

She spoke forceful, strong words. He focused, drawing forth magical power and joining it to hers. A blue hemisphere of energy leaped up over the Riders.

The dragon breathed. A roaring wave of flame shot out at them. It hit the blue globe and curled around it. Eric felt the heat through the magical shield, but it held. Nearby bushes and logs burst into flame, filling the air with wood-smoke and the stink of brimstone. The dragon banked away. It spat another stream of flame at Khyron and Connor as they raced to the edge of the glade.

Heart in his throat, Eric saw both his friends hurl themselves to the side and then scramble to a halt under the nearby trees. The bull-satyr leaped at them through remnants of flaming grass.

The remaining Skullhead Legionaries charged at Eric's group. The next few seconds were occupied with just trying to survive while keeping a weather eye out for the dragon. Eric knew that Khyron and Connor battled the remaining bull-satyr but he couldn't spare them a glance.

"Coming around again!" shouted Buck, slamming aside a Legionary's shield and running him through. Andyn ducked under a slash and crippled a Skullhead with a strike to the leg.

Eric tried to get to Andyn to combine their magical skills again, but their enemies intercepted them with blades and shields. The dragon swooped low for another pass. Just as they did the previous time, the skull-helmed warriors withdrew.

Eric raised his hand and called forth a quartet of acorn-sized comets, aiming them at the approaching dragon. Five more streaked out from Andyn's outstretched fingers.

The fire darts tracked the dragon, hitting it and detonating with sharp cracks. The creature snarled and opened its mouth wide on the approach.

Intense fire shot out at them. Eric waited until the last possible second, then threw himself to the side. He felt Andyn's magical protections waver and vanish and searing pain hit his legs. He struggled to his feet and hurled the spear as the dragon shot past. With a satisfying thunk, it slammed into the beast's side.

The dragon emitted a stone-cracking shriek and veered away.

"Fidelis!" Eric called, holding out his hand. The spear, still penetrating the dragon's hide, glittered and faded. In Eric's fist, a spear-shaped cloud of light answered and in a second he held his weapon again. The dragon climbed, trailing a stream of dark blood.

Now Dar and Buck took the initiative and charged at the warriors, closely followed by Andyn. Swords and maces flashed in the morning mist. Eric spared a glance at his legs. His chainmail was scorched and all that remained of one boot was blackened shreds of leather.

He gritted his teeth against burning pain, but limped forwards to help. Waiting for his opportunity, he ran through a Skullhead with his sword as Andyn smashed him in the nightmare helm with a mace.

"Look out!"

Eric jerked his head up. Connor and Khyron raced towards them as the dragon came by for another run, swooping low.

It was too low. As a matter of fact, its belly skimmed the tall grass in the glade and it landed at a run, charging into Eric and his friends. Buck crouched behind his shield, his sword flaring bright gold.

Eric managed to get his spear up in time to take a shot at a glaring dragon eye before something massive and scaly slammed into him. The world tumbled all around and he lost count of how many stones and branches he hit. Finally, the sky stopped spinning. He groaned, levering himself to his feet and holding onto a nearby tree.

"Fidelis," he whispered and the spear teleported to his hand again.

He stumbled towards the others. Buck picked himself up from a thicket and Dar put a boot onto the dragon's skull, jerking his black sword out from between its eyes. Eric found a largish boulder and plopped on it wearily. A decidedly bruised and bloodied Connor and Khyron joined him.

Andyn came to Eric's side in an instant. "You took quite a pop," she said, replacing her maces and shrugging off her backpack.

He grimaced, feeling the pain of his burns. "At least we don't have to worry about getting roasted."

He took a deep breath, closing his eyes and laying hands on his wounds. He focused, gathering healing power and trying to see his injuries in his mind. He envisioned the burned tissue sloughing off and new muscle and skin growing to replace it. A cooling sensation flowed into his feet and legs. He sighed as the burning pain eased and faded.

He opened his eyes. Andyn gave him a tiny vial of deep purple liquid. She gauged him with a critical eye as he popped out the stopper. "You'll live. I'll go see to the others."

The taste of bacon, lemons and cherries assaulted his tongue and he almost gagged on the potion, but managed to swallow it anyway.

Wizards who make potions are psychotic. I think they invent these flavor combinations so they can laugh themselves silly imagining us trying to choke them down.

Slowly, an invigorating wave of energy flowed through him and he let out a deep breath. The pain receded to a memory, but the fatigue of battle remained.

He assessed his equipment. His armor was scorched and his boots were a total loss, but at least he could walk normally.

A light breeze wafted the odor of burning grass and flesh and dragon stench to him. He wrinkled his nose.

Could have been worse. He stood and joined the others.

Khyron met him first. He removed his scorched cloak and shook it out. His forearm bore a bandage and part of his dark brigandine showed even darker scorch marks.

"Better?" he asked with a raised eyebrow.

"Yes, thanks to your girl," Eric said with a grin.

Khyron opened his mouth for a rejoinder, then shot a glance at Andyn. She knelt next to Buck, her hands glowing mild blue as she held them on his injuries.

"Don't say that out loud for a while, if you don't mind," Khyron said. "We're still, er, working things out."

Eric considered teasing him but relented. Khyron had only recently come back into Andyn Eleandir's life after an absence of several years. It was only natural that the couple had to deal with the intervening separation. That would take time. "Is Connor okay?" he asked.

Khyron nodded towards the smallest member of their group. Connor knelt by the dragon. "You know halflings. Practically indestructible, plus they're so small, it's damned impossible to hit them."

"Being the smallest helps sometimes."

"Connor will never admit to that. He thinks he's our size."

Khyron nodded. Eric thought he looked entirely too serious. "But that won't stop us from making short jokes."

Eric grinned.

The pair rejoined the group around the dead dragon.

"Did you say one of the humans had a companion pin of a ferret?" Andyn asked.

Buck held up a shattered silver brooch. "Well, 'had' is the right word. Sorry, Andyn."

She sighed, disappointed. "I would have liked to have that. I used to have a ferret when I was a kid. I named him Bueller."

Buck gave her a sidelong look. "You had a ferret named Bueller?"

She put her hands on her hips. "Yes, I did. My ferret, Bueller."

Eric decided not to meet Dar's gaze and turned his attention to the dead dragon instead.

"Good shot, Eric," said Connor, rising from inspecting the corpse. "Right through the eye."

"I'm surprised I hit anything," Eric answered.

Dar smiled and finished wiping his bastard sword in the tunic of a Skullhead. The blade shimmered with tiny stars against a night-black surface.

He slipped it back into its sheath. "You made it miss me so I could plant the Starblade in its brain."

"Glad to be of service," Eric said. "Let's get into the tower."

Connor led them to the door at the base of the structure. They waited as the halfling inspected the doorframe, the lock and the area in front of the portal.

"Any traps?" Buck asked. Connor shook his head.

Eric tried to figure out how to make a serviceable pair of boots from the scraps and gave up. He removed his backpack and rummaged in it, coming up with a pair of low shoes for going about town. They were not nearly as protective as the boots but they would have to do.

Connor took out a small packet of tools from his belt purse and had the door lock open in seconds.

Buck stepped inside first. He scanned left and right, the Eye of Truth shining with rainbow colors.

"Clear," he said.

Eric joined the others inside. It was pitch black until Dar called forth a small globe of light in his palm. With a whispered word, he sent it up to hover under the ceiling.

Eric scanned the area. A large number of long boxes lay on the floor and a curving set of steps led to an upper floor.

"Well," Buck said, "No Skull Gate, but three guesses as to what all *that* is for." He nodded at the crates.

"Check it please, Buck," said Andyn.

The tall warrior scanned left and right, the Eye of Truth glittering in its setting.

"Nothing hidden, no illusions. Just the aura of evil, as you'd expect."

Khyron went to guard the steps to the upper floor while Andyn and Dar opened a box.

Eric peered inside and his stomach tightened. Dirty bones gleamed in the magical light. Femurs had been somehow welded together to form long spars. Metal joints and fittings also held sections in place. He counted five skulls before he could take no more and turned away.

Knowing the Ja'al, those bones weren't stolen from a graveyard.

Connor shook his head. "Looks like a staging area. They haven't built anything yet."

Andyn's eyes flared as she gazed at the skulls and bones. "And they won't, if I have anything to say about it."

Buck opened the other boxes. Khyron came to join them, face grim. Andyn sighed and closed her eyes.

"Holy Verian, god of all life and the forests of the world, have mercy on these poor souls slain by the forces of evil," she prayed. "Please know that we mean no irreverence by what we are about to do, but that our actions come from desire to see that they did not die in vain."

Eric added his own prayer. "Give them eternal rest, O Lord, and may your light shine on them forever."

"Amen," murmured Dar.

Andyn hefted her maces. "Let's make sure this never becomes a Skull Gate…"

Chapter Two – Alliances of Old

"Druidess Carine Del Rio to see you, Your Excellency."

"Show her in, Lawrence. And make sure we are not disturbed."

The blue-liveried servant bowed and departed.

Lady Arlene, Countess of Harlinsville, regarded her reflection in the mirror. A tall woman with grey hair and narrow, aquiline features gazed back at her. Jeweled rings flashed on her fingers as she smoothed the front of her blue and white gown.

A single knock on the door announced the arrival of her guest. A slender, pretty young woman with black hair entered and bowed. She wore the simple brown robes and boots of a druid priestess. Lawrence closed the double doors behind her.

Arlene watched the druidess in the mirror. The top of her head probably came up to Arlene's forehead. The Countess saw a flash of apprehension in the woman's bright green eyes.

She's nervous. Good. I chose the right gown. Sapphires always outshine dull brown rocks. Arlene gave a thin smile.

"Thank you for seeing me, Excellency," Carine said.

Arlene turned around. "Why shouldn't I? Our family has been a supporter of the Old Faith for years."

She gestured at a padded couch in front of the library fireplace. "Would you care for some tea? I can have it brought in."

"Thank you, milady," Carine said, shaking her head. "But I must decline.

My errand is urgent."

"Urgent? Well, then, please tell me all about it."

The countess slid onto the seat. Carine hesitated, then joined her, eyes on her hands in her lap, as if gathering her thoughts.

Arlene waited.

"My lady," Carine said, looking at her, "the unrest in the free lands is increasing. There are handbills with inflammatory language and protests even in the smaller villages. People are anxious. But it isn't just in the towns and cities. I see signs of it every day in nature. The animals are restless and afraid. The Earth Mother is disturbed."

"Ah yes," Arlene answered with a sigh. "Unfortunate signs of the times. King Phillip and the Senate are indeed under a lot of stress. But how can I help? My husband and I are responsible for Harlinsville. We cannot affect anything beyond our own city, after all."

Carine twisted the front of her robe, eyes downcast. "Your family connections with the Druid Council are long-lived and deep."

Arlene's eyes flickered towards the drapes by the big picture window overlooking her gardens. A slight bulge near the window frame told her all she needed to know.

Good. Now all he needs to do is stay quiet.

"And you need assistance in the Council?" Arlene asked.

Carine stood, her brow furrowed, her hands still worrying the fabric of her robe. "I… yes. I have tried all the usual methods of appealing to them, but I am not high enough in rank."

"I'm sure they will do the right thing, Druidess."

Carine's eyes wandered to a painting of a verdant mountainside. "I am not so sure."

"What makes you say that?"

Carine didn't reply for a few heartbeats. Arlene watched her.

"The religions of the Light have asked for assistance in combating both the unrest and the threat from the Dark Faiths," Carine said. Her mouth set in a firm line and her eyes flashed.

You're a fighter, that's for sure, Arlene mused.

"In the past, when all Nature was threatened," Carine continued, "we have allied with them. But not now. Their requests are delayed in committees and the Council still debates. It doesn't make sense. Something is not right and I have to make it right."

You're also a bit too clever for your own good, Carine.

"Ah," Arlene replied with a nod. "Well, that is odd, I'll grant you. I wonder if perhaps their attention is diverted by the potential threat to Nature you mention. After all, their first duty is to the Earth Mother, not to the other faiths, no matter how benign their intent."

Carine shook her head. "No one will tell me anything. Please, Excellency, can you help?"

"I can make inquiries. We haven't met with the Council since my husband's grandfather's time. I'm not sure if it will help that much, but I can try."

Carine let out a breath. "Thank you, Your Excellency." She looked relieved.

"I will send a message to your grove," Arlene said, rising from the couch. "It is northwest of Oakmoor, correct?"

"Yes."

Arlene regarded her reflection in the mirror again and kept one eye on Carine. "By the way, aren't you affiliated with those warriors who ride the pegasi, the Grey Riders?"

"I am a mentor to Sir Buckminster." Carine's cheeks flushed, but she held her head high.

Arlene pretended not to notice. *A mentor? I think quite a bit more than that, my dear. Or you wish it to be quite a bit more.*

"Couldn't you appeal to them?" she asked instead. "I'm sure they could be of assistance, no matter what the Council decides."

"They are not in Deran at present, milady."

"Pity. Well, I will send Lawrence when I receive a reply."

Carine bowed low. "Thank you again, Your Excellency."

Arlene watched the door as it closed behind her.

"I found that interesting, Kili," she said to the air. "I assume you heard everything."

A halfling in dark leather armor slipped out from behind the curtains. His black eyes glittered. "Of course."

"Good. Our friends on the Council will, of course, be contacted. I am quite certain of their reply to our young druidess. You know your task."

Kili Mikman ran a hand over his chin. "She seems to have some kind of connection with Bydecy. Too bad. I'd rather watch Connor Lomin suffer instead. I hear he's quite fond of the sister of Handor Lervion. Maybe I should pay her a visit after we take care this little forest wench."

Arlene frowned. "Don't be ridiculous. Hannah Lervion is extremely well-guarded and besides, she's in Gorostol. That's very far away."

Kili shrugged. "I have connections."

Arlene looked down her nose at him. "Your personal vendettas don't concern me. Don't get distracted. After all your obligations for me are complete, if you want to get yourself spitted on a pike while trying to take out Hannah Lervion, be my guest. But that's on your own time."

Kili's eyes assessed her. For a moment, she thought he would protest but he bowed instead. "As Your Excellency commands."

"Good." She lifted her head with a sniff. "Alert the Shrikes. If my assessment of Carine is accurate, you will need additional blades."

***

Edward Cardinal Simpson breathed deeply of the crisp, clean air and sighed. He always liked this part of Astarel. Though it was not quite so dry as the land near his hometown, the tall mountains and valleys brought back fond memories. His eyes wandered over the towering peaks - capped with snow even now in late spring - and the afternoon light casting shadows on the crags and rills.

His chances of seeing the land of his birth again diminished with each week he spent in this world, yet he had no regrets. As Papal Nuncio to Damora, his vocation was to serve and to go to the ends of creation to bring the word of God to all peoples.

As I have tried to do, O Lord. I pray you will have mercy on me for my failings.

He gathered his black robes around him and sat on a large boulder. A breeze ruffled the tall grass in the meadow and a butterfly danced by.

Iron Thunder said he would be there. Edward could wait and enjoy the sunlight in the meantime.

Not long afterwards, he sensed a presence in the woods behind him and stood. A tall, white-bearded old man with amber, cat-like eyes strode towards him from the sheltering woods. He wore a plain dun robe and no shoes.

Edward stood and smiled. "You would be Donnervassilianelikilandra."

The man's eyes twinkled and he bowed. "Your Draakon pronunciation is better than most, Eminence."

Edward bowed back. "It took a lot of practice and much correction by one of my staff, Excellency."

"An Elf? Their knowledge of languages is extensive."

"Father Gideon, a dwarf. The librarian at the Chancery."

"He has done well. You may call me Iron Thunder if it is easier."

"Thank you."

"Your choice of meeting place is very picturesque, Your Excellency," Edward said. "From what Lord Melinor told me, I imagine your news is not nearly as pleasant."

"You are correct. What would you like to hear first? The bad news or the worse news?"

"Is there any good news?"

Iron Thunder pursed his lip. "Actually, yes. I'll start with the worst. Some of the dragon clans have taken the Blood Sign against the religions of the Light."

A chill raced down Edward's spine.

Just what we need.

"I see," he said. "And their stated reason?"

"They see the religions of Christianity, Kurental, Verian and Irial to be oppressive and intolerant. In particular, they take issue with persecution of people who hold what they term 'enlightened ideals'. Of course, their idea of 'persecution' means 'not accepting everything we say'."

"Not very original of them."

"No argument from me. Also, some are tired of what they consider encroachment on their lands by 'lesser peoples'. Again, not very original."

Edward clasped his hands behind his back. "Is the latter a valid one? Be honest."

Iron Thunder shrugged. "I have never given it much credence. Ours is a big world. There is always a way for people to learn to live together in it. I think it is just an excuse for some embittered parties."

Edward returned to his seat on the boulder, leaning backwards and resting his hands against the stone. "Well, philosophical differences aside, what do you think?"

"I think they are subverted."

Edward shot him a glance. "By whom?"

Iron Thunder sighed. "The Ja'al, most likely. There have always been those among dragonkind who are susceptible to the blandishments of evil. When prompted by agents of the Dark Faiths, they are only too ready to jump to conclusions and accept what is presented if it will get them what they want. I'm sure you recognize the pattern."

Edward gazed out at the peaceful scene before him, not speaking for several moments. "How bad is it?"

"Five of the Twelve Great Clans have taken the Blood Sign."

His heart sank. "And the others?"

"Six of the remaining have opposed them. One is undecided, the Twin Star Clan. I have no idea how they will go. They have always been a bit… mercurial."

"I see."

Iron Thunder made as if to speak, then reconsidered. He stared off into the distance for some time. "Your Eminence?"

"Just Edward, if you like."

"Fine. Edward, I sense a tension in the Clans. They are expecting something major, something cataclysmic."

"Just like the other peoples," Edward murmured. "Just like all the free lands. Disagreement turns to rancor, then to bitterness, then to spite, then to hatred. It is getting worse. The Count of Deorfast survived an assassination attempt last week, although Lady Sidara was injured. I know the Ja'al are behind it, but to what end? They are expending considerable resources to keep up the tempo of discord. The longer they pursue this course of action, the greater the chance we will find and entrap their agents, and then what? What is the end game?"

The pair remained silent among the wind and gently rustling trees.

Edward thought over Iron Thunder's news in his mind. *The Skull Gates are involved somehow. I'm sure of it. End game indeed.*

With a start, Edward noticed all birdsong ceased and no more insects flew nearby. His senses tingled and he raised an eyebrow at Iron Thunder. "Who else knows you came here?"

The dragon-man stood. "A few in the High Clan Council. You?"

Edward stood as well. "Some people in the Chancery and a few nobles in Oakmoor."

The wind blew.

Edward's senses tingled again, more powerful this time. Then he felt it: a malevolence emanating from the trees two hundred yards away. It lurked like a prowling lion, hidden among the shadows.

"Three of them," he murmured to Iron Thunder. "In the trees. They are shielded. Probably invisible."

Iron Thunder nodded. "Understood." He raised his arms over his head, then gestured in a wide circle. The air around him vibrated and his form shimmered and warped. It grew and grew.

Edward blinked. Now, a huge dragon with amber-gold scales and immense wings crouched next to him. It regarded him with the same golden, cat-like eyes.

"What are they?" the dragon rumbled.

"Give me a moment." Edward closed his eyes. He held up his crucifix. "*Malum reperio.*"

A globe of mildest white light expanded out from him, racing over the meadow with the speed of an arrow shot from a bow. The arc hit the forest. Three lizard-like shapes with bat wings flashed in his Sight. One towered over the other two, but even the smaller ones were about thirty feet long.

"One true dragon and two drakes. One must be a wizard if they're this well-hidden."

The dragon grinned. "They won't be hidden for long."

He trotted forward and leaped into the air. Soaring over the glade, he gestured with his forepaws and a golden light flared. Three draconic figures shimmered into being at the edge of the woods. With hissing snarls, the two of the dragons took wing, heading for Iron Thunder. He obliged by soaring higher.

The third enemy, a drake with reddish white scales and a ruff of black horns around his head, flew towards Edward. The drake's red eyes flashed with anger.

The Nuncio waited. "Saint Michael the Archangel, defend us in battle," he whispered. "Be our defense against the wickedness and snares of the Devil."

A peaceful, vibrant power built within Edward. It surged and surrounded him, forming a faint white light on his skin. He felt uplifted, almost weightless.

The drake closed the distance in a few heartbeats. He opened his jaws and blue-white acid boiled within.

"*Confuto*," the Nuncio said, pointing at the drake.

In the blink of an eye, a giant sphere of white light surrounded the drake. The creature floated down to the ground inside the globe, eyes wide in amazement as he tried to shove his way through. The sphere held him immobile.

Roars, blasts of fire and the sizzle of lightning echoed in the sky high above him, but Edward kept his eyes on his captive assailant. "Now perhaps we can discuss this in a civilized manner."

The drake's visage contorted into a sneer. "Civilized discussion? With you? You little, sawed-off runt of a creature! Unfit to clean the cesspits by my lair!"

He hurled himself forward and Edward applied more power, gritting his teeth to maintain the sphere.

"That's not very civilized," he chided. "Perhaps you can tell me why you're attacking me."

Now the drake laughed, clawing at the globe with wicked talons. He spat a stream of acid at his prison walls. The shield of light wavered.

"Why? You idiot! The days of your false religion are at an end! The gods of the Ja'al will rule Damora! Only willing servants or slaves will survive the wave of darkness to come."

Edward's control of the magic sphere weakened further. He rebuked the drake. "*Taceo!*"

The sound of his voice reverberated in the glade, making the very air vibrate. The drake staggered backwards into one wall of his prison, eyes glassy.

A sudden wave of tiredness washed over Edward. Pain stabbed his midsection and he grimaced. His sphere of light flickered and he concentrated to maintain it.

A screech drew his eyes to the sky. Iron Thunder grappled the true dragon and the other drake in mid-air, tumbling and spinning through the puffy white clouds. All three creatures trailed smoke.

Edward regarded his opponent. "We'll never get anywhere if you insist on being nasty."

"Oh, we'll get somewhere, all right," the drake retorted, struggling to his feet. He gestured with his forepaws and muttered vile-sounding words.

Time for a different approach, Edward mused. "*Salve Regina, Mater Misericordie,*" he murmured.

The drake finished his spell and a bright purple light burst within the pale sphere.

A jolt of energy surged through Edward just as the imprisoning globe vanished. With a shout of triumph, the drake charged. Edward sidestepped and the creature's jaws clashed on empty air.

The drake's eyes widened. He lashed his tail but Edward leaped lightly over it. The drake spun, slashing with his claws. Edward focused power into his palms. With sharp pushing motions, he slapped the dragon's attacks aside.

The drake charged again. Edward dodged and hopped up onto the nearby boulder.

"Fight me!" the creature roared, whipping his tail overhead. Edward jumped off the boulder just before the strike pulverized the rock. He tucked into a roll and stood, then sidestepped again as a stream of acid sizzled past, melting a sapling and another boulder.

"Oh Saint Joseph, whose protection is so great, so strong, so prompt before the throne of God," he whispered, "Aid me in my hour of need."

Another surge of power pulsed through him. As the drake sprayed acid at him, Edward formed a shield of light on his left forearm. He thrust his arm at the deadly stream, deflecting it into a stand of trees. They melted and burst into flame.

"You're ruining a perfectly lovely meadow," he scolded the drake.

The creature's eyes flared in rage. "I'll gnaw your bones, false priest!" He bellowed and hurled himself through the air.

Edward dropped flat on the ground. The drake sailed into another stand of larger trees, splintering them. All that remained of one giant pine was a sharp spike of wood pointing at an angle into the air like an admonishing finger.

The drake stalked out of the wreckage, bleeding from several wounds where shards of wood had pierced his hide. Edward circled away until the ruined trees stood behind him.

"This makes no sense," the dragon snarled. "I am imbued with the power of the Blood Sign! How are you doing this?"

Edward shrugged. "Prayer. It seems to be working. You should try it."

The drake's eyes burned. Spitting a blast of acid, he charged again, flailing with his claws.

Edward knelt. "*Obsto.*" A hemisphere of blue light leaped up over him. The acid jet burst into a cloud of steam and mist.

The drake hurtled headlong into the cloud, shrieking curses. Edward ducked and rolled. He heard a mighty crash, an agonized scream, and a wet gurgle.

As he had expected, the drake had impaled himself on the giant spike of wood that remained of the large tree. Steaming white blood poured onto the ground and the drake slumped forward.

Edward sighed and stood, brushing his robes. "The wages of sin is death."

From above came another echoing scream. The true dragon tumbled downwards, trailing flames, smoke and a stream of blood. With a thud that Edward could feel even at this distance, it slammed into a nearby mountainside. Iron Thunder beat his wings and raced after the remaining drake, but faltered. The remaining enemy bellowed an obscenity at him and winged away over the mountains.

Edward met Iron Thunder as he landed. The gold dragon was winded, panting and limping.

"Nicely done, Iron Thunder." Edward placed a hand on the dragon's foreleg. He whispered and a golden aura covered a bloody slash. The injury slowly faded.

"Harrumph," Iron Thunder said, eyeing the dead drake balefully. He placed a paw on one of his wing injuries and the wound sealed in a glow of pale blue light. An angry scar remained. "Seems you did pretty well your-self."

Edward placed one hand on a bleeding wound in Iron Thunder's chest and another on a painful-looking patch of melted dragon scales. He murmured softly and two lights glowed. The dragon's injuries diminished though the scales remained warped and deformed.

"All I tried to do was talk to him and get out of the way," Edward said, shaking his head against a sudden dizziness. "He did the rest to himself."

With the worst of his wounds now treated, Iron Thunder transformed back into a human. He helped Edward sit in front of an undamaged pine tree.

Edward's head swam and throbbed in pain. The now-familiar ache in his abdomen intensified. He closed his eyes, forcing himself to relax and control his breathing. He opened his eyes to see Iron Thunder regarding him.

"Not as young as I once was," Edward said.

Iron Thunder raised an eyebrow. "Nor as healthy. I sense illness."

"It is nothing."

"Clearly. And I'm a Christian goblin."

"I actually know one of those."

That got him a scoff of derision but nothing else.

The pair sat in silence in the remnants of the meadow. Birdsong slowly returned and the butterflies resumed their fluttering among the tall grasses.

Edward waited until his dizziness faded, then applied a pulse of healing to his head. The pain subsided to a dull ache. "We are getting close if they need to try an assassination. Now, however, we have an added problem: spies in our ranks."

"The Dragon Council has dealt with spies before."

"As have we, but one that can set up an ambush like this worries me." Edward stood, feeling a little better.

Iron Thunder helped him stand. "We had best get to work. The Ja'al will not rest."

"Neither will we. Can you give me a lift to Saint Martin's Town?"

The dragon-man smiled and raised his hands over his head. "I think I can arrange that."

Chapter Three – Dissension in the Ranks

Late afternoon sunshine slanted through the nearby woods into the stable yard. A light breeze ruffled Buck's hair and blew dust motes into the shafts of sunlight. He felt the difference in the climate now that summer approached. He patted Shadowbane on the neck, running a brush over the pegasus' back.

"We'll be off and flying soon, fellow," he said.

The winged horse gave him a sidelong look as if to say "I'll believe it when I see it."

Buck sighed. He had to cool his heels while Khyron met with the garrison commander in Evonald about the Skull Gate staging area. Buck didn't expect him back for at least an hour. In addition, since it was Sunday, Dar and Eric attended services at the local Christian church. Andyn and Connor toured the local shops somewhere in town.

Buck dropped the brush into a case hung on a nearby post. He leaned his forearms on the fence rail and gazed over the corral, suppressing the urge to fidget. At least it was a pleasant day.

With a last pat on Shadowbane's side, Buck strode towards the corral gate. As silly as it sounded to keep a flying animal in a corral, the pegasi enjoyed the company of horses, so the Riders had learned to just stable them as if they had no wings at all.

A fleeting movement behind a shed caught his eye. He faded back into the shadows of a nearby stall. With memories of attacks by Ja'al assassins fresh in his memory, he gripped his sword, nerves on edge.

When nothing moved after a while, he wondered if he had imagined it. *I'm being ridiculous. Eric's birth parents are dead, thank the Earth Mother. There are few left alive from their guild.*

Then he saw a flicker of motion and something slipped around the corner of the shed. He whipped out Khelios. Golden fire ran along the edge of the blade.

A beautiful black doe limped towards him and his eyes widened. The creature's form shimmered and warped and became a raven-haired young woman in tattered robes of dark brown. Blood and dirt marked her pretty, oval features and he saw bleeding wounds on her legs, abdomen and shoulder.

He stared, dumbfounded. "Druidess Carine?"

She stumbled against a post and turned bright green eyes to him. "Buck…"

He ran and caught her just before she hit the ground.

***

"How is she?" Buck asked. He bit his lip, afraid to ask too much.

Andyn smoothed Carine's hair back from her forehead and returned a potion vial to her medical kit. "She'll live."

Buck took a seat next to the bed. He wanted to move closer but hesitated. "How bad was it?"

"Multiple lacerations, broken rib, mild concussion, some evidence of poison," Andyn said with a shrug. "There are signs she used magical healing on herself, so it must have been a lot worse earlier."

The door to Andyn's room opened. Khyron and Connor entered, followed by Dar and Eric.

Khyron frowned. "Dar and Eric just found us. Who is she?"

"A druidess," Connor said before Buck could speak. The halfling shot him a glance. "She's been a mentor to Buck for some time."

Buck's mind flitted back to a snow-covered hilltop near Oakmoor, when Carine had given him insights and advice. But then, he thought he had detected something else: true affection, more than that expected of a mentor and counselor.

Did I imagine it?

Andyn closed her medical case. "We should let her get some rest, but we can't leave her alone."

"I'll stay with her," Buck said. "You go on and get some dinner."

"We'll bring you something from the tavern," said Dar.

Khyron elbowed Buck, "Was she coming to see you, then?"

"Let's discuss later," Andyn interrupted. She patted him on the shoulder and guided him out.

Buck watched Carine's chest rise and fall under the blanket as the door closed behind them.

"We'll have to get you new clothes," he murmured, pulling the blanket up to her collarbone. "Those rags won't do … at least, not in a conservative Elven town."

Crickets chirped outside and a breeze filtered in through an open window. He watched her sleep as evening deepened into twilight.

Unfamiliar feelings surged through him. Sure, he had known other women — some quite well — but when he was near Carine, he felt an overwhelming urge to protect her and ensure her happiness.

Where is this coming from?

The room darkened. He lit three oil lamps and returned to her side. Knowing Andyn's impressive skills, he trusted Carine would recover, despite the extent of her initial injuries.

Not knowing what else to do, he took a damp cloth and patted her forehead and neck.

She stirred and her eyelids fluttered open. "Buck."

He smiled. "Right here."

She gazed at him, eyes intense. "Thank you for helping me."

"Don't mention it."

She said nothing more, her gaze growing distant. The lamplight flickered on her features.

"What happened?" he asked finally.

A tear traced a shiny line from the corner of her eye down past her temple.

His heart skipped a beat. What kind of tragedy would bring strong, wise Carine to tears? Buck hesitated, then reached out and caught the teardrop before it reached her ear.

She smiled at him and he drew back. "I'm sorry, Druidess," he said. "That was presumptuous."

She gazed at him. "No. It was kind. I am Carine to you from now on."

Carine?

He let out a deep breath, smiling back. "Carine it is. What happened?"

Her smile faded and her jaw set in a firm line. "The Druid Council has split."

"What do you mean?"

Carine closed her eyes. "Civil war. Druids have chosen sides between the religions of the Light and Darkness. They stalk each other now in the hills and forests."

Buck's stomach felt as if an ingot of lead had dropped into it. "I don't understand. Why?"

She shook her head. "The turmoil in the free lands has worsened. The Council was undecided and debates became hot and harsh and endless. Accusations flew. Soon, druids charged each other with conspiracy and treason."

Buck tried to remain calm. "I'm sure politicking is normal for a high council. They'll come to their senses."

"No, Buck. They would never turn to violence to resolve differences. I am convinced some have been subverted by the forces of evil."

"How do you know?"

"From evidence I have gathered. For example, do you believe Christians would try to sow unrest to frighten people into joining them?"

Buck thought of Dar and Eric, the Alenar women, and of their employer, Cardinal Edward Simpson. "Well, I'm sure some might, but I doubt if there would be many. Besides, I know the Papal Nuncio. He would never approve of something like that."

"Well," she continued. "I uncovered proof that someone has been planting false evidence of such scare tactics. Accusations were brought up in the Council and they became the focus for some of the most rancorous shouting matches. While I can understand distrust, it is quite a leap from distrust to conspiracy. Ultimately, that was what convinced me this level of discord was the work of the Ja'al."

She lapsed into silence. Buck digested her words, mind whirring. "I can't believe it. Every druid I know is calm and reasonable," he murmured.

Carine kept her eyes closed but he heard the amusement in her voice. "I hope you're talking about me."

"Of course!"

"Good."

She lapsed into silence again and he waited.

"As you noted, politics are strong in the Council, even for the best of the Great Druids," she continued, opening her eyes. "Still, I would have thought our people strong enough to resist the lies of the Ja'al. I was wrong."

"How could they be so blind?" he blurted.

"Everyone is blind in their own way, Buck. The Ja'al are well-named as the Manipulator Church. Some of the members of the current Council are not the first to be taken in by them."

"But what happened to you? How did you get hurt?"

Her voice became bitter. "I produced my evidence at the last meeting and was shouted down. When I, and others, protested, we were told not to contradict those in authority over us. We were removed from the Grove of Meeting. Not long afterwards, Shrike assassins paid me a visit."

Buck gaped at her. "Shrike assassins! They work for the Ja'al. That's madness. You think the Council set them on you?"

She nodded, opening her eyes again. "Some of them, I am sure. The Shrikes had assistance: the plants and animals nearby would not defend me but helped my attackers instead. I suspect druidical magic."

Buck found his hands clenched into tight fists and he forced himself to relax.

"For all the good it did them," Carine spat, eyes flashing.

Buck shook his head. "Don't they understand what they're doing? I've known firsthand what the Ja'al are capable of …We have lost…"

He stopped, a lump in his throat. He remembered the funeral of one of the Grey Riders, Handor Lervion, buried in a cemetery in his homeland of Gorostol. He saw again the anguished eyes of Handor's sister, Hannah, now all alone, her last family member dead.

"We lost one of our own to them," he finished.

Carine's eyes grew soft. "I know. I received Hannah's message."

He sighed. "But you. Your grove is hundreds of miles away, isn't it? Near

Oakmoor? Why come this far? And how did you find us, anyway?"

"I knew that you would be somewhere in north-eastern Terenai. I summoned animals when I arrived and their memories told of a fierce battle between a dragon and warriors who rode winged horses. I found the ruined tower and guessed you would come to the nearest village."

"Why didn't you go to the town guard here in Evonald, or find a healer?"

"Where do you think I was going when I saw you? No matter. You have quite a fine healer here already."

"Yes, Andyn is very good."

Her hand slid out from under the blanket and took his. Startled, he met her gaze. There he saw great affection, sadness and a little fear.

"You have many powerful enemies," she said. "I had to make sure you were safe."

Keep me safe?

She squeezed his hand.

But she's my counselor. We can't be anything more.

He smiled. Her eyes grew shiny and she turned away.

Can we?

"I am fine," he reassured her. "You don't have to worry."

She nodded. Seconds passed. She opened her mouth, then closed it, then tried again. Her voice broke. "My whole world is coming apart, Buck. Everything I've ever known is upside-down. You're one of the few people I can trust."

"I think you overestimate me," he replied, gazing down at the floor. "I'm no rock of stability."

Her hand disengaged from his and moved up to touch his face.

He met her eyes again, heartbeat quickening.

"No. You underestimate yourself, Buck. For so long you have tried to walk a line between good or evil. Finally, you have chosen, and chosen well. You told me about your ordeal in the Chamber of Decision last summer. You have committed to fight against the Darkness. Evil will not claim you."

Out of words, he sat quietly at her side. The crickets continued their serenade.

"I also have made my choice," she continued, her voice now weary. "I will stand with the religions of the Light. Someday we will rebuild the

Council, but not until it is purged."

Her eyes closed.

"You need to rest, Carine, and to heal." He took a chance, raising her hand to his lips and kissing it.

She smiled, eyes still closed. "If you are here, then I will."

She slept.

Sir Buckminster Bydecy, Sword-knight of Astarel, kept watch.

***

Connor drained the last of the ale from his mug as Dar and Eric left to take Buck his dinner. Magical lamps carved in the shape of sunflowers glowed with white light. Dark wood furniture and cream-colored upholstery gave an air of casual elegance. A few couples lingered in the tavern, but by now most of the patrons had left for their homes. Only the barkeep and a pair of waiters remained to clean up.

Khyron leaned back in the booth and put an arm around Andyn. "So, Carine and Buck are close then?"

Andyn shrugged. "From what little Buck has told us. She counseled him when we were up in Oakmoor, and I gathered that he knew her back home in Astarel. He doesn't say much."

Khyron pursed his lip. "Is she connected in any way with the other two who traveled south?"

Connor shook his head. "No, Carine is not a Grey Rider like Brandi and Megan Alenar."

"And have you heard from them?" Khyron asked.

Andyn and Connor exchanged a look. The halfling noticed the sadness in her eyes.

He toyed with his ale mug before answering. "No, nothing since late winter. Brandi and Megan used to exchange letters with Eric and Dar every couple of weeks."

"You're worried," Khyron said.

Andyn interlocked her fingers with Khyron's hand on her shoulder. "You know their mission, Khyron. Torosc is dangerous in and of itself. Searching for the rightful heirs to the old kingdoms makes it even worse."

"But their aunt and uncle are with them," Khyron noted. "I've heard of Daphne and Stephen Alenar. Anyone who stands against them had better make sure their last will and testament is in order."

A twinge of anxiety made Connor shift in his seat. "I know, but it's just not like them. Brandi and Megan care very much for Eric and Dar. They should have written by now."

The trio sat in silence for a while. Connor's eyes wandered to tapestries on the walls between the windows. They depicted leaping deer or the Silver Tree of Verian. One showed a verdant forestland and snow-capped mountains.

One of those looks like Whitehorse Peak.

Connor thought back over the months, to the time when he had first met Dar Cabot and the other Riders. Sometimes it felt like their lives were a long epic poem recited by a bard at a festival.

Was it really more than a year ago?

"Life was easier when we were still freelance sell-swords," he noted with a sigh.

Khyron raised an eyebrow. "Was it? Well, there are sell-swords and then there are sell-swords. Some just take the work from the highest bidder and others have a more highly developed sense of morals, like all of you."

Connor remained lost in thought. He remembered the heady feeling of freedom and possibility when he had arrived near the Deranese borderlands. Now, with all their new-found responsibilities...

"True, your 'lances' aren't 'free' anymore," Khyron continued, "but that's not necessarily bad. Dar and Eric are members of knightly orders, Andyn answers directly to the Emperor of Terenai and Buck serves the King of Astarel as a Sword-knight. All these come with some advantages. You have an impressive support system."

Connor had to admit he had a point. He and the other Riders had access to resources that would be the envy of free-lances with years more experience. He shot a glance at Khyron. "Speaking of which, why didn't you take the freelance profession? You certainly have the ability."

Khyron shrugged. "The ways of a freelance mercenary always seemed so uncertain. I guess I just need a more structured life. Besides, mine is a military family, and Andyn's father encouraged me when I was younger. But you have gained some wonderful friends along the way, haven't you?"

Andyn kissed his hand.

Connor smiled. "We've been through a lot together."

Khyron chuckled and released Andyn. "Do you think? The last year or so has been crowded, to say the least."

He held up a hand and counted on his fingers. "First, you meet Dar, Buck and Eric up in Deran. With Brandi and Megan and Andyn, you uncover a Ja'al plot to find a secret weapon from the Esten Empire. Then you find out that your lives were predicted by this 'Song of the Grey Riders'. You win the race against the Ja'al and claim the prize—which happens to be a herd of battle-trained pegasi held in temporal stasis. Then Brandi and Megan leave on their mission with their relatives."

He eyed Connor. "Do I have this right so far?"

Connor nodded. Khyron continued to count on his fingers. "Handor Lervion joins your group. You nearly get killed trying to clear Buck of false charges. Later, hunt down the man who ordered Andyn's husband murdered. You find a clue to something called the Helm of Shadows, which can teleport its bearer great distances."

He paused, but the halfling just waved a hand for him to continue. "Then—surprise-surprise—you discover that a lich-princess, Zhinia Margoth, is going to invade Deran. Since this Helm of Shadows seems to be the key to it all, you set off to find it."

"You forgot to mention that the Helm was evil," interjected Andyn. "And that it would have just taken over our minds slowly and destroyed us all one by one."

"A minor omission. Where was I? Oh yes: Margoth. Well, on your way to find and destroy the Helm, you stumble across an ancient fortress and get transported to, well, I'm not sure where this 'Chamber of Decision' was, but you had to choose between cooperating with the forces of evil or sacrificing everything in order to fulfill the predictions of the Song of the Grey Riders. Choices made."

He straightened in his seat and shook his head. "Now, this is the part that really amazes me: a Celestial, of all things, gives Andyn the Crown of Saint Alyssa. Let's all ignore for the moment that we're talking about an *Elohir*, a creature of incredible power from another world, taking the time out of her busy day to give Andyn a crown. But this is not just a piece of jewelry. It's a Christian relic."

Connor smiled at Andyn, who traced a pattern on the tabletop with her finger.

Khyron continued counting. "Margoth invades Deran with about fifteen thousand troops, there's lots of clanging metal and fire and smoke and magic flying around, but in the mean time you find the Helm. I thought that you would have just smashed it and that would be the end of everyone's favorite lich princess, but there's a curse on it that teleports you right to her at the Battle of Hillton. There, Andyn uses the Crown's powers to blast Margoth into fragments."

Andyn pinched him in the side. "You make it sound so easy, Khy."

"You mean it wasn't?" He winced from a harder pinch.

Connor lifted his mug in salute. "You forgot the part where Margoth killed us all, except for Andyn. And the part where Andyn used the Crown to bring us back to life."

"Ah yes, silly of me. Well, with Margoth blasted into a pile of steaming ash, her invasion falls apart. There is lots of pomp and ceremony, la-la-la, you're all knighted, etcetera."

Andyn nodded. "But Handor steals the Helm to try to rescue his sister from false imprisonment."

"I was getting to that. No one knows for sure where Handor teleported off to with the Helm. So, while various agencies puzzle over that, you set your sights on a simple task of destroying the Crossed Swords Assassins guild, which happens to be led by Eric's birth parents. Then, with that little distraction out of the way, you catch up with Handor only to find out he's been killed by his no-good uncle and you rescue Hannah."

Connor grinned. Khyron had gone through the fingers of one hand three times.

"It makes me tired just thinking about it," Khyron said, letting his hands drop. "How is it that you're not all perpetually exhausted? Or just dead? "

Andyn elbowed him but she smiled. "By the Blessings of Verian, Khy. Nothing else."

A waiter approached. "Will there be anything else? We will be closing soon."

Connor shook his head. "No, thank you."

The waiter nodded and left.

Connor stood. "Come on, you two. Let's see how Buck's girlfriend is doing."

Andyn took a swipe at him as she rose. "Don't you go playing match-maker, Connor Lomin!"

"And why not?" he asked with raised eyebrows.

"Because we can make a lot of comments about you and a certain Han-nah Lervion, can't we?" Khyron asked.

Connor felt his face grow warm but he kept his expression neutral. "Wipe that grin off your face, Major Demaris," he said to Khyron. "There's plenty of that to go around. You too, Miss Eleandir."

Andyn's cheeks colored and she made a face at Connor.

"Truce," Khyron said, raising his hands and laughing.

The trio left the tavern. They entered Andyn's room just as Buck fin-ished his supper.

Connor nodded to Carine as Andyn went to her side. "Did she wake up?" he asked.

"Yes, she did," Dar replied. "And had plenty to say, none of it good."

Buck related what Carine had told him.

Connor listened to the whole story, then slowly lowered himself onto the top of a nearby footlocker. "Is the entire world unraveling?" he asked.

Andyn sighed. "One thing is certain. She can't stay here. The Ja'al will figure out what's going on and set the Shrikes on her again."

"And the Blue Mark is expecting us to report tomorrow," Dar added.

"I suggest we send her to your parents, Andyn." Khyron said. "Eleth-Anor is on the other side of the country and your father has the connec-tions to make sure she won't be caught on her own again. I have contacts here and at the other military bases in Terenai, so transport is not a prob-lem."

Buck shrugged, eyes on his boots. "I don't want to impose on your fam-ily, Andyn."

Andyn put a hand on his shoulder. "You *are* family as far as my parents are concerned. Any friend of yours will be well-guarded."

Buck shot a glance at Carine's sleeping form. "She probably won't like the idea."

Something in his eyes made Connor look closer.

Because she wants to be with him! Ah, Buck, you lucky man. You have a strong-willed woman interested in you and she has a mind of her own. You may as well resign yourself to it: you're caught.

"I think I can convince her," Andyn said. "Let me talk to her in the morning."

"Do you need me to stay here with you?" asked Khyron.

"No, Khy," Andyn replied, kissing him on the lips. "You're just next door and I can magically ward the room."

The men filed out and dispersed to their chamber. They didn't say much as they prepared for bed. Just before he put the light out, Connor saw Buck staring out the window. He carried a lamp with him as he joined him.

"Hey."

Buck looked down at him.

"She's going to be okay," Connor continued. "Andyn is really good at what she does."

"That's not what worries me," Buck said, staring into the night again. "It's what might happen after she leaves me. I feel like I have to be at her side."

Connor nodded. "I know what you mean."

"Sorry. I know about you and Hannah."

"We have to trust in something greater than ourselves," Connor replied, extinguishing the light. The room plunged into darkness.

"Otherwise, we'd go mad," he finished.

Chapter Four – The Blue Mark

"Whoa, Medianox," Andyn commanded, reining in.

Her pegasus landed in the meadow and cantered to a stop. Hoofbeats thumped in the turf behind her as the other Riders stopped alongside. Andyn shaded her eyes against the bright sunlight, patting her mount's neck.

Buck pulled up in next to her on Shadowbane. "Whatever you said to Carine, she was agreeable about leaving."

Andyn smiled. "Just girl-talk. She realizes that she could better help you if you aren't worrying about her attracting the attention of assassins, rogue druids and worse. Carine is a smart woman."

Buck nodded. She stole a glance at him.

Andyn couldn't resist. "Congratulations."

Buck shot a look at her. "For what?"

She kept smiling but said nothing. Buck stared at her for a while, then shrugged. He flipped down the Eye of Truth, looking left and right. Still they waited. A couple of purple and red butterflies floated past and birds chirped in the trees. Andyn breathed in the scent of wild sage and lavender.

"They're here," Buck said.

The air around them wavered. More than three dozen flying figures shimmered into view. Each only about a foot tall, they resembled naked male and female elves with dragonfly wings. Each carried a spear or bow and they had swords strapped to their thighs.

Hill sprites…

One of the males flew forward. "Who approaches?"

Andyn inclined her head. "We seek the Blue Mark."

The male sprite nodded. "And the password?"

"Lady Belinda makes no scones," Andyn replied.

Now the sprite grinned. "Good to see you again, Lady Andyn."

She smiled. "Good to be back, Captain Varon. Please, lead on."

Varon alighted on Andyn's saddlebow. The other sprites sped away into the nearby woods. Together, the Grey Riders cantered into the forest.

"One question, Captain," Buck asked.

"Yes?"

"We've been here before," Buck continued. "Why do you still ask the password?"

Varon nodded. "The Ja'al are masters of deception. They could easily disguise some of their agents to look like you – and even to make normal horses appear to be pegasi. Also, giving the password delays you just enough so that our mages can finish scanning you."

"How is Lady Belinda?" asked Khyron from Andyn's other side.

Varon smiled. "Better. The fever is past and she is eager to be a proper hostess to you this time."

Their path through the forest widened and soon they emerged into a vast region of green hills. Herds of horses galloped in the distance, accompanied by riders. A great house of wood and stone sat atop the largest hill two miles away.

Andyn smiled. Sir Rhonin Handor, otherwise known as the Blue Mark, retired here with his wife, Belinda, after a long career as a free-lance warrior. They now had a handsome business providing horses to the military of Terenai.

"And the children?" asked Dar.

Varon's smile widened. "You will see for yourselves. They've talked of nothing but your visit for two days."

The aforementioned youngsters made their appearance as soon as the Riders drew up to the circular gravel pathway before the front door. A brown-haired lad of seven and a girl of five careened down the steps.

"The Riders are here! Daddy! Mommy! The Riders are here!"

Andyn couldn't keep the smile from her face as she dismounted. "Ah! I see we can never approach in secret, can we, Roger?"

The boy beamed from ear to ear. "I was watching for you from my special spy-post!" He pointed at a tiny wooden structure in the lower limbs of a tree by the house.

The girl tugged Andyn's tunic. "And I used my magical looking glass! See!" She brandished a worn and tarnished silver hand mirror.

"Yes, Mary!" Andyn put her hands on her hips. "You are certainly excellent sentries."

"Now if only they would be as good about obeying when they are to clean up their rooms!" boomed a voice from the front door.

Andyn couldn't keep herself from grinning at that voice. Rhonin Handor strode down the steps, black-bearded and broad-shouldered, as tall as Buck. A slender woman with soft brown eyes walked hand-in-hand with him. She stood a head shorter than her husband and waves of lustrous chestnut hair framed a delicate, heart-shaped face.

Despite Rhonin's words, his eyes sparkled. His children smiled shyly.

"Now, dear," said Belinda, laying a hand on his shoulder. "You have to admit they are getting better."

"You are right, my love," he replied with a kiss on her head. "You only had to scold them three times this week. What improvement!" He winked at his children.

The couple reached the bottom step and both bowed to Andyn.

"It is an honor to host you and your companions again, Light of Justice," said Belinda as she straightened. Her eyes twinkled.

Despite only having known them for a few weeks, Andyn warmed to them immediately. She felt that, no matter how formally they spoke, the Handors regarded everything within range as a source of amusement.

It's better than looking for rivals behind every shadow and taking offense at every perceived slight.

She inclined her head. "It is an honor to be here, Sir Rhonin, Lady Belinda. I fear the Riders are becoming spoiled on your hospitality."

"Good!" Rhonin said, reaching out to clasp hands with Buck and Eric in turn. "That's as it should be."

Buck lifted Roger on his shoulders and Dar hoisted Mary in his arms.

Connor bowed over Belinda's hand. "If you ever come to Evendale, my family will return the favor."

Belinda smiled. "I will very much look forward to that, Master Lomin. Please, come inside, all of you."

Rhonin nodded to Captain Varon. "Thank you again, Captain. Would you care to join us?"

The hill sprite considered. "I may be able to do so. I have reports to provide to Lord Hirion but might have time afterward."

"Well, you are always welcome," Rhonin said with a broad smile. "As are all the fae-folk at my home."

"Thank you, Sir Rhonin." Varon bowed and flitted off.

Andyn linked hands with Khyron as they entered the home. She reveled in the sounds of the children's excited chatter, the sight of warm wooden floors and walls, the gleam of silver, and the aroma of newly-baked bread.

This is what I want. When all this nasty business is over, I want this. A home. A family of my own. Will Khyron want it too?

She gave his hand a squeeze.

He smiled at her. "I like it here too."

Belinda led them into a dining room, where tea, jam, honey, cheese, fruit—and scones—awaited. Suddenly ravenous, Andyn joined in the small talk as little as was considered polite. Her hunger sated, she sat back in her chair.

As Khyron's hand found hers again, her pulse quickened. *Easy, girl.*

She smiled at Belinda. "It is good to see you feeling well again."

Belinda Handor made a face. "I don't get sick often. It happens so seldom that I need to remind myself to let healing happen and not try to force things."

Her husband gave her a look over the rim of his mug.

She sighed. "Well, yes, Rhonin has to remind me too."

His eyes twinkled at her but he turned to Eric. "So, tell me the latest news."

Eric's eyes flickered to the children, engrossed in telling stories to Connor and Dar. "Maybe later, Sir Rhonin."

Rhonin watched his offspring for a moment. His expression softened but then his eyes took on a hard sheen. "Yes, of course."

When teatime ended, Connor and Buck headed off with the kids to explore a copse of woods nearby. Rhonin nodded to Eric.

They gathered at the dining room table.

"Well?" asked Belinda.

Dar pulled their map out of his shoulder bag. "Your intelligence was right."

Andyn joined her friends in telling of the Ja'al staging area. Rhonin and Belinda asked few questions, but she detected a note of agitation.

"Well," Rhonin said, pressing his fists into the table. "This is a two-edged sword. I am glad that the sprites weren't mistaken, but it means the next step is even more perilous."

"What do you mean?" asked Khyron.

"Hopefully, Captain Varon can explain it to you tonight," Rhonin said, nodding at the picture window. The afternoon's light deepened into evening and Andyn saw the twin moons. "He is the one who led the scouting party. If not, we will see him in the morning. Until then, relax."

"And I'll help with dinner," Eric and Dar said at the same time. Belinda looked at them in surprise.

"You were ill not long ago," Dar said, with a sheepish smile, "But you tended to us anyway. We owe you."

Belinda laughed. "I was going to refuse since you're guests, but with both of you volunteering to help at once, I don't think I can. Come along then. The rest of you should go get settled."

Andyn did as she suggested. She washed her face, brushed her hair, then emptied her saddlebag onto the bed. It only took a few minutes to lay her extra clothes and toiletries in a bureau drawer. With a sigh, she stepped onto the balcony to watch the sunset. Khyron joined her after a while. She held him wordlessly as the sky shifted from mauve and gold to deep blue.

Please, Verian, grant me a life like this when the Ja'al are defeated.

A flurry of knocks at her door made them turn. Roger and Mary stood there, grinning like imps.

"Um, Mom said to call you for dinner," Roger said. Mary hid giggles behind her hand.

Khyron coughed into his fist. "Yes, well," he began.

"We will be right there," Andyn finished with a mischievous glance at him, "Thank you for coming to get us."

They found a pleasant feast waiting at the table and she was glad to see Captain Varon seated on a small pillow at Lady Belinda's side.

"Dispatches delivered, Captain?" Khyron asked.

The sprite smiled. "Yes. We don't hear from our kin in Tokkab very often and this was important."

"Tokkab?" Dar and Eric said at the same time.

Varon frowned. "Yes. Do you know of it?"

Eric nodded slowly. "Megan and Brandi wrote to us about you."

With a start, Andyn remembered. The sisters had sent letters to the men last summer, telling of a disturbing incident while on their mission.

Rhonin stroked his beard. "This sounds interesting. What happened?"

"Well," Dar began. "There is a small Elven village named Tokkab near Marolpeth, in eastern Alenar. Apparently, troll warriors attacked it and killed or drove off the townsfolk. Megan and Brandi arrived soon after, looking for the town wizard. They tracked the refugees to a marsh that had been corrupted by an evil undead sprite called a Hell Wisp. After some difficulties, they freed the refugees."

"How are the sprites involved?" asked Belinda.

"We have a village near Tokkab," Varon replied. "Our people helped the Alenars after they emerged from the swamp."

"And the Hell Wisp?" asked Belinda.

"They destroyed it," Eric replied, eyes distant.

"Well," Varon answered, leaning back on his hands. "That's no small feat. Anyone who can destroy a Hell Wisp is to be reckoned with."

"Have you heard from the Alenars lately?" asked Rhonin.

Dar shook his head. "Not for weeks."

Rhonin and Belinda exchanged a look. "Well," the big bearded man noted, "They just might not be able to communicate with you for now."

Eric nodded but Andyn could see the tension in his shoulders and neck.

No one said anything.

"Shall we begin?" Rhonin said finally. He bowed his head. "Thank you Lord, for the bounty of our meal. Bless the ones who prepared it and bring Your favor and love on our honored guests. Please extend Your protection to Megan and Brandawyn, who are not here but who we hope will be reunited with us very soon."

They began the meal in silence. Andyn watched Dar and Eric. *We need to get them to stop worrying.*

"I see your assistants were busy," she said to Lady Belinda.

"Very busy," Belinda said, nodding at Eric and Dar. "Dar helped roast the venison and boar and Eric made the vegetable stew, cooked the rice and made the cheese bread. I hardly had to lift a finger. They have future careers as chefs."

"Yes, this is excellent," said Connor, scooping up a serving of wild rice with peas and onions.

Dar's somber demeanor faded and he smiled. "The Lady Belinda tells fibs."

"I think we were the kitchen knaves helping the master," Eric agreed.

The conversation flowed soon after. With Dar and Eric now engaged and distracted, Andyn let herself relax.

They all repaired to the sitting room for dessert. Roger and Mary stacked wood in the fireplace, then closed the grate. Their faces shone with anticipation. Belinda aimed her finger at the logs and spoke a quick word. Flame leaped from her fingertip and a fire blazed. Captain Varon took a seat on the arm of Rhonin's chair.

Dar and Eric brought around pie and tea and little cakes. Andyn settled back into a couch next to Khyron, drowsy and happy.

Khyron put his arm around her and she leaned into him, eyes watching Dar and Eric playing a game with Roger and Mary. Rhonin, Belinda and Buck sat in a group, talking in low tones. Something about Buck's posture made her pause. He shook his head while speaking to Rhonin. Belinda laid a sympathetic hand on his arm. Rhonin removed his pipe from his teeth and said something, to which Buck nodded in return.

He's really worried about Carine, Andyn mused.

She closed her eyes, listening to the murmur of conversation, punctuated occasionally by a pop and crackle of the fire. Eric teased Roger and Mary and their giggles made her smile.

Somewhere along the way, she fell asleep.

"Andyn?" That was Khyron's voice. "The children are in bed. We're going to meet with Varon."

She blinked. Roger and Mary were gone. She cuddled with Khyron alone on the sofa.

"Yes," she said, wiping at her eyes. "I should have stayed awake. I'm sorry."

"Don't be. You obviously needed the rest."

He helped her to her feet and took her hand, leading her to the dining room again. She yawned. Dar raised an eyebrow.

"Don't say it, Darius Cabot. I'm warning you."

He winked.

Rhonin joined Belinda, Captain Varon and the Riders at the table. He unrolled a thick parchment and they set heavy mugs on the corners.

Andyn stared down at a very meticulous relief map of the surrounding area. She recognized the town of Evonald, the nearby Bethyn River, and the local highway. Rhonin and Belinda's home and their stables were drawn in minute detail.

Eric ran his fingers over the elevation lines, trees and waterway. "This is probably one of the best maps I've seen yet."

Rhonin grinned broadly. "I would love to claim the credit, but the fae-folk had a major role in its creation. I depend on their help for many things."

Varon waved his hand. "We all work together, Sir Rhonin." The sprite captain flitted over to a section of the map and knelt down. He tapped on a drawing of a tiny village in the forest north and west of Rhonin's home, close by the river.

"Here is Essefae, our home." He pointed farther east, into a dense section of forest. "Here, the forest is very old and murky. The place is called the Darkhollow. Our people patrol nearby but do not enter."

Andyn's sleepiness faded. "That doesn't sound very good," she said.

"It isn't," Varon replied, eyes narrowing. "Legend tells of a mighty wizard during the time of the Esten Empire who dabbled with forces beyond his ken and corrupted the land. Deep in the Darkhollow lie the ruins of some structure, presumably the wizard's manor. From time to time, an evil force will try to gain a foothold there."

"The Empire ended over a thousand years ago," said Belinda flatly. "The only way that wizard remained is if he became a lich."

Andyn shivered. Zhinia Margoth's hateful, skeletal visage hovered in her memory for a moment. Khyron gave her hand a squeeze.

"Our scouts reported activity on the borders a few days ago," Varon continued. "Independently, two of them reported groups of bull-satyrs. You encountered them at the Ja'al storage depot. I am willing to bet that there might be others trying to construct a Skull Gate there."

Andyn shot a glance at Dar. His brow creased and his mouth set in a thin line.

Rhonin stroked his beard. "It does make a certain sort of sense, to base something as vile as a Skull Gate in an equally vile place like that," he mused.

Andyn wondered. "You don't sound convinced, Sir Rhonin."

He said nothing, continuing to stroke his beard.

Belinda elbowed him. "Out with it, dear."

He frowned. "I'd rather wait and let everyone else have their say."

She watched him, then shrugged and turned back to the map.

Dar and Eric quizzed Captain Varon, asking about the best approaches to the Darkhollow. Andyn listened with half an ear, content to let them put their heads together with Khyron.

She studied the map. Something bothered her. She used a ruler to measure the relative distance between the staging area and the construction site.

"Why put them so close together?" she murmured.

She didn't notice that the room fell silent until Rhonin spoke. "My thoughts exactly, Lady Andyn."

Khyron, Dar and Eric watched her, their expressions thoughtful.

Buck shrugged. "Well, it could be to disperse the number of targets so that we can't take them out at the same time."

She shook her head. "Then why not have four or five staging areas? It's hardly dispersing them to send the materials to one additional place. A single attack, like we accomplished, can upset their plan, unless that place is hardened. It looks like the Darkhollow is very difficult to get into. Why bother with a depot at the tower? Why not just ship the components directly to the Darkhollow?"

No one spoke.

Eric laughed. "Well, Andyn, you've come up with something we can't answer. Can't say that I disagree with you, though."

Andyn turned her attention to Belinda and Rhonin. "What do you think?"

The Blue Mark and his wife exchanged another look. "I think it is something to consider as you continue," Belinda said slowly. "I'm with Eric. You raise a good point. However, it doesn't change the fact that something is going on and we have no idea what that is."

Andyn stared at the representation of the deep forest on the map. Now even the woods shown in the sketch appeared sinister. All her doubts and misgivings collided together in her mind.

"You're going to have to go in there," Rhonin said, leaning his hands on the table. "Into the Darkhollow."

She shuddered…

Chapter Five - Red Moon Rising

After traveling with Captain Varon and his scouts, Khyron decided two things: one, he was not nearly as good in the forest as he thought and two, anything that made Varon and his people edgy made him nervous.

He crouched behind a boulder near a large raspberry bush and stared downslope into the Darkhollow. Tall trees with mossy trunks grew close together, their boughs intermingled overhead, shutting out the sunlight. Vines and creepers draped the lower branches, making an odd sort of leafy veil in places. In contrast to the green, bright forest behind them, he heard no birdsong in the dense woods below.

He sniffed the air. In addition to the more familiar scent of wood, fungus and earth, he detected something almost metallic or acidic, mixed in with a musty odor that reminded him of old cemeteries.

Instinct told him to give the place a wide berth.

"Well?" whispered Dar next to him.

Khyron shook his head. Twelve years in the Elven Special Guard had given him a lot of experience and he thought of himself as a reasonably competent commander. The Darkhollow bothered him. "It's not right," he murmured.

"Agreed," said Andyn on his other side.

"What do you feel?" Dar asked her.

Andyn placed a hand on a nearby tree trunk and closed her eyes. "Death," she murmured. "Evil. Corruption. The living forest, a gift of Verian, is defiled."

Khyron tapped Buck on the arm. "What about you?"

Buck flipped down the metal arm on his helmet. He swept the area with the Eye of Truth, left and right, the gemstone shining with an aurora of colors.

"I second that," Buck added, flipping up the arm again. "The problem is that there's a mild aura of evil on the whole area. Nothing specific."

Captain Varon whirred up to a branch next to Khyron. Twelve sprites crouched in trees nearby, bows at the ready.

"That doesn't surprise me, considering its reputation," Varon said. "We've stayed away from here for generations, just watching to make sure nothing profane got out."

Connor nodded and stepped forward. "Let's get going then. We can't see anything from here anyway."

The smallest of us is the bravest.

"You're right, Connor," Khyron said, fitting an arrow to his bow.

"We'll be watching for you," Varon murmured, "If it gets too hot in there, come back out and we can regroup."

The Riders drew weapons and crept from cover, heading down into the hollow.

Buck barked a short, low laugh. "The Grey Hikers strike again. Let evil-doers beware."

Khyron grinned and his mood lightened.

They slipped into the Darkhollow with Buck, Dar and Eric in front, followed by Andyn, Khyron and Connor. The silence and gloom increased the farther they travelled. Khyron's eyes flitted from one shadow to the next. He focused his nervousness into vigilance and relied on his training, watching their back trail as well as the sides and forward.

The oppressive silence made every footfall seem like thunder and every clink of mail like the clash of arms. He cast an eye on their group, nearly invisible in their camouflage cloaks.

Come on, soldier, he berated himself. *You've been in worse places.*

Dar's hand shot up and they halted. He and Eric leaned their heads together and Dar scooted back to the second rank.

"Vampire roses," he whispered.

Something in Dar's tone made Khyron take notice. He met Andyn's eyes. "I take it you've run into them before?" he asked.

"Months ago, near Twinspire Peak," she replied. "When we found the Helm of Shadows. You?"

"Never."

"Well, they're real trouble."

Dar nodded at her. "Eric thinks we should form two scout teams of two each and go on either flank to see if there's a way around them. Buck and Andyn can hold position here. Khyron, you come with me and Connor goes with Eric."

Khyron joined Dar and they sneaked through the forest to the right of their position. Part of his mind balked at leaving Andyn but he reminded himself that she had done quite well in his absence.

She's a big girl. And a Lichslayer. And Light of Justice. And a Knight of Mindra. And you've seen her in action, so stop worrying.

He flowed through the woods with Dar. They came to a field of rose-bushes growing in the filtered shafts of light under the towering trees. Without ever having seen a Vampire Rose, he identified the blood-red blossoms and black leaves immediately.

"What do they do?" he asked.

"The flowers mesmerize you and then the branches slice you to ribbons so the plant can feed on your blood."

"Lovely. Great for the country garden."

"If you're Ja'al or Vardish."

They continued on their arcing path, looking for an end to the field of deadly flowers.

Dar stopped short. "Well, this is unexpected," he whispered.

The field of murderous rosebushes stopped and a wide pathway led deeper into the Darkhollow. At first glance, it looked like it was made of black rocks. Upon further observation, Khyron realized someone—or some-thing—had burned a path through the Vampire Roses.

"At the risk of sounding foolish," Dar mused, "that's a trap or we've stumbled on someone else's way of getting into the Darkhollow."

Khyron chewed his lip. "Either way, we can avoid the roses."

"Agreed."

They rejoined Andyn and Buck and waited for Eric and Connor, who both arrived moments later. When asked about their reconnaissance, Eric waved a hand at the area they had scouted.

"More Roses, and then Ghost Creepers mingled among them. That's not the way in."

Khyron nodded. At least he had encountered Ghost Creepers before. They attacked by wrapping tendrils and vines around intruders. Their touch weakened. Worse still, in the presence of non-evil creatures, they set up a thin wailing that alerted anyone in earshot. The combination of Creepers and Vampire Roses would be a potent deterrent.

Dar knelt and drew in the dirt with a stick, indicating the burnt pathway leading deeper into the Darkhollow. Khyron listened with half an ear as his companions discussed their discovery. He mulled over various possibilities but he had no ready answers.

"It's too easy," Buck said.

"My feeling exactly," Connor agreed. "If it's a pathway, then it's for someone else to follow—probably not us. If it's a trap, I'm pretty sure I can find it or the Eye of Truth will tell us. Either way, we have to go in there. This would be the perfect place to put a Skull Gate."

Andyn's voice sounded doubtful. "But Varon and his patrols are always around this place. They would have seen anyone bringing the Gate components. They're not small and neither are bull-satyrs."

"Unless the Ja'al turn the porters invisible," Eric pointed out. "The Ja'al have mages. Even though invisibility magic is short-lived, it's certainly long enough to let a team sneak in when the hill sprite soldiers pass by."

"Invisible bull-satyrs?" Buck scoffed. "Now I've heard everything."

Khyron pointed at the burnt pathway. "I say we go past it and see if there are Vampire Roses on the other side. If the way is clear, we can always go in parallel to the path. If it isn't, Buck can scan our way on the path and make sure we're not about to run into a magical ambush."

The Riders considered the map, lost in thought.

Finally, Dar stood. "I agree with Khyron. We have to find out what's going on and this is the most direct route."

"Well, if we're going in to that hellish place," Andyn interjected, "I'm going to make sure we have every advantage."

She held out her hands over the group and murmured gentle phrases. As before, glittering nets of color wafted down over them and Khyron felt invigorated, protected and more clear-headed. The lights vanished.

"We should have Buck on point," Eric said, activating Fidelis.

Buck lowered the arm with the Eye of Truth. Dar drew his bow and stood on one side of him while Eric took the other side.

Khyron fitted an arrow to his own bow and followed them. Dar directed their path to the burned Vampire Roses. They picked their way between the blackened stumps. The lurking forest pressed in around them.

Buck led them through the eerie silence. The rainbow lights from the Eye of Truth sparkled whenever he turned his head. After about a hundred yards, the trail of burned Vampire Roses ended. Now they saw a more normal-looking track through the woods.

"On the trail?" asked Buck, eyes still focused ahead.

"Yes," Dar murmured.

The terrain dipped eventually but they kept on moving along the path. The trees grew more gnarled and misshapen, the moss darker, and the creepers and vines more tangled. They had to pause a couple of times to hack through growth or wait until Dar and Eric could find a clearer way.

Then the path led up the side of a densely wooded hill. As they approached the crest, the forest fell away and now they viewed a broad mesa with a ruined manor house.

Khyron's eyes widened. It looked like the manor had been actually made of clay or cake and that giant hands had scooped massive sections out of it. Blackened stones scattered the ground on the approach. Four gigantic leafless trees squatted close to the ruin. Noisome purple grass with glittering tips grew in scattered clumps.

Buck said something obscene.

"My thoughts exactly," Connor said.

"And look at that," Dar said, pointing.

Khyron's grip tightened on his bow. Set up against one of the remaining walls of the manor, a white structure of bones loomed.

"Could that be a Skull Gate, or a part of one?" Connor asked.

Andyn shook her head. "I'd said no, based on the drawings we saw—even from this distance. It looks more like an altar of bones."

"What's going on here?" asked Eric, his eyes darting all around. "Do the Ja'al have another plot in the works? Or is this something else?"

"Wouldn't surprise me," said Buck.

"All right then," said Dar. "Let's see what all this is."

He set an arrow to his bow and drew back the string, then advanced. Buck followed to his right and Eric came after. Khyron followed with Connor and Andyn on the right flank. They moved cautiously, eyes flitting around.

Khyron kept his attention on the rents in the manor walls, sighting along his arrow shaft as he went along. As they approached, he spied jumbles of stone amid ruined furniture. Rags of curtains shifted in the mild breeze.

Would be a good place to hide.

Buck's hand shot up. "Evil on the stones in front of us."

Khyron aimed at one of the nearest boulders, feeling a little ridiculous as he did so.

"Which one?" asked Connor.

"All of them."

Something prickled the short hairs of his neck and Khyron felt an odd foreboding.

"Something's not right," he said.

Then one of the blackened stones vibrated.

A memory flashed in his mind—a memory not of the Ja'al, but the Vardish.

"Down!" he screamed, all pretense of stealth gone. "Down now!"

To their credit, the Riders reacted as well as any troopers he had ever commanded. They dropped as one. The blackened rocks leaped up and detonated. Shards of hot, flaming stone lanced the air where they had stood moments ago. As it was, several corkscrewing fragments pinged off Buck's armor plate.

"What in Dolmide's Beard was that?" Connor yelled.

"Up now!" Khyron shouted. "The attack is next!"

Just as he had feared, figures loomed up out of the rents in the manor walls. His eyes widened.

They were bull-satyrs, but not like the ones they had vanquished days ago. Their blackened horns were cracked and broken. Their eyes glowed a baleful red. They opened their snouts, showing fangs dripping a steaming acid. Claws gleamed dully in the pale light and they wore no armor or clothing.

A horrid stench wafted out at the Riders. Khyron's heart clenched. The hide and skin of the satyrs was decayed and warped, as if they had been recently exhumed.

"Saint Kira protect us!" Dar breathed.

With inhuman speed, six creatures leaped out from the ruined manor and charged. In the span of two heartbeats, they covered half the distance.

Andyn held up her silver symbol of Verian's Tree. "*Verian, ald-adani!*"

A blue-white disc of energy shot out from her hand and struck the warped bull-satyrs. With rasping bellows, they covered their faces and slowed their headlong charge. The light tore pieces off them, but they struggled onward. Two stumbled, falling to their knees.

One shouted something harsh and vile. An object on the bone altar flashed red in response. The undead satyrs leaped to their feet and thudded forward.

Andyn's magical protections vanished and Khyron's heart grew cold. *What the hell?*

He loosed two arrows. They thumped into a satyr's chest, but the creature snarled and snapped them as if they were twigs. The other Riders also let fly, but only two shafts from Eric's bow hit the target, flaring with magic. The beast roared in pain.

Then the creatures were among them.

The clearing rang with the echo of distorted roaring, the sizzle of magic and the voices of his friends. Khyron saw Dar Cabot retreating steadily, parrying the attacks of his opponent with his dark-bladed sword.

This is going to get a bit sporty…

Khyron tossed his bow away and tumbled to his right, away from his companions. Leaping to his feet, he drew his sword and dagger. The edges of his blades glittered with silver fire.

A massive form loomed up at him. A meaty fist swept the air near his head and he tumbled away again, his weapons up.

Damn, it's fast!

A corrupted bull-satyr surged at him, swinging, clawing and goring. Its crimson eyes blazed. Khyron spun, ducked and parried. He slashed with his weapons, but every time he hit the creature, it felt like he hacked boiled leather. No blood flowed and the wounds didn't seem to slow the creature down.

He scrambled back to get some distance.

The monstrosity snorted and charged, head down. Khyron dodged. Too late, he saw a hoof lash out and a heavy blow hit him in the ribs. He flew to the side, landing in a heap, fighting for air. The bull-satyr spun and rushed at him again.

He rolled to his feet and leaped to the side, just avoiding the impact of both hooves as the bull-satyr jumped in the air to stomp him. The creature stumbled on a rock and righted itself, eyes flaring.

Khyron backpedaled, ribs aching with sharp pain. This was insane. If the creature really was some kind of undead, it shouldn't be able to move this fast.

It leaped forward again, arms swinging. An ear-splitting bellow of pain echoed off the walls of the manor.

"The eyes!" screamed Andyn. "Hit them in the eyes!"

Khyron sidestepped the charging beast, then moved in. As he expected, it spun towards him.

He planted his dagger to the hilt in one of its eyes and the weapon flared with white light. The bull-satyr went wild, shrieking and jerking its head to the side. Khyron's shoulder popped and searing pain shot through him. He lost the grip on his dagger. The creature staggered. Despite the pain, Khyron gritted his teeth and lunged. His sword flashed white fire as it punctured the creature's other eye and burst through the other side of its skull.

The corrupted bull-satyr froze in mid-stride and keeled over. Khyron went with the motion, slipping his sword out as it collapsed.

Panting, he retrieved his dagger and bow, wincing from the pain in his ribs and shoulder. His friends stood over the dark forms of their enemies. Five more bull-satyrs littered the ground. One of them had no head. Instead, a smoking stump remained at the top of its neck.

"You okay?" asked Eric as he approached.

"Got one in the ribs," Khyron said with a grimace. "Pretty good hit, too. And my shoulder isn't doing so well."

"Fidelis," Eric said. His golden spear shrank to the size of a dagger and he motioned for Khyron to sit.

"How's everyone else?" he asked Eric.

Eric's eyes closed. He laid his hands on Khyron's ribs and shoulder. "Dar got a horn in the leg. Andyn has him. He'll be all right. You sit still."

From long practice of being laid out in medical tents, Khyron did as he was told. Soon a wave of healing entered his body. It felt a lot like when Andyn did it, except not as powerful. Eric moved his shoulder gently and Khyron felt it pop back into place. His vision swam and he gasped from the pain, but the ache started receding almost immediately.

Eric opened his eyes. "Better?"

Khyron waited until the spots in his vision faded, then rotated his stiff shoulder. The sting in his ribs faded to a raw soreness. "I'll live."

They rejoined the others. Buck helped Dar to stand. Connor jumped to steady Andyn as she rose from the ground.

"It must have been bad," Khyron fretted. He lifted her chin to meet his eyes. "You look drained."

She nodded, face pale. "The beast nailed him right in the thigh and cracked his femur. I had to get to him pretty fast. Everyone else is a little banged up, but we're still breathing."

"We should draw back to the woods, as much as I hate to say it," said Eric.

They moved back and sat among a clump of bushes and rocks. Dar used his healing magic on Andyn. Soon, her color returned.

"Thanks."

Dar gave her a wry grin. "No, actually. Thanks to you. Again."

She smiled at him.

"Now, for the question no one is asking," said Buck, leaning on a nearby tree. "What in Hades were those things?"

"Darkspawn," replied Andyn.

"Wonderful," said Connor. "And those are…?"

"Greater undead made by powerful evil clerics. They use bigger, stronger creatures because the sacrificial rite destroys smaller corpses."

Dar paled and Khyron didn't blame him.

"Ja'al?" asked Connor.

She shook her head, jaw tight. "Sometimes. But this is usually the calling card of the Vardish."

"Wait," Buck said. "You mean the Ja'al aren't responsible for this?"

"No, I don't think so," Andyn said, standing. "I think we'll find that the bone structure is a shrine to Vardu, not one of the Ja'al pantheon."

"So now we're up against the Ja'al *and* the Vardish?" Eric asked, his tone unbelieving. "They're working together?"

Khyron stared down at his hands, trying to comprehend that possibility. One of the Dark Faiths was bad enough.

"I don't know," Andyn said putting her hands on her hips. "Vardu and one of the Ja'al gods are rivals. They both claim overlordship of death and the undead. Not that the two religions can't cooperate, but it would have to be something pretty serious."

She snatched up her maces and strode forward. The other Riders scrambled to their feet.

"Where are you going?" asked Khyron, loping to catch up with her.

"I have a feeling we'll find an answer at that shrine," Andyn said, pointing with Eleison. "I intend to search it. Something flashed red when I used Verian's power against the Darkspawn and I want to know what it was."

Khyron and the other Riders joined her. The white structure was indeed an altar of stone, decorated with skulls and bones. Flowing runes in some unknown language curved and entwined on the surface. Something metallic lay in a dark smear of dried blood on top of the altar. Malice emanated at them in waves.

Khyron forced himself to relax his grip on his sword.

We need different weapons.

"I wish Brandi were here," Andyn said. "I need another cleric with power enough to help cleanse this. She had excellent talents at this sort of thing."

Khyron's eyes flicked to Eric, who nodded, his eyes solemn.

"You can't do it yourself?" asked Connor.

She shook her head. "Not an altar like this. If these Darkspawn were created in this location, a Vardu high priest probably had a hand in it. The protections would be very strong."

Buck picked up a dry branch and hooked the metallic object. He laid it down on the rocks nearby.

A medallion of gold gleamed in the wan sunlight of the Darkhollow, flecked with dried blood. Khyron took a good look at the motif on the front.

A red moon carved of solid ruby hovered over a blackened tree. Skulls hung from the branches like some macabre fruit.

"Any ideas?" Dar asked.

Andyn shook her head. Without touching it, Connor wrapped up the medallion in a spare tunic, then placed it in a sack.

"Do you think the Blue Mark or the sprites might know?" asked Eric.

"Maybe. Let's get out of here and find out," Buck replied. "This place gives me chills."

With one last look at the ruined manor and its evil altar, the Grey Riders drew back into the Darkhollow.

Chapter Six – Toil and Trouble

The warm, humid air clung to her like a blanket.

Megan Alenar sighed and watched three birds flit past the narrow window in the sunlight. Their bright green, violet and yellow plumage looked almost too colorful for living creatures.

She remembered this environment—spring in the southern realms. Eventually, the heat of summer followed behind it, bringing nights as warm as summer days in the northern realms. She knew it well from her childhood in the Republic of Torosc, before the death of her parents, before she and Brandawyn had fled for freedom in the north.

Megan leaned on the wooden laboratory table by the window. A washcloth, cleaning solution and crucible sat next to her hands. Outside, below the tower, a pathway of black paving stones led through a garden to an iron gate in a stone wall. Guards in brigandine armor bearing spears stood watch at the entrance. Beyond the compound, the city of Catrin, Morlan, stretched off into the distance. Whitewashed buildings gleamed like bones in the sun. Tall trees lined the boulevards and other wizard's towers dotted the landscape.

It could be worse, she thought with a sigh. *I'm not overworked to exhaustion. He wants me alert and able to help with his experiments. And he is beyond the usual desires of men—or so he says.*

Oxbridge's attitude puzzled her. She was just a slave — technically, his property — but sometimes, she felt as if he regarded her like a prized but inexperienced apprentice. He refused to let his guards or guests have her for their pleasures, telling them that she was too valuable to damage. At other times, he treated her like a trained animal, or a valuable tool he kept locked in a drawer.

He's probably insane.

Her eyes drifted to a blocky temple not a mile away. Fashioned of deep purple stone shot through with veins of white, it squatted among the smaller structures like a brooding spider. Even at this distance, she easily made out the screaming daemon-head insignia of the Ja'al cult.

Her hands clenched into fists. Memories flooded her mind and she squeezed her eyes shut, willing the images away.

It didn't work. Her aunt and uncle's faces hovered behind her eyelids. She half-expected them to appear in the complex somewhere, ready to spirit her from this place of toil and lingering apprehension.

She knew they would not. Their eyes had closed for the last time.

At least Uncle Stephen and Aunt Daphne died clean and are with our parents now. And we destroyed a Skull Gate. Even if I never leave this place, we will have done that.

She let out a deep breath as her thoughts wandered to her sister. Her stomach tightened and she fought to maintain her composure.

God, please help Brandi. Give her strength and help her resist. I know You will do it. I trust You. You will free her, in whatever manner You choose. She loves You and will never serve the Ja'al willingly.

Brandi was a fighter.

Just like Dar…

Despite the months of separation and the distance, she heard his voice as if they had parted yesterday.

"I will wait and watch for you to return…"

Her vision swam and she shut her eyes.

"I won't cry," she whispered. "I won't cry. I will find a way to get free and make my way back to him, and we will rescue Brandi."

Footsteps sounded behind her. She wiped her eyes and turned around.

George Oxbridge raised an eyebrow at her expression. A white-haired, bearded old man, he wore deep green robes with gold piping and brown boots.

The wizard regarded her with intent brown eyes. "Is it all clean?"

"Yes, Master."

In the weeks since her capture, Megan had repeated those words many times. At first, they were bitter, but now she was used to them.

"Bring them into the laboratory."

Without a word, she gathered up crucibles, beakers, mortar and pestle and various utensils, packed them into a wooden box and followed him.

Megan considered a spell to distract or disarm him, but for the tenth time decided against it. The first attempt had not ended well. He had made sure she was locked in her cell for three days with only a few cups of water as punishment.

The second time he had feigned defeat, only to recapture her when one of his traps pinned her to the wall with glowing cords of magic.

I need to know more before I try again.

Oxbridge led her down a hallway. "We will repeat yesterday's experiment, with some modifications. We mustn't fall behind schedule. We have time for one more test this afternoon, then I have to get ready for a Council dinner. As usually, you will prepare all the materials while I gather my energies for the proper incantations. Then you will lend me all your magical power for the final fusion."

"Yes, Master," she said as they passed through another workroom.

Oxbridge's Elf apprentices labored over glass test tubes filled with bubbling pink liquid. Kantar and Olik glared at her, red-tinted eyes following her every move. Megan avoided their gaze. Oxbridge kept his employees away from his slaves, but that didn't prevent them from scheming ways to harass or injure her.

Olik aimed a kick at her legs. She skipped to the side, striking her bare foot against a chair leg. The box of implements rattled in her arms.

"Is something wrong?" Oxbridge said, turning with a raised eyebrow.

"No, Master," she said, trying to ignore the shooting pain in her foot. "I just slipped."

Oxbridge's gaze rested on the apprentices for a moment and they averted their gaze, returning to their work. He considered them for a moment, then strode away.

Megan followed him into a large circular chamber. Varienne spared Megan a little smile. A slim blonde human woman, she bowed to Oxbridge. Like

Megan, she was barefoot and wore an identical slave's tunic.

"Varienne," Oxbridge said, waving a hand to Megan. "Make sure slave Megan stays conscious."

"Yes, Master."

Megan shot back a tiny smile of her own to Varienne. She set the box down on a side table and began unloading it. The blonde woman stayed back near the wall, well clear of Oxbridge.

At least Varienne can put me back together after he wrings the magic from me like a wet towel.

Ever since she had met Oxbridge's healer-slave, Megan had wondered about the girl's name. It sounded familiar.

Megan prepared the special powders and liquids according to the sheet of parchment on the table next to her.

Another reason he values me, I guess. I can make sense of all the equations.

She doubted Olik or Kantar could.

Oxbridge stalked around a complicated series of glittering symbols etched into the floor, murmuring arcane words under his breath. The symbols flashed in sequence.

He stroked his beard. "I think I may have unraveled one of the equations," he mused to himself, "but there are a couple of other ways to solve it, so I'll have to try an experiment to make sure."

What does he see? What is he after?

She knew that Oxbridge's experiments had a lot to do with the signatures of discontinuities in the space-time continuum, particularly those associated with teleportation and planetary gates. She puzzled over the purpose of it all. She had seen many of his calculations and equations and she had managed to figure out one thing in particular: Oxbridge was not working on a Skull Gate. Though he used an impressive amount of power (and leeched much of her own), Megan had done some calculations on her own and the equations didn't match up.

"Attend, slave Megan," Oxbridge said. He indicated the equipment on the table. Megan pointed at two burners on the table and little sparks of flame lit them. She set about mixing powders and liquids per the instructions on the sheet. The wizard pulled a small notebook out of his robes and scribbled in it with a thin charcoal pencil as she worked.

Oxbridge folded his hands and closed his eyes, breathing deeply and regularly. Megan brought an acidic gel to a boil in one of the beakers, then added a few dark blue stones. When the stones turned yellow, she used levitation magic to pull them out of the gel onto a stone platter. She dipped a spoon into a tiny jar of white powder and sprinkled it onto the stones. They sizzled and their surfaces changed to deep black.

Oxbridge murmured arcane syllables under his breath, raising his hands over his head. The air warped and Megan's magical senses tingled uncontrollably. The back of her head felt hot and she held onto the table for support. Varienne moved to her side and took her hand.

Oxbridge's eyes snapped open, glowing with pale green light. "Now, slave!"

Megan focused her energy on the stones. The universe spun around her. Raw power such as she had never felt coursed through her body. She gasped.

The stones doubled in size.

The magical field forces switched off like a snuffed candle and Megan's legs shook. Oxbridge paled and he leaned both hands on the table, arms trembling.

Megan's vision swam and she slumped down to the floor. Varienne knelt next to her. Through misty eyes, Megan could barely make out her feet on the tiles.

"Excellent," Oxbridge grunted. She heard him pick up the platter with the stones and stumble to the etched floor symbols.

"Even if this doesn't work," he rasped, "we will have gathered important data. We will complete one of the greatest works of magic in history!"

Megan blearily watched him lay the stones down onto a twisting line of script.

"I have you," Varienne murmured, lifting Megan and helping her lean against the table. Her head now ached and pounded with every heartbeat.

Mage-exhaustion, she thought. *Great.*

"Hold still, Megan," said Varienne. She placed her hands on Megan's head, with one thumb on each temple.

The girl whispered soft words and a blessed coolness filled Megan's head, driving the pain away until only a bare shadow of it remained.

She's good. Not as good as Brandi, but good.

Megan's throat constricted and she felt tears sting her eyes. She pressed her fingernails into her palms.

"Are you all right?" Varienne asked, cornflower blue eyes concerned.

Megan shook her head. "It's nothing. I'm just very tired."

Oxbridge stepped back and barked out short, sharp words. The line of script flared and the stones reduced back to their normal size. A ribbon of darkness snaked up into the air, splitting into several tendrils. The dark strips flew out the open windows.

Oxbridge stared at something she couldn't see, smiling broadly. His eyes shone. "Ah. Well, this is a lot closer. Good. Very good."

Megan waited. She hoped he would forget about her and go off to some other experiment.

He let out a deep breath, draining a cup of wine on a nearby table. Some of his color returned. "Your power and skills are significant, slave, though I can't for the life of me figure out where you got them. You're just an ordinary female half-breed. You're very intelligent, but otherwise completely unre-markable. Where does it come from?"

His eyes measured her. She felt as if her simple tunic had been stripped from her and she stood naked in front of his piercing gaze. She wouldn't put it past him to dissect her to satisfy his curiosity.

Instead he spoke to Varienne. "See that this slave is treated for exhaus-tion. I think I may have tried to use too much of her energies and she will need to recuperate in time for the demonstrations."

Varienne nodded and came to Megan's side, lifting her with gentle, strong arms. Megan shot an alarmed glance at her master.

He noticed her eyes and smirked.

"Yes," Oxbridge said. "I have spoken of your considerable talents to some of my colleagues and you will demonstrate your skills for them at a conference in a couple of weeks. I will need you to be at your best, but our experiments also must continue. Varienne's skills will come in very handy."

Varienne bowed and helped Megan out of the experiment chamber. In-stead of leading her back through the workroom with her Elven tormentors, she took a different route through the kitchens and up a back set of stairs.

"Thank you," Megan whispered.

Varienne only smiled in reply. She led her through a door into a hallway, then along a covered bridge between the tower and the slaves' quarters.

Megan's legs felt like lead weights by the time Varienne got her to her cell. She flopped down on the cot.

"I'll be right back. Lie still."

As if I could move now anyway.

In a few seconds, Varienne returned, carrying a satchel. She unrolled a leather medical case and selected a potion vial. Eyeing it critically, she pulled out the stopper and held it to Megan's lips.

The taste of grapes, beef and cumin stung her tongue, but she swallowed. A bright warmth spread throughout her body. In seconds, she felt her energy returning.

"Better?"

Megan smiled at Varienne. "Yes, thanks." She sat up.

Varienne helped her. "Dizzy?"

"Not much now, thanks to you."

Varienne sat on the cot next to her. For a long time, she said nothing, her lovely face showing only concern. Then, she replaced the potion vial and medical case in the satchel.

"You are suffering from more than just mage-exhaustion," she said, placing a hand on Megan's shoulder. "What's bothering you?"

Megan kept her eyes on the afternoon sunlight streaming in through her tiny window. "We all have our sorrows. Mine are no greater than anyone else's."

"Sometimes it helps if you share them."

Megan regarded her silently for a while. Some part of her reached out to Varienne — measuring, assessing, gauging. Then, as had happened several times since the battle at the Skull Gate, a mild aura surrounded the person before her. In times past, with Olik and Kantar, the nimbus was a lurid red. In Varienne's case, it was gold.

As before, she wondered. For her Elven tormentors, the aura came with a sense of foreboding and evil. For Varienne, Megan only felt kindness and strength.

Deep within her, she felt Varienne could be trusted, but she hesitated to expose her to further danger by sharing too much. "There are some things I can't reveal to you."

Varienne nodded. "Fair enough. Tell me what you can."

Megan took a deep breath. "My parents are dead. They were killed in the Christian persecutions in Torosc, in Coastwatch, as a matter of fact. My sister and I fled north, where we became freelance sell-swords. I met the love of my life there, but two of our relatives came and recruited us for a special assignment. We…"

She pressed her lips together. The sorrow threatened to overwhelm her and she took a deep breath. Varienne's hand covered her own.

"You don't have to —"

"No, I can do this." Megan said. "My aunt and uncle died in battle. My only sister was captured by the Ja'al and warped into an undead servant, a vampire. They took her away, but I saw the spark of life in her eyes. I know she's in there still. I will escape, find her and free her from the curse."

"And your love?"

Megan sighed and swallowed the lump in her throat. "He promised to wait for me and I believe him. I will be reunited to him, by God's providence."

Varienne gave her hand a squeeze. "I know your God will aid you. Do not give up. While life remains, hope remains. What is your sister's name?"

"Brandawyn."

"A lovely name. I'm sure she's as beautiful as you."

Megan squeezed her hand in return. "And what about you? Do you have family?"

"I did, in Eastbluff, in Deran. I was captured at age fifteen and held by a slave-dealer. That was four years ago. But I have hope. The great god Irial will give me strength and provide a way for me to escape and return home."

"I will help you if I can."

Varienne's eyes danced. "Indeed! Of course, there is the small matter of the wizard. I'm sure he is more concerned about you escaping than me."

"I beg to differ. You're his only healer. At any rate, if we at least reach Gorostol, I know people who could keep us safe."

"I wasn't even thinking of getting that far. In Kentridge, Altus would help me."

"Altus?" Now something more tickled at Megan's memory. Her mind whirred.

"Yes, Altus Volan. He was one of the sons of the slave traders. I think he was disgusted by the whole business, frankly. If he could have bought me for himself and freed me, he would have. He was under the thumb of his father too much, though."

Her memory cleared and Megan's heartbeat quickened. "Altus Volan? Was he a soldier at one time?"

"I think so. He may have gotten in with the wrong crowd. I think the Skullhead Legion wanted to recruit him and his father and mother were difficult to deal with. I was always afraid he would join up just to be free of them."

"I know him!"

Varienne's jaw dropped. "You do? How?"

"We were hot on the trail of… well, I can't tell you. But it is enough to say that we rescued some slaves and, in the process, I was captured by Skullheads. Their commander was Altus Volan."

Varienne's eyes widened and she gasped, turning pale. "What? He was? Where? When?"

"Months ago, in Gorostol, near Shark Bluff."

"What happened? Please say he's alive!"

"Well, he was roughed up a little in the end, but he was fine when we left him. You see, he protected me from some vile and heartless men under his command. I could tell his heart really wasn't in what he did and I think he secretly wanted a way out. Eventually my sister and relatives defeated the Skullheads, freed me and captured Altus. We spoke to him and found out he was ready to renounce that part of his life, so we let him go. He searches for you now, I think."

Varienne covered her mouth with one hand. Tears leaked out of her eyes. Megan embraced her.

"Oh, praise Irial!" Varienne said finally. "I knew he would break away! I knew he had a good heart!"

She began to cry and Megan held the younger girl in her arms, trying unsuccessfully to stop her own tears.

Finally, Varienne shook herself and raised her head. "What happened then? Where did he go?"

Megan smiled. "We gave him the means to make a new life for himself and he was in Gorostol when we last saw him. My aunt gave him a reference to someone who could help him get a reputable job."

Varienne's eyes welled up again and she caught Megan in a tight hug. "Oh, thank you, Megan! Thank you! I have prayed so many nights that he would change and be free! You are truly a blessed one. Irial the Creator himself sent you to him, I know it."

Megan hugged her back. "I think he is a good man. I know he will find you."

Varienne pulled away. "I am sure of it! And you. Who is your man? What is his name?"

"Dar."

"Well then, your Dar will find you. And I will help you until he does."

"We have to find a way out of Oxbridge's clutches first. That's not easy. I've tried, twice, but he's outwitted me each time. I just have to be more careful the next time."

She patted Varienne's hand, frowning. "There is something else. I know he is in contact with Brandi's captors. He's used threats against her safety to bully me when I'm too tired or in too much pain. When we make our move, it will have to be sudden and swift so that he doesn't know where we went."

"I will work with you," Varienne said, rising and lifting Megan up with her. "So help me, Megan, I will attend at your wedding and you at mine. Let us promise each other."

This is madness. Brandi is a vampire, Dar is far away, I'm enslaved to an unscrupulous wizard deep in the heart of one of the most evil nations in the world… I'm making wedding plans?

She met Varienne's eyes and saw fire of such strength and fierce determination that her smile returned.

"I promise."

<h1 style="text-align:center">Chapter Seven- Profaned</h1>

The magic called. She resisted, squeezing her eyes shut. The call strengthened.

No. I won't do it again.

The magic thrummed with an insistent tempo, piercing the shield of her will. She held her hands to her head, praying for strength. The headache began and a red haze swam behind her eyelids.

"Delilah," Adina's voice sang from outside her room. "Time to get ready, my dear."

She gritted her teeth. "That is *not* my name! I am Brandawyn Alenar!" A knife of pain struck between her eyes and she gasped.

"Your name," Adina said with a hint of steel in her voice, "is whatever I choose to call you."

Another white-hot stab hit Brandi. Adina sighed. "Frankly, I don't know why you're complaining. It's even a name straight out of that religious book of yours. Now stop being obstinate. We have work tonight."

"No!" Brandi hissed through clenched teeth. "I refuse!"

The magic doubled in intensity and Brandawyn bit back a moan of agony. It felt like her brain would split in two.

"Now, that's not very cooperative, is it? Ah well. I guess I can always contact George Oxbridge about your sister, Megan. She's a fine slave, I'm sure, and quite able to help him in his laboratory, but she can always perform more than one duty, can't she? The old man may be beyond the usual appetites of men, but I'm sure his visitors and guests would love for her to entertain them. What do you want, Brandi?"

The magic receded. She relaxed, feeling overwhelming relief as the pain diminished.

"Megan is stronger than that. She will defeat you," she breathed.

"Perhaps. But the bargain was her life for your servitude. And you will serve, or she will suffer."

An iron clamp of magical power seized Brandi's mind and it was all she could do to stay conscious. She felt herself recede into the background. Another personality came to the fore: base, violent, arrogant, greedy, selfish.

The real Brandawyn Alenar retreated to a small core of her being, a little oasis of happy memories and diamond-hard faith where she still remembered that God loved her.

The magic warped and twisted and Delilah, the servant of the Ja'al, took control.

She stood. "Yes, mistress," she said.

"Good, my darling," Adina purred. "Now, get dressed. Wear the ivory gown with the gold decorations. It complements your hair and I hear that our newest target likes girls who look pure."

Delilah complied. She stripped off her plain black tunic and slipped into a form-fitting cream gown that left her shoulders bare. Mechanically, she took up a brush and ran it through her strawberry blonde hair.

Her violet eyes held a light sparkle of red. She gave a wicked smile. In the recesses of her mind, the real Brandawyn cringed.

Her gaze drifted to a medallion lying on the worn little table by her cot. It glittered in the moonlight drifting in through the tiny window. She would not need it to protect her from the sun, so she left it there.

"What shoes, mistress?"

"The ivory sandals. It won't matter really."

Delilah slipped her feet into the sandals, then knocked on the door to her cell. "I am ready, mistress."

The edges of the portal sizzled with purple light and it popped open.

Adina, resplendent in a deep indigo dress, smiled in approval. She fingered a ring on her pinky finger, a garnet carved in the shape of a skull.

"Very nice, Delilah," she said, turning to go in a swish of long brown hair.

"You will serve well tonight."

Adina led the way out of the cellar, up the stairs to the main hall of the mansion. Bright spheres of light held by statues of nymphs and satyrs dazzled Delilah's eyes for a second, but she kept up with her mistress.

Two guards in dark brigandine awaited them, armed with dirks and short swords. Their eyes watched her appreciatively but warily. She smelled their blood even from this distance and felt their life force. She favored them with a wink and a demure smile that hid her fangs.

They stood no chance whatsoever. The guards knew enough not to even think of touching her. Few people knew of her true nature, but the rumors ran rampant. That and her service to Adina kept them at a distance.

It didn't stop her from tempting them with her body. Their uncertainty and apprehension made it all the more enjoyable. She knew they were attracted to her but afraid.

Delicious.

"*Cruel!*" the real Brandawyn cried.

Delilah felt a rush of warmth and light and her step faltered.

"Something wrong?" Adina waited for her in the foyer, a frown on her face. She lifted her hand with the pinky ring. It flared orange-red.

Delilah, servant of the Ja'al, regained control. She shook her head.

"Good," Adina said. "Come along."

A short walk down the steps led to a waiting carriage. Delilah let one of the guards assist her and she slipped inside.

Berek greeted them with a slight smile on his lips. His eyes glittered in the light of the carriage lamps.

"Magnificent," he said as Adina entered. "Both of you."

Adina stroked his cheek and lingered over a kiss. "Good boy."

The guards mounted nearby horses and they set off.

Adina fluffed her hair and inspected herself in a little hand mirror. "Delilah, your target for the evening is a Mister Arless Octavio. He is a merchant of considerable fortune and has political connections here in Fenbluff."

Berek nodded. "We need him subverted. He has a liking for delectable half-elven girls. You will ensure that he is sufficiently distracted, then deliver your, er, special gift."

Images of past assignments flooded her mind. Brandi cringed at the memories of other men who had become the recipients of that "special gift".

"God, help me! Don't let them force me again!" Brandi whimpered.

Still under the influence of Adina's magic, Delilah ignored her. From her access to Brandi's memory, Delilah knew that a blond half-elven man with violet eyes was very important to Brandi.

Maybe I'll get a blond one. Won't that be delicious? Delilah felt an exhilarating anticipation of the night's activities. She lounged back in her seat, smiling languidly. "Is this one handsome?"

Adina sniffed. "He could be a toad for all you care."

"Yes, mistress." Delilah pouted. She preferred the handsome ones. They tasted better.

Brandi fought against the iron bands of Adina's spell but it remained strong, for now.

Berek's smile turned icy. "Do not, under any circumstances, let it get too far and kill him. We need his resources. Understood?"

Delilah shrugged. "As you say, Master Berek."

She gazed out the window as they clattered off into the evening. As a vampire enslaved to Adina, she had several ways to affect victims. She could use her bite to drain someone's lifeblood or enslave them to Adina. She could also infect another person with vampirism or create a thrall loyal to Delilah alone. These last two, of course, Adina kept under strict control using her magic ring. It wouldn't do to have Delilah creating a small army of other vampires or loyal slaves with which to challenge her mistress.

The carriage pulled up in a line of other carriages at a splendid mansion at the end of a cul-de-sac overlooking the Great Sea. Guests streamed up a curving staircase that led to the front door, where attendants stood waiting to assist them. Guards in shiny plate mail watched from vantage points along the route.

Adina and Berek exited first. Delilah followed them, smiling sweetly at the attendants.

They entered the main hall crowded with guests. Delilah played the role of attentive servant, fetching drinks and dainties for Berek and Adina.

Twin hungers made her feel faint. The scent of the food made her stomach rumble— Brandi had not been fed very much that day. The proximity of so many potential victims made Delilah fairly drool in anticipation.

Delilah wavered, overcome with physical hunger and vampiric desire. Maybe if she at least took care of the physical part it might assuage the dizziness.

"Mistress, may I have a snack of something?"

"No." Adina spared her a disdainful glance. "We need you hungry."

"Maybe just a little morsel?"

"I said no, Delilah. Obey."

"Yes, Lady Adina."

Her masters worked the room with charm and aplomb. Despite her hunger, Delilah continued to play her part. Many eyes followed her and she reveled in the attention.

Adina snapped her fingers. As Delilah approached, Adina nodded to one corner of the room. "See the blond one talking to the old man with the beard? He's your target. Go get him. We will be monitoring you, so make sure you let us know when you slip away with him."

Ooh, perfect: blond and handsome. This one's for you, Brandawyn…

Delilah sashayed through the crowd towards her selected victim and his elderly companion.

"Mister Arless Octavio?" she asked with a curtsey.

Octavio's eyebrows rose as she straightened. "Yes?"

"I am Delilah, a servant to Lady Adina. She told me to arrange your next meeting. May we discuss the details?"

The men's eyes roamed over her figure and she smiled coyly at Octavio.

He inclined his head to the older man. "If you will excuse me, Councilor."

The councilor measured Delilah with his eyes and smirked. "We will continue our discussion later, when your activities of the evening are concluded."

"Indeed."

Octavio turned his full attention to Delilah. "Now then. When does Lady Adina wish to meet again?"

Delilah looped an arm in his as he set his goblet down on a nearby table. She shot a glance at Adina. "I think we need to schedule something for next week. However, some of the particulars are, shall we say, delicate? Is there somewhere more private we can go?"

Octavio's smirk changed to a leer. "Certainly."

With another quick glance to make sure Adina and Berek followed,

Delilah let him lead her across the ballroom. He walked up a curving staircase past other couples deeply engaged in conversation. At the top of the stairs, they arrived at a carved wooden door.

"This should do," he murmured.

She demurely lowered her gaze and preceded him inside. A chamber with a large bed, a round wooden table and a pair of open doors to a balcony greeted her eyes.

"Very nice," she commented, walking out to the balcony, where statues of nude dancers stood frozen in the moonlight.

"Yes," he replied, following her out into the fresh air. "More importantly, we won't be overheard or disturbed."

"We wouldn't want that."

Octavio leaned on the railing and sized her up again before speaking. "Your mistress is very interested in my support."

"Naturally. You are an important man in society."

"There are costs incurred by providing such support. I fear that your mistress is unwilling to meet these costs. Also, I would be taking sides. That is risky."

"But there are rewards too." Delilah traced her fingers on his arm and went back into the room. The touch of his warm flesh under her hand pulsed with lifeblood. It took all her reserve to prevent her hunger from overcoming her.

"Like beautiful women?" he asked, following her.

She glided up to the bedpost and stood with her back to it. With her toes, she slipped the sandals off her feet and nudged them under the bed. "You think I'm beautiful?"

"So far."

"I have more to show you."

He approached. She ran a hand up his arm to his shoulder, then cupped the back of his neck and kissed him slowly and languidly. A tingle inside her brain told her Adina lurked not far away.

Her pulse quickened at the feeling of his heartbeat, so near. She pulled him in tighter. His hands moved down her ribcage to her hips, then lower. Both her vampiric and womanly sides responded.

Brandawyn Alenar struggled to free herself from Delilah. "*No!*" she screamed. *"I won't do it!"*

Warmth surged through her. Delilah pulled back from the kiss and blinked. She felt dizzy and uncertain, as if she were trying to remember something important that she had to avoid doing.

He frowned, tightening his hold on her. "Too much wine this evening?"

"No, I don't think… it's nothing."

He raised an eyebrow. "I hope so. I am sure Lady Adina would not send someone who is ill."

Adina's order echoed in Delilah's head. *We need him subverted.*

"I'll be fine. Give me a moment." Delilah took a deep breath.

A sudden, intense wave of magical force rocked her and Brandi faded. Delilah gave Octavio a seductive smile. "There. I'm better. Where were we?"

She loosened the ties on the back of her gown and let the material glide down her body. She placed Octavio's hands on the fabric. He obliged by sliding it down her hips and legs. The dress slipped to the floor.

Octavio's eyes flashed. "Well, well."

"You like?"

He grinned wolfishly and slipped out of his tunic, revealing a slim, muscular frame. "Yes, but I think a closer inspection is warranted."

She slid onto the bed, enjoying the way his eyes devoured her body. "Then let me show you some other beautiful things."

"This is wrong!" Brandi screamed.

He removed his boots and trousers and tossed them aside. Soon they lay entangled on the bed, arms, legs and feet intertwined. Delilah enjoyed the feeling of his hands and lips on her body. Soon she would feed.

"Don't!" wailed Brandawyn.

"Yes!" moaned Delilah. "More!"

"No!" Brandawyn struggled to exert herself. *"This isn't me!"*

Delilah faltered. Then a flash of magic burst inside her and she regained control, flipping Octavio onto his back.

"Oh, you're a strong one," he purred, his hands on her firm, round breasts.

Delilah laughed. "I'm just getting started." She lowered her lips to his neck.

Fangs snapped out in her mouth. Octavio bucked and moaned.

"My turn!" she hissed and bit down hard.

Octavio froze with a gasp.

Ravenous hunger rose up in Delilah. She eagerly lapped up his hot life-blood. All the pent-up tension of battling Brandawyn and hours of starvation and deprivation drove her. Her control wavered.

If I can't stop this, Brandi realized, *at least I can ruin it.*

"Delilah! *Defy Adina!*" she called. "*Delilah! Do what you want! Feed! He's there for the taking!*"

Yes, Delilah exulted. *To hell with Adina!*

She began to drain his life force. A lurid red glow lit the room and Octavio's eyes filled with it.

A voice rang out. "What do you think you're doing, you slut!"

Delilah raised a bloody face towards the door to the room. Adina stood there, furious, with Berek at her side.

"I said turn him, you brainless whore! Not drain him!"

Delilah snarled, dipping her head down to Octavio again.

"*Stop!*" shouted Brandawyn. Delilah wavered, dizzy and unsure.

Adina raised her hand. The pinky ring flashed. For a split second, Delilah battled both Brandawyn and Adina.

With an irritated hiss, Adina thrust her fist at Delilah. A misty red globe shot out. It struck her with an audible pop and hurled her backwards. Delilah flew off the bed and hit a rug on the floor, sliding into a heap in the corner.

Berek and Adina leaped to Octavio's side. Delilah sat up, licking the blood from her mouth.

"He can be saved." Berek took out a tiny silver vial and spread an ointment on the blond man's neck.

"Did it work?" Adina snapped.

A mild blue glow lit Octavio's neck and his wounds faded. The man's eyes glazed over with a purple sheen that faded in a couple of heartbeats. With a deep gasp, he rolled on his side and coughed.

"What?" he muttered, putting a hand to his head.

Berek tapped Octavio's forehead with his middle finger and a yellow spark flashed. The blond man's eyes rolled back in his head and he flopped down on the mattress.

Berek checked his pulse and nodded. "The medicine worked. He'll survive. And yes, he has been turned." He shot a venomous look at Adina. "No thanks to you."

"Me? What did I do? It's her fault!"

"If you hadn't starved her, this wouldn't have happened!" Berek shot back.

Adina glared at him, then at Delilah, lounging on the rug. "I know what I'm doing. There's something else at work."

She crouched in front of Delilah. "Look at me," she commanded. Her pinky ring flashed again.

Delilah snarled but held still. Adina stared into her eyes, then cursed and stood.

"It's that bitch, Brandawyn," Adina snapped. "Damn her miserable soul to Hades! How is she able to interfere?"

Berek joined her and frowned down at Delilah. "This is the fifth time, Adina. We've had trouble from the start. Somehow, Brandawyn is in there, working against us. We can get her to start seducing a target but it always gets disrupted."

Adina ground her teeth and swore.

"Maybe it's time to get rid of her," Berek said, sliding a hand towards a dagger at his belt. "She's more trouble than she's worth."

"No," Adina snapped. "I spent a lot of effort to turn this wench into a serviceable thrall and I'm not about to give up on the project."

She bent, took Delilah's chin in her iron grip and hauled her to her feet.

"You will submit, you filthy trollop," she purred. "I have all the time I want and the might of the Ja'al gods are on my side. You have nothing."

Something in Adina's eyes belied her words.

She's unsure, Brandi realized. *She doesn't understand what's going on and it has her off balance. I can do this.*

Delilah wavered. Brandawyn grew stronger and stronger. Delilah faded and vanished.

"I have God," Brandi whispered.

Adina dealt her a ringing slap in the face. "Your god is weak. Otherwise you wouldn't be in this position, harlot. How does he allow you to come into my power if he cares so much?"

Brandi gave a tiny smile. "He permits it because he offers you the chance to repent. Through your evil, His glory will shine all the brighter."

Another hard slap made her head ring again. "Don't play the pure maiden with me. You've bedded five men at our command."

Brandi met her eyes calmly though her stomach twisted at the memories. "You had to force me. What does that say about your gods?"

Adina's grip tightened and pain lanced through Brandi's jaw. "Your blasphemy will not avail you. You will submit. I guarantee it."

Brandi met her eyes calmly. "You have already lost, Adina."

Adina's hand shot back for another strike but Berek grabbed her arm. "Let's go. We have what we came for. Every minute we stay means we could be discovered."

He threw the dress and sandals at Brandi. "Get dressed."

Brandi slipped back into the clothing.

Berek watched her like a hawk. "What now, Adina?"

"First, help me with Octavio." She cast a scornful glance at Brandi. "I have a different plan for her, later. I think maybe a change in venue and assignment will be in order until I can figure this out."

Brandi pressed her lips together and didn't say anything, watching them attend to their latest victim.

I will never surrender…

Chapter Eight – Convolutions

Connor Lomin leaned back against the tree trunk with a sigh. His eyes wandered to the opposite side of their campsite. Buck dozed against a pair of trees with his backpack as a pillow and Khyron kept watch, recurve bow at the ready. Andyn brushed out the mane of her pegasus.

Connor drew a letter from his pocket and opened it. The blocky script looked like Dwarven. The symbol of a snarling badger at the bottom of the page drew his eyes and he smiled.

Now that I have a chance, I can take another look…

He took out a pair of spectacles from a small flat box. Tiny red jewels near the tops of the lenses flashed as he put them on. The letters on the page transformed to an elegant, flowing script in Humana.

He recognized the handwriting immediately.

"*My dearest Connor,*" he read. "*I hope this finds you well and that your mission continues to be successful. Agents of the Alliance tell me of your victories in Terenai and I am glad, though I am worried and pray for you every night.*

I think of you often. Last night, Mindy made that crab cobbler you liked so much when you were here. Do you remember that? I should hope so. You had three helpings! I think Buck was peeved that he didn't get the last little bit of it. I have fond memories of our time together despite the pain of Handor's passing. Having all of you with me made a difficult time much easier.

You will be happy to know that I had the gazebo rebuilt after our battle with Beol and his minions. It looks better than ever. I hope you can visit me before the summer ends to see the flowers in full bloom in the garden. Your favorite, the Gold Dragon Rose, is not doing as well as when you were here. I think it misses you. So do I.

My cousins have returned home but I now have two helpers: a married Elven couple from Terenai named Caridan and Caria Meraloy. They were both sell-swords and retired three years ago, but came here at the behest of the Alliance. They are both lovely people and very competent. I feel completely safe with them at the mansion, though it is not the same with you gone.

I would love to write about more pleasant things, but I must turn this letter to our most recent business. Caridan and Caria have been assisting in rooting out unpleasant elements within the company still remaining from my unlamented Uncle Beol's time. During one of their more recent forays, they procured a small book with writing in code. Though it was damaged by fire, they managed to decipher some of it and it mentioned something related to a red moon. I trust you will know what this means, since you also mentioned it in your recent correspondence. There was also a set of coordinates in latitude and longitude that I have included at the bottom of this letter. The location is in eastern Terenai, near the Blue Mark's area of operations. Lord Melinor and I agreed that it would be prudent for you and the other Riders to investigate.

I have to admit all this is perplexing. Knowing what we do about the significance of the red moon, this adds an ominous aspect to the whole business. We have sent the book on to Mil-Tereth for analysis and continue on our work.

Our rebuilding of the Lervion Shipping Line is going very well. We have renewed the old accounts and business is picking up. At least Beol did something right: he set up a network of safe-houses throughout the lands which is coming in very handy. To date, however, we have not found anything more about the focus of your particular mission.

Please write back to me when you can. I know you are busy and your work is very dangerous. I offer sacrifices at the Temple of Irial every day on your behalf and pray night and day. I hope to see you one day very soon.

Ever Yours,

Hannah"

"Ever yours," he whispered, running his fingertips over her signature. He replaced the lenses safely in a box in his backpack.

He sat quietly for a while, tapping the letter in his hand. The afternoon deepened. Long shadows from the dense forest striped the ground with shafts of dark and light among boulders and shrubs.

He questioned if his affection for Hannah was not simply empathy at the loss of her brother. Her attachment to him had certainly seemed genuine and, deep down, he had to admit that he felt a strong connection to her during the weeks after the funeral.

Would her feelings fade as time passed and her grief abated? Maybe he was just letting his sympathy get the better of him.

Yet, he saw her lively green eyes reflected in the bright forest and heard her gentle laugh in birdsong. He knew exactly which wildflowers she would like among the many he had seen.

Can I really find a future with her?

He imagined himself settling down at the manor, helping to run the Lervion Shipping Line at her side, seeing the sun set over the lake by Meridian. He smiled, envisioning a life of peace and family like the one he had known in Glen before the Plague.

What would Janey think?

He gave a low chuckle at the thought of his deceased wife's probable reaction. She would raise an eyebrow and tell him that she never intended him to live out his life alone, thank you very much, and, furthermore, that she didn't appreciate being used as an excuse to avoid a relationship with another woman who was perfectly capable of making him happy.

Yes. That's exactly what she would say…

Andyn shot Connor a glance. "Re-reading the mushy romantic parts?"

Connor's face flushed. "How do you know there's anything romantic in there?"

She merely gave him an enigmatic smile. "I don't, of course."

Khyron grinned at her and raised his eyebrows at Connor.

He decided to ignore them both and closed his eyes.

"Don't get too comfortable," Andyn said. "Dar and Eric should be back very soon." She lifted her saddlebags onto Medianox.

"Not sure we should do this so close to nightfall," Connor said.

She shrugged. "More of a problem for the humans than the rest of us."

"I heard that," said Buck.

Connor considered flicking a pebble at him but settled more comfortably in his place instead.

"They're back," said Khyron. Connor's eyes snapped open and he sat up. Like green-and-brown dappled ghosts, Dar and Eric rejoined them.

"Well?" Khyron asked.

"There's a mine," Eric said, lifting back his hood. He held out his forearm and Stealth alighted on it. He spoke to the construct and it transformed into a cloud of light that merged into the brooch on his cloak.

Connor's eyes widened. "Here? On the eastern border of Terenai? Hannah didn't mention a mine."

"Well, there's one down the valley, with an abandoned town. Everything looks run-down."

Buck sat up. "Anyone there?"

Dar shook his head. "No. Eric used Stealth to scout around. And it's not on the map."

"Really…" Andyn mused.

"Really." Eric pursed his lip. "The one that Captain Arad gave us is the best the military has of this area, though it's two years old. Of course, the town could have been built in the intervening time, but it looks too decrepit."

"That's very odd," Khyron said, taking up the reins of Zasural.

"Agreed." Connor slipped Hannah's note into his saddlebag and swung into the saddle. The Riders gathered up their gear.

Phantom nickered softly and he patted her nose. "We should at least get a look before night falls," he remarked.

Eric and Khyron concealed the campsite and mounted up.

"How far?" asked Buck as they trotted their pegasi through the woods.

"About three miles," Dar said, "Still, I don't think we should fly. The town may look abandoned, but someone may be watching and we'd certainly attract attention."

Buck smirked at him. "At least we're not hiking."

That got a guffaw from Dar. They rode off two by two: Dar and Eric in the front, followed by Khyron and Connor, then Buck and Andyn.

Connor tried to keep an eye on the thick forest, but mostly watched the two scouts. After all this time in their company, he learned to rely on their uncanny ability to sense danger out in the wilds. Also, Andyn was attuned to the living forest and would alert them if she detected anything.

His mind wandered to a mansion in a mighty city by a lake, to the south, in Gorostol. He imagined a lovely halfling woman standing on the balcony of her room, gazing at the waters of the Kaljirre, praying for him.

Maybe I should return the favor.

He sighed. He hadn't prayed since Janey and Rose died years ago. He wasn't sure if Irial would even listen to him now.

Then he smiled, imagining his mother's voice.

"Irial always listens. We're the ones who don't."

He jerked his thoughts back to their trek and forced himself not to think about Hannah. Missing her just distracted him anyway. He would have to use a possible reunion as a motivation to not get himself killed.

They traversed down hollows and up slopes thick with vegetation, following the leaders. The afternoon had truly deepened into evening when Dar's hand shot up. Connor reined in, hand going to his bow.

Eric and Dar dismounted. The other Riders did likewise.

"There," Dar said, pointing with a gloved hand. Past the trees, Connor saw a thin road overgrown with weeds. A few dilapidated wooden buildings huddled near the thoroughfare. The road continued beyond and ended at the face of a short cliff that loomed up on the left. A large, dark opening yawned at them.

"Your turn," Eric whispered.

Without another word, Connor looped his bow over his back and lifted his hood over his head. He slipped between two large trees under the cover of a massive growth of ferns.

He fell into a familiar pattern of movement, pauses, and movement again, using shadow, cover and line of sight to skulk between hiding places. He varied the pacing, sometimes waiting for only one heartbeat, sometimes for several or even a dozen. Always, his eyes flicked from one shadow to the next. Often, he stopped to listen. All other thoughts faded into the background: the Ja'al, the mysterious town, possible ambush… even Hannah's smile.

He reached one of the buildings. A door hung off its hinges and he scooted around to a tree from where he could look inside. Nothing moved and his heat-vision showed nothing living.

That doesn't help with undead, of course.

He kept one hand close to the enchanted brooch of the Devoted

Defender, pinned to his tunic. Not trusting to chance, he slipped away again and repeated his reconnaissance of each of the eight buildings. He noticed several other structures that had collapsed completely.

Nothing moved save a few rats and lizards. One of the rodents regarded him with opalescent, beady eyes, then scampered away towards the cave.

He crept up to the entrance. There was no cover before the cave mouth and he would make an easy target, so he approached from the side.

He peered inside. Total blackness permeated the cavern.

Wait. What's that?

He sniffed. It smelled faintly like a dog kennel—and something else.

Brimstone?

His pulse quickened and the hackles on his neck rose. Careful to make no noise, he returned to his companions via a different route. As he went, he cast glances over his shoulder at the town.

It was almost dark by the time he got back to them. In as few words as possible, he described what he had found.

Andyn scowled. "Brimstone? I can think of a few things that have that scent. None of them good."

"How do we approach so Buck and Dar can see?" Eric asked.

Khyron chewed his lip. "The best way may be to send them in first with glow-globes. We follow in the shadows and if anything attacks, we'll be ready."

"Let's go," Buck said. "I want to get a good sleep tonight and the sooner we smash a Skull Gate the better."

Andyn cast protective and augmenting spells on all of them. When the magical auras faded, Buck produced a small glass sphere with a metal clip from his belt purse. He shook the ball and it glowed brightly. He clipped the sphere to his shield and hefted Khelios. Dar set an arrow to his bow and nodded. Without another word, the two humans marched around the edge of the ruined town towards the cave.

Connor and Khyron flitted through the shadowed woods on either side while Eric and Andyn followed Dar and Buck. At the cave entrance, the two humans paused. Dar knelt to examine the ground. He glanced back at the other Riders and made a "walking man" sign with his hand, then held up five fingers twice.

How can he tell how many people are in there? Oh, never mind.

Dar tapped Buck on the shoulder. They entered the cave. Connor and Khyron followed next. The globe spoiled their heat vision, but they were more concerned about potential targets leaping into the light than seeing beyond it. Connor kept his bow at the ready, eyes flicking to every shadow.

Buck and Dar advanced into the tunnel. The sphere glimmered like a giant firefly amid the total darkness and silence. The limit of its light barely reached to the twenty-foot high ceiling.

Nothing leaped out at them and the light moved on. Connor kept his focus, looking for anything out of the ordinary. He licked dry lips, remembering the brimstone smell.

Dar and Buck halted, then darted forward. When Connor followed them, he emerged in a large cavern with three exits.

Dar knelt to examine the ground. "Traffic to the right," he whispered.

"Buck!" Andyn hissed. "Look sharp!" She slapped a metal bullet into the pouch of her sling.

At the same moment, Khelios flared to life. Twelve pairs of glowing red eyes glared at them out of the darkness of the rightmost tunnel.

Creatures stalked into the light. They looked like wolves, except that they had lizard tails and tusks. Bony ridges ran down their backs and their saliva steamed when it hit the ground.

Connor's jaw set in a firm line. *Fell-beasts… great.*

The largest one snarled. The others charged.

The Riders let fly. In rapid succession, glittering arrows and a sling bullet sizzling with electricity shot out. Flares of light burst where the arrows hit and three of the beasts dropped. Andyn's bullet hit the alpha male with an explosion of tiny lightning bolts. The monster howled and writhed in agony.

Connor activated his dancing sword brooch and the misty blade sprang to life in front of him. He moved to his right, firing arrows as two wolves raced towards him. His arrows sang through the darkness, puncturing the chest and eye of one of his assailants. The dancing sword lashed out at the other wolf. The beast dodged and snapped at it. The sword stabbed and slashed again. The wolf's jaws clashed on the sword and hurled it to the side. The blade vibrated and leaped back into the air in an eyeblink. It buried itself to the hilt in the wolf's neck. With a gurgle, the creature dropped.

Connor continued moving to his right, arrow ready. The swirl of combat made it hard to pick out a target. He bided his time, his glowing sword standing guard nearby.

His friends methodically struck down the mutated wolves. Khyron jumped over the charging alpha male and landed on its back, stabbing deep with his blades. It dropped and he stabbed twice more to make sure.

Connor shot an arrow into the back of one that leaped at Andyn from her blind side. It yelped. She spun and slammed it into the stony floor with her maces.

The cavern fell silent again. Andyn saluted Connor with Eleison. She and Eric examined the corpses.

Connor took a quick look around, then knelt at the side of a dead wolf. It wore a leather collar with metal studs and an iron ring. The stink of brimstone hung in the air.

"Fell wolves with collars," Andyn muttered, her eyes flashing. She glowered at the corpses. He knew why. Fell creatures were usually the result of some forbidden combination of magic and science and it pained Andyn to see animals warped into evil thralls.

Connor didn't blame her. He dusted off his gloves and trousers. "Well, now we know the mine isn't abandoned. It's just serving some other purpose now, maybe even a Skull Gate. And these things are guards for someone."

Eric joined them. "In that case, let's go smash the Gate."

As they left, a motion caught Connor's eye and he raised his bow, sighting on a small shadow.

Just another rat, he mused, relaxing. The rodent watched him with glowing eyes and then scurried away down the passage.

Connor resumed his place in their formation. as before. They advanced more slowly this time, with Dar checking the ground at intervals. Several times, he made hand signs to indicate that he still found tracks of people.

Connor shook his head. He knew little of tracking, but Dar and Eric found signs in the dirty, dusty floor where he saw only scuffs in the gloom. How they did it was beyond him.

Dar's hand shot up. Connor waited.

Dar waved. He and Buck disappeared into a side passage. The other Riders raced to follow.

The tunnel opened into a wide cavern. A jumble of disused mine carts clustered in the center. Two ramps led up to a wooden balcony about twenty feet up on the far wall. A dark opening loomed behind a wooden railing.

Connor activated his brooch and the misty sword sprang up again at his shoulder. He slipped to the side, eyes darting to every shadow.

Dar and Buck crept to the base of one of the ramps, but Khyron hissed a warning. Connor aimed at the opening.

Four hulking figures emerged from the darkness into the circle of light from Buck's globe: shaggy bear-like shapes with bulging, burning red eyes and dripping maws. Their paws ended in curved talons and spiny ridges ran down their backs. Collars of steel chain shone on their necks.

Connor sighted on one of them, but they merely stopped at the top of the ramp. Then a squad of warriors in red-enameled scale mail marched out from the tunnel, their helmet visors closed. They halted at the railing, shields up and hands on sword hilts.

When a grey-haired human in red plate mail emerged next to them, they all snapped to attention. Connor's eyes locked on a symbol on the leader's breastplate: a red moon over a blackened tree.

Dar and Eric drew back their bowstrings, but the leader raised a hand.

"Hail, riders of the pegasi," he announced, his voice echoing in the cavern. "I wish to parley."

Connor's eyes narrowed. "Who says we ride anything?"

The man smiled, blue eyes flashing. "We have ways of knowing who comes into our valley." He gestured and the large rat with opal eyes scampered up to him. His lips moved and the rat vanished. A pin on the man's tunic flashed in response.

"Why should we parley with you?" Dar challenged.

The man's smile grew wider. "Well, you made short work of the fell-wolves, so you are very capable. We can help each other."

"With what?" Buck shot back.

"The destruction of a Skull Gate."

Chapter Nine – The Enemy of My Enemy

Boy, she's mad, Buck thought.

"I don't like this," Andyn muttered, amber eyes flashing. She glowered at the Vardu priest, some twenty feet away. He didn't look in their direction, instead nodding at something Eric and Dar said. The two scouts gestured at the cavern entrance.

Buck leaned against a tree next to her. The Red Moon cultists had agreed to a conference just outside the mine entrance, mostly on Andyn's insistence. Out here, under the night sky and stars, they could meet with less risk of subterfuge. He had his reservations: this was still their territory.

"I don't like it either, but I think we should hear him out. Don't forget, I have a way to make sure he isn't lying." He swiveled down the arm on his helmet with the Eye of Truth.

Andyn scoffed but said nothing. An owl hooted deep in the forest behind her and the shadows of the abandoned town loomed like giant tombstones in the torchlight.

Khyron sidled up next to Andyn. "You're right, Buck," he murmured. "But it won't show if he's omitting something important."

Buck used the Eye to scan the Vardu priest and his four guards. They glowed with mild purple light. Khyron was right: the Eye of Truth had limitations. "Well," he said, placing a hand on the hilt of his sword, "We'll just have to make sure we ask very specific questions."

Andyn maintained her fiery stare. "You do it. I don't trust myself to speak to that degenerate. He's probably the one who mutated those animals."

Khyron put his arm around her and kissed her golden locks. "Done. Keep watch on his cronies and make sure nobody tries anything."

Andyn gave a curt nod and stalked away, her hands on her maces. She leaned back against Medianox, the night shadows enveloping her just outside the circle of firelight.

"I'm glad she's not mad at me," Connor said.

Khyron's lips curved in a sardonic smile. "You should be. I've been on the receiving end from time to time. It's not pleasant."

They waited as Dar and Eric conferred with the Vardish cleric. Finally, Dar waved at them.

"Conference time," Connor said. He led Buck and Khyron to join the conference with the Vardish leader.

"Now that the truce terms are set out," Eric said to the Red Moon Priest as they approached, "You can tell us what you know about the Skull Gates."

"This is Ilyan Kalik," Dar said, jerking his head at the Vardu priest. Eric drifted around behind Kalik's shoulder, looking right at Buck. He gave a slight nod.

Kalik inclined his head at them and smoothed his beard. He had a round, pleasant face that reminded Buck of a greengrocer he had known back home in Tyler. If it weren't for his eyes, dark blue and cold, Buck might have felt inclined to trust him.

"I think we can help each other," Kalik began, then stopped. "Er, your female companion is welcome to partake in the discussion. Vardu is a very tolerant religion."

"She prefers to remain in the shadows," Khyron said in a mild tone before anyone else could speak. He smiled but not with his eyes.

Kalik's gaze lingered on Andyn for a moment, then he shrugged. "Well, then, in that case, let us proceed. Ask me anything."

"How is it that you know about Skull Gates?" Connor asked. He gripped the collar of his cloak with both hands.

Good idea, Connor. Keep your hands near that magic brooch of yours.

The Vardu priest nodded. "It may surprise you, but the Ja'al actually asked the Church of Vardu for help with the project at the outset. Specifically, they asked for our cult of the Red Moon. We did some initial work together."

Buck watched carefully with the Eye of Truth, but Kalik's aura remained mildly purple. Nothing indicated that he lied.

"And?" prompted Dar.

Kalik made a helpless gesture. "We quarreled. I was not in the council meetings where the discussions took place, but we had a falling out. To be perfectly honest, I think our leaders wanted more control over the project and we can be rather adamant in our beliefs. I will admit it. We were greedy."

Nothing in the man's aura indicated a lie. Buck blinked. He met Eric's eyes and shook his head very slightly.

"I'm sure the Ja'al didn't take kindly to that," Connor observed.

Kalik sighed. "Well, there were several, shall we say, energetic confrontations between our respective supporters. The casualties mounted so we left the contested areas and resumed our previous activities."

"Why the sudden interest now?" Khyron interjected, raising an eyebrow. "You had broken with them, so your involvement ended, right?"

Kalik shook his head. "If you are after the Skull Gates, you know what they can do, correct? Our High Council did some research and realized that the Ja'al would not stop at using daemonic allies for local conquest. They were interested in eliminating all opposition. While the followers of the god of Death would not lament the damage to the faiths of the Light, we also realized that we would be next on their list. This did not sit well with leadership."

Buck thought of Carine lying injured on a bed in a tavern room. He gripped his sword tighter but said nothing.

"Why can't you destroy the Skull Gate yourselves?" Dar asked.

The priest hesitated, his brow furrowed in thought. "My team is a security detail for a different project, not a strike force. In our scouting, we found a Skull Gate assembly area not far away, but it is guarded by more Ja'al than we can handle. It is also very difficult to access."

He regarded the Riders with his cold blue eyes. "Difficult, that is, unless you can fly."

Buck scoffed. "What does that mean? Is it on top of a mountain or floating in the clouds or something?"

Kalik chuckled. "Not exactly. The Gate is in a gully with two narrow ravines. Though they have the ravines well-guarded, airborne infantry would have no problem simply flying in from the north onto the plateau above the Gate."

Again no lies showed. Buck's mind whirred, trying to think of some way Kalik could be bending the truth.

"Is it a real Gate or just a decoy?" Connor put in.

"A real one, I assure you. I can tell the difference."

Still no lies? Buck couldn't believe the Vardish would just hand them a Skull Gate.

"How do we know you're not going to attack us after we're done with the Ja'al?" Dar asked.

Kalik grinned. "You don't. Our churches, after all, are enemies."

"No deal," Buck barked. He turned away.

"Wait!"

The Riders paused.

Kalik hesitated. "What pledge can I give you that will satisfy you?"

Eric nodded at the pendant of the Red Moon lying against his chest. "Swear that neither you nor your men will attack us during or after we destroy the Skull Gate."

Kalik hesitated, then nodded. "Very well." He placed the medallion against his forehead. "May the god of death eat my soul if I speak falsely: I pledge that neither I nor my guards will attack the riders of the pegasi who serve the church of Verian and of Christ before, during or after they destroy the Skull Gate."

The medallion glittered and he let it drop to his chest again. "Anything else?"

Buck's eyes narrowed. "What do you get out of it? And what's in it for us?"

Kalik spread his hands. "To be blunt, I want a promotion and an assignment away from here. If the Gate is eliminated and I incur no losses, that will be guaranteed. As for what you get, well, one of the Gates will be destroyed. I'm sure your churches will reward you."

His eyes flicked to Andyn and his smile turned wolfish. "In many ways."

Khyron's eyes flashed. "Typical. I say no deal."

Kalik examined his fingernails. "Or you could just leave it here. I'm sure the Ja'al will be glad when it's fully operational."

The Riders stared at him in silence. Buck's stomach tightened. He was sure Kalik was bending the truth or omitting something, but the man was devilishly clever, no mistake.

"Give us a few minutes," Eric said. He beckoned to the others and they strode off to join Andyn.

"I heard what he said," Andyn said before anyone could speak. "I don't trust him."

"Was that a real oath or just a magic trick?" Dar asked.

"It was real. I could sense it from here. There's major pain in his future if he breaks that vow."

"Buck, what does the Eye show you?" Connor asked.

Buck gritted his teeth and rotated the gemstone up to the top of his helmet. "Nothing. He hasn't lied. Either he's telling the truth or he's really good at not giving anything away."

Eric took a long look at Kalik and his troops. "Well, Melinor told me that there are some magic spells that can confuse truth-reading, but they're difficult to use. I don't think this guy is powerful enough. He's telling the truth on what he's answered, in all probability. Opinions?"

"I'm with Andyn," Dar said. "He could easily have left out some critical information without lying."

Connor shrugged. "If he's only telling half of the truth, we can't let this opportunity pass by."

Khyron shook his head. "They're Vardish. They'll keep their word on an agreement only until the deal is concluded. Then they're likely to turn on us if they can manage it."

All eyes regarded Buck. He bit his lip. He didn't really trust anyone from the Dark Faiths — doubly so, now that Carine had been attacked by their allies — but if it really was a Skull Gate?

Daemons on Damora? He suppressed a shudder. *Evil incarnate set loose on the world?*

"I'm with Connor. We can't take the chance that there really is a Skull Gate," he said finally. "But I don't trust him either."

The other Riders nodded. Andyn stayed behind again as they approached Kalik.

"Very well," Khyron said. "Tell us how to get to the Skull Gate and we'll take care of the rest."

"Excellent." Kalik beamed. He sent one of his guards to bring a map case from his personal quarters.

The Red Moon priest's eyes wandered towards Andyn again. "I am glad to see that we are able to set aside personal philosophical differences in favor of a mutually beneficial arrangement." He smiled.

"As long as we ruin the Skull Gate," Dar said, "We can part ways amicably enough. For now."

"For now. Of course."

They waited silently as a breeze ruffled the trees and stars sparkled overhead.

The guard returned and Kalik handed over a parchment. "I have marked the location of the ravines and the Gate, along with approximate guard estimates."

Eric handed it to Dar, who perused it for a while, then nodded. "It matches with our other information. I know how to find it."

Kalik bowed low, hands out at his side. "May your enemies find Death and may you find Victory."

Without another word, the Riders spun on their heels and rejoined Andyn. She remained still while her companions mounted up. Her eyes bored into Kalik and the Red Moon cultists as they returned to the mine. When they had disappeared inside, she swung into the saddle.

Eric unrolled the map and showed it to Dar, who perused it. He nodded. "There's a place we can set up camp not too far from the Gate. We can rest and plan an attack tomorrow. Riders up!"

Six winged horses trotted forward, then launched into the night sky.

***

A few minutes later, Ilyan Kalik came out of the cave with a guard.

"What do you think, Sergeant Major?" he asked.

The guard nodded. "They'll do it, sir. Too much risk to them if they don't."

"I agree." Kalik touched the brooch on his tunic.

"Bloodflit," he said. The brooch glowed and a bat materialized in the air. He held out his arm and the creature alighted on it. Kalik locked eyes with the tiny construct.

"Find Captain Goldbriar at the Blacktomb Temple. Tell her the following: Assistance with eliminating SG project in sector 15 has been procured. High-level Christian and Verian operatives on the way. Send two platoons immediately for post-engagement cleanup."

The bat blinked its red, beady eyes.

"Repeat," Kalik ordered.

The bat's mouth opened and Kalik's own voice came out. "Assistance with eliminating SG project in sector 15 has been procured. High-level Christian and Verian operatives on the way. Send two platoons immediately for post-engagement cleanup."

He flicked his wrist. The bat shot up into the night sky and winged away.

"A bold move, sir," the guard said. "This might help you with the Council."

"It certainly will," replied Kalik with a relaxed smile.

***

"I hear from Sister Karen that you are an awful patient," Melinor said, taking a seat next to the bed.

Edward Simpson gave him a wry look. "I won't presume to debate her."

"Can you at least take your medicine?"

"Speaking of awful..."

Melinor sighed, resting his hands in his lap. "And stubborn."

"My mother's own words back at me."

Melinor hid a smile and instead faced the window overlooking the Chancery gardens. He remained silent. Only Father Edward's breathing and the ticking of a grandfather clock broke the stillness. Evening slowly faded into night, shadows deepening into darkness.

A particularly large and well-fed pigeon fluttered to a tree branch by the window and peered into the room.

"Sir Buckminster's bird has found a home here," Melinor observed.

Edward sat up and Melinor moved a pillow to support him. The Papal

Nuncio nodded at the bird with a wry smile. "Yes. Buck was very reluctant to leave him, but I think Puup has found some lady pigeons that react favorably to his tales of derring-do with the Grey Riders. He's quite the celebrity."

The bird fluttered up to a nest higher in the tree and settled in, tucking its beak under its wing.

In the world outside, stars glowed in the night. Kaliri, the smaller moon, waxed in the low horizon and Diometrios, her mate, ambled placidly not far behind.

"How long?" Melinor asked.

Edward adjusted his position and winced. "Weeks. A month or two, maybe. Not long."

Melinor's heart sank. His mind flitted back to memories of Father Edward when Saren had first come into his life: his gentle yet uncompromising questioning of the half-daemon girl, then his unwavering support for her when she had been accused of treason. It seemed like yesterday when Edward officiated at her wedding.

"Give me something to think about besides my aches and complaints, Melinor."

"Well, some of the news will probably make you sicker," Melinor warned him.

"Not if I can help it. What is the latest?"

"Well," Melinor said, eyes on a corner of the ceiling, "Unrest has subsided in some areas while it has intensified in others. The Grand Duke of Rokon is facing a vote of no-confidence from his council, which will spur an election if successful. There are rumors that bribed voters are being imported secretly from Eldir. On the positive side, the ringleaders in the plot to assassinate Lord and Lady Faldanor have been apprehended and will go to trial despite carefully orchestrated street protests to set them free."

"Are they under secure guard?"

"Very. We think at least one is a Ja'al agent, so we are prepared."

"Good. What else?"

"Let's see… there was an outright rebellion in the province of Gilran in Kortos. It seems that a priestess of Neralia tried to take parts of the region by force and had assembled an army including goblins, dark elves and hobgoblins.”

Edward grunted. “Shades of Zhinia Margoth.”

“With similar results,” Melinor agreed with a smile. “The Duke of Gilran’s son, Justin Martin, led an army to defeat her. The Duke is convinced it was all a diversion to get attention away from investigations into spy networks in the cities.

In addition, Targanon is turbulent. The Sultan sent an army to the eastern desert to confront an army of ogres, of all things, led by a fire drake. Two days ago, Caliph of Shemhajal narrowly escaped an assassination attempt.”

Edward didn’t reply and bit his lip, turning pale. Melinor sighed and picked up a tumbler of water and two pills the color of goldenrod from the side table. Without a word, he pressed the medicine into Edward’s hand and gave him the glass.

Edward responded with a sidelong look and Melinor raised an eyebrow. The Nuncio downed the pills with a grimace, then drank the water.

Melinor took the glass back and gave his friend’s shoulder a squeeze. “Think of it as avoiding some time in Purgatory.”

Edward winced and smiled. “I’ll need a lot more than this to compensate the Lord for my many sins.”

Melinor watched Edward’s pale, wan features and his heart clenched. He tried to imagine his world without him and came up with only a sense of being lost, without guidance.

He’s been there for me, through Saren’s troubles, Eric’s life and Anne’s death. Thank you, God, but could you leave him here for a little while longer?

He cleared a lump in his throat and placed the tumbler on the table. “In my experience, those who speak of their many sins with any level of humility actually have very few.”

Edward chuckled. “Then we’ll have to enlarge the circle of your experience.”

As he rested, his color returned bit by bit. Melinor sat quietly, listening to the ticking of a large clock next to the window.

“Melinor?” Edward asked.

“Yes?”

“I had a strange dream and I think something must be done about it.”

"We might have to adjust your medication." Melinor tried to hide a smirk and failed.

Edward scoffed. "Not that kind of dream, you dotard. I'm serious."

Melinor turned his chair to face him. "Tell me."

Edward gazed out at the night sky. "I saw a young man with dark hair and blue eyes. I don't recall ever seeing him before, but his presence seemed familiar somehow, and comforting. He led me into a barren place of mist and shadow where the Grey Riders stood facing the darkness. As I watched, they put forth their hands and cast golden nets of light over each other. The darkness tried to consume them but the gold nets held it back. Then I awoke."

"What do you think it means?"

Edward's brow furrowed. "I am not sure. The golden nets I recognized. However, it doesn't make any sense."

"What were they?"

"You're familiar with Preservation Nets? Well, you will doubtless also be familiar with their portable version, the Preservation Bead."

Melinor nodded.

"Well, that's what confuses me. A Bead just casts a Net over whatever the user designates. It inhibits the passage of time to one ten-millionth of normal. It has no ability to deflect attacks of Evil. *That's* the part that doesn't make sense."

Melinor stroked his beard. "Interesting. But the Riders don't have any Preservation Beads."

"No, they don't," Edward mused, lost in thought.

"Should they?"

Edward was silent for so long that Melinor thought he hadn't heard.

Finally, the Nuncio set his mouth in a firm line. "Yes, they should, for whatever reason the dream was brought to me. Do you have any?"

"I think I can prevail upon Queen Ahlana to relinquish a few."

"Good, please do it." Edward lay back against the pillow. "I am getting tired, Mel, but I want you to think on a couple of things tonight. First, the families of the Riders need to be warned and assigned guards, if possible. Second, we need to find the snake in the grass that leaked the location of my conference with Iron Thunder to the Blood-Sign Dragons. I'm convinced it's one of the nobility here in Oakmoor."

His eyes closed. Melinor stood, then bent over his friend and patted his hand. "Rest. It will be done."

Melinor dimmed the lights with a wave of his hand. The room faded into darkness as he shut the door.

"Lord Melinor?" asked a gruff voice next to him.

"Oh. Gorlak. What are you doing here?"

The goblin fidgeted and shot a look at the door. "How is Father Edward?"

Melinor considered sugar-coating his condition then decided against it. Of all people, with his arduous past life, Gorlak was most equipped to deal with the unvarnished truth.

"He is slowly dying, Gorlak."

The goblin looked stricken. "Can healers help him?"

Melinor strode down the hallway and Gorlak followed him. "Healers can repair wounds and neutralize poison but they don't do any better with diseases than medical doctors," he said with a sigh. "His own body systems are failing and some are turning against him. There is no spell to defeat this."

Gorlak said nothing and they emerged in a foyer that led out to the gardens. The goblin twisted the fabric of his tunic in his hands, shiny black eyes gazing into the distance.

"You realize he is quite old," Melinor said gently. "He was never going to live forever, you know."

Gorlak wiped his eyes and nodded, exhaling a deep breath. "I guess. He look old, but not like ancient one."

Melinor smiled. "Would it surprise you to know he is over a hundred and ten? Yes. It's true. He was old when Saren was a baby and even when Emily and Brendan were young."

Gorlak's jaw dropped. "He look good for eleven decades. How he do that?"

Melinor clasped his hands behind his back, gaze wandering to the night sky outside the glass doors. "I think it has to do with his home world. And no, before you ask, I have no idea where it is. All I know is that it is the same world of the Savior, with places like Nazareth and Bethlehem and

Rome. That is all I know. But I believe it."

"Take great faith to believe that when you not see it."

"That's what faith is, Gorlak."

The two of them, goblin and wizard, silently watched the night.

"Father Edward needs anything?" Gorlak asked.

"He mentioned a few things."

"Anything a goblin can do?"

Melinor started to shake his head, then paused. He pursed his lip, eyeing Gorlak. "Are you up to a little spying?"

The goblin grinned, showing sharp little canines. "Was Zhinia Margoth a miserable bitch?"

Melinor clucked his tongue in disapproval. "Now, now. Charity, Gorlak, even towards miserable bitches. What I have in mind will require you to do some skulking."

Gorlak's eyes shone. "I like skulking. Tell me."

"It seems there is a spy in the Royal Court…"

Chapter Ten – First Contact

"Well, that's a few," Dar noted. He crouched behind bushes and tall grass at the top of the cliff. "Twenty Skullhead Legionaries and two Ja'al priestesses. The two elves in light armor are probably wizards."

"It matches Kalik's notes," Connor remarked.

The early morning sun cast long shadows among the boulders and scrub oaks. At the cliff's edge, the ground plunged into the hollow seventy feet down. Dar bit his lip, lost in thought.

"I can understand why Ilyan Kalik didn't want to try this himself," Khyron said. "Look at those barricades at the ravine. Even if he had four times the number of troops, they'd have a hard time getting in here."

"Seems like too few Ja'al to guard a Skull Gate, though," mused Eric.

Dar eyed the barricades in question. He shook his head. "It's out in the middle of nowhere in a very defensible area. Besides, they're Ja'al. I'm sure they have tricks up their sleeves."

Andyn sniffed. "Too bad we can't induce that Red Moon cleric to charge in here with his gang of thugs. We'd be well rid of all of them."

"Yes, it's a pity, but we're not here to increase the body count," said Khyron, pointing. "*That's* what worries me."

Dar frowned. A hundred yards away, the Skull Gate crouched like a bony spider against a cliff face opposite them, a menacing altar of death crafted of bones and skulls and misery.

Well, he thought with a twinge of anxiety. *Now we get to earn our pay.*

"Do you think it's operational?" Connor asked.

"Well," Eric said, "I'm willing to say it's complete, based on the engineering drawings. Is it operational? I have no idea. We don't even know how it's activated."

Andyn sounded doubtful. "They'd need a high cleric to control the daemons, at least, and probably some pretty strong mages and warriors in heavy armor. I think we caught them at an early stage, maybe before testing."

"It's a gamble," Khyron agreed, "but we have the element of surprise for now. Buck, can you see any wardings or traps nearby? Try the Eye."

Buck lowered the Eye of Truth, peered down at the Gate and pointed. "It's faint at this distance but there's a semicircular band of red in front of it and two small glyphs on the cliff face above. Looks like they're aware of the risk of someone climbing down from the mesa."

They watched the Ja'al in silence. Dar's anxiety grew as he mulled over various possibilities. "I think they'll take the same tactics we saw near the ruined tower," he said finally. "If the Skull Gate is threatened, they'll fall back to defend it. I say two of us get their attention, then the rest of us fly in from the east, with the sun behind us."

"Mages and clerics first?" asked Connor.

"The guards have crossbows," Eric said. "Even if they're average shots, they can still hit us from three hundred yards. Unless the mages are arch-wizards, which I doubt, their spells won't go much past one hundred."

"Who goes first?" Andyn asked.

Dar gave his companions a once-over. "You and Buck are probably the most threatening. We can use spells to cut into the archers first, then hit the spell-casters. Andyn, you'll also have to cancel the traps by the Gate as soon as you can."

Andyn raised an eyebrow. "Is that all? You don't want me to conquer Torosc single-handed? Well, then, it's child's play."

Buck looked at Andyn and shrugged. "Save at least a dozen for me though. I need the practice."

"Deal."

Eric put his hands on their shoulders. "Whatever you do, make sure that you keep an eye on the priests. They might have some way to warn their superiors of an attack. As soon as their attention is on you, we'll strike."

The Riders withdrew from the cliffs towards the shelter of a dense tree line. Among giant boulders, the pegasi waited in the shade.

Andyn swung into the saddle and held her hands out over Buck. "Hold still." At her soft words, colored nets of light drifted down on him.

Eric gave her a wry grin. "What, none for us?" he asked.

"You're not going in two-against-two dozen," she retorted, but her eyes danced. "Just look sharp. I don't want to turn into a flying pincushion."

She turned Medianox to join Buck on Shadowbane.

Dar mounted and readied his bow. He licked dry lips and tried not to fidget. The clash of battle, the pain of wounds, the shock and horror of facing evil – these he could handle. He hated the waiting before the fight.

Never has a battle plan survived contact with the enemy, especially the Ja'al.

Buck and Andyn cantered away to a relatively clear spot in the high grass and took wing. Dar walked his pegasus forward to the ridge.

When Buck and Andyn made their appearance, they approached so quietly that they were almost to the Gate by the time sentries saw them. Ja'al soldiers shouted and scurried about, snatching up crossbows. The clerics and wizards scrambled to their feet.

Andyn unloaded a fireball spell at a knot of troops taking aim at Buck. The blast blew them into the air. They crashed into boulders and rocks with metallic thumps and lay still. Buck dropped another crossbowman with a pair of arrows. He and Andyn soared upwards, dodging and whirling away from a hail of bolts and two spears of lightning.

"Now!" Dar shouted and spurred Virasi forward. The pegasus leaped off the edge of the canyon. He loosed arrows as fast as he could, dropping two soldiers. Eric unleashed a fireball spell of his own, blasting more Ja'al warriors into smoking heaps. Connor and Khyron dropped others with arrow fire.

A Ja'al cleric cast a red-hot beam of light at Dar and he banked Virasi away. Curving around for another pass, he got a good look at the battlefield.

Many of the Ja'al warriors lay still on the rocky ground. Five crossbowmen reloaded from the cover of a large boulder.

Ah, the element of surprise! Maybe this will be easier than we thought. Urgency and the need to destroy the Skull Gate drove him.

Then one of the Ja'al priestesses and both wizards scrambled towards the rock wall behind the Gate. The priestess raised her hands and a portion of the wall shimmered and disappeared. She ran into a dark opening. The wizards raced inside after her. The crossbowmen covered them, firing bolts at Andyn and Buck as they swept past. A bolt glanced off Shadowbane's leg and the pegasus whinnied in pain.

Dar's memory clicked, going back in time to when he and the Riders had become trapped in a Ja'al chapel near Forester, long ago.

Damn it! They're going for help! I knew this was too good to be true.

He made a motion with his hand and pointed down at the Gate. The other Riders wheeled around in a diving arc. Andyn and Buck took the first pass again. She pointed her fist as they dove past the Gate and a hemisphere of white light pulsed forth. Where it touched the vile bone structure, red lights flashed and dull booms sounded. Clouds of smoke puffed into the air. She and Buck soared away.

Dar led the next charge. He narrowly missed taking a bolt in the head and one missile glanced off Virasi's barding, cutting a thin red line in the pegasi's neck. Dar dropped a warrior with two arrows and pulled up into evasive maneuvers.

By the time he came around for another pass, the remaining Ja'al archers lay dead on the rocks. The Ja'al priestess jerked a pair of arrows out of her armor, laying a glowing hand on her injuries.

"On the ground, everyone!" Dar shouted to his friends, pulling Virasi into a hover. He pointed at the gaping cave mouth. "We have to find out where they went!"

The Ja'al cleric and wizards charged from the cave. The priestess carried two wet objects in her hands. They were human hearts. Impossibly, each throbbed with a phantom heartbeat, pulsing with purple light. Dar's stomach convulsed.

The cleric hurled the heart at the skull at the apex of the Gate. The skull's jaw opened and clamped down on the heart. The Gate crackled to life. Pink and orange radiance exploded from several skulls around the perimeter of the structure. A swirling, dark void sprang up.

Dar's heart froze in terror. *Oh my God! The activators!*

Eric and Andyn peppered the cleric with fire darts and she dropped, screaming. The wizards returned fire and the magic missiles detonated on their armor. Eric and Andyn reeled in the saddle and pulled away.

The void constricted and flexed, vomiting forth a nightmare. Vaguely man-shaped, the creature stood at least as tall as Buck and wore black-and-red striped scale mail. It gripped a falchion. A black glove encrusted with jewels glittered on its other hand. A tiger-like face surmounted by a ruff of black horns whipped around to follow the Riders in the air. Purple eyes burned and it voiced a snarling howl. The remaining priestess shouted something at it. The daemon nodded, then unfurled deep indigo wings and leaped into the air.

No, no, no, no! Heart in his throat, Dar scrabbled in his arrow case for a shaft with shimmering green feathers. He pulled it out and set it to his bow.

The daemon soared upwards, roaring a challenge. A wave of pure malice crashed over Dar and he fought the urge to panic. Part of him wanted to run away and hide, to cower in a dark corner and pray that the thing would forget about him.

"Damn it, no!" he growled, pulling on Virasi's reins and bringing him around.

Andyn, Connor, Eric and Khyron zipped past, heading for the Gate. Dar and Buck banked around to meet the daemon. Buck shouted something and Khelios burned with golden light. He charged.

Dar took careful aim and loosed, but the daemon dodged and the arrow sailed away.

At the last second, Buck pulled Shadowbane into a corkscrew maneuver. Khelios flashed. The daemon's sword answered with a red flame. A double clang echoed in the canyon and the two combatants shot past each other.

Buck sagged in his saddle, then recovered and pulled Shadowbane around. Dar saw a deep cut in Buck's shield.

Another one like that and he won't have one any more.

Dar pulled Virasi into a climb, pulling out another green-feathered arrow. It sparkled and vibrated in the wind against his bow. The daemon banked and headed back towards Buck, who likewise swung around to meet him.

Dar looped behind the daemon as it charged, then said a quick prayer to Saint Sebastian and loosed. The arrow struck the daemon in the back with an explosion of white radiance. The creature howled and swept out of the way. Buck shot past, his sword swishing through empty air.

The daemon turned so that it fell with its back towards the earth. The gemstones on its glove sparked and a veritable blizzard of tiny glowing stars rushed out at Dar.

Dar pulled on the reins, heart in his throat. The miniscule darts struck with stinging impact, burning through his armor. The stench of melting metal surrounded him. Virasi screamed in pain and faltered, his wings smoking. The daemon climbed towards him, but Buck swooped down. The pair exchanged a ringing pair of blows, then parted again.

"Come on, boy, we'll be all right," Dar gasped.

It felt like he had been lacerated with a dozen tiny blades coated in acid. His armor smoldered and steamed. Tears sprang to his eyes and he pulled Virasi aside, heading towards the Skull Gate. The pegasus gamely beat his wings, trailing a plume of smoke. Dar gritted his teeth against the pain. He pulled his mount in a wide arc, trying to get some distance to catch his breath.

Buck and the tiger-daemon charged each other again. They exchanged another ringing set of blows and Buck's shield fell to pieces. He leaned against Shadowbane's neck as the pegasus raced away. With a howl of triumph, the daemon pursued.

"Enough," growled Dar. He swung Rindara Starblade's scabbard around to the front.

As if sensing his determination, his pegasus surged into a charge. They closed the distance fast. Seeing his opening, Dar swept in from below. He drew Rindara and stood in his stirrups.

The tiger daemon whirled, eyes wide. The glove of gems shone again, but Dar ignored it. Star-filled Rindara struck once, twice. The first blow cut off the creature's left hand and the glove exploded in white light. Pain seared Dar again, but his second blow took off the daemon's head.

The corpse froze in mid-air, trailing steaming white ichor, then arced gracefully downwards. Dar turned to watch. The dead daemon exploded into flaming chunks of meat and bones.

A ghostly shriek echoed off the walls of the canyon and a deathly chill ran through Dar's bones. He pulled Virasi into a dive.

The blood drained from his face. His friends were dismounted, standing over the corpses of the last Ja'al. Eric limped noticeably. The void inside the gate warped again. A deep black mist with glittering silver tendrils and six red eyes slithered out. It was easily the size of a large wagon.

The creature floated away from the Gate, its eyes darting about as if sizing them up. The Riders backed away from the creature, weapons held on guard. Then the mist-daemon pulsed and emitted another piercing shriek. Virasi whinnied and bucked in mid-air and Dar fought to control him. He landed the pegasus with difficulty, then unfastened his flying straps and dismounted.

A harsh, hissing voice echoed in his mind. Dar winced from a sudden headache.

"You think this will end it?" the voice mocked. "You have no idea what you face. We are coming, you fools!"

Dar's stomach knotted. *Where are the Elohir? They're supposed to know when a daemon arrives on Damora! Why aren't they here?*

His wounds burned and his eyes felt like they were filled with sand. He raised his arm to wipe sweat and tears out of his eyes and felt the stickiness of blood on his forehead.

Dar took his place next to Buck. "Take out the Gate while we have it occupied," he muttered.

Buck's left arm hung loose at his side but he shook his head. "I won't leave you."

"Rindara and Fidelis are Celestial weapons. Khelios and Tiuz are not."

"No! I can — "

"Buck! The Gate has to be destroyed. Besides, you might distract it."

Buck hesitated, then stalked to the side, sword up. He paused by Connor and whispered. The halfling nodded and backed away.

"Now," Dar said. Buck and Connor raced towards the Gate.

The daemon hissed and surged forwards to intercept, but Eric stabbed it with Fidelis. The spear penetrated the fog, burning a hole in it. The daemon screamed and recoiled, flailing at him with its tentacles. Eric leaped backwards. Dar charged, Andyn and Khyron at his side.

The daemon spun into a massive dust-devil shape, its tentacles lashing out. One of its arms slammed into Eric, hurling him backwards. Dar ducked, leaped, and came down slashing. The sword cut through the fog and he felt a resistance, almost as if he attacked a firm mattress. A silvery light flashed and a cloud of stinking, freezing cold mist sprang up from the daemon's wound. The creature shrieked. Dar staggered backwards, dizzy and deafened.

The daemon detached its arms and hurled them at the Riders. Where they landed, explosions rent the earth, casting rocks and dirt everywhere.

Several large stones pummeled Dar. Already disoriented from his loss of hearing, he lurched and fell, slamming into a boulder. He felt a rib crack and gasped, pain lancing through him like a dagger.

He struggled to his feet. He heard Khyron and Andyn shouting something but their voices sounded watery and distant. Eric picked himself up from a pile of rocks and threw Fidelis from a kneeling position. The spear shot through the daemon and a gush of white gas streamed out. The monster screeched.

"Fidelis!" Eric shouted, but to Dar it sounded like he muttered from inside a barrel. The spear flashed back to his fist.

The daemon produced six more tentacles. Khyron and Andyn drove it back, slashing and hammering it with their glittering weapons.

The daemon lunged, entwining them in its tendrils. They screamed in agony. Andyn twisted but the daemon slammed her into a rock and she dropped her maces, head lolling back. Khyron stabbed his sword and dagger into the tentacle around his waist. Both blades melted and flowed into a pool of steaming metal on the stones.

The daemon wrapped two more tentacles around him and Khyron turned sheet white.

"No!" Dar charged, Eric beside him. They simultaneously impaled the daemon. Silver and gold light burst as bright as the sun. The daemon let out a hissing scream and exploded, hurling the Riders back. Khyron landed in a heap on top of Andyn.

Dar flew through the air and hit the ground, the air escaping his lungs. His helmet smacked into something hard. He saw stars and groaned, rolling onto his side. Through misty eyes, he peered at the Gate.

The skull at the top of the structure snapped shut and the void faded, then winked out like a snuffed candle. Dar felt pain and weariness overtake him and he rose to his knees.

Buck and Connor ran to him. "We can't break the Gate!" the halfling gasped. "Khelios and Tiuz are barely damaging it!"

A grey mist crept in on the edge of Dar's vision. He handed Rindara to Buck.

"Try this," he croaked.

Connor grabbed Eric's spear.

Buck shrugged off his backpack. "I have healing medicine."

"Forget me! Destroy the gate!" Dar went down on all fours as his friends raced away. Through gritty vision, he saw the glitter of stars on his blade. Fidelis shone so bright he could barely look at it. To his vast relief, Andyn and Khyron moved and Eric crawled towards him.

Dar summoned a weak grin. "Congratulations, Daemon-slayer." Then everything went black.

***

Dar felt the wind coursing over him and the rhythmic motion of Virasi's wings. He tried to sit up and take the reins, but something held him pinned to his pegasi's neck. Someone had tied him into the saddle. Dark green forest whisked by beneath him.

Where are we going? Where is everyone?

He turned his head. Connor rode Phantom right next to him, almost wingtip-to-wingtip.

The halfling stared straight ahead.

Did we destroy it?

He heard someone moan in agony and realized it was he. A wave of nausea gripped his gut and he slumped against Virasi.

"Get us home, boy," he choked.

The world went dark again.

He saw Andyn's face hovering over him, then a cool, sweet liquid that tasted like a cross between Gorostoli jekka and salt pork, then another with the flavor of pickles and hazelnuts. He passed out, then awoke as Eric and Andyn spread soothing ointment on his body. They looked haggard. He tried to rise and help, but couldn't move.

He blacked out again. Through a fog of pain, he heard Melissa the Elohir's voice, then a wave of warmth and peace and power. He slept naked below towering green trees.

Seemingly centuries later, he felt the ground against his back under a blanket. Another blanket covered him.

He opened his eyes. Eric Indidarc smiled. "Welcome back," he said.

Dar felt a hundred years old. Every muscle creaked with soreness and his mind struggled through a fog. He tried to sit and Eric helped him up. Dar remained that way for a while, breathing deeply and enjoying the luxury of not having to pay attention to anything.

After a time of nothing more than listening to the wind in the trees, he sighed. His head felt better and some vitality crept back into his limbs.

"Did I dream it or did Melissa make an appearance?"

Eric nodded. "Yes, she tracked us down. It took her a while to get here. She had to do some searching around to find us."

"I thought she was up in Saint Martin's Town."

"She came to find us at the request of the Nuncio. She's been in Terenai for a couple of days. She flew back towards the location of the Gate to see what's going on. Said she'd be back before nightfall."

Better late than never, Dar thought. Instead, he asked, "Where's my armor?"

"You mean the melted slag we peeled off your body? We might use it for some abstract art project. Don't worry. Nobody got off scot-free. Andyn and Khyron don't have armor anymore and Buck needs a new shield. You saw what happened to Khyron's blades."

Dar groaned. "Great. I hope we get paid well for this. That armor was expensive."

"Well, Buck's instinct to turn a profit came in handy. He looted the Ja'al facility like a bandit. Connor was busy too. He took a lot of scrolls and books. The Nuncio's staff will have quite a bit to pore over."

"At least you found my spare clothes. Any more nudity from me and the local squirrels will arrest me."

Eric scoffed. "If they don't run screaming in terror." He held out a hand and helped him stand.

"How are Khyron and Andyn?" Dar asked.

"You can ask them yourself," Eric replied with a nod towards a small fire near one side of the glade. Khyron sat behind Andyn, one arm curled around her shoulder and across her collarbone and the other across her middle. She leaned her head back into his chest, eyes closed, hands clasped over his.

"When's the wedding?"

Eric gave him a sad smile. "Not soon enough. We have bigger problems, unfortunately."

Dar hobbled over to join them at the campfire.

"You had us worried there for a while," Andyn said, standing to embrace him. Her eyes measured him as if she would doubt any response.

"I'm fine," he said and almost believed it himself.

"Two daemons in the span of a few minutes is a lot to ask," Khyron said, clasping his shoulder.

Dar made a wry face. "I didn't ask."

Khyron grinned. "That's our Dar."

"Where are Connor and Buck?"

"Making sure the area is safe."

Dar took a look around. Early evening beckoned from the west and tall trees crowded around their little meadow. Six winged horses placidly cropped grass nearby.

"Where are we?"

Eric sat on the fallen log. "About forty miles southwest of the Skull Gate."

Dar joined him as Khyron and Andyn resumed their seats. "And the Gate?"

Andyn smiled. "Fidelis and Rindara were just the tools we needed. The Gate is a pile of metal and bone."

Dar let out a deep breath. Much of his tension melted away, replaced by a great relief that left him almost weak. "That is a *very* large load off my mind."

"Ours too," Eric said, flicking a twig into the fire.

Khyron nodded. "We had to move fast."

"Why?" Dar asked.

Andyn put an arm around her man and leaned her head on his shoulder. "The Vardish."

Dar swore under his breath. "I don't know why I'm surprised. I knew Kalik would betray us, just not this fast. What happened?"

"I sent up Stealth after Andyn healed me," Eric said. "I spotted some movement in the woods to the east and hung around long enough to see forty Red Moon troops on the move."

"Kalik was just waiting for us to take out the Ja'al," Dar spat.

"Or for us to kill each other off," Andyn said. "In any event, we tied you and Khyron to your saddles, gathered up as much as we could pack into our saddlebags, and took off."

Dar raised an eyebrow at Khyron. "You too?"

"Andyn was very busy for a while. So was Eric. The Ja'al had some healing potions in their stash in the caves. We collected what they had left."

"How much did we use?"

"All of it," Khyron said. "It's a good thing Melissa found us or we'd all be whining lumps of pain huddled around the campfire."

Considering how Dar had felt upon awakening and his current level of fatigue, he wondered how close to death they had come.

Andyn bit her lip and held Khyron's hand in two of hers. He pulled her close and kissed her head.

Too close to suit those two. Dar wondered how he would feel if Megan were with him and he had seen her go under the tendrils of the fog-daemon. A lump started in his throat and he swallowed with difficulty.

Approaching figures near the edge of the glade caught his eye. Connor Lomin strode towards them, followed soon thereafter by the larger armored form of Buck.

Dar stretched, feeling some more life return. He shook his head. "We look terrible," he said. "And we stink too."

Andyn's serious and worried demeanor vanished and she opened her mouth in shock. "I never stink. I just emit a different aroma from time to time."

Dar grinned back at her. Khyron chuckled. They really did look a sight: covered in dirt or daemon ichor or their own blood or all three. Eric sported a bruise on the left side of his face and Buck's forehead showed a darkening scar.

"Well," Connor said, "Now that you're back in the land of the living, we can at least return to Evonald and get some rest before we head back to St. Martin's."

"We're going to need every bit of the loot from the Ja'al," Buck added, nodding at a pair of bulging saddlebags at the base of a tree. "Whoever said they could get rich being a freelance was a lousy liar."

Dar sighed. "Speaking of liars, did the Red Moon troops see us leave?"

Eric shook his head. "I don't think so. I scouted with Stealth as we took off. They were still about a mile away, in the forest and outside of the ravines."

A flash of motion on the low horizon drew their eyes. A bright figure soared low over the treetops towards them, faster than a pegasus. Soon, a winged woman gently alighted on the grass in the meadow.

Dar's eyes widened. He had gotten used to seeing Melissa barefoot, wearing her short white robe and a golden belt. Now, fine, shiny chainmail armor covered her sleek figure from head to toe. She wore boots of metal and leather and bore a silvery shield with the symbol of a triangle and a flame. A steely helmet glittered on her head in the evening light. A longsword hung at her hip.

She removed the helmet and tossed her head, loosening her lustrous, shoulder-length blonde hair. She smiled, jewel-like eyes sparkling. "It's good to see everyone up and about."

The Riders stood as one.

"Yes, thanks to you, my Lady," Dar offered with a bow.

"What news?" asked Andyn. Khyron stood wide-eyed at her elbow.

Dar hid a smile. He had forgotten that Khyron had never met Melissa, nor likely any other Elohir. He remembered his own initial reaction.

"The Vardish have withdrawn," Melissa replied, setting down her helmet and shield. She took a seat on the log and motioned for them to do likewise.

"Did they do anything unusual?" Eric asked, sitting on the ground near the fire.

Melissa pursed her lip. "Well, they entered the cave, looted the bodies and piled them up, severed all the heads for trophies and set the corpses on fire. Fairly typical for followers of Vardu. Then they headed back the way they had come."

"What did the leader do?" Connor asked.

"Ah, yes," Melissa said, snapping her fingers. "He had a Companion Pin of a little bat. He sent that up into the air and had it fly a great circle over the area. When he recalled the bat, he ordered them all to leave."

"Good riddance," hissed Andyn. Melissa laughed and Dar grinned.

"You do not varnish your opinions, Andyn," Melissa said with a twinkle in her eye. "I am also glad they have gone."

She clapped her hands on her knees. "I have to commend all of you. To vanquish not one, but two, of the Fallen Ones is a tale for bards to sing of. Though your other weapons are mighty, without the help of Rindara and Fidelis, some of you doubtless would have perished."

"What were those daemons?" Buck asked.

"A Tigris Infernales and a Deathmist — but enough of that for now. You must rest. This has been an exhausting day for all of you."

"Great," Dar said with a sigh. "Who has first watch?"

"I do." Melissa coiled her hair up on top of her head and settled her helmet back in place.

"Well," Eric began. "We can't ask you to — "

Melissa held up a hand. "I volunteer. Rest the night through." She hefted her shield and drew her sword. The blade rang like a church bell and pulsed with blue light.

"Nothing will harm you."

Chapter Eleven – The Fate of Chattel

"Stand here," George Oxbridge commanded.

Megan complied, hands clasped below her waist, head down. The anti-magic collar around her neck sizzled with energy. The lawn under her feet was manicured, thick and even. She resisted the urge to wiggle her toes in it.

Five wizards lounged on gold-filigreed couches about fifty paces away, attended by guards in shiny plate mail and two apprentices each. A hooded, solitary figure lurked behind the chairs.

"Now, my friends," Oxbridge announced. "You will see the remarkable abilities of this slave girl. Despite her youth, she has astonishing talents."

"Look up, slave," said a husky female voice.

Megan again complied.

A middle-aged woman eyed Megan up and down with bright blue eyes. She frowned, flipping a lock of blonde hair over her ear. "Not much to her. Slender girl with nice tits and a good shape, but those are ten coppers a pound. Looks more like a dancer or a pleasure slave."

"I assure you, Lady Ravida," Oxbridge responded, holding up a hand, "she is very intelligent and has impressive talents."

"Talents? I'll wager," drawled one of the other mages, a round-faced dandy with jewels glittering on his fingers. He smirked and fixed Megan with warm brown eyes. "Have you tried her out, yet, George?"

Oxbridge made a face like he had bitten something sour. He fixed Jeffries with a glare. "Please, Lord Jeffries, don't be so common. You know I have grown beyond such carnal pursuits. In their time, they were amusing enough, but magic and power are far more important."

"Pity," Lord Jeffries said, eyes following the curves of Megan's figure.

Megan's cheeks burned and she forced herself to stare straight ahead. The buildings of the Catrin Magical Academy surrounded them on all sides, brooding grey edifices crowned by statues of wizards and daemons. She kept her eyes on the elegant carvings on the university library across the central plaza.

An elderly, one-eyed dwarf with blue-tinted hair scowled. "Enough of this bar-room nonsense. Are you here to show us her abilities or not?"

"Just so," Oxbridge said with a bow. He strode away and stood next to the assembly. "If my lords and ladies will assist me?"

The wizards stood and raised their hands, chanting together in a sing-song melody. A fifty-foot tall dome of iridescent colors swirled and arced over Megan.

"There," Oxbridge concluded, looking satisfied. He handed a sapphire key to one of the apprentices.

"Remove the collar."

A slit in the multicolored dome parted for a brown-haired man not much older than Dar. The attendant approached, eyeing Megan warily. She didn't even twitch.

Megan wondered what Oxbridge had told the apprentice. *He looks as if he thinks I'll bite his head off or something.*

The man touched the key to the collar and it snapped open. He snatched it as it fell from Megan's neck. With a wary look in his eyes, he backpedaled towards the barrier. The slit in the dome closed behind him.

Megan couldn't help but sympathize. The junior wizards were probably just as powerless as she, and frightened of whatever rumors Oxbridge had spread in advance of the demonstration.

"Now, we begin," her master intoned. "Apprentices, attack. Slave, perform countermeasures! Do not kill!"

Megan retreated as the dome parted for wo of the apprentices to advance. They moved their hands in intricate patterns. Fog clouds and fire-darts materialized in their hands. She mimicked their gestures in reverse and the spells winked out. Next the apprentices conjured up lightning and acid, but she unwound those spells as well.

"Nicely done!" chortled Lord Jeffries. "Now use fire, George! Burn her tunic off!"

Lady Ravida laughed. "I was wondering when you would suggest that, William."

Both apprentices gestured in unison and balls of flame grew in their palms. Megan waited.

They hurled the fireballs at her. Megan focused her power and unleashed a Spell-breaker Shield. The flaming comets detonated on the Shield and flared to the sides, crisping the nearby lawn. Megan allowed herself a little smile. All they had managed to do was singe her tunic.

Go ahead, you sadistic fiends. I'll show you a demonstration.

Lady Ravida laughed again. "Well, the little whore has more upstairs than I gave her credit for. Add two more apprentices, George."

Two women joined the men. All four wizards chanted, hands in motion.

Megan licked dry lips, her heart skipping a beat. How was she going to take on all four at once?

Lord, please defend me, she prayed. Then, just as on that fateful day when her aunt and uncle had perished, Megan felt serenity and surety come over her. She reached out with her mind. Power built up, warming her heart and calming her soul.

Every little nuance of her adversaries' gestures took on a sharp clarity. She quickly calculated how long it would take to complete each spell.

She created two illusionary duplicates of herself. One of the women changed her spell.

She's dispelling my illusions! Megan realized. *Her first, then.*

Megan crafted a Storm Force spell and blew her off her feet into the iridescent dome. The woman hit the wall. All the air left her lungs in a whoof. She flopped to the ground.

Both of the male apprentices motioned and glittering cords snaked out at her illusions. The cords wrapped around the images and they vanished with a pop.

The other woman thrust her hands over her head and the earth churned under Megan's feet. The ground erupted in a cloud of rocks and lawn and dirt. Megan leaped back and rolled.

The last female wizard skittered to the side, low to the ground, her fingertips glowing. Megan drew back and, when the woman advanced, Megan charged.

The woman's eyes widened. She gestured and a glowing fist of light materialized before her. Megan slammed her shoulder into the wizard, hurling her into the dome. The fist of light winked out of existence and the woman bounced off and fell. She rolled on the ground, holding her head in pain.

A force struck Megan from behind and she lurched, then spun and dodged. Another glowing fist hurtled at her and she threw up a Shield. The fist thudded into it and a lightning bolt hissed in at her from a male wizard's pointed finger.

Megan moved her open hand in a shunting motion and redirected the bolt into the fist, blowing it apart. The blast hurled her back. She tumbled against the glowing dome.

Her head rang. Megan scrambled to her feet just in time to receive a blast of hot wind that pinned her to the dome. She twisted and struggled. The two male wizards advanced, muttering and moving their fingers in time with the gusts of wind. The wind grew to gale force. Her tunic ripped at the shoulder and whipped to the side, torn in half. Her anger rose and a glowing red haze crept into the edges of her vision.

Fine! They want me to fight nude? I'll accommodate them!

She cast a Spellbane again. The constricting wind vanished and she pulled off her ruined tunic. Both men's eyes immediately locked onto her body.

Red tinted the edge of her vision. A feeling of hot, languid seductiveness came over her.

Hmm… she thought. *This will be fun.*

"Like what you see, gentlemen?" she murmured in a husky voice, gliding towards them. They both started as if stung and raised their hands.

Part of her exulted in raw feminine power. With a sly grin, Megan cast a spell on the tunic. It leaped to life and shot out, wrapping one of the men in a tight embrace, pinning his hands to his sides.

Wait… what's happening? She struggled against lurid thoughts dancing in her brain.

The last mage retreated, throwing a wall of fog in front of her. Megan waved a hand to the side and the fog dissipated. The mage's eyes bulged with fright and Megan blasted firedarts at him. They pinged off his shields and she followed with an Acid Bullet that also spun off into the dome.

"Master!" the mage yelped. "Help! She is a daemon!"

The dwarf laughed. "You idiot! She's a half-breed Elf slut, not a daemon. Knock her down!"

"Slave!" roared Oxbridge. "I said no killing spells!"

The fear in the apprentice's eyes made Megan pause. She shook her head as if waking from a bad dream.

Wait. He's forced to do this as much as I am. Why am I trying to kill him? What's wrong with me?

Megan struggled against the urges raging within her, taking a deep breath and focusing on calmness and confidence. The red haze faded and the feelings vanished.

The apprentice raised his hands and a void of inky blackness formed in front of him. He darted to the side, hand crackling with frost. Megan planted a magical ball of light on his eyes and he fell backwards with a cry. His frost spell blasted into the dome and rimed it with a sheet of ice. He tumbled to the ground and the disk of darkness disappeared with a pop.

Megan leaped forward and tapped him on the forehead. "Sleep now," she said.

He relaxed onto the grass.

Megan faced the assembled wizards, head held high.

"Well, well," rumbled the dwarf. "She analyzes attack modes, uses countermeasures as commanded and even masters her own anger. Extraordinary. Four against one couldn't beat her. I owe you an apology, George."

"Bring them out," Oxbridge ordered and some of the other attendants entered the dome cautiously, then helped the vanquished wizards exit. Megan remained where she was.

An Elf wearing robes of black and silver put a hand on Oxbridge's shoulder. He tilted his head to the side. "She can defend against magical attack well enough. What about other challenges?"

"I thought of that. I have a visitor for her," said Oxbridge with a cold smirk and Megan's heart chilled.

Without taking his eyes off her, Oxbridge nodded to the hooded figure.

"The globe, please, my lord."

The figure handed him a milky white orb. Oxbridge smiled and rolled the glass ball into the iridescent dome. It stopped about twenty feet from Megan.

The figure nodded. Oxbridge shouted a guttural word and the sphere shattered.

A horror from another world burst forth and grew to its full, eight-foot height. Four clawed legs gripped the earth, crushing the grass beneath. A frog's head with five horns pivoted around to regard her. Frothy blue drool flowed out of a jaw filled with double rows of dagger teeth and tusks the size of short swords. A part-insect, part-reptile body connected to a long neck and lashing double tail. A ridge of spines ran down the armored back.

Megan froze. *Dear, sweet Jesus…*

"Let's see how she does against a dark reaver, even a young one," said the Elf with a sniff.

The creature growled and vanished.

Megan's senses tingled and she used Eagle Magic, soaring overhead. Twin claws slammed into the earth where she had stood.

Again, the calmness and surety washed over her. Despite the danger, Megan smiled. She formed a counter-spell, unwinding the reaver's invisibility. The air in the dome wavered and the reaver popped back into view. It lashed its tail and snarled.

To her immense satisfaction, all the wizards started and their eyes widened.

More than you bargained for, am I?

The reaver leaped into the air, tail lashing and claws extended. She flew to the side and fired off a spell. A pair of multicolored pinwheels whirled out and burst on the monster's face. The reaver landed awkwardly on the ground. It tried to pounce on her again but its eyes wandered all around the dome and it stumbled, falling half-prone.

She soared over it. The reaver shook its head and lurched to the side. Megan cast a shielding spell on herself, adding protections against acid and fire.

The dark reaver regained its feet, growling and slavering. Megan responded with a cloud of thick fog, then darted behind the creature. The reaver howled and lashed out in all directions. Megan stayed away, preparing her next spell in her mind. She pinched two fingers into the palm of her other hand.

The reaver burst out of the fog cloud, head twisting around to locate her. She drew the fingers away from her palm and a glittering cord of light followed. She gestured and the rope of light whisked out, wrapping around the thing's legs.

The reaver opened its mouth and hissed. A storm of tiny, needle-like teeth shot at her. Megan dove towards the ground, heart in her throat. Stinging pains burned in her legs, back and buttocks. The sound of the teeth pinging off the iridescent dome rang loudly in the university square.

The reaver tried to charge but entangled its legs in the magical cords and fell on its face. Megan landed, grimacing against the pain. She reached around to her back and legs, focusing her power. Warm, healing energy erased the pains of her wounds and the tiny dart-teeth fell into the grass. The creature struggled to rise, but Megan commanded the cords and they tightened. It fell back down.

The reaver opened its mouth again. Megan planted a light ball on its eyes and it howled in anger, unleashing a storm of tiny darts to the side. Again, the miniature missiles pinged off the dome.

Megan set her mouth in a firm line, then clenched her hand, murmuring the words of a spell. A ghostly fist of light materialized next to her. She stepped forward and punched. The kinetite slammed into the reaver's skull. The monster's head jerked backwards and it gave a wilted squawk. She punched again. The creature's head dropped to the grass.

"Finish it," Lady Ravida sneered.

"No." Megan said, eyes on the reaver prone at her feet. "It's just a dumb beast."

"I said finish it, you little whelp!"

Megan whipped around, glaring at her. "It's a slave, just like me. It can't help that it's here anymore than I can. It lives."

Ravida's face flushed. "What? Insolent whore! Oxbridge, is this the behavior you allow from your slave girls?"

Instead of getting angry, Oxbridge actually grinned. "Lady Ravida, this slave can back up her impudence with magical skill. I'm perfectly happy to let her have a bit of leeway if she can perform like this."

Megan deliberately knelt to pick up her torn tunic.

"Too bad about that," Oxbridge sighed. "I won't give you another one, you know. I can't have my slaves ruining what I give them out of sheer generosity."

Megan's eyes narrowed. She held up the tunic and concentrated. A mild green glow lit her index finger and she touched it to the fabric, tracing the tear all the way around. The fibers of the cloth knit back together and soon she held an intact piece of clothing. She slipped the tunic back on, smoothed the fabric and raised her eyes to the assembled wizards.

Oxbridge gave her a sardonic smile in return.

"Well, I'm convinced," the dwarf grunted. "Anyone else?"

The cloaked figure nodded. "Let's see how she deals with a mature challenge." It lifted the cloak back and cast it aside.

Megan froze in horror.

A beautiful man in bone-white scale mail stood before her. Two black horns poked up from his forehead under honey-blond hair. His cat-like eyes regarded her with a frigid stare. Deep purple bat wings spread out behind his shoulders.

"Dear Jesus, protect me," Megan whispered, crossing herself.

A real daemon from Hades.

"Greetings, slave girl," the daemon said. "I am Balris, emissary and observer to the city of Catrin. You have some impressive and interesting abilities."

Megan's mouth felt as dry as paper and words caught in her throat.

Balris nodded. "Yes, you know what I am and realize your danger. Good. This shows you are learned and have a realistic appraisal of your own abilities. Now, defend yourself. Lord Oxbridge, if you please?"

Oxbridge motioned with his hands and Balris entered the dome. A wave of pure malice swept towards Megan.

She staggered backwards, trying to think of a spell. Already tired, her breath came in gasps. She wavered and stepped first to one side, then another.

Balris frowned. "Come, come, girl. Defend yourself. Don't disappoint me."

He thrust out a hand and a swarm of firedarts shot out. Megan leaped to the side and cast a shielding spell. Most of the darts detonated harmlessly on the shield. Three got through, hitting her with sharp cracks in her thigh, breast and shoulder.

Savage agony seared through her and Megan fought for breath.

Relax. The thought came unbidden to her mind. *Heal. Think.*

As before, the calming feeling of certainty suffused her being and her fear receded. She pressed a hand to her wounds and golden light washed over them. They vanished and she cast a protective spell over herself.

Balris stopped in mid-stride. "Interesting. A single healing I expected, but multiple? And complete recovery. This is odd."

He leaped forward and Megan found herself in the fastest, deadliest, most exhilarating magical duel in her life. She used counter-spells, shields, illusions and disruptors faster than she had ever imagined.

"Not really a fair test," drawled Lord Jeffries, sounding bored. "She can't counterattack."

"Fine then," Oxbridge retorted. "Slave, attack to kill."

Gladly. Megan smiled and was gratified to see Balris' eyes narrow.

She went on the offensive, casting lightning, cold and fire at the daemon. He methodically countered, dodged or deflected her spells. She kept moving the whole time, not pausing.

And she noticed something. Every time a magical attack missed its target and hit the iridescent dome, the barrier shimmered. The wizards didn't seem to notice.

A wild thrill of hope surged through her. *Maybe…*

She unleashed a series of firebolts, driving Balris back, then cast a cloud of fog on him.

Megan gathered her power, then sent a blast of hot light at the dome. It burst into shards of rainbow-colored fragments. Megan used Eagle Magic and shot out over the plaza, heart in her throat.

"Fuck me!" screamed the one-eyed dwarf. "She's getting away!"

"Son of a bitch!" Balris roared, lunging out of the fog.

"Damn her to hell!" Ravida yelped. Jeffries burst out in peals of laughter.

Megan swooped this way and that. Sizzling bolts of darkness shot past her.

Dar! Brandi! I'm coming!

She heard Oxbridge's voice. "Move, you fools! We need to bring her back!"

She heard chanting behind her as she zoomed over the library, heading for the beckoning green jungle beyond the city.

Then six loud voices erupted in a shout. A wave of pressure and sound slammed into her from behind. She lost control and tumbled through the air. A tower loomed up at her and she frantically tried to regain her bearings.

The tower whipped past not two feet from her head and she corrected her course, slowing to avoid another building.

Then a flash of red light burst all around and she felt weak as a kitten. The ground rushed up at her. Everything went dark.

***

Slowly, Megan regained consciousness. The first sense to return was hearing.

"…not possible for someone this young to have this much power!" That was Lady Ravida, sounding peeved.

"Many things are possible." Oxbridge replied. From his tone of voice, she could imagine him shrugging.

"Aren't you at least curious as to the reason?" asked Jeffries.

Megan opened her eyes. She lay on a table in a room lit by magical globes, her hands and feet held down by double straps. The wizards surrounded the table.

The dwarf held a slim, silvery wand over her body and passed it back and forth. The tip of the wand glowed blue, then green, then red and violet. He chewed his lip and shook his head.

Megan fought back tears. *Are they going to dissect me next?*

"Thirty-five thousand," announced the Elven mage.

The wizards gasped.

"That's insane," retorted the dwarf. "You could buy a fully-trained war pegasus for that. And for a slave?"

"No deal," replied Oxbridge, sounding entirely too pleased with himself.

"The Wizard-King will be most favorably inclined to you, Doctor Oxbridge," the Elf said. "How about forty thousand?"

Oxbridge shook his head. "I need her for the project. I'm almost done."

Another voice answered from the end of the table above Megan's head. "George is right. His project is more important."

A clawed hand rested gently on her head and Megan shuddered, squeezing her eyes shut.

"But her abilities intrigue me," said Balris in a soothing voice. He came around so that she could see him. "Tell me, my dear, where did you get those impressive skills?"

Megan shook her head. "I don't know," she managed. "I have always been this way."

"Preposterous," snorted the dwarf. "I detect traces of diabolical, Elven, and natural magic. I think I might have even found something Celestial. How does one get all those in combination at once?"

"Magical contamination," Jeffries proclaimed. The room fell silent.

The other wizards rounded on him. He shrugged. "That many different types of magic? Doesn't make sense that it would occur naturally. Contamination is the only real answer."

Balris stroked his chin, eyes thoughtful.

"Well," Oxbridge admitted. "That is possible. 'When' and 'how' would be my first questions."

"Indeed," Balris mused. He took Megan's chin in his hand. "Tell me, my dear, were you exposed to a magical accident or contamination?"

Megan shook her head, avoiding his eyes.

"We have ways to encourage you to be forthcoming," Oxbridge said with a raised eyebrow. "I am above such methods, but I assure you that Lord Jeffries, for example, is not."

"I'm telling you I wasn't!" Megan snapped, her heart clenching in fear. Her hands gripped the restraints so tightly she thought she would rip them.

Balris frowned. His hand stroked her cheek and ran down her neck. A tingle of magic rippled through her body where he touched her. His eyes burned and a nimbus of crimson light surrounded him. "Then how about your parents? What did they do?"

Megan trembled violently at his touch. A sly seductiveness returned, bubbling under the surface of her mind. She struggled to remember the feelings of peace and confidence instead.

"I… my father was a guard," she answered. "He didn't use magic."

Balris caressed her breasts with his claws, one at a time. Megan fought a rising panic.

"What about your mother?" The hand went along her ribcage and down to her stomach.

Megan's throat constricted in terror. "Yes, but she wasn't very power-ful," she rasped. "She was more of a laboratory assistant or an apprentice."

Balris' eyes locked on hers. She couldn't look away. His hand went lower and tears sprang to Megan's eyes, misting her vision.

Oh God! Please, don't let him violate me! Please, I beg You!

"Where?"

Megan whimpered at his touch. She felt herself dry heave and gasped to control it.

"Where did they work?" he repeated.

"At… at one of the academies in Coastwatch," she choked out. "Lords and Ladies Magical Conservatory."

"I see. Were you aware of any accidents?"

She shut her eyes, tears leaking out of the corners. "No! Mother never said anything about any accidents."

Balris leaned his hands on the table next to her, one eyebrow raised. "Nothing at all?"

"Probably didn't want her children to know about it, like all the others," Lord Jeffries offered. "Not that I blame them. It was an embarrassing epi-sode for the Academy, actually."

"Really?" Balris remarked. "You are a wealth of news, Lord Jeffries."

"There was a series of accidents at that academy about forty years ago." Jeffries examined his fingernails. "Released all kinds of energy. Rather nasty for the mages involved. Some of them were polymorphed into hybrid muta-tions that didn't live long, fortunately for them. There was some caretaker staff at the facility at the time. They also might have been affected, but to a lesser degree, obviously. If this girl's mother was an apprentice or assistant, she might have been one of the ones who survived."

"Interesting," Balris said. The daemon straightened and brushed his hands together as if he had just been digging in the dirt.

The revulsion left Megan like a snuffed candle and she let out a sob of relief. She took deep breaths, willing the calmness to return.

"Well, that could explain a lot," Oxbridge mused now, sounding disappointed. "If the contamination didn't kill her mother, it would have remained latent for years. This girl could have been affected *in utero*. She certainly wouldn't remember it and it could stay dormant for a long time."

He shot a look at the Elf. "Too bad."

"Why?" asked the dwarf.

"Magically contaminated persons don't usually live past forty years," Ravida interjected.

Megan couldn't breathe. A jolt of despair shot through her.

Forty years old? No…

Balris cupped her face with his hand and peered into her eyes. "How old are you, girl?"

"Thirty-six," she whispered.

"So, she has about four years left," Balris mused. "Well, George, you'd better wrap up the experiments quickly. She doesn't have long."

Oxbridge actually looked disappointed. "Very quickly. The deterioration sets in rather fast the closer you get to the end."

She was amazed to find his gaze almost sympathetic.

"Such a shame," he said finally. "Such a marvelous specimen. Well, slave Megan, we'll make sure we complete the tasks to the end. Have no fear."

"My Lords and Lady," he announced to the other wizards, "I have refreshments and amusements in the rooftop lounge of the library. If you'd care to accompany me?"

He turned away.

"Well, at least he got good use out of her before she wasted away," sniffed Ravida as she left on the arm of Lord Jeffries.

"Indeed," he remarked, his voice fading off into the distance. "Just think what a disaster it would have been if she started to fall apart just when he was almost done…"

Tears flowed down Megan's face. Her throat tightened.

I'm a lab animal — a valuable lab animal, or a working horse — nothing more.

"Four years?" she whispered to the empty chamber. "Four years? Even if I get out of here, what kind of a life is that for me and Dar?"

She thought of her sister, enslaved to the Ja'al as a vampire — and Eric, so far away, ignorant of her doom. She remembered her slain aunt and uncle. All of it seemed so futile now.

She fought back tears and stared at the stone ceiling. *Think, girl, think!*

Her mind whirred, going over the wizards' discussion in her head. When she considered all they had said, some small glimmer of doubt remained. Why hadn't her mother or father shown any signs of contamination? If what the wizards said was true, then they should have.

That was the part that didn't add up. If magical contamination was such a devastating fate, surely she would have noticed something odd about her parents. She remembered nothing. She held onto that fact like a drowning swimmer clutches a floating log.

Still her mind lingered on Oxbridge's words. "Forty years?"

She lay unmoving, her lips moving in silent prayer, struggling between doubt and hope and despair. The tears finally ran down her face.

"Why?"

The silent chamber didn't answer.

Chapter Twelve – Gifts of Many Kinds

The sun shone through the window with unnatural brilliance. Andyn watched the branches on the trees outside her window wave in the breeze. Shadows bobbed and weaved on the bed, on her blankets and the wooden floor, as if in a dance with the light.

She yawned and her stomach rumbled. Remembering her past meals at the Chancery, she grinned. *That's motivation enough to get up and not laze around, young lady.*

Bouncing up out of bed, she stood and stretched, enjoying the feeling of the morning's warmth on her skin. With a sigh, she padded over to the bureau, removing a clean shift, leggings, tunic, and socks. Dipping a washcloth into a basin of water at the bedside, she cleaned herself up and dressed quickly.

She brushed her hair and gave herself a critical once-over in the full-length mirror. *Not nearly as bedraggled as when we got here. A good sleep will do that for you,* she thought. *I hope Khyron and the boys rested as well.*

The thought of her man made her smile and she saw her image in the mirror with new eyes. Now instead of a sad widow exhausted from battling the forces of darkness, she saw a younger self. Her eyes fairly sparkled and her smile widened.

"'A woman in love glows with life'," she quoted. *Blessed Mindra, you had that right.*

She felt so close to Khyron now, as if the years of separation had been only days. Their shared talks and time together seemed to bond them ever tighter, and their recent brush with death joined their souls in mutual devotion. She did not ever want to leave his side.

Andyn wondered about his feelings as she dressed. Certainly, his declarations of affection were genuine, and she knew he cared deeply for her. Where would it lead?

She knew where she wanted and hoped for it to lead, but was this really the time and place in their lives to take the next step? Everything was so uncertain now.

In her heart, she knew now that she wanted to marry Khyron when all this was over, more than anything. Titles and wealth and fame meant little if he didn't share life with her.

She pulled on her low boots and, after a pause, strapped on her belt with her magic mace. There was little chance she would need Eleison here, but its familiar weight comforted her.

Khyron awaited her in the antechamber with Dar. She embraced both of them, adding a sound kiss on Khyron's lips.

He grinned. "That's a nice way to say 'good morning'."

"Get used to it. But no more talk. I'm starving."

Dar elbowed him. "I'm with her. Let's get to breakfast before Connor. I don't want to have to hunt for crumbs on the tablecloth."

She laughed and linked her arms in theirs. They marched down the hall to a set of double doors that soundlessly opened at their approach. A table set with white dishes and an array of mouth-watering treats awaited them — as did a familiar figure.

"Gorlak!" she cried.

The little goblin grinned widely and set down the last of the silver goblets. "Lady Andyn is up early. She must be hungry."

With another laugh, she scooped him up in a warm hug. "You are still a rascal."

The goblin smiled shyly but his eyes danced as she set him down. "Gorlak is guilty again."

He led them to their seats. "Melinor asked kitchen staff to make something special for great heroes, so this is for all of you."

"Hmm…" Dar mused, dropping a napkin into his lap. "I'm glad we got here when we did."

Pancakes with pecans and honey caught Andyn's eye, as did fruit salad of berries, peaches and plums, bacon-wrapped Dwarven sausages, three kinds of toast with apricot, strawberry and grape jam, crispy fried potatoes with herbs and red onions and eggs with chopped peppers and leeks. Oatmeal steamed in a ceramic tureen. Small jars containing walnuts, currants, raisins and dark Elven sugar crowded around it. Then Andyn's eyes alighted on a silver pot with a dark liquid.

"Gorostoli jekka!" she exclaimed at the same time as Khyron. He laughed and pinched her ribs. She smacked him in the arm.

Dar shook his head. "Your kids are going to be a handful."

The very thought of conceiving children with Khyron caused her heart-beat to accelerate, but she instead shot a warning look at Dar. "That's a little premature, isn't it?" she asked as she poured herself a mug of jekka.

Dar pretended not to hear, ladling up oatmeal and sprinkling sugar and walnuts over it. His eyes flicked to Khyron, who suddenly found his pancakes and fruit salad very interesting.

Now what are those two up to? Andyn mused.

They studiously ignored her and served themselves. Andyn shrugged, taking some eggs and potatoes herself. Sometimes, men mystified her.

They were so engrossed in the meal that the arrival of the other Riders made them start in surprise.

"Damn! You beat us to it," said Buck as he entered. "Well, at least Connor's with us, so we can keep an eye on him and make sure there's something left. Even Dar can't eat all that."

"Want to bet?" Dar shot back around a mouthful of eggs.

Eric, Connor and Buck came around their side of the table. Andyn kissed each of them on the cheek, then motioned to their seats. "I think the Nuncio was expecting a platoon," she said, "There might be enough for a halfling."

Connor raised an eyebrow. "Like Dar said, want to bet?"

The Riders made small talk as they dove into breakfast, their best meal since leaving Rhonin Handor's home.

"I haven't seen the Nuncio yet this morning," Buck noted, buttering a slice of toast. "He was in bed when we got here last night. I wonder if he's all right."

The doors opened and Melinor strode in. "He is feeling better now that you are here."

The Riders started to rise but he waved them down. "Don't let me interrupt. You have been in the field for weeks now and you need to recuperate."

"Will His Eminence be down soon?" asked Eric.

Gorlak met the wizard's eyes and Andyn stopped chewing. Something in their expressions made her apprehensive.

Melinor noticed her reaction and smiled. "Don't worry. He is probably in his library by now. He had an early start himself and is eager to meet with you."

He slid into a seat next to Connor and helped himself to a sausage, a couple of pancakes and oatmeal with raisins. Andyn watched the wizard as he chatted with the others.

Melinor seemed a bit off last night too, she mused.

Finally, Dar leaned back in his chair. "Well, that should last me a while."

"Good," said Melinor, popping the last bit of pancake into his mouth. "Off we go."

They trooped after him, following the now-familiar path to Father Edward's study. A thin, pale figure awaited them behind the massive desk. Andyn's heart froze.

Sweet Verian. What's wrong with him?

They all bowed. Andyn saw the shocked expressions on her friends' faces.

Father Edward gave them a wry smile. "Please, sit."

The Grey Riders did so. Melinor and Gorlak took up positions on either side of the Nuncio.

Father Edward coughed into his fist and maintained a straight face, but his eyes twinkled. "Well, I am sure you notice the difference in my appearance. I will explain. First, I hope you are all rested and well-fed?"

Buck nodded. "Yes, Father Edward. Thanks to you."

"Excellent. Speaking of well-fed, Buckminster, your feathered friend has found a happy home."

Buck smiled. "I'm glad. It was getting a bit too dangerous for a pigeon."

The Nuncio's smile returned. "Even for one so valiant as Puup."

His eyes rested on each of them in turn. "Now, on to less pleasant matters.

First things first: yes, I am changed. Yes, I am ill. And unfortunately, it is terminal."

Andyn tried to think of something to say but no words formed in her mind. She grappled with the concept of a world without Father Edward.

Something in her face must have given her away because he turned gentle eyes to her. "It was bound to happen someday," he said in a soft voice. "Do not fear for me. I will look forward to the life in the world to come, if only I am found worthy."

"Worthy? That's the last thing that you, of all people…" Words failed her and she clamped her lips together, eyes stinging.

"Are you sure?" asked Eric, looking stricken. "Isn't there something the healers can do? I mean, you're an incredible healer yourself…"

Edward shook his head. "The time for that type of healing is over. I must make the best of what time I have."

"Maybe you should delegate some duties to others," Dar suggested. Andyn saw his hands clenched into fists on his knees. "There are people who can take over for you so you can rest."

The Nuncio smiled. "Christ didn't get down off the cross, my boy, so how can I give up my duties to someone else while I'm still able? Besides, my wits are as sharp as ever, no? Come, we have plans to make and things to consider. Tell me what you found. Leave nothing out."

Taking turns, the Riders told him about the abandoned mine, the Red Moon cultists, the Skull Gate in the ravine, the battle against the daemons, Melissa's arrival and their departure with the records.

Edward asked only a few questions, content to listen to their account, nodding occasionally and making notes on a paper. "Well," he said finally, "You are to be congratulated. You found an operational Gate and destroy it. You slew two of the Fallen Ones. If it were up to me, your feat would be heralded throughout the lands. Unfortunately, I cannot publicize this for obvious reasons."

"Have other teams found Gates?" Khyron asked.

"Several, but some were decoys. We think we have destroyed a total of eight Gates."

"That leaves five," mused Connor.

Melinor and Edward exchanged a glance.

"We may have made assumptions in our original estimate that were incorrect," the Nuncio replied. "I know that we concluded that there were thirteen gates and our analysts concurred. However, now that more data is coming in from other freelance teams, we are not sure that was the maximum number. The symbol with the thirteen paths that we found in the Ja'al records from Colonel Alenar may have been a ruse. It would fit the pattern of the Ja'al: misdirection, deception and lies."

Andyn forced herself to take a deep breath. *More than thirteen, spitting out monstrosities like those we fought? How are we ever going to find and destroy all of them?*

"Not all is grim," Melinor told them. "The records indicate that the Ja'al have a weakness. They are very keen on finding something called the Dome of Glass. In fact, they are worried that we would find it first, because it supposedly guards something that can overthrow all their schemes. If they are this concerned, that is good news for us."

"What is the Dome of Glass?" Dar asked.

Edward shifted in his seat and winced in pain. Melinor's eyes flicked to him. "Well, it is a bit involved," the wizard replied, "so I'll tell you what I know later today. I don't want to hold up our conference."

Dar looked worried and Melinor chuckled. "It's not as bad as you think. And, Domes of Glass aside, don't forget that there are eight ruined Skull Gates. That is eight less access points for daemonic spies to enter our world and wreak havoc."

Andyn's mind churned like the emotions racing through her. What was the Dome of Glass hiding that could pose such a threat to the Ja'al's plans? Despite the peace and rest at the Chancery, the memories of the battle at the Gate haunted her. She saw anew her Khyron lying pale and broken on the shattered earth, barely breathing.

She felt a sudden urge to know everything. Any information that could thwart the Ja'al loomed in her mind as the highest priority. She thought about asking more questions about this new revelation, but one look at Edward's pale face stopped her.

"What about the Celestials?" she asked instead, forcing herself to unclench her hands. "It took Melissa quite a while to get to us. Will they be able to intervene fast enough?"

Father Edward nodded. "The Elohir are familiar with the unique signature of the Skull Gates now that more than one has been activated. They are using their new knowledge to detect any further tests or summoning of daemons. They will be faster to react now that they know what to look for."

At that, Andyn let out a deep breath and some of her tension left her. If Melissa and other Celestial watchers would be able to reach a Skull Gate quickly, the daemons could be countered more easily.

It won't happen again. Melissa will be there to help. The thought of their heavenly ally calmed her. As mighty as the daemons were, she knew they would be no match for the power she sensed in Melissa.

"What should we do now?" Dar asked.

To Andyn's surprise, Father Edward regarded Gorlak. "I had it in my mind that you work with Gorlak on ferreting out a spy in the Royal Court, but I think he has his own opinion."

Gorlak shook his head. "Not enough known. I still work on it. Need to be cautious and slow. Ja'al very alert now. They know Skull Gates detected and some broken. Not time yet."

"I trust to Gorlak's judgment," Father Edward said. He motioned to Melinor, who strode over to a chest against the wall beneath a window. "In the meantime, I understand that some of your equipment was a bit… battered, to say the least."

Melinor opened the chest and brought out a silvery metal shield. The front face was embossed with a ring of stars with a pair of trees in the center. Despite its size, he hefted it easily and handed it to Buck. "I think this will suit."

Buck's eyes widened. He stood and fitted the shield on his arm. It protected him from shoulder to knees yet he moved as if it weighed little.

"What's it made of?" he asked, tracing one of the trees with his fingers.

Melinor smiled. "Star-silver, crafted by the dwarves of Merdail. It is enchanted to protect you from fire and also floats in water, so, no matter how heavy your armor, you need not worry about drowning. It also has a fitting at the top for attaching a torch or a glow-globe or a small lantern, should you need it."

"Thank you," Buck said, eyes still on the shield.

Melinor handed a long, flat box to Khyron. "Replacements," he said.

Khyron opened it and whistled. Two swords, one long and one short, lay on padding. The hilt of each glittered with one ruby, one emerald, one sapphire, one opal and one diamond. Elegant, alien script wound down the scabbards, which were made of a strange dark wood with white highlights. He drew one of the weapons.

Andyn gaped. A mirror-bright blade reflected their astonished faces. A thin strip of a reddish metal ran down the center. The same script that decorated the scabbards was etched into the surface of the weapon.

"They are called the Changelings," Melinor said, looking immensely satisfied with their reaction. "When the Emperor of Terenai heard of your great victory, he felt compelled to release them to you in recompense for your bravery. I will give you the keywords. You can use them to charge the weapon with either fire, acid, lightning, cold or holy power. They are Celestial."

Khyron slid the sword back into its scabbard, looking stunned. "I don't know what to say."

Melinor smiled. "You needn't say anything. The Emperor's letter said enough." He paused. "Congratulations, Lieutenant Colonel Demaris."

Khyron stared. Andyn's heart swelled with pride and love and she threw her arms around him. "Oh Khyron! That's wonderful!" She gave him a firm kiss on the cheek, then rested her head on his shoulder.

Khyron still looked dazed. "Wait. You mean I… really?"

Father Edward nodded, smiling broadly.

"Really, my love," Andyn whispered. "You deserve it."

Maybe things aren't so grim after all…

"Hey," Dar said with a grin. He slugged Khyron in the shoulder. "Don't question it. Just accept it, and the increase in pay. Speaking of which, can I borrow fifty gold?"

Khyron laughed and swiped at Dar's head. Dar ducked, his grin widening.

"Speaking of pay," Melinor continued, reaching into the chest again. "There's something in here for you too, Dar."

He lifted out a suit of silvery chainmail, including coif, byrnie and leggings. Andyn peered at it. Instead of the traditional design, it was constructed of tiny, closely-spaced plates linked by rings. At the throat of the neckline, a silver plate bore the figure of a reclining lamb with a white pennon decorated with a red cross.

Dar took the armor and his grin faded to amazement as he lifted it. "Is this made of the same material as the shield?"

Melinor nodded. "Yes. The armor is named Habakkuk, after the prophet from the Old Testament. And there is one other feature. Upon command, it will perform a short-range teleport of you and a mass equal to about one other person whom you touch."

Dar stared at him. "Wait. What?"

"Yes. You can teleport. Its range is limited to about fifty feet, but you can choose any distance up to that. Of course, you'll be subject to the usual disorientation, but then again, in a pinch, that would be the least of your worries."

Dar held the armor in front of his chest. "Anything else I should know about it?"

"Don't overdo it," Melinor admonished with a wagging finger. "If you teleport twice in a day, it requires two days' worth of time in direct sunlight to renew its energies."

"Thank you," Dar murmured, running his hand over the silvery mail.

Father Edward nodded. "Now, until we further analyze the records you brought back, you are encouraged to rest here or wherever suits you. I will probably need you to confer with the intelligence ministries of the Northern Alliance nations. I tire easily and you are just as qualified to brief them. When we know more, we will meet again."

He rose and Melinor took his arm, handing him a cane. Father Edward took a step away from his desk, then snapped his fingers.

"I almost forgot. Melinor, the other box, if you please."

"Drat," said Melinor with a grin. "I forgot too." He reached to a coffer of dark wood on a nearby bookshelf. Father Edward laid it on the desk and opened it. Gorlak craned his neck to look, black eyes glittering with undisguised curiosity.

Six amber beads the size of grapes lay on a cushion. Andyn's magical senses tingled like the strings of a mandolin played by a minstrel. The tiny beads radiated waves of powerful magical energy. She turned wondering eyes to the Nuncio.

He smiled. "I will not tell you the full tale of why you need these, but believe me when I say I feel they will come in handy, though I can't say how. These are Preservation Beads. They have the same effect as the Preservation

Net spell, with which I believe Andyn is familiar from her battle with Zhinia Margoth."

She nodded. She had used just such a spell to preserve her friends after the lich queen felled them with vile magic. The spell had slowed time to a miniscule fraction of normal, permitting her to resuscitate them after Margoth's destruction.

Father Edward handed one bead to each of them. "You are not the freelance mercenaries you were when you started your careers," he said with a note of pride. "I am fully confident that you will be wise in using them. Merely crush one in your hands and then hold your palm over whatever you want to preserve."

"Thank you," Eric said. Andyn murmured her thanks and placed the bead into her belt pouch. She would put padding over it, or even get a small box to protect it during her rough-and-tumble adventures.

Now Father Edward took up his cane and raised a hand in benediction. "I leave you for now. May the Lord bless and keep you and make His face to shine upon you now and always."

Andyn bowed her head. Edward looked tired and frail as he shuffled away from the Riders with Gorlak and Melinor guiding him.

Her heart skipped a beat. Something broke within her. She intercepted Father Edward, wrapping him in a hug.

"Please…" she couldn't finish the sentence for the tightening in her throat and the tears blurring her vision.

His lips pressed against her forehead. "Peace, my dear, brave priestess of Verian," he whispered. "All will be well."

She released him and watched him go with misty eyes. Khyron's arm encircled her waist.

He gave her a squeeze and she sighed, wiping her tears. "I can't believe he's this sick."

Dar and Eric exchanged a look. "It was bound to happen, Andyn. Melinor told us how old he really is."

Connor raised his eyebrows. "He appeared to be about seventy before his illness, but I'm willing to bet from your expressions it's more than that."

"He's over a hundred and ten."

Andyn shook her head. "How?"

Dar shrugged. "No one knows."

"Well," said Buck, "I have a letter to write."

Connor gave him a bland look. "Do I know the recipient?"

Buck tried to look mysterious and failed as they exited. "You might."

Connor chuckled as he and Eric joined them. Dar shot a look at Khyron and gave a tiny nod, then closed the door.

"Hey, what are —" Andyn stepped towards the door but Khyron's hand on her arm stopped her.

"Andyn, please wait."

Maybe this is the mystery… she gave him a measuring look. "Okay, Khyron, what is this about?"

He fumbled with his belt purse and dropped his gaze to the floor. "I just…well…um… I need to talk to you about something."

She took his hand. "About what? Are you feeling all right?"

He shook his head. His hand trembled and she wondered, then realized he was laughing.

What in the…?

He squeezed her hand and raised sea-green eyes to hers, still smiling. "All right? Yes. I'm all right, more than all right. The best."

He took a deep breath. "I have something very particular to ask you."

She gazed back at him. Her eyes widened at something in his expression. Her knees felt like water.

He drew something out of his belt purse and opened his hand. Andyn's heartbeat thundered in her chest. She stared, a wild joy breaking out in her soul. He held two matching gold rings with bands of emerald twining around them.

Oh my God! Betrothal rings!

"Andyn Josette Fallbrook Eleandir, will you marry me?"

Chapter Thirteen – Wolf in the Fold

"She'll be your problem for a while, Kelani," Adina said with a glare at Brandawyn.

"I'll see what I can do," replied a blonde woman in a wine-red cloak. She motioned towards the door of the cottage and it swept open.

"In, Delilah," Adina ordered.

Brandawyn complied. Her eyes darted all around the sitting room. It was furnished with large cushioned couches, elegantly carved tables, lace curtains, crystal decanters, Elven ceramics and burnished brass. A statue of a fire giant crafted entirely out of red crystal sat on a cherry-wood pedestal.

Kelani swirled the cloak from her shoulders, revealing a simple country woman's dress. She regarded Brandi with a raised eyebrow. "A vampire, you say?"

Adina nodded. "Yes, with the usual abilities, but very rebellious." She handed a skull-shaped garnet medallion to Kelani. "This matches a ring I have. It will control her. Don't be afraid to inflict maximum pain."

Kelani's lip curved in a gentle smile. She rang a bell on a nearby table and soon a door on one side of the room opened. Two tall, muscular brown-haired men swaggered in. They wore scale mail and had longswords at their belts. Their dark eyes shot to Brandi, devouring her every curve. One of them filled a crystal goblet with wine from a dragon's-head decanter.

Kelani handed her cloak to one man as the other brought her the goblet. She sipped, green eyes glinting at Brandi over the rim. "I'm sure that punishments won't be necessary, will they, Delilah?"

"No."

"Excellent."

Brandi's eyes flickered to the men.

Kelani giggled. "Oh, no dear. Those are mine. They aren't for you. I might have you to entertain them, if you're not cooperative. But cooperating shouldn't be too hard. Besides serving us here, you will provide surveillance to make sure we aren't disturbed, nothing more."

Kelani's form shimmered and Brandi's heart froze. Instead of a slender blonde human girl, someone else faced her: a taller, voluptuous brunette with dark purple horns jutting out from her forehead. Deep red bat wings unfurled behind her shoulders.

"Yes," she murmured. "You see what I am. Well, I may not be full-blooded — no thanks to my dear departed dad — but I have my share of daemonic abilities. Don't cause trouble and we'll get along famously."

Adina sniffed. "I was hoping that some torments in isolation would give her perspective and improve her obedience. I hate the idea of wasting all that magic."

"Less than optimal results, Adina?"

Adina spun on her heel and fell onto one of the couches, lounging against the pillows. "Well, we did get our objectives, for the most part, not without headaches. She resists us at every turn and it's exhausting. Even more exhausting, I have to leave in the morning to join Berek at the Regional Council."

Kelani slipped onto another couch and flicked her fingers at one of the men.

"Barnard, show Delilah her room. Then return to us. Adina and I require some… *refreshment* after our journey."

Barnard's lips curved in a smile and his eyes flashed. "As you command, Lady Kelani."

Brandi followed him down a hall. Her vampiric senses detected the pulse of the man's blood in his veins. Her eyes wandered from his shoulders, down his back to his buttocks.

She gritted her teeth and tore her gaze away. *I am Brandawyn, not Delilah.*

Barnard stopped at a small room at the end. "Here you are, Miss Delilah," he said with a mocking bow.

"Thank you."

She put her hand on the doorknob but he barred the way with his arm. "I'm sure Lady Adina didn't mean for us to be complete strangers to each other."

Brandi have him a honey-sweet smile as her vampirism boiled to the surface. "I'm sure we'll be great friends," she whispered, showing her fangs.

His smugness melted away. Brandi nodded and entered the room, making sure to sway her hips. She spun around, her dress belling around her as she leaned against the door frame. She ran her tongue over her fangs.

Disgust and fear warred in his eyes. After a few heartbeats, he clenched his jaw and backed away. She watched him go down the hall.

A red haze swam at the edge of her vision and hunger for blood rippled through her body. Her heart raced and she found herself practically gasping for air.

With an effort, she regained control. *Damn it! No! I am Brandawyn!*

She grimaced, closed the door and collapsed on the small bed. Cradling her head on her arms, she tried to pray, making it all the way through the Our Father before the hunger faded.

With a deep sigh, she sat up and examined the room. Only a bed, a single chair and a bureau with a washbasin occupied it.

Brandi stared at the wall, wondering what odious tasks Kelani might add to her chores. The looks on the men's faces made her stomach lurch. She gazed out the solitary window. Woods stretched away from a cleared space around the house. A flat mesa loomed in the distance. Even from a mile away, she clearly noted three enormous boulders on the plateau.

From Adina's conversation with Kelani on the way here, she knew they were somewhere in eastern Deran, probably near the metropolis of Eastridge. She wondered if she could just break the window and run.

Brandi frowned, looking down at her simple grey frock. Adina hadn't even given her shoes.

The Ja'al cleric's voice echoed in her memory. "You run slower without them, dear, and we wouldn't want you to get away from us, would we?"

We'll see about that. I can make my own shoes. Brandi inspected the window frame, looking for a weak point. Then she saw a curling symbol etched in purple on the window frame and wall. She murmured an arcane syllable and waved her fingers at the glyph. It sparkled and glowed and a part of her brain tingled with magical power.

Brandi ground her teeth. *Great — a Glyph of Entanglement. If Adina placed that in here, I doubt if I can dispel it. But there may be other ways to escape. If I can get away from Kelani, I might be able to find someone who could help. Eastridge is a big city. Maybe I can find a wizard who knows Melinor Indidarc. I can tell him I know his foster son.*

Even as she thought it, she knew what a slim chance that was. Away from the controlling power of the garnet-skull jewel, she had no idea if she would be able to manage her vampiric side.

She clenched her fists. "I *will* find, you, Eric," she whispered. "If only to see that you're alive and well, and to set you free from me."

No one can marry a vampire and live. Her heart sank at what she had become and her eyes stung. Trying to focus on something else, she stared at the landscape, thinking of possible escape routes.

In the silence, she became aware of voices. She paused, listening, then reddened.

The voices were Adina and Kelani and, she presumed, the two men. There were few words but a substantial amount of other sounds, including moans and giggles, interrupted by rhythmic motion.

She lay down on the bed, put the pillow over her face, and tried to pray. At least it might drown out Adina and Kelani with their lovers.

After a while, she heard a bell. With a muttered curse, she rose, smoothed her dress and retraced her steps to the living room.

She opened the door and blinked.

Adina and Kelani lay naked in the arms of two equally naked men on the couches. Kelani gave her a languid smile.

"Delilah? Be a dear and go into the kitchen. Barnard tells me there are some dainties laid out in the cold box and more wine. Bring them here."

Keeping her eyes on a painting of a dragon soaring over a mountain, Brandi did as she was told, ignoring the snickers.

"Oh my. She's quite the prude, I'm guessing," the other man said.

"Well, Harlan!" Adina replied. "You wouldn't think so if you saw her with some of her victims!"

That got a round of laughter.

Her ears burning, Brandi retrieved two platters, a bottle of wine and four goblets and brought them to the living room.

Kelani waved at a sideboard. Brandi set everything down.

"Now go clean up the kitchen. We'll call for you when we need you."

Again, she tried to ignore various vulgar comments as she departed. She steadied herself and made an effort to breathe evenly. There would be no benefit in tipping her hand before she had an idea of how to escape.

Patience, she told herself as she washed dishes.

Over the clink of ceramic and silver, she caught a tone in their voices that made her pause.

"If we only knew where the damned Gate of Stars was —" said Adina.

"My lady," Barnard interjected. "The slut in the kitchen will hear."

"Her? Bah!" Adina sneered. "She can't even wipe herself without my say-so. It doesn't matter what she hears."

"Besides," replied Harlan. "The Gate is guarded by the Dome of Glass. We all know what happens to anyone who tries to pass it."

"Quite so, Harlan," purred Adina.

Glasses pinged in the living room.

"Still," Kelani mused, "The Gate is very powerful. The High Command says Oxbridge's magic will work on the other targets, but the Gate of Stars? Probably not."

"It doesn't matter," Adina replied. Brandi heard her voice muffle as she stretched. Adina sighed. "No one knows where the Dome is, much less the Gate. Don't worry: Oxbridge's magic will see to it that the Final Solution is implemented."

Brandi put away the dishes, her mind whirring. What did *that* mean? She felt an immediate urge to record every detail. She shot a glance into the living room, but they were completely occupied with other matters.

Paper and a pencil or marker, she thought. *Could there be some in the kitchen?* She furtively searched drawers and shelves but found none.

Maybe in one of the other rooms near mine?

She peeked into the parlor again, then smoothed her dress and adopted a resigned expression.

"Done, mistress," she announced as she entered.

"Good," Adina said, rolling over on top of Barnard. "Now, back to your room."

Brandi walked away.

"What is the Final Solution, my lady?" asked Barnard as Brandi departed.

Brandi heard the wet sound of a kiss. "A plan to eliminate our enemies or make them slaves," Adina said. "Then we will have as many pleasures and riches as we want. We will rule everything."

"As long as I can serve you, milady Adina."

"That you will," drawled Kelani, "But for now, you get to serve *me*. Adina, let's trade."

"Marvelous idea. Let's do."

Brandi closed the door behind her, then tried the first door in the hall on the way to her room. It was locked.

She tried another and another until she found an open one.

Boxes, barrels and crates greeted her eyes in the windowless chamber. She pointed a finger at the ceiling and a mage-light flickered into being.

A thick stack of papers and a cup with charcoal pencils sat on a shelf.

Yes! The housekeeping ledgers. She stole three sheets and a pencil, extinguished the light, and stole back to her room.

Her door didn't lock, but she wedged her chair under the knob and sat on her bed.

"*My Dearest Eric,*" she wrote, "*If you find this, it means that I am no more, but I will be glad, because I will be free…*"

***

"Okay, rest stop is over," Buck announced. "If we hurry, we can make it to Eastridge before nightfall."

Eric nodded. He cinched the straps on Niveral and vaulted into the saddle. As he buckled in, his eyes flickered to Andyn and Khyron and he smiled.

They were now inseparable. After Andyn's joyous acceptance of

Khyron's proposal, the Grey Riders had treated them to a night on the town for a celebratory dinner, accompanied by a beaming Melinor Indidarc.

Andyn glowed with happiness and Khyron's usually serious demeanor melted into relaxed joviality. Eric sometimes felt a twinge of pain in their presence and he recognized it as envy.

Will I ever have that?

Thoughts of Brandi entered his head. He saw the light in her lavender blue eyes and her gentle smile. His throat constricted. For some reason, he remembered the way she walked: lithe, balanced and strong.

The most beautiful girl I've ever seen.

He shook himself. He had dreamt of her again and the barely-remembered impressions unsettled him. To refocus his thoughts, he drew a parchment from his belt purse and unfolded it.

"*Proceed to Eastridge,*" he read. "*In the woods nearby is a location that the Ja'al records designated as a 'transmission site'. The exact nature of this site is unknown, but it is doubtless related to the current plot. Your instructions are to infiltrate the location, gather intelligence, neutralize Ja'al agents and collect any contraband that might be useful. If it is a functional Gate, your previous mission orders stand.*"

His thoughts drifted back to a fireside chat with Melinor prior to leaving Saint Martin's Town.

"Well, the Dome of Glass is shrouded in mystery," the wizard had told the Riders, "In antiquity, during the Paragon Wars, it was supposed to have been a structure devised by the forces of evil to guard something, to keep it away from the Allies of the Light. No one is quite certain what that thing is. Some theories include an enchanted armory for making powerful magic items, or a gate to some other world, or an army of steel golems, or a flying fortress. Most of the theories are based on legends, and those are rather tenuous at best."

"What do you think it is?" Connor had asked.

Melinor had shrugged. "I really don't know. It wasn't exactly my area of expertise. I don't need to tell you that any one of them would be extremely helpful in any conflict with the Dark Faiths. If the Ja'al are concerned, that means that they take it as a serious threat, so it will be very beneficial to find out whatever we can."

Their discussion had left him only with more questions. Melinor had advised them to thoroughly interrogate any captured Ja'al agents.

Eric brought his thoughts back to the present and tried to imagine any of the wonders Melinor had mentioned. He shook his head. *From the Paragon Age? That was over three thousand years ago.*

He folded the parchment and replaced it, then nodded when Dar beckoned to them.

"Riders up!" Dar shouted.

Eric urged Niveral into a canter. The pegasus beat his wings and they rose into a twilight sky touched with ochre and gold. They soared over foothills, keeping the Eastern Pass Highway below them. The city of Eastridge nestled against the towering Silver Mountains some twenty miles away. Thickly forested slopes darkened as the day deepened into evening.

Eric tried to keep his mind off his most recent dreams of Brandi, instead studying the topography below. If there was a secret Ja'al safehouse somewhere in there, it was going to take some effort to find it.

City lights twinkled from towers and spires as they neared Eastridge. Eric's eyes wandered to a plateau about a mile away. Three enormous rock formations clustered near the edge of the mesa like petrified giants. He banked Niveral around, following Dar on their landing approach.

Dear Lord, he prayed, *please help and protect Brandi until I can find her. And don't let me lose hope…*

Chapter Fourteen – Reunion

"Observe and report only. Avoid contact and don't kill." Kelani's admonition and the subsequent searing pain echoed in Brandi's mind. While not interested in simply using the medallion to inflict torture, Kelani certainly wasn't shy about its powers.

At least I don't have to worry about Adina. Until she comes back, anyway.

Brandi crouched in the bushes by the thin hunters' track. Her eyes flickered over the woods. Nothing moved. She slipped through the undergrowth.

Kelani had seen the practicality of providing Brandi with a suit of leather armor in mottled green and brown with matching boots. Although the half-daemon didn't have Adina's penchant for humiliation, Brandi was just a tool to her, little different from a hammer or a corkscrew.

At least she gave me a dagger, Brandi thought sourly.

She clambered atop a boulder and slipped under the overhanging boughs of a nearby willow. After three patrols, she had found the most advantageous locations for spying. So far, she had alerted her new mistress about one air patrol from Eastridge, a pack of fell wolves, and a trio of trappers with their mules. None approached close enough to warrant alarm and Brandi felt glad she was prohibited from attacking. She didn't want to contend with Delilah again.

Her senses tingled and she froze. She heard a low voice — an oddly familiar voice.

She whispered arcane syllables and a moving curtain of air swirled before her. Anyone looking in her direction would see only boulders and vegetation.

She waited.

A male halfling in black leather armor and hooded camouflage cloak flitted between two trees. He glanced in her direction and her heart caught in her throat.

Connor Lomin?!

The realization took her breath away. She opened her mouth to call to him and then winced as red-hot magic lanced through her temples.

"Observe only."

She bit down on her lip to keep from crying out. It was Connor! That meant that Eric might be near.

Another figure slipped out from the undergrowth and she glimpsed blond hair underneath the cloak hood. For a wild, exhilarating moment, she thought it was he. But an unfamiliar Elven man flicked sea-green eyes towards Connor. The Elf made a hand signal to Connor and the pair retreated.

Her heart hammered in her chest and she sat back heavily against the tree trunk.

Connor Lomin! Obviously, the other man was an ally, but who was he? Where were the other Riders? Had they broken up, divided their forces, or gone on separate assignments? A dozen different thoughts rambled around in her head.

She calmed her racing pulse and adjusted her position to see further down the path. Soon, she heard the thump of hooves.

A pair of winged horses approached through dappled sunlight. Her heart soared. Connor rode one. The familiar figure of Dar Cabot rode the other, his bow at the ready and his eyes scanning the forest.

Oh God! Dar is alive! Good, brave, foolhardy Dar! Wait for my sister, blessed man. She still lives!

Two more pegasi followed, one bearing the unfamiliar Elven man and the other, a smiling Andyn Eleandir. Andyn spoke to the man at her side. He smiled back and Brandi could feel their joy.

Dear, sweet Andyn too! And who is that man?

To her delight, another pegasus trotted into view with the tall, lean form of Buck Bydecy, wearing banded mail armor underneath his cloak. And at his side…

All the love in her soul swelled up, threatening to overwhelm her. As handsome as ever, Eric Indidarc rode with an easy confidence and casual alertness that made her proud. A strange, golden dagger sat at his hip and he held a bow in his left hand with an arrow nocked.

How much he must have grown and changed over the intervening time!

Every fiber of her being urged her to leap up and announce herself. Finally, after all this time, they would be reunited. Then vicious agony ripped through her and she squeezed her eyes shut, gritting her teeth.

"Observe and report only!"

Kelani's order rang in her ears and the compulsion of her magic echoed in Brandi's head. Brandi clapped her hands over her ears, praying desperately. For what seemed like centuries, she fought. She reached inward for the calmness and surety that had served her so well in the past when resisting Adina. The magic faded, then dwindled to nothing.

Brandawyn's ears still rang and her head spun. She rested on hands and knees on top of the rock, breathing steadily and deeply. She heard only the sounds of birds in the trees and the breeze through the leaves.

When she opened her eyes, the Grey Riders were gone.

She choked back tears. Her love was alive! And yet, he was as inaccessible to her as if he were in Targanon across the Great Sea. How could she warn him of Kelani and the warriors? She felt confident of their ability to defend themselves, but against a daemon? And Kelani's countermeasures could prove a challenge to anyone.

What if she intercepted the Riders just as they approached the lodge? After all, her orders only applied when she was on patrol, not when on the property. If she could get to the Riders before they met Kelani, could she warn them somehow?

I have to be patient. God will show me a way.

As far as Kelani's instructions were concerned? Brandi pressed her lips together. *I saw nothing in the forest today. Nothing at all.*

She marched back towards the lodge...

***

Eric crouched behind a tanrin bush, watching the building. He felt an

150

unexpected sense of foreboding. Everything certainly looked normal, even picturesque: a grey structure with white painted shutters, glass windows with curtains, a sturdy stable, a garden with a gated fence, even a well near the corral.

"Well?" Buck asked Khyron.

Khyron stroked his chin. "Looks ordinary to me. Four horses in the corral. I don't like that pile of reddish rock on the north side of the house, though. Anything could be hidden in that."

Eric's unease intensified the longer he surveyed the scene.

"It's the only place for miles around," Dar said.

"It could be just what it seems," offered Andyn. "Maybe there's nothing special here."

Eric bit his lip. From using Stealth earlier, he knew there was at least one occupant: a tall, burly human with long brown hair. With four horses, there were likely others.

"We'd tip our hand if all of us went in there," Connor mused. "Maybe a more subtle approach? How about if Eric, Dar, Buck and Andyn go up and just knock on the door? Tell them you're agents of the government looking for smugglers of contraband."

Dar grinned. "In a certain, legalistic way, that's exactly what we're doing, so we wouldn't technically be lying."

Khyron winked. "Unless they're all lawyers, we're in the clear. Buck, give it a look with the Eye."

Buck swung the arm down on his helmet. For long moments, they waited while he stared at the lodge and its surroundings.

"Harrumph," he finally said. He frowned and flipped the arm back up. "That doesn't help much. Well, it does and it doesn't. There are symbols on the ground in a ring around it. And I know one thing at least — it's not a simple hunting lodge. There's an aura of evil, like I saw in the Darkhollow."

That stopped them.

"The Darkhollow?" Dar asked. "Oh. Great."

Eric still said nothing, watching the building and the four horses. The feeling of dread remained.

"Eric?" Andyn asked. He broke his reverie to find them all staring at him.

"What's wrong?" asked Khyron.

Eric shook his head.

Dar made a face. "Come on. Out with it. Something's bothering you."

"I don't know," Eric said slowly. "I have an unsettled feeling, like there's a violent storm just over the horizon and I can't see it."

The others exchanged looks, then eyed the building again.

"Hmm…" Khyron said. "Maybe we try to infiltrate through a back door or window? Eric saw at least three doors and five windows with Stealth."

Andyn shook her head. "Without knowing the nature of the evil, we could be running right into a trap."

"In that case," said Dar, rising, "We should go with Connor's original plan. If we run into trouble, any attackers from the lodge will be surprised when he comes running with Khyron."

Eric hesitated. Andyn pulled him to his feet, eyes narrowing as she gazed at him. "Eric, if you have another idea, even if it's just a hunch, tell us."

"Nothing specific," he answered. "Let's do it."

She held her hands up, praying as misty colored nets wafted down over them.

Eric gripped the handle of Fidelis with a hand suddenly gone clammy. Buck flipped down the Eye of Truth again. As they neared the garden gate, the air around Eric tingled and he felt magical scanners sweep over him. It felt very much like the type of threat assessors that guarded Northern Alliance safehouses.

Someone's taking care to guard this place as well as hide it.

At the door, Andyn and Dar took the lead while Eric and Buck stood behind them. Andyn knocked and they waited.

The door swung open and a tall man with brown hair raised his eyebrows. He wore a grey tunic over scale mail. A longsword with a black gem in the pommel hung at his belt.

"Yes? May I help you?"

Andyn inclined her head. "We are sorry to disturb you, sir, but we are officials of the King patrolling the area for smugglers of contraband. Have you noticed any unusual activity nearby?"

"Who is it, Barnard?" asked a woman's voice from within the lodge.

"Royal agents, Lady Kelani," Barnard answered without taking his eyes off the Riders. "Searching for smugglers."

"Really? Way out here? Well, that is news. Bid them come inside."

Barnard stood aside and waited as they entered. Eric's eyes flickered around the interior of a sitting room, passing over lace curtains, enameled ceramics, dark woods and plush upholstery. A high ceiling arched almost twenty feet overhead.

A golden-haired human woman entered from a side hallway, smiling brilliantly. She wore a white dress and a skull-shaped garnet pendant lay on her shapely chest. Another muscular, brown-haired man entered, bearing armor and weapons identical to Barnard.

"Well! Royal officers? Here at my humble lodge?" Her green eyes danced as they flitted over the Riders. "What an honor. How can I help you?"

Andyn nodded to her. "Our apologies, Lady. We are searching for smugglers in the area. Have you seen any suspicious activities nearby? Unfamiliar persons moving about, perhaps at night?"

Kelani shook her head, moving over to a pedestal that held a red crystal statuette of a giant. "That sounds ominous. What would they be smuggling?"

"We are not at liberty to say, milady," Dar replied. "But they might be using carts or large creatures to move containers of considerable size."

Again Kelani shook her head. "I haven't noticed anything. Barnard? Harlan?"

The two men exchanged a glance and shrugged. "We have not, lady," replied Harlan. "Perhaps Delilah has seen something?"

"Ah yes." Kelani rang a little bell next to the statuette. "Delilah? Come to the parlor, please. We have guests."

Eric shot a look at Buck, who gave in imperceptible shake of his head.

Not lying? Then what is really going on?

A red-haired woman entered the parlor from an exterior door, clad in a suit of leather armor in camouflage patterns with matching boots. A silver pendant with a dark purple gem rested between her breasts and a dagger hung at her belt.

Eric gasped. The universe ground to a halt. His heart stopped beating. His friends froze.

Brandawyn Alenar held her head high. A mixture of intense happiness, deep longing and despair shone in her piercing lavender-blue eyes.

"Brandi…" he breathed, unable to believe his eyes.

***

Oh God! How did they get here so fast? How do I warn him? Brandi thought frantically.

Though her heart thundered in her chest, she answered calmly. "Hello, Eric."

"You two know each other?" asked Kelani. Her eyes glittered.

Brandi watched Eric's hand creep towards the strange golden dagger at his belt. He found his voice. "Yes, we do. We parted ways months ago. She…"

Kelani's gaze darted from Eric to Brandi and back. Brandi saw the other Riders tense and realized Connor and the other Elven man were absent.

"… we were friends," Eric finished.

"Delilah, dear," said Kelani with a smile not matched in her eyes. "I didn't know you were acquainted with our guests."

"I just returned from my rounds, Lady Kelani," answered Brandi. Her mind whirled desperately for a way to warn the Riders.

Kelani gave a carefree laugh. "Well, then, this is a merry reunion! Delilah works for me here at the lodge. A most attentive servant, I might add."

"How did you get here?" Eric blurted out. "And where's Megan?"

How do I tell him about Kelani? How do I tell him about me?

Brandi smiled at him. "We went our separate ways before I came into the service of the excellent and most *devilishly* beautiful Lady Kelani. You remember how Megan was always eager to visit exotic places and work for new employers. She's such a free spirit."

A flash of understanding shone in Andyn's eyes. The Verian priestess pressed her lips together, then smiled with a gentle nod of her head. "Well, this is a happy accident, Lady Kelani. However, we must continue our patrols. We will take our leave of you. Perhaps Eric and Delilah could renew their acquaintance some other time."

No! God! How do I warn them? They need to know about the Dome of Glass and the Gate of Stars! I'm so close! Brandi's thoughts winged to her hidden notes.

Unbidden, memories of Delilah came to the fore.

154

That's it. Delilah! Yes! Delilah! Come out, come out! I have victims for you! You can feed!

A red haze burned at the edges of her vision. Brandi smiled, showing her teeth, feeling her fangs come in.

***

Eric stared in horror. Brandi's skin paled, her canines lengthened into fangs, and her eyes flashed red.

"Don't go just yet," she whispered. "You've had a long journey. I'm sure you're hungry. I know I am."

"Stupid bitch!" Kelani shrieked, snatching up the statuette of the giant. She transformed, gaining fangs of her own while ebony horns sprouted from her forehead. Dark red wings unfurled from her shoulders. With one hand, she smashed the statuette against the table.

The ground shook and the entire cottage lurched. The front wall bucked and a window shattered.

"Delilah! Attack!" the daemoness shouted, clasping the medallion. Lurid orange light burst out between her fingers.

Brandi's eyes flashed red and she staggered. She snarled, clenching her fists.

God! Help her! Eric held forth the silver crucifix she had given him. "Brandi!" Eric pleaded. "Don't give in!"

Her eyes locked on the crucifix and tears ran down her face. "No!" she screamed and hurled herself out of the broken window.

"Damn it!" Kelani screamed. She thrust a hand at the Riders and spat a foul word. Fire blasted out from her palm.

Buck drew Khelios and leaped forward, shield up. The inferno curved around his shield and hit the carpet instead, setting it ablaze.

"Idiots!" screamed Kelani. "That was Adina's favorite rug!"

Barnard and Harlan whipped out their swords and charged.

The Riders moved as one. Dar swung Rindara in its scabbard to his front, drawing the blade. Andyn's maces flicked out.

Eric dropped his hand to his belt. "Fidelis!" The spear transformed to its full length, bright with holy fire.

"Fucking hell!" Kelani swore, eyes wide. She leaped up. With a single beat of her wings, she shot towards the ceiling.

Eric hurled Fidelis. To his amazement, Kelani spun, deflecting the spear with her palm. Fidelis penetrated two feet into the far wall.

The daemon shot down one of the hallways. Dar and Eric lunged after her.

Barnard and Harlan blocked their way, slashing. Buck and Andyn charged the two men, driving them back. Eric dodged and dove past a hissing blade, calling to his spear. It glittered to life in his hand. He ran into the hallway, Dar at his side. He heard the sizzle of magic behind him and the voices of Harlan and Barnard crying out in pain.

Several doors stood open in the hall. On instinct, Eric raced into the first room just in time to see Kelani flit out of a door on the opposite side. He raised Fidelis but she made an obscene gesture and smoke filled the room.

Dar chanted a quick phrase and the smoke dissipated. The men charged into another hallway, turning back into the parlor.

Kelani hovered near the ceiling. "How dare you bring that piece of trash into my house!" she raged. She darted toward Eric. He dropped to a crouch, spear planted into the singed floorboards. Dar leaned back, Rindara held point-up near his shoulder.

Kelani swept up at the last second. She latched her claws onto a ceiling beam and swung out of the way. Dar swung at her but missed, shattering a chair instead. Eric raised his spear again. A globe of pure blackness surrounded him.

Stinging energy crackled. He gasped from the pain.

"*Lux Domini!*" he cried. The darkness vanished. A globe of grey mist shot out at him and he hurled himself to the side. The sphere splatted into the wall, dissipating into an ill-smelling fog.

Kelani hissed, casting a hail of firedarts. Eric and Dar staggered back. Andyn's magic protections vanished under the onslaught.

Kelani smiled sweetly and drew a jade dagger from a sheath attached to her thigh. Her other hand crackled with electricity.

Eric's blood ran cold. *This is a problem.*

***

In the yard, Brandi rolled out of the way of a massive axe. The blade bit deep into the earth. She leaped to her feet and raced towards the forest. A ten-foot wall of brambles burst up at the limit of the forest edge and she scrambled to a halt. She spun but the wall of thorns encircled the lodge.

"Blast!" she fumed.

The ground shook behind her and she darted to the side as the huge axe slammed into the ground again. She raced away from the cottage at inhuman speed towards the corral. The horses plunged in fear and strained at their bridles.

A two-headed giant lumbered towards her, eyes blazing. He stood as tall as a castle wall, armored in an enormous coat of metal rings. In one hand, he swung an axe longer than her body and in the other, a club the size of a small tree.

She sensed his pulse and her vampiric urges burned. *So much blood!*

"Brandi?"

She whirled at the voice. With a desperate effort, Brandi submerged Delilah.

Connor and the unfamiliar Elven man hacked themselves free from the brambles and stumbled near her.

The halfling gaped at her. "Brandi?"

The Elf drew two shiny swords. "You know her?"

"Yes, Khyron! It's Brandawyn!"

"Invaders!" both heads of the giant bellowed in a weird, throaty chorus. "I will kill you all!"

"Never mind that!" Brandi shouted. "We have bigger problems! Run!"

The two-headed behemoth thundered closer. Connor, Khyron and Brandi split up, heading in three different directions. The giant lashed out at Connor with the club and missed. Khyron slid under an axe swipe, slashing with his blades. The swords scored deep cuts in the giant's armor but didn't draw blood.

Brandi tried to find a way to help them, then realized she had only an ordinary dagger.

Well, maybe I can distract it.

"You there!" Brandi shouted, her tone haughty and imperious. "I command you in the name of Adina! Stop your attack!"

Both heads swung around and four red-rimmed eyes narrowed. "You do not wear the sign of the skull. You are a slave."

Brandi dodged an axe swipe. *Well, it was worth a try.*

Connor placed a hand to his chest. To Brandi's amazement, a glittering sword materialized out of nowhere, hovering in the air next to him. The dancing sword darted in at one of the giant's heads, then slashed at a thick neck.

The monstrosity recoiled, swatting at the blade with his weapons. "What witchery is this?" he roared, both mouths twisted in anger.

"Where the hell did the ettin come from?" Brandi called to Connor. She vaulted into the corral, ripping the horses' ropes in half with vampiric strength. The steeds galloped away, leaping over the fences. They darted towards the bramble wall and veered away from the thorny mass, eyes rolling in terror.

"He transformed from that big pile of red rocks!" Connor called back, tumbling between the giant's legs. A huge club slammed into the ground near him. "Can we talk about this later, please?"

"Hideg! Shavash!" Khyron shouted. Ice rimed one of his swords and bright blue acid covered the blade of his other weapon.

Wow. Nice toys! Brandi thought.

She ran out the corral gate, watching Khyron and Connor dance and slash at the giant, wishing she could do something to help.

***

Whatever confidence Eric had gained from defeating the daemons at the Skull Gate faded rapidly. He dodged, launched counter-spells and parried, desperately trying to stay alive. Kelani anticipated their moves before they even tried them.

"Any ideas?" Buck called over his shoulder, shield up.

"I have one!" Kelani called. She hovered in the smoky air. "Surrender to me and I let you live."

"For how long?" Dar shot back.

A loud thud and double-voiced bellow sounded from outside. Eric fought the urge to race outside.

A mocking smile curved the daemon's lips. "Long enough. I might even allow you to be a slave. You look tasty."

"I don't serve daemon sluts," Dar growled.

Kelani laughed, eyes darting to Andyn. "No, I can see you have other tastes. Harlan, Barnard, your turn."

The two men drove Andyn and Buck back with a flurry of blows. Then they dropped their blades and undid the straps on their scale mail. They tossed the armor to the side. Andyn and Buck charged but both men opened fanged mouths and roared.

Eric gaped. Within the span of a couple of heartbeats, the men's bodies warped, grew and twisted, ripping out of their clothing. Now, two massive cave bears faced the Riders.

"Oh shit," said Buck.

We have to end this, Eric thought, hefting Fidelis.

"Ever hear of an Old Testament Prophet named Habakkuk, Dar?" Eric called.

Dar nodded. "Now that you mention it, yes."

Kelani gestured and a sizzling ball of electricity formed in her hand.

"This might hurt a bit in the morning," Dar announced.

Eric launched Fidelis. Kelani danced away. The spear thumped into the wall again.

Dar dropped his sword and touched the metal plate at the throat of his chainmail. "Habakkuk!"

The universe twisted around Dar and he vanished. A split second later, he materialized in mid-air above Kelani, then landed on top of her.

Kelani yelped in surprise and rage. She and Dar plummeted down to flatten another couch. Kelani's lightning ball shot to the side and blew a hole in a wall.

"Fidelis!" Eric called. The spear reappeared in his hand. He lunged.

Kelani stabbed Dar in the side and hurled him aside. Her eyes widened. Sun-bright Fidelis struck the skull-shaped garnet medallion, burst it into fragments, and continued on, impaling her.

"No!" she wailed. Her voice trailed off into a weak gurgle.

Dar, cursing with pain, swept up Rindara and beheaded her.

The cave bears roared and lashed about in wild rage. Andyn and Buck battled desperately, falling back under the hellish onslaught.

Eric pulled the dagger out.

Dar's face was pale and his limbs shook. "Poison," he gasped.

Eric closed his eyes and pressed a hand on the wound, praying he had remembered Andyn's lessons. His mind raced through equations and chemical combinations. Finally, he recognized the poison's molecular structure. He poured magical energy into Dar, unwinding the venom until it collapsed into harmless hydrocarbons.

He opened his eyes. Andyn smashed the skull of one of the cave bears with an overhead strike. Buck thrust Khelios deep into the side of the other. It howled and he thrust again. It shuddered and dropped.

Eric helped Dar rise. A woman's hellish scream from outside the cottage froze him in his tracks.

"Brandi!" He raced outside, just behind Buck.

***

Brandi darted at the ettin, ducking under the swooping club. She leaped aside from the axe. Connor and Khyron kept up their assault while she tried to divert the giant's attention.

If I only had a sword! Her attempts to stab the giant with her dagger only resulted in a couple of rips in his armor. Brandi wished for one of Khyron's blades but didn't dare ask him.

Despite her frustration, their tactics seemed to work. The giant bled from a half-dozen wounds. His two heads tried to coordinate their attacks but Connor's dancing sword kept them off balance.

Brandi's constant motion also kept her mind off Delilah. She had control for now. However, if she paused for even a few moments and caught the scent of blood she feared the worst.

Delilah might lock onto Connor or Khyron.

I would rather die…

A ripping blast from the cottage made them all whirl to look. The remnants of one wall collapsed under the explosive force of a lightning ball. Seconds later, a woman's shriek echoed through the air.

A rush of energy filled Brandi and she staggered back towards the corral. Her pulse pounded in her ears and her vision grew misty red.

Yes! Delilah's voice howled in triumph. *I am free! Good riddance, Kelani, you stupid bitch!*

"No!" Brandi stumbled against the gate. Vampiric bloodlust intensified and she shook her head.

"Look out, Brandi!" Khyron shouted.

She raised her head. A massive club swept down on her. She rolled out of the way. The club shattered the corral gate and fencing into firewood.

A lust for blood threatened to overcome her like an ocean wave. She struggled for the familiar feeling of surety and calm. The giant swung again, interrupting her thoughts.

Connor slashed the giant in the ankle. His dancing sword thrust at one of the heads. The ettin recoiled, dodging the hovering blade. Khyron leaped up and stabbed the ettin in the hip. He spun out of the way as the axe pulverized a nearby water trough.

Brandi's eyes locked on a bleeding wound on the giant's forearm. Delilah cackled with glee in her mind. With an inarticulate howl, she launched herself into the air. Like some kind of vampiric gnat, she clamped onto the monster's forearm and bit deep.

Warm lifeblood poured into her. Delilah laughed. The giant stumbled backwards, waving his arm frantically, trying to dislodge her. The world spun crazily, but Delilah clung to him, drawing out his blood.

No! Brandi screamed inside her mind. *Not now!*

Her vampiric senses alerted her a fraction of a second before the giant tried to sweep her off his arm with the club. She let go and landed in a crouch on the ground.

Her chest heaved with deep gasps as Brandi and Delilah battled for control.

"Brandi!"

A beloved voice cut through the bloodlust haze and she blinked, her vision clearing.

Eric raced towards her, a bright spear in his hand. Buck ran past, his Dwarven sword blazing with golden light.

"No, Eric," she pleaded, scrambling backwards. "Stay away!" She felt

Delilah surge to the surface, calling for his blood.

"We can help you, Bran." He slid to his knees before her.

"Son of a bitch!" Buck's exasperated voice made them whirl around.

Khelios danced in the air like Connor's sword. Buck lurched this way and that, desperately trying to maintain his grip on his weapon. The giant flailed away with his club and axe, eyes wide in terror.

Khelios stabbed the ettin in the leg, in the stomach and the hand. The creature let out a double bellow, dropping the axe. Buck planted his feet in the ground, trying to regain control. Khelios shot at the giant like a steel arrow. Buck cursed and flew through the air. The sword impaled the ettin in the heart. The giant gasped, then four eyes rolled back in its heads. It keeled over backwards, crashed on top of the bramble-thorn wall, and smashed it flat.

Buck wrenched the sword out and leaped clear.

Brandi shuddered at the sight of all that blood.

Delilah assumed control. She locked her eyes on the Riders, slowly gathering near her. Her eyes flicked from Eric's crucifix to the cross on the shoulder of Dar's tunic to the silver tree of Verian in Andyn's hand. She bared her fangs and hissed.

Eric paled. "Brandi! It's me. Eric. Remember me?"

Delilah's lip curled in a leer. "I'm quite sure I'd remember you, darling. Why don't you come over here and we'll get reacquainted?"

Andyn glowered at Delilah. She stepped next to Eric. "*Verian, ald-adani!*"

Her silver tree of Verian burst with light. A wave of warmth and holy power crashed over Delilah and she wavered, then retreated.

Brandi gave a moaning gasp and went to hands and knees. A hand raised her up and then two strong arms enveloped her in a hug she had dreamt of for months.

"Brandi!"

"Eric?" She wrapped her arms around him, finally feeling the bliss of his presence.

"I'm here, Brandi."

She felt his heartbeat and Delilah surged again. Desperately, she pushed him away.

"What's wrong?" His dear face showed only anguish and concern.

"She's still here," Brandi rasped, scrambling away until her back struck a fence post.

"Who?" asked Dar.

"Delilah!" Brandi put a hand to her forehead.

"The vampire?" asked Andyn, eyes narrowing.

Brandi nodded. "Is Kelani dead?"

Dar sheathed a black-bladed sword that glittered with stars. "The half-daemon? Very definitely."

"Where is the skull-shaped medallion she wore?" Brandi choked out.

Dar shrugged. "Shattered into a hundred pieces. Why?"

Brandi's heart sank. Delilah threatened to overwhelm her again. "She used it to control me, to control Delilah, just like Adina."

"Who's Adina?" Connor asked.

Brandi shook her head angrily. "That doesn't matter now. You have to find my notes. I wrote it all down."

The Riders exchanged bewildered looks. "Wrote what down?" asked Buck.

Eric took a step towards her, hand out. "It's going to be okay, Brandi. One thing at a time. I'm here. No matter what's wrong, we'll figure a way out of it."

She pressed against the remnants of the fence. "Stay back, Eric! I can't control her!"

They all stopped. She rested her eyes on them, one by one. The sound of their heartbeats echoed in her brain. The edges of her vision stayed crimson and she struggled to retain the feeling of peace. With a deep breath, she focused on Eric's crucifix.

Delilah retreated again. Despair washed over Brandi. *I'll never be free of her.*

The Riders froze in place, their expressions a mixture of confusion and worry.

"She'll always be there, lurking, waiting, watching," she explained. "I can make her go away for a time, but she will come back, over and over again, seeking blood."

The wind blew and the residual smoke from the cottage drifted over them. Still her friends hesitated.

"Don't you see?" Brandi pleaded. "Unless and until you can find the cursed item that changed me into a vampire and destroy it, I will be a danger to you. I will try to kill every single one of you."

She met Eric's beautiful eyes. "Especially you, my love. You would trust me and let me close to you, and that's exactly what Delilah wants. She knows I love you and is just waiting for a chance to hurt me by destroying you. I couldn't live with that."

Eric gazed back at her, stricken and lost. His eyes glistened with tears and he tried to say something but no words came out. Then something changed in his expression and he gave a tiny nod.

Her vision misted over. *He knows. He understands.* She blinked and tears ran down her cheeks.

"We can find the item," Dar interrupted. "We can set a trap for this Adina person and take it from her and destroy it and set you free."

Now she smiled at him. "Brave, headstrong Dar! How? She answers to the Ja'al High Council. I don't even know where to start looking for her and the one person who might know is dead. No, my friend, there is only one way to set me free."

She selected a piece of broken wood as long as her forearm and held it out to Eric.

A teardrop traced a shiny line down his cheek. "Bran, isn't there another way?"

Delilah saw his hesitation and she snickered. *Trusting boy. I will enjoy him.*

"You have to!" Brandi hissed, struggling for control again. "I can't fight her every second of every day! It takes more energy and vigilance than is humanly possible."

The look in his eyes tore her heart in two. Her vision tinted red again and she clenched her fist, forcing herself to breathe evenly. "You need to set me free. Find my notes. Stop the Ja'al. Find the Dome of Glass."

Eric shook his head and the other Riders stared at her.

Brandi's gaze sought Andyn. "Andyn. You know. You understand. Tell him."

Her eyes shiny, Andyn set her jaw and slowly nodded. "She's right. Unless we find the device that corrupted her and obliterate it, she will destroy us."

Brandi held out the jagged stake to Eric again. "Please."

***

Eric took the broken wood. "Why?" he asked. A vast, empty ache spread throughout his soul.

Brandi smiled. He could still see her fangs. "So that you can be free too. You won't need to worry about me anymore. You can have a new life. And I will be happy forever."

"Eric, let one of us do it. We can't ask you to — " Connor began.

Eric raised a hand. "It's okay."

Brandi's smile faded and her eyes flashed red. "Please, love. Be quick!"

He hesitated. Brandi's smile transformed into a sneer and she reached for him, mouth agape, fangs gleaming. Her eyes showed a titanic internal struggle.

Almost as if he were observing someone else, Eric raised the pointed wood to Brandi's heart. Time slowed. He impaled her with it.

The red light flashed in her eyes and disappeared. Her fangs receded and she relaxed.

***

"No!" Delilah wailed. Her voice faded into the distance and then winked out like a snuffed candle.

Intense pain wracked Brandi's body. She smiled. "You did it!" she whispered. "She's gone!"

She felt Eric cradle her in his arms as he lay her gently on the ground. An image of him laying her down on their marriage bed flashed before her eyes, then vanished.

Tears streamed down his cheeks to match the ones flowing from her eyes. She reached up a hand to cup his face.

"Thank you, love."

His lips met hers in a glorious, warm kiss. The sky darkened and she saw a beautiful, welcoming light.

***

"Stand aside, you fools!" Andyn barked.

Eric drew back. He could barely make out Brandi's face through his tears as her eyes fluttered closed. Then he heard a crisp, hot pop next to his face. A golden glimmer lit the air.

He wiped his eyes. A glittering net dropped from Andyn's hand. As Brandi's chest relaxed, the net snapped down around her like a second skin. An intense wave of otherworldly power shook him to his core, then he felt only silence and stillness.

"Good thinking, Andyn," Khyron said. "Bravo."

Eric stared down at Brandi, her beautiful face at peace under the Preservation Net, the wooden stake still in her heart. He felt like an identical one pierced his.

A black emptiness and a raw, blazing pain such as he had never known in his life seared through him. Despair clouded everything. His vision misted over again and he tried to speak but only managed a ragged sob.

The universe shattered and went dark.

Chapter Fifteen – Memoirs, Cloaks and Daggers

"First his birth parents and now Brandi." Dar murmured. "How much can one person take?"

"I don't know," Andyn sighed. "I *do* know I won't leave his side."

And where is Megan? Cold fear gripped Dar's stomach at the thought of Megan in the clutches of the Ja'al. *Please, God…*

He gathered with Khyron and Andyn near a stone table outside Saint Mark's cathedral in Eastridge. Eric sat in the sunshine on a bench about fifty feet away, his back to them.

"Has he finished reading her journals?" asked Khyron. He stretched and propped his booted foot on a bench. "I don't mean to sound callous, but Brandi's notes might have something we really need."

"I know, I know," Dar replied, then held up his hand when Khyron opened his mouth again. "We'll have to ask him gently, when he's ready."

Khyron nodded and picked up a dry stick, snapping it in his hands. "Like I said, I feel for him," he muttered. "You said they were close."

Dar forced himself to unclench his fists. The silence lengthened. Andyn shot him a look and squeezed his shoulder.

"I thought they were going to get married," Dar said finally, his throat constricting.

Khyron raised his eyes towards the nearby mountains and tossed the stick fragments at a rock. "Do I assume you were also that close to Megan?"

A lump in his throat choked off Dar's next words so he just nodded again.

Andyn put her arm around him.

Khyron's sigh came from his boots. "The Grey Riders have had more than their share of tragedy. But I promise you this: if Megan lives, I will help you find her, no matter what." He fixed Dar with sea-green eyes.

"Thank you, Khyron," Dar managed. "That means a lot."

All the worries he had pushed to the back of his mind now surged to the fore. He tried to relax and not fixate on the many horrible fates his nightmares had conjured up for Megan.

The round leaves of the towering doriff trees fluttered in the warm summer breeze. Eric lifted his head and stared out at the mountains for a long time, then raised a hand to his face and covered his eyes. His shoulders shook.

Dar's heart broke for his friend and he felt his own vision grow misty. *Damn it! She was like a sister to me, but as much as it hurts me, it must be unbearable for him.*

He thought about praying again, but he had already prayed so much for Eric — and for Megan — that he felt spiritually exhausted and drained.

"Do you think you were fast enough?" Khyron asked Andyn.

Her hand tightened on Dar's shoulder.

"I hope so, Khy, I hope so," she managed in a wavering voice. "I might have frozen her in time. Maybe I saved her just before her spirit fled, but I just don't know! I feel so helpless!"

The hand on Dar's shoulder trembled. Andyn bit her lip, eyes flashing. "Damn those Ja'al!" she spat, then burst into tears.

Khyron drew her close. She released Dar and buried her face in her fiancé's chest. He cradled her gently, kissing the top of her golden tresses as Andyn wept. She sagged into him and he held her up, his eyes glistening.

Dar realized how much she had held inside the last couple of days, trying to be the strong anchor of stability for Eric, the spiritual counselor, the emotional support. He also remembered how close Andyn had been to Megan and Brandi during their time together on the Borderlands. She had loved them like sisters.

He brushed away his tears, feeling the empty ache anew. *Why, God? Why?*

Suddenly, Eric heaved a great sigh. He stood tall and made the Sign of the Cross. With that, he spun on his heel and headed back towards them.

Dar tried to get himself into a semblance of order. Andyn hurriedly wiped her face as Eric approached.

Eric's eyes were red but resolute. "It's time I told you what she wrote in her journals. Some will be hard to hear, but she had vital information she wanted to pass along. We should get Connor and Buck."

"I'll bring them," Khyron volunteered. He trotted off.

Andyn wrapped Eric in a hug. For a moment, Dar thought Eric's composure would break again, but he put his chin on top of Andyn's head and sighed.

"Thank you, Andyn. Time enough for grief later."

They stood in silence. Dar spied Khyron returning with Buck and Connor and waved to them. Eric released Andyn.

Buck and Connor took places on the edge of a great stone planter across from them. Eric faced them, hands at his belt, toying with a thick scroll. Connor stood on the bench next to him and put a hand on his back, his dark eyes solemn.

He knows exactly what Eric's going through, Dar realized, watching the halfling's expression. *He even had a child to mourn.*

Buck cleared his throat. "Before you say anything, Eric," he began, "I know this is hard, but I hope you aren't blaming yourself. You had to do it, man. She needed you to free her."

Eric nodded. "I know. I've gone over it all in my head a hundred times. Thank you, though."

Connor curved his arm around Eric's shoulder. "You know where to find me."

Eric's eyes dropped to his boots and nodded. He let out a shuddering breath. "Thank you, Connor. I will need your help."

"All you have to do is ask."

Eric composed himself. He smiled at Dar. "First, and most importantly, there was something in her letters that will make you all happy. Megan is alive."

A sudden rush of emotion came over Dar, so strong that the world spun. He felt weak with relief.

Buck slapped his knee. "I knew it! You see, Dar?"

"Where is she?" Dar asked.

"A wizard named George Oxbridge took her into Morlan to be a slave apprentice," Eric said.

"Morlan?" Dar straightened, then fell back against the bench seat. "That's south of Torosc! Even if we could figure out where she is, how would we get there?"

Despair replaced his joy. He stared at the paving stones. The ships of the Pirate Kings of Jered prowled the seas south of Gorostol and even the Terenaian Navy would be hard-pressed to make inroads there. To get to Morlan, he would have to traverse Torosc, a land controlled by the Ja'al, Vardish and Cla'agik churches. Then there was the matter of Morlan itself, a perilous realm steeped in magic and ruled by a Wizard King.

How in God's name am I going to pull that off? How do I even start?

"Hey."

Dar looked up.

Eric took a seat next to him. Buck joined him.

"We will find her." Eric said, eyes burning into Dar's. "Brandi would want us to. Melinor and Father Edward will help us figure it out. Don't worry."

Dar felt strong arms encircle him. Khyron and Andyn knelt at his side and Buck gripped his shoulder.

Andyn laid a gentle hand on his head. "We will help you, Dar. All of us, together."

As quickly as the despair had set in, it now faded. Instead, looking at his friends, Dar felt a strong, quiet peace and a familiar warmth that he had missed for many days. He took Buck and Andyn's hands in a firm grip.

"You're the best friends I have ever had," he said, voice breaking.

They surrounded him with a ring of smiles.

Buck gave him his trademark, homespun grin. "And you might just live to regret it."

Dar couldn't help from smiling at that. "Thank you. All of you."

He let out a deep breath and swallowed to regain his composure. "Let's get to it. What else was in Brandi's journal?"

"She was clever," Eric said, absently turning the scroll of Brandi's journal in his hands. "She wrote everything in Elven. That tells me that none of the people in the hunting lodge knew the language or she wouldn't have risked it. She also jumbled up the paragraphs and put a key on the last page in Elven to tell me the order of the sections."

Dar's smile widened. Even though Brandi had always said she wasn't as smart as her sister, this confirmed his suspicion that she was simply selling herself short.

"Anything in there about those black stones we found in the box under the hunting lodge?" Khyron asked.

Dar eyed him. "You mean the ones in the box that had six layers of trapping spells? The box that took everyone's combined magic power to open? The stones that almost blinded Buck when he inspected them with the Eye of Truth?"

"Yes. Those."

Eric shook his head. "Nothing specific, just the box and its location."

Andyn sniffed. "Whatever they are, they're evil and very powerful."

"Another mystery for Melinor and Father Edward's analysts," Dar added. "I'm glad I'm not on their laboratory team. Anything else?"

"Well, the Ja'al used the threat of Megan's well-being as an additional incentive to control Brandi when she got difficult to manage," Eric continued. "There are also some things in the diary that I don't understand. Andyn, it looks like Brandi was able to interfere with the Ja'al plans somehow, even though she was a vampire under their control."

Andyn's brow furrowed. "I can't imagine how. Maybe Father Edward has some ideas."

Dar mulled this over as Eric continued.

"The Ja'al used Brandi as their servant and agent," Eric said. "She was a sort of temptress to get their targets into her power and then make them thralls to this Adina, who was her mistress and controller. I think Adina has a similar skull pendant to the one that Kelani wore. It was what she used to control Brandi by bringing out her evil alter ego, Delilah."

"Oh Eric," said Andyn. "I'm so sorry."

Eric pressed his lips together and nodded. "She's free now. That's what matters."

"Here's the part that relates to our latest assignment," he continued, "Apparently, Father Edward was right. Kelani and Adina talked about the Dome of Glass. The Ja'al *are* worried, but Brandi found out something more: it guards something called the Gate of Stars."

The Riders exchanged bewildered looks.

"Gate of Stars?" Connor mused. "Didn't Melinor say something about an interplanetary gate?"

Khyron nodded. "Yes. If the Ja'al are worried about a Dome of Glass, guarding a Gate of Stars, I'll bet you my weight in gold that the Dome is evil and the Gate is good."

Dar steepled his fingers in front of his mouth and leaned his elbows on his knees.

"Is the Gate of Stars connected with the Skull Gates?" asked Andyn.

Eric shrugged. "A counterbalance, maybe? If this new Gate is good, maybe it's a portal to Celestia?"

Andyn shook her head. "One more wouldn't make that much difference. There are already hidden Gates to Celestia on Damora. Besides, Melissa and her companions can recognize the Skull Gate signature by now. They'll be on hand to help out, and they can always get reinforcements through their own Gates. Why would the Ja'al care so much about this one?"

Dar shook his head. "That's a good point. Maybe it's special somehow?"

"Well, I know that we won't puzzle it out here," Connor stated. "We should get this to Father Edward."

"Agreed," Andyn said. "Anything else, Eric?"

Eric shook his head. "No. The best news is that Megan is alive. That gives us hope."

Yes, Dar thought. *Megan is alive. By my life or death, I will free her, so help me God.*

He stood. His friends arose with him. "Then let's go find her…"

***

Gorlak sipped his beer, eyes on the glass bottles on the shelves across from him, behind the bar. All around him, the clientele of the Lusty Griffon Inn swirled in a veritable storm of conversation, laughter and ribald songs.

He saw his reflection in the mirrored glass behind the shelves — or, rather, that of a dark-haired halfling man with black eyes. Behind him, near the windows, another pair of halfling men sat at a table, heads bowed in deep discussion. The fading light of the day washed over them, glinting on brass rims of their tankards.

Gorlak adopted the weary expression of a laborer at the end of a long day. He peeked up from under his hat brim, using the mirror to monitor everything in the tavern.

So far, he marked the two halflins; he knew one of them as Kili Mikman, some-time Ja'al agent and, according to Melinor, the avowed enemy of Connor Lomin. The other he only recognized from descriptions, but the bushy eyebrows, portly build and perpetually amazed expression identified him as Vidi Darkwater, Kili's cousin, a known cutthroat.

Gorlak finished his beer in appreciation. Used to the hearty and often bitter ales of his own people, the rich Dwarven concoction in his mug brought a variety of flavors, including nuts and honey.

Much better taste than Goblin drink.

Kili and Vidi tossed back their tankards and set them down on the table, pushing their chairs back. Gorlak motioned to the barkeep, depositing five silver coins on the worn countertop, plus an additional two.

"Thank you, good sir," boomed the burly human, giving him a toothy grin.

Without a word, Gorlak smiled, tipped his hat and hopped off the stool. As long as he didn't speak, no one would suspect him of being a goblin instead of a halfling. The Nuncio's medallion saw to that.

He headed outside. He scooted between carriages and horses and people to the other side of the avenue and slipped into the shadows of a shuttered vendor's cart. He leaned against a wall and waited.

His quarry didn't appear as soon as he expected. The minutes dragged on and evening darkened the neighborhood. Gorlak chafed, wondering if they had sniffed him out and left by a different route. Then he breathed a sigh of relief when both men emerged.

Kili nodded to Vidi and placed something in his hand, then the two marched off in different directions.

Gorlak growled a curse in Goblin under his breath. Which one should he follow? Both were dangerous, both were Ja'al spies, and both could hold the key to his mission.

Kili, he decided. Vidi was more of a tool for the highest bidder. He didn't care about strategy or the long game. Kili, on the other hand, had worked for the Ja'al high cleric Halkith, who had lost the race against the Grey Riders for the pegasi of Whitehorse Peak. Kili moved in loftier circles than Vidi.

Gorlak grinned at the idea of anything the Ja'al did even remotely resembling "lofty". He headed off down the street to parallel his target.

Kili marched up the road away from the merchant sector of Harlinsville and then turned down a side street. Gorlak pulled his cloak tighter around himself despite the warm night. He whisked unseen between pedestrians and carts, crossing just in time to see Kili flit down an alleyway. He hustled after him and peeked around the corner.

Only stacked crates and empty barrels greeted his eyes.

Damn and blast!

Then he heard a click and scrape and looked up. His jaw dropped. Kili scrambled up the side of a nearby building like a spider, then disappeared over the edge of the roof.

With another muttered Goblin curse, Gorlak ran down the alleyway, then leaped into the air, spreading his cloak. The fabric snapped out, transforming into bat wings. He flapped his arms and ascended, hovering below the roof. He peeked over.

Kili scurried along the rooftops, hopping across the gap between buildings with alarming agility. His boot heels flashed green with every leap. Gorlak gaped again.

This one has very good toys.

Gorlak fluttered up into the air, careful to stay well back and not too high. Not that he was afraid of local air patrols, but it wouldn't help to attract attention.

Kili's path led him over the working-class section of Harlinsville to the more established neighborhoods. Then the halfling made a beeline for the Count's Manor.

"What?" Gorlak muttered.

Kili disappeared over the edge of the roof of an estate across the street from the palace. Gorlak landed on the roof and peered down. Kili crouched behind a manicured hedge. The halfling pulled off his outer garments, revealing servant's livery in grey and hunter green. He folded the clothes and stashed them under the hedge.

Kili shot a look down the street, then marched to the front gate of the manor. He spoke to the guards. They sized him up, gave a perfunctory search, then admitted him.

Gorlak's eyebrows rose. *Very interesting…*

He drew back from the edge, stroking his chin. Finally, he leaped into the air, fluttering along out of sight of the guards until he reached the rear of the manor. There, servants lugged bundles of garbage to a horse and empty wagon.

Gorlak gave a wicked grin and drew out a blow gun. Selecting a pebble from his pocket, he inserted it into the tube, aimed it at a horse's rump, and huffed.

The rock snapped off the horse's flank. The animal whinnied and stamped forward, taking the cart with it. The driver and servants yelled and clutched for bridles and falling bundles.

Gorlak soared into the air and over the gate. Occupied with calming the horse, the servants never even noticed.

Keeping a wary eye out for guards, Gorlak landed on an empty balcony of the manor.

Who would Kili talk to? Guard? Count? Attendant? He ground his teeth, wondering if he should fly down to one of the other balconies in hopes of finding Kili.

He peered down into the garden and froze. Kili conversed with a tall, middle-aged human woman in an ivory dress.

Countess Arlene!

Gorlak took wing. He hovered over one of the towering trees nearby, then wrapped the cloak around himself and dropped. About eight feet from the ground, he opened his arms and the cloak arrested his fall. It took all his agility to avoid crashing into a bush.

Holding his breath, he listened with racing heart. He sneaked as close as he dared, hiding behind a stone bench near a fountain.

"… Riders went south-east." Kili finished.

"Good," sniffed Arlene, swirling her wrap around her slim shoulders. "They're not likely to cause trouble here. What is the word on the Druids?"

"Turmoil," Kili replied with a wolfish grin. "Some of the groves are falling into ruin while the leaders fight each other. Delegations from the Veriani, Irial or Christians are dismissed or ignored outright. The Earth-worshippers are well-occupied."

Arlene smiled. "Good. What about that little forest wench, Carine?"

Kili shrugged. "The Shrikes swear they killed her, but they haven't produced a body."

"What do you think?"

"She's alive. The Shrikes just don't want to admit it. If she were dead, they would have sent us her head."

Arlene frowned, muttering several obscenities.

"I couldn't agree more," Kili said with a bland expression.

She spun on him. "Don't be impertinent. That little bitch will get what's coming to her. Now, I have another assignment for you. Rumor has it that the Papal Nuncio is ill. I want you to find out just how ill. If he's as sick as they say, the Christians may be ripe for some turmoil of their own. Are the assassins in place at the Archbishop's palace in Darlon?"

"Ready and waiting."

Arlene appeared to calm. "Good. We don't want that ass-goblin taking Edward's place. Not only is he young and strong, but he's an Elf. He'd be a chore and a half if he took the miter of Papal Nuncio."

"We'll make sure he doesn't."

Arlene folded her hands at her waist. "See that you do. But not until Edward croaks like the old bullfrog he is. What news about the trial of the ones who tried to kill Faldanor?"

Kili shrugged. "The Deorfast city guard caught our agent trying to bribe jurors. She's in jail now, but they don't know she's Ja'al. They think she's just an over-eager activist."

"How much is her bail?"

"Five hundred seventy-five."

She frowned. "Faldanor is not taking chances." She handed him a bulging belt purse. "Here. Ryland Sommers has the rest for the bail. Tell him I'll refund him tomorrow at the meeting."

Kili hefted it, eyebrows raised. "Nice."

She frowned, then gave him a smaller purse. "This one is yours. If the two get mixed up, I will hear of it, Kili."

"I wouldn't dream of it."

"Good. Now get going."

He sketched a deep bow. "As Your Excellency commands."

Arlene swept off towards the manor without a backward glance. Kili stuffed the larger of the two purses into his shirt, tucked the other in his belt and strode off, whistling a bawdy drinking song. Gorlak waited until both of them were out of sight, then opened his arms and swept up to the roof again.

Kili left the way he had entered, returning to his discarded clothing. He changed clothes in the shadows, then slipped down the street.

Gorlak flitted over the nearby houses, keeping Kili in sight. The halfling didn't make any attempt to skulk through the alleys as before, but Gorlak noted his path: towards the riverfront section of town.

Gorlak's mind whirred. Lady Arlene, involved in bribing jurors? Did that mean the Count was also involved?

And Ryland Sommers? Gorlak knew the name. A former member of the aristocracy stripped of his title for conspiracy, he was a known Ja'al operative. Apparently, he and Lady Saren had a history.

This means Lady Arlene works for Ja'al. She is the spy in Court.

Gorlak set his mouth in a firm line. He had to tell Melinor. He launched himself into the air, flying as fast as he could.

Chapter Sixteen – A Little Rebellion

"Brandi!"

Megan's eyes popped open and she gasped for breath. A strange, light-headed feeling surged through her. She knew that something dreadful, yet glorious, had happened.

She sat up on her cot and rubbed her temples, head spinning. Only fragments of a dream remained. Prominent among them was the image of her sister enveloped in golden light, eyes closed and smiling.

Dear Jesus, what's happened to Brandi?

The light of early morning broke through the cracks in the wooden shutters on her window. She stood and ran a hand through her hair. Blinking against the sun, she opened one shutter.

It was a dream, nothing more. She let out a deep breath and her heartbeat slowed. Megan leaned on the window sill, watching the city of Catrin come to life.

It looked the same as always: a green expanse of stately trees and flowering bushes interspersed with white houses and brooding grey towers. The air felt cool, but she knew cloying humidity would not be long in coming.

She turned at a tap on the door. Varienne's face peeked around the corner. "Oh. I see you're up. Mind if I come in?"

Megan smiled. "Please do."

Varienne entered, smiling shyly, and joined her at the window.

After Megan's aborted escape attempt, Oxbridge decided to move her closer to Varienne in order to protect his "most valuable and intriguing asset", as he put it. This suited the girls just fine since they could communicate easier.

"Sleep well?" she asked Varienne.

The girl nodded. "Yes, but I still don't know about sleeping naked."

Megan's eyes drifted off to the city again. "I grew up a little north of here. You get used to it. Otherwise you wake up miserable and drenched in sweat."

"I can see why." Varienne also leaned on the windowsill. "At least he gave us tunics. It looks like yours got ripped and you repaired it. I can still see the seam."

"Mending spell," Megan replied, smoothing her tunic.

"You'll have to teach me that one."

"Done."

Varienne contemplated the cityscape for a while. "Did Oxbridge say where we would be going?"

Megan shook her head. "No. Just that he needed to consult with a colleague in another city. I can understand him taking me along if it's another examination, but you?"

Varienne shrugged. "I'm his only healer. He's cautious."

Megan said nothing, watching the city. The suddenness of this new "consultation" bothered her.

Again, Varienne paused before continuing. "Does he really think you're magically contaminated?"

Megan fought down the panic in her middle. "Well, he suspects, but I don't think he's convinced. He keeps muttering to himself and looking in books and scrolls and asking me questions."

Varienne put a hand on hers. "Don't worry. We'll escape and find someone who can cure you."

Will we?

A bell rang and the girls exchanged a glance. Steeling herself, Megan took Varienne's hand and led her out the door. They padded quietly down the hallway to another, locked portal.

A small hatch in the door opened. Olik's face appeared. His eyes lingered on their figures.

"The master is waiting," he barked. "You should be here faster."

Megan raised her chin and met his eyes. "Does Professor Oxbridge require our assistance?"

Olik's expression became surly. "Prissy little bitch."

The door swung open. "Follow me," he snapped. They trailed behind him through the workroom to the experiment chamber.

Oxbridge awaited the girls, a book in his hands. "Ah. Good."

He indicated a stack of scrolls and a few other books on the table, then handed a backpack to Megan. "I will need these for our journey. Fill the backpack and follow me."

As Megan complied, Oxbridge motioned to Olik. "Return to the storeroom. I want an inventory from you and Kantar by lunch time."

Olik bowed and left with one more venomous glare at Megan.

Oxbridge led them outside into his gardens without speaking. Near a tinkling fountain in the shape of a succubus, he stopped. He made a circular arc overhead with both hands, ending at his hips. A misty yellow sphere of light sprang up around him and the women.

An Inscrutable Globe? Megan wondered. *What does he have to say to us in secret?*

The professor waited in the silence. A couple of purple-and-red butterflies flitted past him. He stroked his beard, eyes on a nearby cluster of rosebushes.

He nodded at them. "Those are Vampire Roses, you know. Fascinating plants: beautiful, deadly, magical. Some scholars think they were originally brought from Hades."

Varienne's eyes flickered towards Megan.

Oxbridge clasped his hands behind his back. "They are a lot like you, slave Megan. Do you also come from Hades?"

Megan blinked. "Um, no. No, master."

He pursed his lip. "I wonder." He regarded the Vampire Roses for a while, then shrugged. "Well, in any case, your unusual qualities remain in the minds of many. It may have been a mistake to take you to the University. Speculation is now rampant about the magical accident that could have contaminated your mother, and, by extension, you."

Megan said nothing.

Oxbridge actually sighed. "I have a problem. The Wizard King is keenly interested in you and his offers to purchase you are becoming more insistent. The oaf is bored, I think. He won't risk angering the Ja'al High Council by simply taking you away, but there's nothing to stop him from hiring someone *else* to steal you."

For a while, he said nothing, eyes distant.

He spun back to them. "I think I should remind His Majesty that I'm not beholden to him for anything. I'm going to take a little trip, and both of you are coming. I have a special place north of here. No one knows of it and they won't be able to trace us. After the King has had a chance to think it over, we will let him know that we will return on certain conditions."

Where no one can trace us? Megan didn't like the sound of that.

"But what about your project, Master?" she ventured.

He smiled thinly. "All is in readiness. The system can be used in a matter of days. I can afford the time away."

"How will we get there?" asked Varienne in a quiet voice.

Oxbridge's smile broadened. He reached into his robes and produced a ring of black metal with many tiny diamonds. He slipped it onto his finger. "The backpack, slave Megan."

She lifted it onto her shoulders.

"Take Varienne's hand."

She did so and Oxbridge placed his hand on the blonde girl's shoulder. He spoke a sharp word.

Megan gasped as the universe convulsed around her. The gardens, Oxbridge's tower, the surrounding jungle and the city of Catrin swirled and melded into a riot of color. She squeezed her eyes shut and her stomach lurched.

She felt herself falling and tried to scream but no sound came out. Her feet landed in soft and yielding sand. Varienne staggered.

Megan tasted bile. She fell to her knees and heard Varienne throw up next to her.

"Hold on, Varienne," Megan hissed through gritted teeth. The world rotated in directions in which it had no business rotating. She willed herself to peace and calmness and her nausea vanished. She opened her eyes.

She knelt on a dune among wispy patches of grass. Seagulls screeched overhead and she smelled salty air. The surf crashed somewhere past the dunes.

Poor Varienne was on hands and knees, gagging. Megan put her arm around her.

"Easy, Vari," she said, willing some of her peace to transfer to her friend.

Varienne's breathing eased. She sat back on her heels, hands on her thighs and face up to the sky. She grimaced. "By Irial's Tears, what was that?"

"Teleportation." Oxbridge smirked down at them. "The disorientation will pass. Get up. The cabin is just there."

About a bowshot away, a small grey beach house with blue trim perched on top of one of the taller dunes. A porch curved around the front of it, facing the sea, and Megan saw a rocking chair.

"Come on, Vari," Megan said, hauling the younger girl to her feet.

"I'm okay," Varienne murmured. She wiped her mouth with the corner of her tunic, then whispered a prayer. A mild glow flashed at her temples for a split second and she opened her eyes.

Megan smiled at her, hefting the backpack. "At least we'll be far away from Olik and Kantar."

"Thank Irial!"

They fought their way through the dunes to the cottage. To her surprise, Megan found the house quite pleasant and clean — not what she had expected, considering Oxbridge. Potted plants clustered on the porch near the rocking chair, the windows had real glass, and the structure looked very sturdy.

"Cozy," Varienne murmured as she entered. "Very pleasant."

Megan nodded, taking in the padded couches, carved wooden chairs, and embroidered draperies. "And black widows are pretty when you first see them," she whispered.

Oxbridge stopped in the center of the room, turning in a circle on a large rug. "Ah, yes!" he proclaimed, a smile on his face. "Every intellectual mind needs a refuge, a haven away from the demands of a hectic world."

"Master," Varienne offered, "I don't have any of my curatives. Will we get some from a nearby town?"

Oxbridge waved his hand. "I doubt if you'll need anything specific as all that. I have a medical kit in the downstairs pantry you can use if you need it. For the most part, you will be helping Megan if any of our experiments are too much for her."

He appropriated a crystal decanter from a side table and poured a dark brown liquid into a tumbler. He eyed the drink critically, swirled it in the glass, and tasted it. With a satisfied nod, he downed it.

"Besides," he added with a sigh of satisfaction, "the nearest village is Carville and that's three miles east. I don't feel like walking there just yet."

"Now," he continued, "For the time being, both of you will serve me here. Your room and the pantry are just there through the left door. The center door leads to stairs up to my bedroom, the study and the laboratory on the second floor. The kitchen and bathroom are through the right door."

He whirled on them, eyes flashing. "I am not to be disturbed unless I expressly allow it. And you will report any persons moving in the vicinity to me. Understood?"

"Yes, master," the women chorused.

"Good." He stretched. "I think I will rest a bit and then head down to the beach for a swim. Clean up the place and take inventory. I'm sure we won't have to go to town for a few days at least, but it never hurts to be prepared."

With that, he stamped upstairs.

Megan dropped the backpack on one of the couches. "Well, it could be worse."

Varienne's eyes shone as she peered out the front window. "Megan! Come look! We're very close to the sea. What is that great city there?"

Megan joined her, mind whirring. Her eyes followed the coast to her left. There, a metropolis gleamed by a natural harbor. Many ships plied the waters nearby with belled sails.

"Carville…" she whispered. "Wait! I think I know where we are! That's Northpoint! We're in Torosc, in Coastwatch Prefecture."

Varienne spun to her in surprise. Her eyes flicked to the door to the upper floors. "Coastwatch?" she asked in a low voice. "That's very close to Gorostol."

Megan's heart beat faster. "And, unless I miss my guess, we're not twenty miles from the border."

"You mean…"

"Yes. This could be our chance."

Varienne's hands gripped hers. "He is aware how close we are to freedom. He will be vigilant."

Megan nodded and bit her lip. "Then we will be careful. A chance will present itself. I know it."

"Let's do exactly what he says, every day, and put him at ease," Varienne murmured, "I'll examine the pantry."

She departed. Megan stared at nothing, creating and discarding a dozen wild plans in her mind. Finally, with a vexed shake of her head, she headed towards the kitchen.

I don't know enough yet. I have to be patient. She finished tidying up, then checked the supplies.

Varienne returned shortly with a list. "That's quite a pantry. It even has a cold box with a permanent block of ice powered by a magical generator."

"That doesn't surprise me," Megan said. She read the list. "We have enough for a few days at least. He'll have to make a trip to Carville after that."

Varienne raised an eyebrow.

"I know what you're thinking," Megan said, "And no, he won't send only one of us or leave us here on our own. He'll keep us close, especially me."

Footsteps sounded on the stairs and they returned to the main room. Oxbridge emerged, carrying a bag, a towel, a couple of books, and a small dark bottle — and nothing else.

"Off to the beach!" he declared, handing the articles to Megan. "Varienne, bring a bottle of wine, a goblet and the sun umbrella from the pantry."

Megan placed the towel, bottle and books into the bag and stared at the sea. For an academic and an older man, Oxbridge had aged quite well. It was a good thing he had no interest in the "baser instincts" as he called them.

"Anti-aging potions." She heard the grin in his voice.

"Master?"

"Anti-aging potions. They take a couple of years off each time I drink one. Damned expensive to make though. You need the brain of an unborn child, unicorn's horn and some other very costly ingredients. Even then, it doesn't always work. I might give you one if I thought it would help — which it wouldn't."

Varienne rejoined them.

"Right then. Off we go," he announced, marching off.

Megan kept her eyes on the sea instead of Oxbridge as they trekked off to the beach. She also made sure not to look at Varienne either — she wasn't sure she could keep herself from giggling. Knowing Oxbridge's lack of humor, that would not end well.

The beach was empty when they arrived. Oxbridge had them lay out the towel, blanket and wine while he dove into the waters.

The two women spent the next few hours filling Oxbridge's wine, toweling him off, putting sun oil on him, and listening to the sound of seagulls and surf as he wiggled his toes in the sand and read the books. He even sent them into the sea with a wave of his hand.

"You haven't bathed since yesterday," he sniffed. "And leave the tunics. Salt water will ruin them."

Megan hesitated, casting a nervous glance around the beach. They were still alone.

Oxbridge raised an eyebrow at her. "I already told you: I won't give you another one if you ruin that one."

She whipped off her tunic and cast it on the towel. She headed to the water as fast as possible, imagining the wizard's eyes on her.

Varienne took her hand. "Try not to think about it, Megan," she said, pulling her along to the surf. "Remember that he really doesn't care about us as women. We're just useful tools."

The feeling of warm ocean water on her skin took Megan back to her childhood and she fought back tears, remembering. She could see her mother and father in her mind's eye, their bodies shining in the sunlight, her mother's golden-red hair slicked back over her head, laughing as she played with Brandawyn. They had been so beautiful and strong and alive. Megan had felt protected and happy, even though the specter of persecution lurked in every shadow in the city. There in the ocean with her family, none of that mattered.

"Hey."

Megan wiped her tears away and smiled at Varienne.

The younger girl's eyes were soft and gentle. "You okay?"

"Memories," Megan said, walking into the ocean until the water reached her breasts. "I grew up not far from here."

"Good memories?"

"Yes. But that life ended all too soon."

Varienne remained silent and followed her. They didn't speak, instead ducking under waves and moving through the water.

"Slaves!" Oxbridge called. Megan turned to go but Varienne's hand stopped her.

"You will make new memories with Darius," she said, eyes intense. "I will see to it."

Megan's vision misted over and she nodded, then wiped her eyes again. "Thank you."

"Slaves!"

They splashed up to the shore and jogged back to him.

He frowned at a small, dark grey book. "I need you to go back to the cottage. This isn't the treatise on dark energy after all. It's one of my journals."

He handed it to Megan. "Return this to the study and get the little black book with the gold lettering. The author is Townsend."

She reached for her tunic but he waved her away. "Just get it. There's no one here to ogle you anyway. Hurry now."

With a muttered curse under her breath, Megan trudged through the sand to the cottage.

"Damned idiot!" she fumed. "Not only do I have to put sun oil on his aged ass, but now I have to fight through the dunes, stark naked, to this stupid cottage to get some meaningless book that he forgot."

She jerked the front door open and took the stairs two at a time. In his study, she snatched the correct text and shoved the journal into its place on the shelf. In her haste to leave, she knocked one of the other ones off. It fluttered open and landed on the floor.

She sighed and picked it up, leafing through the pages. *I wonder what the old goat writes in these things anyway.* She scanned the pages with little interest. Most of it was esoteric ramblings on magical theories, some of them so outlandish that she rolled her eyes. Then one particular entry caught her attention.

"21 Aprilis, 1079 PIY- The barring spell will not be effective on a multi-directional portal, like the Gate of Stars," she read. "However, such portals are very rare and attempting to block one is not worth the effort. The encryption routines are a daemon's own whore and they have automated recovery sequences that are hard to counteract."

Megan's pulse quickened as she read on. "Ancient records suggest that the Gate of Stars is either in Rainbow Valley or the Elethi Rin. Either location would be difficult to access in any event. By Gariil's fortune, the so-called Faiths of the Light don't even know how to find them. No, the most effective method would be to block all other gates instead. Let the Ja'al figure out how to deal with the Gate of Stars — if I even decide to tell them anyway. As a matter of fact, it's probably best to keep it from them. One never knows when he will need an extra bargaining chip!"

Megan's heart started pounding for some reason. Her hand trembled as she replaced the journal and headed back to the beach.

What is all that about? And why is Oxbridge keeping it a secret?

Her mind spun. Something about this latest revelation and Oxbridge's experiments in Catrin formed a tantalizing pattern if she could only just think —

All at once, it came to her and she froze. Perspiration beaded on her forehead and she realized she had stopped breathing.

Oh, my God! The Celestial Gates! That's what the stones are for!

Feeling dizzy, she had to sit down on a nearby chair. A wave of desperation surged through her and she clenched her fists. This information had to get to the right people, and right away — or the entire world was in peril.

But how?

Her eyes alighted on a box next to the bookshelf. It held some of Oxbridge's supplies, including spare journals and charcoal pencils.

Megan leaped to her feet, snatched a journal and three pencils and raced towards the door, almost forgetting Oxbridge's desired book in the process. She bounded down the stairs, slipped into her room, and hid the journal and pencils under her mattress.

Heart pounding again, she formulated a plan. If nothing else, she could record her conclusions and figure out a way to get it out of the country. A book would be much easier to smuggle than a person.

She returned to the beach. It took all her mental control to shove this new knowledge into the back of her consciousness and not give a hint that she suspected anything.

Now we need a break, a way to escape. Wait for the right moment…

***

Two days later, an opportunity arose.

Oxbridge stumped down from the upper room, his expression frustrated. "Slave Megan! Where are the vials of Thivin's Wort extract?"

She continued dusting a glass display case. "All the bottles are on the shelf in the workroom, master."

"Damn it," he muttered, scowling. "We're out. Used too much yesterday on the designer poisons."

He ascended the stairs again. "We'll have to go into Carville and get some more. Tell Varienne. We leave in ten minutes."

"Yes, Master." Megan poked her head into the kitchen. Varienne removed some meat pies from the oven.

Megan explained Oxbridge's orders. "What's Thivin's Wort?"

"An herb," Varienne replied. "It's used in making designer poisons."

Megan's eyes widened. "Designer poison?"

Varienne shuddered. "They're specially keyed toxins that can't be neutralized by a healer unless they have at least part of the keying pattern. I didn't know he knew how to make those. The more I learn about George Oxbridge, the more disgusted I get."

Megan's mind whirred. "I agree, but there's an opportunity here. This could be a scouting expedition for us to try to figure out how to escape. If we follow his commands to the letter, he won't suspect us of anything. We can even make comments about how it's nice to be away from Olik and Kantar. Make him think we're enjoying being here."

Varienne gave her a wicked grin. "That will be easy." She widened her eyes and adopted an adoring expression. "Oh, Master Oxbridge! Your retreat is so quaint and the area so beautiful. Thank you ever so much for taking us away from Catrin and those nasty leering dark elves. They made my little heart shake with fear every time I went near them! You are truly the most magnanimous and generous master a poor little slave girl could ever hope for!" She batted her eyelashes.

Megan clapped a hand over her mouth to keep from laughing. "Just don't overdo it," she admonished. "Oxbridge may be a sheltered academic with no libido, but he's not an idiot."

"Yes, ma'am. I'll make it believable."

"Remember: all we need is a way to smuggle my journal out of Torosc."

Varienne's silly demeanor vanished and her eyes flashed. She nodded. "I understand," she whispered.

Megan returned from the pantry minutes later with a list.

Oxbridge snatched it from her hand when he came down, carrying a black wooden staff. "Ah. Good. You have noted a few other items I missed. Capital bit of thinking, slave."

He stuffed the list into his belt purse. "We leave now. If we hurry, we'll make it to town, get our supplies and be back for dinner. Varienne, did you make the pies as I ordered?"

"Yes, master. They are cooling on the table. I also made the fruit salad you like."

"Excellent! If you were my servants, I would give you a bonus this week for superior work. Follow me."

He led them through the front door and out into the sand.

Megan tried to keep her heartbeat from racing.

Jesus, Mary and Joseph, guide and help us…

Chapter Seventeen – A Twisting Road

The Grey Riders trooped into the vast inner courtyard of the Lervion manor.

Connor Lomin's eyes roamed over flowerbeds in a riot of color, sparkling fountains, manicured hedges, verdant lawn and a gleaming white gazebo. Despite the memories of danger and pain and sadness in this place, he felt a curious peace.

"It's good to be back," he said.

"We agree," replied Andyn at his side. She eyed him sidelong, the corner of her mouth quirking up in a smile. "But for different reasons than you, I'm sure."

"I don't know what you're talking about."

The glass doors to the back foyer of the manor house swung open and two slender Elves approached. The woman stood a little shorter than Andyn. A jet-black braid looped over one shoulder. She wore a form-fitting ensemble of a beige sleeveless blouse and black skirt with matching black sandals.

A brown-haired male Elf accompanied her. He was clad in a grey tunic over chainmail with black boots and twin short swords hung at his hips. He was only a bit shorter than Dar.

The woman's amber eyes danced as she and the man bowed. "You honor us, Grey Riders."

Connor bowed in return. "You would be Sir Caridan and Lady Caria

Meraloy."

"Guilty," replied the man as he straightened. Forest green eyes locked onto Andyn Eleandir immediately.

He approached and took her hand, bowing deeply as Caria curtseyed. "Welcome, Light of Justice. We are here to serve you."

Andyn smiled back. "Your gallantry is noted, Sir Caridan, but you can call me Andyn. We have heard all about the wonderful help you have been to Miss Hannah."

"Speaking of which," Buck interjected, "Where is she?"

"Meeting with officials at the Defense Ministry," replied Caria. She didn't expect you until later this afternoon, around supper time."

Caria swept a hand towards the Manor. "Please, come in and rest a while. Your rooms have already been prepared."

"Thank you," Dar replied, "Let us introduce ourselves. I am Dar Cabot — ."

"Oh, we already know you," said Caridan.

The Riders shot looks at each other.

"From the Battle of Hillton," Caria added. "We can discuss it in the grand hall. Please, you must be tired from your journey."

Connor exchanged a look with Dar, who shrugged. They hefted their saddlebags and followed.

The couple led them to a wide hall with a long table and many chairs — some of them fitted for smaller folk such as halflings and dwarves and others fashioned for humans and elves.

"Alvin and Henry will ensure that your gear gets to your rooms," Caria said, beckoning to a pair of dwarves in house livery. The men swooped in, gathered up the saddlebags with many bows and smiles, and disappeared.

A trio of halfling girls materialized out of nowhere and soon Connor sat with a steaming mug of tea and a plate of tiny pastries and sliced fruit and cheese. "Hannah has indoctrinated you in her ways of hospitality, it seems," he remarked.

Caria laughed. "Well, yes, but we have a lot of visitors these days."

She and her husband joined them at the table. Connor noted they left the chair at the head of the table empty.

"So, you were at Hillton?" asked Eric.

Caridan nodded. "I was on a military exchange program between Deran and the Empire. At the time, I was attached to the First Regiment, First Division, the Blue Ravens. Colonel Hatcher came up ill when we were supposed to travel from Oakmoor to Darlon, so the General Staff thought it would be a good exercise for me to take command temporarily. Zhinia Margoth invaded soon after. Since I was already in the field, we diverted to Hillton."

Caria took a sip of her tea. "So, yes, we were both there. We saw everything."

Her eyes met Connor's and his mind flashed back in time. Once again, he saw the lich princess on the hill, exuding a miasma of vile magic, surrounded by her minions. He felt the overwhelming, momentary pain as she ended his life, then the glorious, warm light that enveloped him until Andyn called him back to life using the Crown of Saint Alyssa. He remembered staggering to his feet, taking up his fire-sword, Tiuz, and fighting for his life when Margoth's army tried to overwhelm them after Andyn had destroyed the lich. He saw anew Saren and Terenil DeMey as they literally flew in to help and kept them alive until Margoth's army fell to infighting and disintegrated.

He smelled burning wood, cloth and flesh as if it were yesterday, felt the otherworldly sizzle of magic spells and the pain of goblin spears, tasted the adrenaline in his mouth.

"Master Lomin?"

He shook himself. "Sorry, Lady Caria. Just memories."

"I can only imagine. Even from the other side of the battlefield, it all looked unbelievable. And please, it's just Caria."

They sat in silence for a while. Connor sipped his tea.

"So here you are," Caridan put in. "And Zhinia Margoth is no more. Praise God."

"Praise God," murmured Eric at Connor's side, eyes distant.

Caria smiled brightly. "You will be pleased to know that you aren't the only visitors for the week."

"Really?" asked Khyron. "Who else is coming?"

"Lord Justin and Lady Cassandra Martin, Count and Countess of

Whitmark, Kortos," Caria replied.

Khyron frowned. "Kortosian nobility? Why?"

Caridan plucked grapes off a stem and dropped them onto his plate. "Lord and Lady Martin had to deal with an uprising in the Duchy of Gilran, where Lord Justin's father rules. Apparently, a Ja'al high priestess named Shirina Diyasa raised an army and went rampaging about the countryside. Cassandra and Justin defeated her at the Battle of the Four Hills. They are here to coordinate with our intelligence services and report back to the Dukes of Kortos, who, I think, are afraid they might find a Skull Gate or two in their back yards. The Martins should be here in a couple of days."

Connor nodded, lost in thought. The idea of an international effort to destroy the Skull Gates reassured and alarmed him at the same time. Certainly, if the other nations united, they could bring more resources to bear and put immense pressure on the Ja'al.

He chewed his lip. *On the other hand, if all the nations have to work together this means the threat is very serious.*

From his work with the Deranese Intelligence Service, he knew quite a bit about the capabilities of the other nations. He didn't care to think about something so dangerous to make them unite like this.

The other Riders ate silently. Connor watched them. Caria and Caridan exchanged more than a couple of concerned glances.

We must seem subdued. I wonder what Hannah told them?

As if on cue, the doors to the hall swung open. A familiar young halfling woman with nut-brown hair and an athletic figure burst in.

"Can't you Grey Riders at least send some kind of warning?" she said, grinning. "After all, this is my house."

The Riders rose as one and gathered to greet her. She kissed Andyn and hugged Buck, Khyron and Dar.

Connor waited his turn. Eyes twinkling, she sashayed up to him. He raised her hands to his lips. In reply, she wrapped her arms around his neck and gave him a firm and thorough kiss.

"Well, that's a great welcome," he remarked.

She lifted her chin. "Get used to it."

Her expression changed when she saw Eric standing next to Buck. "Oh, Eric." Hannah took his hands and pulled him down to kneel before her.

He smiled. "It's good to see you again, Hannah."

She kissed his cheeks. "Dear, sweet Eric. I heard the news. I am so sorry, my friend."

His lip trembled but he gazed at her without blinking. "Thank you. I… You know some of what I'm going through."

Hannah closed her eyes and touched her forehead to his. "I understand, dear one. You were here for me when Handor died and I want to be there for you in return. I asked the High Priest of Irial in Meridian to hold a special ceremony in Brandawyn's honor: the Rite of the Risen Hero. I hope you will come."

Eric squeezed his eyes shut and drew a shuddering breath. "Thank you, Hannah," he whispered. "It means the world to me. I will be there."

"We all will," Connor said, sliding up to put an arm over Hannah's shoulder.

Hannah waited for a long moment before she released Eric and kissed his forehead tenderly.

With a sigh, she nodded at Caridan and Caria. "Well, I see you have met my new friends."

The elves bowed. "We have tried to make them feel at home, Hannah," Caria said.

Everyone seated themselves. Hannah took the chair at the head of the table.

Caridan opened his mouth as if to say something, then shook his head.

"What is it, Caridan?" asked Khyron.

"I don't mean to pry."

"Please. Don't worry," answered Dar.

Caridan's eyes flicked to Eric. "Who is Brandawyn?"

Andyn put a hand on Eric's before he could speak. "She and Eric were beloved to each other. She was one of the original Grey Riders. She and her sister went to the south on a secret mission and never came back. Only recently, we found her, but she had been corrupted by an evil spell into a vampire thrall. We had to… free her."

Caria nodded. Connor could almost see her mental wheels spinning. "I see. Were you able to save her?"

"We don't know," Andyn's voice faltered. "She breathes no more but we had special magic to try to preserve her. It is complicated. It is likely that she is with her God now."

Caria inclined her head. "Again, we did not mean to pry. The loss of one of the Grey Riders is a tragic blow to us all."

Eric let out a deep breath. "Thank you. I feel we can honor her by dedicating ourselves to defeating the Ja'al once and for all. It's what she would want."

Silence reigned.

"It will be good to see Justin and Cassandra again," Caria finally remarked. "It's a pity they won't be able to take time to visit Rhonin or Andareth or Mary."

Connor did a double-take. "Wait. Do you mean… Rhonin Handor or Andareth Faldanor?"

"The same."

Caridan laughed. "I'm sorry. We didn't explain the connection. Have you heard of the Four Silvers free-lance mercenary group?"

"Well, yes," started Dar, "but — "

"That was us," Caria stated, laying her spoon on the table. "Rhonin and Andareth were two of the original members. Belinda, Sidara and I joined later. You might also recognize the name of Mary Sarith. She was part of the group, along with Justin."

"Mary Sarith…" Connor knew that name was familiar.

"She rules the town of Sun Plains, Deran," Caria added. "Sir George is her husband. You saw her at Hillton."

"But Four Silvers? There were more than four of you," Buck pointed out.

"It was a joke," Caridan grinned. "We didn't have much money when we started out and Andareth and Rhonin had running arguments about practically everything. They started to wager, but Andareth only ever wanted to bet four silver coins. We started calling him 'Four-Silver'. Eventually the name stuck to the whole group."

The Grey Riders exchanged a look. "Good thing we were named by someone else," Dar quipped, "There are a lot of very… original names we could have taken — though Andyn probably wouldn't approve of any of them."

That drew chuckles from the whole table and the mood lightened.

Hannah laughed. "It's so good to have you all here!"

The dwarven servants returned. One bowed. "The rooms are ready, Mistress Hannah."

"Thank you, Alvin." Hannah rose. "Please, everyone, rest for a bit. We will meet in the study before dinner."

Connor was touched and humbled when she gave him her brother's old room on the second floor. He ran his hand over the badger emblem carved into the headboard of the bed.

"Wish you were in here with us, old friend," he murmured.

To his surprise, he lay down and actually dozed off before a knock on the door roused him.

Alvin poked his head in. "The meeting will start soon, Master Lomin."

Connor washed his face and combed his hair into a semblance of order, then walked to the study. The other Riders were already there. Dar, Buck, and Eric crowded over the desk, examining a map.

Andyn and Khyron talked quietly by the tall windows that overlooked the Kaljirre. The vast lake sparkled in the late afternoon and sunlight glowed on their hair. Andyn rested her head on her fiancé's shoulder.

Connor paused, struck by the couple's beauty. *Made for each other…*

"Hey you." Hannah sidled up behind him and leaned around his shoulder for a kiss.

"Hey yourself," he replied, obliging her. She wrinkled her nose at him, then took his hand and led him to the desk.

"Caridan and Caria have already seen this," she announced, "but they will join us momentarily in any event."

Connor examined the map with interest. The city of Northpoint, Torosc, was circled in red near the western coastline. A larger semicircle of blue curved farther out, encompassing several smaller towns.

"From the records we have seized from the Ja'al when they controlled Lervion House," Hannah began, "and the others you sent from the Skull Gate you destroyed, we were able to get enough information to Alliance spies to enable them to infiltrate some of the areas in Torosc."

Khyron's eyes met Connor's. "A very dangerous assignment."

"That's an understatement." Hannah tapped one of the towns with her finger. "They obtained copies of military documents showing a planned build-up in Northpoint. Then, just a week ago, we intercepted communications about a high-value Ja'al target in Torosc."

"What kind of target?" asked Buck.

"A High Council priest or wizard," Hannah replied.

Eric gave a soundless whistle.

"How do you know?" Dar asked.

"A lot of message traffic between Torosc and Morlan. There's a bit of a dust-up going on, courtesy of the Wizard-King of Morlan. Apparently, the Wizard-King wants something that the target has, and he — or she — is unwilling to bargain. The Morlanese think the target is in Torosc. The Torosians are trying to figure out where the target is while still holding off the inquiries. So far, they're focused on the northern districts."

The door to the study opened and the Meraloys entered. The Riders nodded in greeting.

Khyron indicated the map. "We were talking about this Ja'al official. Could they be somewhere else, maybe farther north in another country, like Gorostol? They might be able to hide out in Meridian or one of the big cities."

Caria shook her head. "It's too risky. Someone like this wouldn't travel outside of the Dark Countries without a powerful escort and that would attract attention. No, we think the target is in Torosc."

Connor nodded at the map. "Northpoint is a big place. Do you want us to go in there?"

"No." Caridan tapped the blue circle. "We have multiple spies already in place in Northpoint. You'll start in disguise in the smaller towns. If we find the target is elsewhere, you can return to Meridian and regroup."

"Why us?" asked Buck.

"Convenience," Hannah replied with a grin. "You're in the area, you can move fast and you have enough firepower to capture the target. Based on what you pulled off when you rescued me, you have a talent for disguise and playacting."

"That won't help if they have wizards scanning for infiltrators," Connor noted.

Andyn shook her head. "They have to be actively concentrating and know what to look for. Besides, we'll use the same types of clothes and hair dye and makeup that actors use. No amount of magical scanning will show anything amiss."

Khyron nodded. "Agreed. We can break up into two groups, then converge on the target if we find it."

"Excellent idea," Caria said. "We have some short-range Sending Mirrors we can lend you. Miss Hannah has enough materials for disguises."

Hannah winked at them and smiled in satisfaction.

Connor gazed at the map, lost in thought. He traced the blue arc with his finger. It would encompass hundreds of square miles, and he counted at least a dozen communities.

How are we going to find one person in all that, especially a person who doesn't want to be found? It will take Irial's own favor to help us pull this one off...

***

I feel ridiculous, Connor groused. *And they look ridiculous.*

"Grigor!" Andyn called out.

Connor remembered to answer to his pseudonym. He looked up from a rack of cloaks.

"What do you think about this one?" she asked, holding up a delicate pink chemise. "Will Kaldor like it?"

He scratched the eyebrow above his eyepatch. "He'll like whatever you wear, Gina. Or don't wear."

She giggled and spun back to the assortment of clothes on display.

Considering Andyn's outfit, the chemise wouldn't be much of a change. Disguised as a priestess of Gariil, the god of chance and luck, she wore a rather skimpy outfit: black sandals, a very short pair of leather pants that fit her like a second skin, and a sleeveless half-tunic that covered her to just below her ribs. Her hair, dyed black with a blue stripe down the middle, lay in a braid down her back. Runic Gariilite designs in silver danced along the side of her leg. An amethyst in the shape of Gariil's male and female aspects bounced against her breasts with every move she made.

She made sure to move a lot. The male patrons in the clothier's shop couldn't keep their eyes off her. This suited the three Riders just fine — it allowed Dar to engage people in casual conversation.

Dar looked fully twenty years older, sporting a salt-and-pepper beard and a dark purple robe festooned with magical symbols about the hem. He leaned against the counter, affably chatting with the storekeeper and a red-haired dwarf.

It's a good thing we're incognito, thought Connor. *If we actually had to fight anything, I doubt if we'd survive.*

Connor tossed down a brown cloak and his plate mail armor clanked. He resisted the urge to shift the metal segments around yet again. He now sympathized with Buck. Even though their resident armored knight wore banded mail (easier on the frame than plate), Connor couldn't imagine having to engage in combat.

He felt like a metal turtle.

"Are you getting that one, Gina?" he asked, picking up his crossbow and clumping over to Andyn.

"I'm not sure." She gazed up at the ceiling, made a face, then smiled. "Let's see what Gariil says!"

Extricating a pair of crystal dice from her belt purse (a move that locked all male eyes on her again), she tossed them on the countertop.

She read the dice and pouted. "Oh blast! Not today, it seems."

She gave Connor a brilliant smile. "On second thought, that must mean that there is something even more tempting elsewhere!" With a laugh, she swept up her dice, grabbed her white wooden staff and flounced out of the shop.

Connor hid a smile. *At this rate, all we need for her to do is start dancing. We could lift everyone's purse and clean out the cash drawer and no one would even notice.*

Dar raised his eyebrows and motioned towards the exit. He paid for a pair of leather gloves and left with Connor.

"She's playing this entirely too well," Connor muttered as they followed Andyn down the street towards the War Axe Inn.

"You weren't there in the plaza in Meridian when we were trying to find Handor," Dar smirked. "She and Khyron could become actors after they retire."

Andyn breezed into the Inn. She waved cheerfully to the desk clerk and spun up the stairs. Dar and Connor joined her in their room, shutting the door.

Andyn set her religious symbol of Gariil down on the table, holding her hand above it and murmuring soft words. A misty globe of white light expanded over it and grew until it reached to the ceiling.

"There, now." Andyn plopped down on the overstuffed couch with a sigh. "At least we can't be spied upon without some extraordinarily strong magic. And I'm tired. Pretending to be a bird-brain is exhausting."

"But you do it so well," Dar added with an innocent look. This earned him a tossed pillow to the head.

"Enough with the jester practice," Andyn retorted. "Just tell us what the shopkeeper said."

Connor clanked over to a wooden chair and pulled it up to the table.

"Well," Dar said, removing his fake beard, "He said there were several older gents in town who could be wizards but none of them had escorts, not even a single bodyguard. He did notice an unfamiliar man with two slave girls a few days ago but the man didn't come into the shop. He thought he saw them heading down towards the apothecary."

Connor pulled a small silver hand mirror out of his shoulder bag. "Let's see what Khyron found."

He held the mirror so that Dar and Andyn could also see. The metal frame of the mirror was made of twisting vines that ended in a closed eye at the top.

"Two, one, two, eight, A, D, C," Connor recited. The eye opened, revealing a blue-white gemstone. The jewel glowed and the mirror's surface warped and twisted, then grew dark.

A very mild ping sounded in the room. Connor sat on the edge of the table with a clank. "Now we wait."

They didn't wait long. The mirror's surface swirled and resolved to an image of Khyron, Buck and Eric, suitably disguised. Connor had to admit that the image of Buck as a Druid, Eric as a black-clad hunter and Khyron as a wizard would have a good chance of fooling enemy surveillance – particularly with Buck as a blond, Eric with green eyes and Khyron with a thin moustache and close-cropped hair.

Dar related his report from the clothier's shop. "Aside from the man with the two slaves, no one at the other shops remembered anything unusual about any recent visitors," Dar said. "They have plenty of traffic in the spring and summer season and are used to the usual crowds."

Khyron nodded. "We'll check at the apothecary. We have to watch it, though. It's Friday afternoon. The Sisters of Gudarta are going to hold a Dance of the Lash in the village square, so we'll have to skulk around the back way."

Andyn made a face. "Look sharp. The Sisters have probably used up all the willing participants in the village so unwilling ones are next."

The image winked out. Dar and Andyn sat back on the couch, not speaking.

Connor laid the mirror on the table, lost in thought. Infiltrating Torosc had been somewhat less stressful than expected: a night landing on the coast, followed by a long trek on foot to Carville, in separate 3-person teams. Thanks to the pegasi and a remote landing site, they felt they had avoided attracting attention.

Connor tried to think of more pleasant things than being in Torosc, but images of the skulls on pikes at the village gate still remained. Justice in the land of the Archons was swift, harsh, and sometimes inaccurate, but effective. He wondered if the executed people were real criminals, in the wrong place at the wrong time, or convenient scapegoats for local officials.

He shuddered. The sooner they found their target and made their move, the sooner they could leave. It seemed hard to believe that Torosc used to be composed of kingdoms much like Deran.

As if reading his thoughts, Andyn said, "There are good people here. They're just in hiding. If Brandi and Megan succeeded in rescuing at least one royal heir from the old kingdoms, that is a ray of hope."

Dar nodded. "In a place that sorely needs one."

Connor found Carville to be a weird place. It wasn't a metropolis — maybe half as large as Hillton, which would make its population a little over twelve thousand. The shops and stores and taverns did a brisk business and though some commodities were a little scarce, he didn't detect any major shortages.

Rather, it was the demeanor of the people. People laughed a bit too readily, welcomed customers a bit too quickly, and wanted to bend over backward to satisfy everyone's needs — for the correct financial inducement, of course. It was almost as if they expected to be arrested for not being cheerful enough.

The brothels seemed to have no lack of customers.

A sure sign of despair, Connor reflected.

A mild ping sounded in the room and the trio sat up. Dar snatched the mirror.

The dark, shadowed image made it difficult to see Eric's face. "We have a lead," he whispered. "The old man with the two slaves bought some herbs and extracts at the apothecary, including Thivin's Wort. It's a plant that is used for analyzing poisons."

Something in Connor's brain prickled in alarm. "Poisons?"

"Yes, encoded ones," replied Eric. "It can also be used for antidotes. He picked up a few more little items that I recognized from Melinor's workshop. Whoever this fellow is, he knows what he's doing and it's not beginner magic. The shopkeeper also thinks he's working for the Ja'al based on a wrist tattoo."

"Where are you?" asked Andyn. "It looks like you're in a closet."

"That's because we are, in the blacksmith's shop. It's closed. Some of the Sisters came around just as we left the apothecary and we had to do a dance of our own to get out of sight."

"Did you get a name for this wizard?" Connor asked.

Eric shook his head. "The storekeeper said he didn't give one and was very evasive. We tried to slip the storekeeper some extra coin, but he wouldn't take it. I think he's scared of this guy."

"Any idea where they went?" Andyn asked.

"The apothecary said something obscure about rich folks and their fancy beach cottages. There are some to the west of town over the dunes. The wealthy keep them for special getaways. The impression I got was that visitors are discouraged aggressively by magical and other means."

"Can you make it back to the Inn?" asked Dar.

"We'll be there as soon as we can."

The tiny eye on the mirror frame closed and the glass reflected their faces once again.

Connor exchanged looks with his companions. "Do you think this is the target?"

Dar bit his lip. "This guy is buying the same magic supplies that Melinor has in his lab? Won't give his name? Ja'al tattoo? No bodyguards but two female slaves? Seems like a decent bet. What do you think, Andyn?"

She sighed. "It could be that this is just a Torosci academic on holiday, but we can't risk not checking it out."

Buck, Khyron and Eric slipped in the open window a little while later.

"We think we should investigate," Connor announced as they took seats on chairs and the edge of the bed. "Do you two scouts think you can track the man the apothecary mentioned?"

Eric and Dar nodded. "As long as the weather is mild."

"Even over sand dunes?" asked Buck, eyebrows raised.

The two rangers shared a grin. "We've learned a few things, Buck. We'll find them."

Andyn reached under the couch. "Let's get something to eat and our real gear. We can leave as soon as the Sisters have had enough bloodletting to satisfy the Mistress of Pain."

She brought out a large sack. Reaching inside, she drew out Buck's armor and weapons, handing them to him, then extricated her own gear. Impossibly, Eric withdrew his equipment from the bag, which seemed to have enough room inside it to house the contents of a small armory.

Buck nodded as Dar pulled out his armor and weapons. "It was nice of Hannah to part with Handor's Quartermaster's Bag."

Andyn gave a sad smile. "Even after death, Handor is helping us."

At the mention of their fallen comrade, the Riders lapsed into a somber silence. They removed their disguises, changing into their own gear. Eric handed out rations and they ate without speaking.

The light outside faded to evening. As the sun drifted lower on the horizon, they heard a deep gong from the town square.

Andyn patted Khyron on the shoulder. "Ceremony is done. Let's go while everyone is scurrying home to lick their wounds."

Connor rose, settled his sword at his hip and picked up his bow. "Ready?"

Looking more like the Grey Riders, they nodded their affirmation and slipped out the window. In mere seconds they disappeared into the lengthening shadows.

Chapter Eighteen – Again

"Well?" Eric whispered. He crouched against a sand dune in the fading twilight, his eyes on a blue-painted cottage.

Buck shook his head, peeking around a screen of tall grass. "I don't like it. Not one little bit."

"What do you see?" Khyron asked.

Buck's brows knitted together and his eyes narrowed. "Remember the place where we found Brandi?"

Eric nodded. *Oh God. Not another daemon.*

Buck rotated the Eye of Truth up over the crown of his helmet. "Well, same thing with this place."

"Where?" Andyn hissed next to him.

Buck gestured expansively. "Everywhere. The entire beach house has evil auras."

Eric's unease intensified. He wiped sweaty palms on his tunic. "Well, we can lay protections on ourselves before we go in."

Khyron shook his head. "No good. If it's a trap, they'll have all of us. Connor and I can sneak in close and see what's going on."

"Good idea," Dar agreed. "You two are nearly invisible when you want to be."

"Thanks," Connor said with a wink. "I'll put you down as one of my references."

Dar smiled, the tense mood broken. The Riders backed away from the dunes to get some distance. Andyn raised her hands, laying protections on all of them. For good measure, Eric added a spell of misdirection on Khyron and Connor. It would make them misty and insubstantial targets if anyone attacked them.

With a nod, the halfling and elf slipped out over the dunes and vanished into the night.

Eric patted Dar and Buck on the shoulder. "Time for Hannah's toys."

Both men nodded, slipping black wooden rings onto their index fingers. Now their eyes glowed with a faint green light.

"So, this is how the night looks to you Elven people," Buck mused. "Now I'm even more jealous."

The waiting seemed to go on forever. The sky over the ocean horizon faded into dark blue, then deep purple. Lights flickered to life in the cottage and a couple of shapes moved inside. A back door opened and a long rectangle of light spilled out onto the sand. After a while, it vanished, to be repeated again a couple of minutes later. Then they saw a woman's form in the light of a flickering torch. She knelt in the sand, touching the torch to something that flared into fiery life. She watched the fire for a while. When it began to die down, she re-entered the cottage.

One of the slaves, probably, Eric thought.

The barest whisper of sound alerted him mere seconds before Connor and Khyron slipped over a nearby dune.

"Well," Khyron began, "This could end up being really interesting."

"Explain," Andyn demanded.

"We watched the cottage. It's quite a place: two-story, fairly new, well-built, glass windows. We saw someone moving inside, but there's a distortion spell on the windows. All you can see are shapes. Whoever this guy is, he's very cautious."

"What was all that with the woman and the torch?"

Connor nodded. "That's our interesting part. She came out first to empty a chamber pot into a pit behind the house. I think she's a mage or cleric or something, because she used magic that looked a lot like one of those detection spells Andyn uses. But she didn't give us away. I put my finger to my lips and she just nodded."

Andyn pursed her lip. "Probably a discernment spell to gauge your intent.

I wonder why she didn't raise the alarm. What is she after?"

Dar shrugged. "She's a slave. Maybe she wants to be free."

"In any event," Khyron continued. "We heard a man inside tell her to dump out the trash and burn it. He called her Varienne, I think. This time, when she did her chore, she whispered to us. She warned us that the cottage is enchanted and can detect when thieves break in. She also said that her master was a powerful and evil wizard, but asked us for help in escaping to the Alliance with the other slave."

Eric shot a look at his companions, startled. "You mean *the* Northern Alliance? Is she a spy who got captured?"

"Maybe it's a trap after all," Buck mused. "We are dealing with the Ja'al, you know."

"You'll be able to tell easily enough, Buck," Dar noted. "The Eye will show you."

"What else did she say?" Andyn prompted. "If she can get us in there, we can capture the wizard and set her free."

Khyron sat back in the sand. "She said she would leave the door open and then she and the other slave would try to distract the wizard. She said they might even be able to help us."

Eric's interest increased. Slaves capable of helping capture a Ja'al Council wizard? The more they found out, the weirder it became.

"Opinions?" Dar asked.

Buck shook his head. "I don't like it. Something's not right. Not to mention that the cottage is enchanted and I'll bet you my pegasus that there's a lot more than just intruder detection going on."

Dar nodded. "Agreed, but we can counteract that if we think ahead. I think this is our best chance while he least expects it."

"We have an insider willing to help." Connor agreed. "We might be able to take this guy down with a minimum of effort."

Khyron and Andyn exchanged a look. "All right," she said. "Let's take precautions. Eric?"

Despite his sudden misgivings and a feeling of dread, Eric nodded. "Let's get him. We can be in and out in a flash."

Andyn added a couple of augmenting spells to make them resistant to magical and mundane attacks. Khyron drew his swords and whispered a short word under his breath. Fire flickered along the edges of the blades momen-tarily and he slipped them into his scabbards.

"Just don't burn the place down around our ears," Dar quipped. Khyron grinned back at him.

The Riders slipped over the dunes and followed the two agents. At the back door, Andyn made them stop. She murmured a spell. Three red symbols flashed in the sand near the lowest step and winked out. Connor sneaked up and tested the door latch.

He nodded.

Eric put his hand on Fidelis, heart pounding. Connor eased the door open and slipped inside, quickly followed by Khyron and Eric and Dar.

They ended up inside a kitchen area. A young blonde human woman in a short slave's tunic stood near the door to the rest of the house, a finger on her lips in warning. Her blue eyes were frightened but determined. She took a deep breath, then entered the outer room. They glimpsed couches, a table and chairs and curtains.

"Master," she said as Andyn and Buck brought up the rear. "Did you see that flash of light over by the beach?"

"What? Where?" demanded a harsh male voice.

Connor eased the door open and they saw the slave go to a window by the front door. A human male in his fifties joined her. He wore a brown robe with silver symbols inscribed on the hem. A black staff leaned against the wall.

"There," the slave said, pointing. "It looked like a large firefly."

"I don't see anything," grumped the man, putting a hand on a dagger at his belt.

***

"Giant firefly?" Megan repeated from the pantry. That sounded odd. What was going on in the living room? She set the jars of preserves back on the shelf and opened the door. Oxbridge and Varienne stared out the front windows.

A question died on her lips.

Connor Lomin and a blond elven man sneaked in from the kitchen, followed by Eric Indidarc and the love of her life.

Dar! Oh my God! He's here? How?

***

The Riders entered the living room. At the same time, another young woman with strawberry blonde hair entered from a door on the far side.

Eric froze. Megan Alenar gaped at them in a mixture of shock, joy and terror.

The wizard turned and saw her. "Ah, slave Megan. Varienne thinks… Wait. What is it?"

He followed her eyes and whirled on them. "Intruders!" he bellowed.

The blonde slave tackled him and Megan's hands moved in spellcasting.

***

No! Not now! Megan thought in a panic. She cast a protective shield in record time. A shimmering globe surrounded her.

All hell broke loose.

The glass windows vibrated madly, then shattered. A storm of broken glass flew at the Riders. Shards of glass hit Andyn's magic shield and ricocheted aside. Oxbridge cursed, hurling Varienne into a corner and struggling to his feet. The two couches, the table, chairs, and the cupboards leaped into action like living things.

Oh God! They don't know who Oxbridge is! He'll kill them all! Megan shot a counterspell at the table and a couch. The animated furniture stopped in mid-charge at Andyn and Connor. Eric disappeared under a swirl of curtains.

"You dare defy me?" Oxbridge thundered at the Riders. He thrust his palms towards the floor, muttering. The foundations of the cottage trembled. His eyes glowed red and three flaming balls of rock swirled in front of him. Eric slashed his way through the curtains with a fiery golden dagger and stared at the wizard.

"No!" Megan shouted at the top of her lungs. Red fire burned at the edges of her vision. "You will NOT harm them!"

Her counterspell shattered one of the meteors into pebbles. Buck slid in front of Eric with a mirror-bright shield. Dar leaped aside. Oxbridge thrust his hands forward and the comets shot out at Buck and Eric.

***

Eric threw the slashed curtains aside as two flaming rocks the size of large dogs hurtled at him.

Buck Bydecy slid in front of him, his shield flaring blue. The comets slammed into the shield and detonated in a cloud of fire and stone. The impact hurled Buck and Eric backwards and shattered the wall. They landed in the sand outside the cottage amid a heap of flaming wood, broken glass and shredded fabric.

"Damn it!" Eric growled. "Fidelis!" His spear transformed. He leaped to his feet and hurdled back into the living room, Buck on his heels.

His jaw dropped.

An animated couch and two chairs slammed Khyron and Connor with wooden limbs. Connor's arms were pinned to his sides by a curtain, but his Devoted Defender sword slashed and ripped through the padding on a chair as he struggled to draw Tiuz. Khyron danced and dodged, each strike from his blades setting the attacking furniture on fire.

The cupboards disgorged a blizzard of plates, cups, saucers, knives, forks and spoons at Dar. He dropped to the floor. Knives and forks penetrated into the wall behind him and china shattered. He regained his feet but a rug leaped up to envelop him. A powerful slash from his night-black sword cut it in half.

Andyn and Megan stood with feet braced, blue lightning arcing from their outstretched hands at the wizard. A circle of purple flames surrounded him. The lightning bolts curved and sparked around him, lighting nearby upholstery on fire. The wizard made a thrusting gesture and a fusillade of fire-darts lanced out at the two women.

Andyn staggered back, her armor flashing with sharp detonations. Megan's eyes burned with a red flame and the fire-darts curved around her body, exploding on the wall behind her. She snarled and Eric's heart clenched. She looked positively bestial. He thought he even saw fangs.

Eric charged the wizard. The fire shield flared white-hot and he skidded to a stop, driven back by a searing blast of heat.

Oh my God? What's happened to Megan?

***

I will kill him! Megan raged. *I will rip his selfish, cruel heart from his chest and roast it before his own dying eyes!*

The red haze in her vision grew stronger and she felt a savage, dark energy surge in her chest.

Part of her recoiled in alarm. *No! Not now! I have to regain control!*

She faltered in mid-spell. Oxbridge spread the fingers of one hand. Night-black spears blasted at the Riders. Andyn thrust her hands forward and a hemisphere of misty white leaped up around them. The black spears burst on the globe and Andyn dropped to one knee, a hand going to her head.

Oxbridge cursed and fired another spear of black magic at Megan. With a speed she didn't know she had, Megan leaped high into the air, her hair brushing one of the roof beams. She snatched the lance of darkness out of the air as it passed below her. She landed on the floor with the spear pulsating in her fist. With a snarl of anger, she snapped it in half and cast the foggy remnants at her feet.

Oxbridge and the Riders actually froze for a split second.

"What the fuck was that?" Oxbridge spat.

***

This is not going well, Eric thought, *and that's an understatement.*

"The floor!" A soprano voice called to him.

Eric jerked his head to the corner of the room. Varienne crouched there. "The floor! His flame shield is anchored to the floor!"

Eric swung Fidelis overhead and brought it down on the floor with all his might. The glowing spearhead sliced into the floorboards, cutting two of them in half near the wizard's flame circle.

The mage cursed, staggering backwards as a portion of the fiery barrier vanished. Buck charged through the gap. Oxbridge swept a hand through the air and two ceiling beams swung down, slamming into Buck's shield. He lurched backward and tripped over Varienne.

Oxbridge glared at the blonde girl. "You're disloyal and ungrateful."

He pointed a finger. Buck crouched over her and intercepted a sheet of flame. Fire curved around him. Varienne screamed in pain as the fire scorched her legs. She placed blue-glowing hands on her injuries, tears streaming down her cheeks as the burns healed. Through the smoky air, Eric saw Connor and Khyron batter the last of the animated furniture into splinters.

"It's like fighting Melinor!" Buck shouted.

"Melinor?" the wizard sneered. "That half-wit excuse for a two-bit conjurer? Tell him George Oxbridge sends his regards!" He peppered the Riders with fire darts.

Eric hurled himself at him, grimacing against the detonations on his armor. Khyron and Dar charged with him.

Oxbridge thrust his arms to the side and bellowed. A sphere of bruising force slammed into the Riders, hurling them all back.

Eric's helmet hit a swinging chair arm and he saw spots. Before he could recover, a hot, driving wind pinned him to the kitchen wall. Varienne and the other Riders struggled against the maelstrom.

All except Megan. She stood alone, her tunic whipping around her, eyes blazing red.

"I've had enough of this!" Oxbridge raged.

"So have I," Megan snapped.

Visions of Brandawyn's alter-ego, Delilah, surged to the fore and Eric felt a sudden panic.

***

Megan struggled against the violent rage within her. Desperately, she sought the peace and confidence from before.

"No! Megan!" Dar called to her. "Whatever it is, don't give in!"

She faltered. Oxbridge waved his hands over his head and nets of purple, red and gold drifted down on him.

"Megan!" Dar called. "It's me! Remember who you are!"

Megan hesitated at the sound of his voice. It felt like she was torn into two people: one of them raging, vengeful and savage and the other brave, hopeful and confident. Both pulled at her soul like opposing tides.

Dear Jesus, help me.

With the prayer, the calm Megan asserted control and the rage faded. She let out a deep breath, focusing on the feeling of surety and peace. The red light snapped off and she shook herself.

She shot a smile back at him. "Thank you, love."

He grinned back and winked and her heart soared.

God, I love that man…

Oxbridge began a chant, low-voiced and harsh. Megan closed her eyes, murmuring a flowing phrase of her own. She felt shield of energy shimmer on her skin, covering her like armor. She opened her eyes.

The wizard clapped his hands on his staff and purple bands of light snaked out to entrap her. Megan waved her hand and captured them in her fist, then jerked them free of the staff.

Oxbridge's jaw dropped. "Not possible…"

Megan threw the magical cords into a corner. Oxbridge fired off a cloud of tiny stars with his staff and Megan raised her open hand over her head. The stars streamed into her palm and formed a ball of crackling lightning. Energy built within her, like when she had fought the daemon prince in Torosc long ago. She floated on a cloud of power.

***

Eric stared. *Megan?*

"You have transgressed long enough, George Oxbridge," Megan said in a voice that seemed to echo across a vast distance. Her eyes glowed silver.

She threw the sphere at the wizard. He held up his staff. The ball of light detonated in a soundless explosion. Oxbridge flew back, blasting through the front door. His protective shields flared and vanished as he lurched against the porch railing

Eric fought against the wind, but he was only able to move his arms as far as his own chest.

Oxbridge used his staff to pull himself to his feet. "It appears I have been too lenient with you," he panted. He slammed the butt of his staff into the porch. The floorboards splintered and burst apart. In their place, a vortex of darkness swirled. At its center, a nightmare landscape loomed and a red-eyed shadow advanced towards them.

"Come, Oh Servant of Hades!" the wizard intoned. "Destroy my enemies and eat their remnants as a reward!"

Eric pulled with all his might, trying to break free. Megan thrust both hands at the maelstrom and it wavered, ceasing its expansion.

Eric met Dar's eyes. "Now," he mouthed.

Dar nodded. His hand touched the metal plate at the throat of his armor. He vanished and reappeared in the air above Oxbridge. He fell, swinging Rindara Starblade.

Oxbridge sidestepped and Dar's black sword shattered the staff.

The world detonated.

Seemingly centuries later, Eric opened leaden eyes. He saw the flicker of flames and smelled acrid smoke. His ears rang. He felt like he had been tumbled down a fifty-foot cliff. Numbly, he tried to turn over but a weight prevented him from moving. He turned a bleary gaze to a halfling in scorched armor lying on his legs.

"I'm okay," Connor croaked in a voice that sounded like he was in a deep tunnel. They both staggered to their feet. Eric called to his spear and it teleported back to his hand.

The ragged remnants of the cottage leaned drunkenly into each other like a pair of sailors on shore leave. Smoke billowed from the building and flames leaped in the darkness, casting a weird, reddish glow.

Where's Megan? He thought foggily.

***

Megan gritted her teeth against the wracking pains. She felt like she had been run over by an oxcart. Dimly, she realized her tunic was a tattered bit of rags. Opening her eyes, she located the most important person in her life and helped him to his feet.

Heedless of her state of undress, Dar clasped her to him.

Glorious ecstasy rushed through her. "Thank you, Jesus," she whispered.

"We need to get you some clothes," he murmured into her hair. Her answering laugh was cut short when she saw Buck approach, carrying Varienne. Andyn placed her hands on the blonde girl's head and chest and golden light glowed. Her eyes fluttered open and Buck laid her down.

"Come on," Megan said, taking Dar's hand in hers and limping towards them.

The unnamed blond elven man pulled himself to his feet, shaking his head and yanking his swords out of the sand.

"You okay, Khyron?" Buck asked. The man waved in assent, wincing in pain.

A crazed voice suddenly echoed in the darkness. "No! I won't have it!"

They whirled.

Incredibly, George Oxbridge stood silhouetted against the sea and the moonlight, eyes wild. Most of his robe was gone and he held only the dagger in his hand. The blade of the weapon glistened with an iridescent slime.

"It's over. Surrender," Khyron commanded, pointing a sword at him. Eric joined Connor and Buck at his side. Connor touched the brooch at his shoulder and his dancing sword materialized.

Oxbridge didn't seem to hear. He pulled back his shoulders and lifted his chin, looking down his nose at the Riders as if delivering a lecture. "This won't end it, you know. The ways will be barred, the Dark Wave will crash upon all the lands, and the Final Solution will be implemented. It is inevitable. You fight only to live a little longer."

"Babbling like an idiot won't help you," Dar said. "You have already lost."

Oxbridge ignored him. His eyes locked on Megan and he sneered. "You. You're the cause of all this. And to think of all the things I did for you, you scheming little trollop."

Dar stepped in front of Megan protectively. "Careful, Dar," she warned. "He has a thousand tricks."

Oxbridge snickered. "I do, do I?" He reached into a pocket of his robe for something that glittered with many diamonds.

"No matter, wench," he continued. "Your days are numbered. Just like your lover's." Oxbridge threw the dagger, then reached for a shining ring in his other hand.

Damn it! NO! Megan's mind wailed as the dagger screamed in like a living thing.

***

Eric's heart clenched.

Several things happened at once. Dar dodged. The dagger followed like a maddened hornet. Megan made a shunting motion with her hand and the dagger veered off course, glancing off her leg and jamming into the remnants of a wall.

Eric threw Fidelis. Connor's sword leaped forward as Khyron and Buck charged.

Connor's enchanted weapon lopped off Oxbridge's hand at the wrist and the glittering ring spun off into the sand. Before he could even scream, Fidelis blew through his chest, Khyron's swords severed his other arm and Khelios decapitated him. Spurting blood, the wizard's corpse keeled over.

Eric stared. Even in the moonlight it was obvious: his body aged the moment it hit the sand, warping into a frail, ninety-year old man.

"Andyn!" Dar screamed. Megan sagged in his arms.

The Riders rushed to his side.

"The dagger hit her leg," he said, sounding panicked. "It's not much of a wound, but something's wrong."

"Poison," rasped Varienne, sitting up.

Andyn cursed and removed her gloves. "Was it one of Oxbridge's?"

Varienne nodded tiredly.

"Eric, Dar, help me!" Andyn put one hand on Megan's wound while the other held Eleison, the mace blazing like a torch. Eric scrambled to her side and put his hand on her shoulder. He concentrated, pouring magic energy into Andyn to bolster her healing arts. He gritted his teeth against his own weariness.

"Dar…" Megan said in a drowsy voice.

"Don't speak, sweetheart. Andyn will — "

Megan convulsed, eyes squeezed shut. "No. I have to tell you."

Perspiration grew on Andyn's brow and she gritted her teeth. "The poison is encoded," she gasped.

"What does that mean?" asked Buck.

***

Through a haze of pain and fog, Megan opened her eyes. The most beloved person in her universe hovered over her, brow furrowed and eyes brimming with tears.

Why can I see my children in his eyes? I won't ever bear them.

She smiled at him and kissed his hand. "Listen well, my love," she said as another spasm of pain seared her internal organs. "You must go to the Rainbow Valley, in Terenai, in the Eastern Wilderness. Find the Dome of Glass. Defeat the guardians. Open the Gate of Stars. I hid my notes. Under the back steps. Take them with you."

"We won't need them," Dar choked, tears streaming down his face. "You can tell us all about it yourself. We'll get you to Melinor and Father Edward."

"Shh…" she smiled again and another convulsion shook her.

"Andyn?" asked Varienne, scooting closer. She put her hands on Andyn's shoulders and they glowed white.

Andyn shuddered, eyes glassy, looking into the distance at something they couldn't see. "I can't… it's too complicated… need the code… I'm losing her! Help me, Varienne!"

***

Additional magical energy surged through Eric from Varienne, but Megan turned paler. Her skin took on a mild green pallor.

Eric couldn't believe his eyes. "No, God," he whispered. "Not her too."

***

"Live for me, Dar," Megan said, her eyelids fluttering shut. "Promise me you'll love again."

The pain faded away, replaced by warmth and glorious light. She heard a million voices singing in wondrous harmony.

"Don't despair," she whispered and pulled him in for a kiss.

***

Time stood still. Dar squeezed his eyes shut and tears ran down his cheeks, his lips still locked on Megan's. He sobbed even as he kissed her. Eric could barely see him through his own tears.

"NO!" Eric screamed. He leaped to his feet, clawing in his belt purse for a tiny amber bead. He smashed it in his fist.

A bright web of gold materialized over Megan and then snapped down over her body. Dar jerked back as if stung, eyes wide in the amber light of the Preservation Net.

"Curse you, Ja'al!" Buck bellowed, fists raised at the night sky. "I swear by the Earth Mother, I will destroy every one of your false gods with my bare hands! Do you hear me?"

Eric stared at Megan's form, covered in shimmering light. He felt nothing, just a dead emptiness.

"Please," Varienne said. She leaned up against Eric, shaking with fatigue. "Get Megan's notes."

"On it!" Khyron sprinted towards the back steps of the ruined cottage.

"Connor," Eric said, "Get a blanket or something for Varienne."

She clutched his arm. "That's not important. We have to get away, and quickly. The explosions and sound will bring someone soon, and I fear it will be the city guards. That much magical power will be of very great interest to them."

"Understood," Eric said. He took a deep breath, submerged his grief and pointed his hand at the sky. At a word, a silvery, twisting band of light streaked up into the night and disappeared in a stream of sparkles.

She shook her head. "No, they will see!"

"Don't worry," he said. "It's our pegasi."

"How long will it take for them to get here?"

"Not long."

Buck joined them, his eyes stormy and haunted. "We're going to have company." He pointed towards the town, where a cluster of magical lights and torches congregated like agitated fireflies.

Varienne tore herself from Eric's grasp and ran to Oxbridge's corpse.

"Wait!" Connor called. "Varienne, what are you doing?"

She stopped and held up her hand. Three of her fingertips glowed and something in the sand flashed in response. She snatched it up and raced back to them. "Here, it's the wizard's ring," she handed Eric a black wooden ring with many tiny diamonds.

"What does it do?" asked Connor.

"Teleport," she replied, fixing them with worried eyes. "Anywhere you want."

Eric shot a glance at the sky and was gratified to see winged shapes approaching in the moonlight. "Anywhere?" he asked. "How far?"

"We transported from Catrin, Morlan, to this place."

Eric's mind reeled as he calculated the distance.

"We're not in shape for a fight," Khyron said, returning with a small black notebook. In confirmation, a set of red twisting lights shot up from the direction of Carville and detonated in fiery blooms. "And I'll bet you anything the air patrols will be after us."

The pegasi circled and started landing. Khyron and Buck ran to get them. Dar and Andyn arrived. He cradled Megan in his arms, her form embraced by the Preservation Net.

"We need to get to somewhere safe," Dar said in a dead voice, hollow eyes locked on Megan's face.

Connor set his mouth in a firm line. "I have just the place."

***

Less than a minute later, the forms of eight people and six pegasi glittered in the night and disappeared.

Shortly thereafter, the same forms coalesced in the courtyard of the Lervion manor house, startling Hannah and the Meraloys as they sat under the gazebo in the rose garden.

Less than half an hour later, a quick-reaction force from Carville found only the mangled corpse of one George Oxbridge, former Wizard of the First Circle of the Ja'al High Council, and the flaming ruins of a magically enchanted cottage.

Chapter Nineteen – Consolation

Melinor took a deep breath and let it out. He raised his hand to the door handle and hesitated.

How do I help? he thought. *Three terrible losses in the span of a couple of months… Megan, Brandi and Handor.*

Other people had brought him comfort when Anne had died years ago, but that was different. Her end had been the result of a latent, undetected heart defect that struck without warning, not the malevolent actions of evil cults. She had lived to see her children and grandchildren peaceful and content and had protected and raised two foster children besides — two very unique foster children.

By now, the pain from Anne's death had receded to a dull ache of longing, tempered by all the happy memories of many good years together. For Dar and Eric, he feared there would only be agony and thoughts of revenge in the aftermath.

That's what I have to focus on, he decided. *I can be strong and guide them. Vengeance will avail them nothing and turn them as heartless as their foes. Justice, not vengeance.*

He opened the door. Andyn sat on a bench in the Chancery gardens, her arm around Dar. His dead eyes focused on nothing, his expression listless. Varienne held his hand, seated at his other side. The other Riders hovered not far away.

A statue of Saint Mary regarded them all with a sorrowful yet beneficent gaze. It was almost as if the saint wanted to tell them that she had been there and understood their pain from her own experience— but she also knew the glorious end of the story.

Melinor squared his shoulders and strolled towards them, hands behind his back. Buck and Connor nodded to him from where they stood under an oak tree. Eric's head popped up from a conversation with Khyron.

"Thanks for coming," Eric said.

Melinor embraced his adopted son. "How are you holding up?"

Eric sighed. "As well as can be expected."

Khyron bowed. "Lord Melinor."

The wizard released Eric. "I'm just Melinor, Khyron. You're like family now."

Khyron's eyes widened and the tiniest of smiles curved his lip. "As you wish, Melinor."

Eric nodded at Dar. "He's barely eaten in three days."

Melinor patted Eric on the shoulder. "You were the same when Brandi fell. You can help him."

Eric sighed, shoulders drooping. "I'm not so sure. But I will be there, as will Connor."

"A question, Lord — I mean, Melinor." Khyron asked. "We have both of the sisters in a safe place now. Why can't we simply remove the Preservation Nets and try to help them? The Alliance has more than enough resources."

Melinor clasped his hands behind his back again. "It's not that simple. If we dispel the Nets, the women will return to their condition at the moment in time before the Nets were activated. That means that we would still have the same problems: namely, how to remove the vampirism from Brandi and the poison from Megan."

Khyron shook his head. "Can't we do something?"

"Well, we have some time to find solutions. the Preservation Net slows time to a ten-millionth of normal, so for every second that passes for the girls, ten million pass for us."

Khyron blinked in surprise. "How many days?"

"About one hundred fifteen, almost a third of a year. It is the equivalent of one second for them."

"That's not a lot of time when you think about it, is it?"

Melinor nodded. "But it could be enough to figure something out. We'd have to solve Brandi's dilemma first. If she's alive and we revive her, she will be fighting her vampirism as soon as we remove the stake."

Khyron's brow furrowed. "She'll revive with a hole in her chest?"

"That's the problem with vampires created by someone else's magic and not another vampire. A stake in the heart is a method to disable, not destroy. As soon as the wood is removed, she will regenerate in a matter of minutes unless we destroy the device that warped her. Otherwise, we would have to imprison her for her own safety."

"And Megan?"

Melinor made a face. "Unless we have an antidote ready, we'd be hitting her almost constantly with metabolic spells to try to slow the poison or interfere with it. She would be in medical isolation or even a coma."

Khyron shook his head. "There's got to be a way to do something!"

Melinor's heart went out to Khyron. Here was the newest of the Riders. Yet he doggedly turned over every possibility in an effort to save people he had only recently met.

Andyn has chosen well.

"As long as there is life," he replied. "There is hope. And we don't know that they are dead, not until we remove the Nets. Don't worry: we will bring every resource to bear. We owe them that much."

Khyron's fists balled and he set his mouth in a firm line.

The door to the Chancery opened and Gorlak approached. The goblin's eyes flicked to Dar, full of sympathy. He came to Melinor's side instead.

"Lord Melinor." He handed him a slip of paper.

Melinor read it. His heart lightened. "Thank you, Gorlak. Please wait here." He strode over to Dar and Andyn. Varienne smiled at Melinor and released Dar's hand.

Melinor embraced Dar and received a half-hearted hug in return. "We are here for you, Darius, and we care for you immensely. Hold onto that."

As Melinor released Dar, the other Riders gathered around in a circle of comfort, arms around Dar's shoulders. Andyn kissed him on the cheek. Dar gave them all a weak smile, tried to speak, then closed his mouth and shook his head.

Melinor watched them, uncertain of what to do. Finally, Varienne smiled at him. "Do you have news, Lord Melinor?"

"Yes," Melinor said briskly. "Good news that may bring light into an otherwise sorrowful time. First of all, Varienne, your debriefing sessions have been most informative. You have quite the visual memory. Thanks to your descriptions, we have been able to recreate many of Oxbridge's equations and algorithms."

The blonde girl blushed and dropped her gaze. "Thank you, Lord Melinor. I was only trying to help."

"Well, you did a creditable job, even if you're not a mage. We are hot on the trail of Oxbridge's work and think that, in a few weeks' time, we will be able to devise a way to counteract the magic of the black stones."

He smiled at her. "But now Gorlak here brings me a note that tells me a certain person has been found. Someone who is important to you, dear girl."

Her head jerked up. "Who?"

In answer, Melinor nodded to Gorlak, who marched to the doors and flung them open.

A tall, dark-haired human man strode in, clad in a dark grey hauberk with a single black star in the middle. His blue eyes lit up when he spotted Varienne.

"Altus?" she whispered. She looked dazed.

With a broad grin, the man bowed before Melinor. "Lord Melinor. I came as soon as I could."

"Just in time, Sergeant," Melinor said, immensely pleased with Varienne's reaction. "Grey Riders, I would like to introduce you to First Sergeant Altus Volan of the Black Star Mercenary Company. I believe you and he are acquainted, Varienne?"

With an inarticulate cry of joy, the blonde girl leaped into the newcomer's arms. He laughed, lifting her up in the air and spinning her around.

"I presume that's a 'yes'," Melinor remarked with a droll look at the other Riders.

To his relief, their somber mood lightened and even Dar smiled.

Altus kissed Varienne soundly and she returned his embrace. Finally, Varienne faced Melinor and wiped her eyes. "I don't understand. How did you find him so quickly?"

"It was Eric's doing. He read through Megan's notes and asked me to make contact with the Black Star Company. It was all rather academic after that."

Varienne took her love's hand and led him to the Grey Riders. She curtseyed before Eric. "I can never thank you enough, Sir Indidarc."

Now sporting a broad smile of his own, Eric waved a hand. "None of that, Varienne. You were such a help to Megan. It was the least we could do."

Varienne took Dar's hand. "I made a vow to your Megan. I intend to keep it."

He smiled through his tears. "I don't doubt it."

"How did you know the Alenars, Sergeant?" Khyron asked.

Altus gave a rueful smile. "From a negative experience opposing them in combat."

The Riders exchanged surprised glances and Varienne laughed. "I think you owe them a bit of explanation, Altus."

They took seats on benches. "My parents were Viper slavers from a district of Torosc named Northmarch," Altus began, "and when I was nineteen, one of our agents brought a certain young lady to our home."

Varienne gave his hand a squeeze.

"Like all teenagers," Altus continued, "I had already been rebelling against my parents. I struck up a relationship with the young lady and found she was studying to be a priestess of Irial. We formed an understanding between us. I went to my parents and asked if I could buy her. They laughed at me. Healer slaves are very rare and command high prices. There is no way I could have afforded her. A few weeks later, George Oxbridge bought her, so I packed up whatever I wanted and left home."

Dar gave him a crooked grin. "Hurray for rebelling teenagers."

Good for you, Darius. Melinor chuckled along with the others.

Altus saluted Dar. "After kicking around with various caravans, the Skullheads approached me. By that time, I was really bitter, not to mention poor, so I took the job. It was worse than I had thought. Skullheads are brutes. However, I must have made an impression; I was promoted to lieutenant and assigned to support a secret Ja'al operation in Gorostol."

"I think I can guess what operation that was," Connor remarked with a raised eyebrow.

"It would be a good guess. In any event, the Alenars basically destroyed a Ja'al compound," Altus said. "My team came along afterwards and captured Megan through a stroke of dumb luck. I knew she would bring an even higher price than Varienne, but Megan talked to me and I really started to have second thoughts about my life."

"She had that effect on people," said Andyn with a smile at Dar.

"By the time that Brandi and Steven and Daphne rescued her and captured me, I had decided not to go through with it." Altus shrugged, eyes on at the paving stones. "Instead of turning me over to the Roadwardens, they set me free and gave me a contact in the Black Star company. I've been there ever since."

He raised Varienne's hand to his lips. "I owe them everything."

No one spoke. Altus gave the Riders a determined look. "I know that Stephen and Daphne are dead. Megan and Brandi are held in some kind of magical stasis and we're not even sure if they're alive. I am here to tell you I've decided to leave the Company and join you in finding a way to help them."

"You don't need do anything that drastic," Melinor interjected. "The Riders will have their own assignments, but I have already spoken to your captain and the Church has purchased your services. We will doubtless need your talents to help protect people in coming days."

"I am ready for whatever task you would give me, Lord Melinor," Altus said, rising and bowing. Varienne beamed at him.

"Excellent. We will be glad for the help. Now, if you will excuse us," Melinor added, also rising. "I have to have a conference with the Riders. We will meet you for dinner."

Hand in hand, the couple left with Gorlak.

"You have something in mind for those two," Connor noted.

"Yes," Melinor mused, staring after them. "Altus and Varienne will be working with Gorlak. We have found a Ja'al agent in the Royal Court. We must be careful and patient, but we think we can capture the agent as well as her superiors if we watch for the right moment."

Melinor spun on his heel and faced the Riders. "Now, as for you, I believe you are familiar with Father Edward's solarium, are you not?"

The Riders nodded.

"Excellent. Come along then." He led them back into the Chancery past the study. He opened a door to a circular, domed room. One wall, composed of tall panes of glass framed by wrought iron, curved up overhead to meet the wooden ceiling at the apex. It gave the impression of a bird cage. Lush green plants grew in pots and containers near the windows and a large round table with wicker chairs sat in the exact center. Beyond the windows, a lawn and trees led to a tall metal fence outside the Chancery.

Melinor removed a simple silver ring from his pocket and slipped it on. He raised his hand up towards the ceiling and a light flashed in his palm. An identical one flared in answer from the apex of the ceiling. Glittering stars of radiance shimmered down the window frames, then flowed across the floor to the back wall and ran up to the ceiling again. In a matter of seconds, a golden light filled the solarium. Melinor blinked to clear his vision. Now, instead of looking out at a green lawn and trees and a street, he saw a wide green field of waving grass, rocky hills and towering pines.

Eric gave him a sidelong look. "I don't suppose you know where we are. Father Edward wouldn't tell us."

Melinor shook his head as he took a seat. "No idea. Father Edward wouldn't tell me. He just gave me his ring and told me to use it. Don't worry. I know how to get us back to the Chancery." He gestured to the other chairs. He measured them as they took their places. While not as somber as before, a definite gloom hung over them.

"I've read over Megan's notes and compared them to Brandi's," he forged ahead in a brisk tone. "This much is certain: Oxbridge and the Ja'al both felt they had figured out how to close Celestial Gates. But we all know that finding them and closing them are two entirely different things."

"There is no shortage of freelancers without morals," Andyn noted. "The Ja'al would have no trouble hiring out agents to deliver the stones to Celestial Gates, once they find them."

"Agreed. However, there is also the matter of how many stones are in existence. There were six in the box near Eastridge. Megan recalls working on at least a dozen others at Oxbridge's workshop, but I believe those were just for testing."

"Why?" Eric asked.

"The research team here in Deran helped me perform some tests of our own and, based on the measurements, I believe that only the Eastridge Six, as I'll call them, are potent enough to bind an interplanetary gate. Of course, we are assuming that there aren't any more than six, but we don't have indications otherwise. Based on the fact that Oxbridge was actively trying to hide from his superiors, he was unlikely to have given them anything concrete, at least not without concessions."

Eric and Andyn stared at him. Connor and Buck looked confused while Khyron leaned back in his chair, eyes hooded.

"How is it even possible to close a Celestial Gate?" Andyn asked.

Melinor considered it, then shook his head. "The technical details would take too long to explain. Suffice it to say I had my calculations independently verified. I consulted with some other wizards, notably Nicodemus Talkir from Terenai and Dorothea Ngolo from Kirdan. Both of them agreed."

"Can the Celestial Gates be freed again later?" asked Connor.

"Well, anything that can be done can also be undone," he answered. "However, if their purpose is to prevent Celestial reinforcements from counteracting raids from Hades, any Elohir on Damora have a quandary. They can either try to break the enchantment on a bound Gate or they can help hunt down daemonic agents running around loose."

"What can we do then?" asked Buck.

Melinor let out a deep breath. "If the Ja'al can get the stones close enough to several gates, they would be able to infiltrate daemons unopposed. The Allied nations and the Elohir will have to deal with them. You, however, will have a different task."

Melinor reached into a pocket in his robes and withdrew a sea-green orb about the size of an apple. The Riders leaned forward, eyes bright with interest.

"It is significant," he said, holding the sphere in his palm, "that both Brandi and Megan mentioned a Gate of Stars and a Dome of Glass that guards it. For whatever reason, the Gate of Stars is feared by the Ja'al. I'm not sure why, but if our initial guess is correct, it could be another, lost gate from the Skyfire for bringing in reinforcements if we need aid in the hunt for daemonic agents. Megan's notes listed both the great Bay of Terenai — the Elethi Rin — and Rainbow Valley, but for some reason she only mentioned Rainbow Valley to you."

Melinor tossed the green glass ball in his palm. "We need to find Rainbow Valley."

Khyron shook his head. "I've been all over Terenai and the Northern Alliance and I've never seen anything like a rainbow valley."

Melinor grinned at him. "That's because you weren't looking in libraries."

They stared back at him. He lifted up the ball in his fingers. "This is an image globe."

"I've heard of them," breathed Andyn.

Melinor whispered a word. The globe flared white light and a translucent map leaped up above it, hovering in midair.

"We have collated the results of several very ancient records and come up with this," he said. "While none of the place names make sense any more, the geographical features are notable."

He pointed at a region of the map. "This is the equivalent of the eastern border of modern Terenai. That ring of mountains beyond it was known as the Titan's Crown in ancient times. We believe that the Rainbow Valley could be there."

"I've never heard of the Titan's Crown," mused Dar.

"True enough," Melinor replied. "But some of our rangers have seen it from a distance. They would have had to traverse miles of dense forest to get to it, but for a group of pegasus riders?"

He shrugged.

"The Empire has riders," Khyron noted.

Melinor smiled and tapped the vision globe. "Yes, but they are regular military troops, not a highly trained special operations team like you. We'd need at least a dozen Imperial air cavalry to equal your abilities. If we suddenly send out an air wing in that direction, it will tip off any spies. I have confidence that you'd be able to slip across the border unnoticed."

He handed the globe to Andyn. "I will teach you the keyword."

He rose, then snapped his fingers. "Ah yes, I almost forgot."

Reaching into another pocket, he removed a flat box as big as his hand. He flipped it open and laid it on the table. A small oval mirror rested against padding inside. Four aquamarines glittered around the mirror frame, equally spaced.

"Another Sending Mirror?" Buck asked.

"A very special one. It can contact similar mirrors here in Deran or Terenai from far away."

Eric's eyes narrowed. "How far away?"

"Very far."

Dar gave him a sharp look. "As far away as the Titan's Crown?"

Melinor nodded and Andyn shook her head. "That's incredible," she murmured.

Melinor smiled and closed the box, handing it to Dar. "It works the same as any other Sending Mirror. I leave it in your capable hands. Do you have any Preservation Beads left?"

Buck patted his belt purse. "Four."

"Excellent. Now, off to meet your travelling companion."

"Who?" asked Eric.

Melinor couldn't resist a conspiratorial look at them but he didn't answer. He raised his hand to the ceiling and the light shone out again. The mountain meadow faded behind its radiance and the windows resolved to the lawn and street outside the Chancery.

"What travelling companion?" Connor demanded.

The scene outside the windows resolved to the lawn and street outside the Chancery. Despite a shower of questions, he gestured for them to follow into the hallway. A tall figure loomed out of the shadows.

The Riders fell silent.

A white-haired, bearded old man in a plain grey robe smiled at them. His golden cat-eyes twinkled.

"Grandpa?" asked Dar.

Chapter Twenty – Changing of the Guard

"Lady Arlene?"

The Countess of Harlinsville looked up from her desk. "What is it, Lawrence?"

"You have a visitor. A halfling man."

She frowned. "At this hour? Can't it wait until morning?"

Lawrence inclined his head. "He is most insistent, milady."

She sighed. "I suppose I have a few minutes. Show him in."

Kili Mikman bowed low as he entered.

She came around to the front of the desk. "It's a little late in the evening, don't you think?"

Instead of answering, he held out a tiny white envelope. With a sharp look from his glittering eyes, he bowed again and left.

Startled, she forgot to be offended and stared at the envelope. The embossed pattern of a thirteen-armed octopus, white on white, was barely visible. She traced it with her fingertips.

Her heartbeat quickened. She opened the envelope and drew out a white card with one word written on it.

Now.

Her hands trembled as she tossed the card and envelope into the fireplace and watched it burn to ashes.

A feeling of immense satisfaction and relief flowed through her. *Finally.*

She opened a desk drawer, worked a catch with her fingernail, and withdrew three tiny ampoules from a secret compartment. Each of them was no bigger than the end of her pinky finger. Palming one and putting the others into her belt purse, she glided upstairs to her bedchamber. Dunston sat in bed, reading a book.

He smiled at her approach. "Finished?"

"For now, my dear. Shall I get your evening brandy?"

"Please."

At the sideboard, she turned her back to him and popped the stopper of the miniature vial. After emptying the contents into a snifter, she added dwarven spirits.

She handed it to him with a brilliant smile and he nodded his thanks. She slid into the bed next to him, propping her head up with her elbow.

"What are you reading?"

"A treatise on balancing the rights of the community with the rights of the individual."

"Interesting?"

"To me, yes. But I won't bore you. I know your interests are in other areas. Thank you for asking, though." He sipped the brandy.

She laid her head on his shoulder. "You are so generous," she said, "Most men your age would be retired and enjoying a life of leisure."

He smiled down at her and patted her hand. "You are the reason, Arlene. I am comforted to know you are with me."

She remained still. He yawned and took another sip. She waited. His eyelids drooped and she removed the snifter, setting it on her nightstand.

"Don't know why I'm so tired now," he mumbled.

"Too much striving to better the life of the common man," she soothed, laying aside the book and propping up his pillow. "You work too hard. Let me take care of you."

"You're so good to me."

"I know. Good night, Dunston."

"Good night, dear…" He drifted off.

She reached under the mattress and withdrew a slender stiletto. "Sleep forever."

***

Melinor leaned against the arched window frame and contemplated the Chancery gardens at sunset. Bright green leaves fluttered like verdant, earthbound butterflies on the trees outside. The ever-present Puup, Buckminster's pigeon, strutted along the crushed rock pathway like a sentry on patrol. He pecked at something among the rocks and marched around a bush, out of sight.

March on, my feathered friend, Melinor mused. He put his hands behind his back and paced back towards Father Edward's room. The portraits of all the Nuncios regarded him from the walls. Melinor contemplated Edward's: he smiled in a friendly yet remote way, almost like a college professor looking on a favorite student. This contrasted with the painting of his predecessor, Father Rodrigo: dusky-skinned with mischievous brown eyes, beaming jovially out at the world.

Melinor had never met Father Rodrigo. He had died when Melinor was just thirteen and he only remembered his parents speaking with admiration about his warmth, kindness and easy way with people.

The door to Edward's room opened and shut.

"I've done what I can." Sister Karen shook her head, setting her black bag on an end table and arranging her medicine bottles. The fading sunlight shone in through the tall windows.

"How much longer?"

"Minutes to hours at most, I think."

"Well," he replied slowly, "At least he had a chance to talk to Saren and Terenil and the Faldanors. Did Konadar make it?"

She nodded, snapping her bag shut. "He left just before you arrived. Said he would be back, but that Father Edward had given him a task to perform after his passing. Edward sent Detlef with him, more to spare the lad than as a help. It will be hard for him."

"For all of us."

Her eyes drifted to the windows behind him and she nodded. "They're here." They glimpsed the Grey Riders hurrying across the courtyard below toward the dormitory wing.

"I worry about them," she said, frowning.

"So do I."

Sister Karen fidgeted with the catch on her medical bag. The pause lengthened. Finally, the nun spoke. "What about their families?"

"Plans are in the works as we speak. Most of the Riders come from families with martial resources at their disposals, like the Lomins and the Eleandirs. They are well-guarded, especially now that we have warned them. For the others, we have assigned special units to protect the Cabots and Bydecys."

"Well," she sighed, "My work here is done." She mad as if to go but Melinor stopped her.

"Thank you, Sister. You have been at Father Edward's side throughout his illness. I know he wasn't the easiest patient, but you did your best."

She turned amused grey-silver eyes to his. "Not the easiest? That's an understatement. Cantankerous old thing."

He smiled at that.

She looped dark hair over pointed ears. "No, his was a life well-lived. He goes to a place where he won't be in pain anymore." Despite her words, Melinor saw her eyes glisten with tears.

Edward's door opened and shut again. A young human priest approached, removing his stole and kissing the cross on it. "All done," he said with a sad smile. "He said to send everyone in when they arrive."

"Thank you."

Sister Karen gave Melinor's arm a squeeze, his eyes another smile, and then departed with the Nuncio's confessor.

Melinor stood alone in the hallway, trying to figure out how to go into Edward's room for the final time.

The sound of boots in the hall made him turn. Gorlak led the Grey Riders towards him. Their eyes were somber, but focused.

Melinor held open the door. "Let's go in, shall we? He has asked for you."

He knew that Edward's condition would shock them. Andyn gasped.

Edward turned his head away from his west-facing window and gave them a weak smile. Even for Melinor, who had seen him deteriorate through the last stages of his illness, the Nuncio looked frail and small.

"You're here at last, you rascals," Father Edward said.

This made the Riders smile.

The Nuncio waved a thin hand. "Come closer. I won't bite you know, not at this stage. Gorlak, sit here."

Melinor stood near the headboard as the Grey Riders gathered around the bed. The scene reminded him of children at the bedside of a parent.

Well, that is what he has been to them.

"I have a surprise for you, Buckminster," Edward said.

Buck's eyebrows rose. Edward nodded. "Indeed. Melinor, ring that little bell please."

Melinor obliged. The tinkling resounded in the quiet room. A side door opened and a pretty young brunette in a brown robe and boots swirled in. She smiled shyly.

"But who… how?" Buck stammered as he rose from the bedside and accepted her embrace.

Carine Del Rio tweaked his nose. "Your Father Edward has many friends. He knew I was in Eleth-Anor and sent for me days ago."

Melinor saw genuine smiles on the faces of the Riders and it warmed his heart. *Another well-needed bit of joy amid the gloom.*

"Carine has been helping us coordinate with some of the Druids who are opposed to the schism in their community and want to work with the Faiths of the Light," he explained.

Carine gazed up at Buck and he cast a self-conscious glance at Eric and Dar. Both men nodded back, their smiles sad but genuine.

"Now," Edward rasped. "Eric and Darius, listen to me."

He reached out and held the hands of both men. "I know your hearts have been wounded," he said, fixing them with a clear gaze. "I will not diminish that. A loss of a loved one is bitter. Yet you and I both know what awaits them at the end. They are good and faithful daughters of the Church and children of God. That is their destiny and they have reached out to claim it."

"Thank you," Eric murmured. Dar didn't speak.

Edward's eyes became soft. "Do not despair, my sons. Look at me."

Dar's head jerked up and his jaw worked. His eyes were haunted. "But they're gone, Father Edward," he managed at last.

Edward sighed and gave their hands a squeeze.

"Are they?" he asked, sounding suddenly tired. "Remember the words of the Archangel Gabriel: nothing will be impossible for God. His words, you know, not mine."

Slowly, Edward pulled the signet ring from his hand and held it out to Gorlak. "My friend, put this in the holder, there by the window."

For the first time, Melinor noticed that the curtains were drawn over that particular window. A peculiar-looking fixture sat on a small table nearby. Gorlak placed the ring into the fixture, oriented so that the large amethyst in the bezel of the Nuncio's ring faced the drapes.

Edward gazed at the fading sunlight through his west window. Gold and ochre and crimson glowed and darkened to deeper colors.

"Such a beautiful place, Damora," he remarked to no one in particular. "Beautiful and dangerous and wondrous and strange all at once. It has been my home these many years."

Gorlak returned to his seat at Edward's side. The Nuncio gave him a side-long look. "You will be fine."

Tears traced shiny lines down the goblin's cheeks and he shook his head.

"No, no. None of that. Not for me, Gorlak," Edward whispered. "You are one of the most faithful, dedicated people I have ever been privileged to know. I hereby release you from my service. You can go do great things for our world, now that I'm not here to worry over you. Lord Melinor will be your new employer, if you prefer. But you are free, my friend. You are a child of the Light, for certain."

Gorlak shook his head, eyes gazing at his mentor.

"Free, Gorlak," Edward whispered. He turned his eyes back to the west. "So beautiful…"

Slowly, he relaxed and his eyes closed. A smile spread over his features and, to Melinor, it seemed that decades of age melted away from his face.

Andyn stifled a sob on Khyron's shoulder and Gorlak covered his face with his hands. Carine clasped her arms around Buck, who shook his head, his fist clenched at his side. Eric and Dar bowed their heads, lips moving in prayer. Connor put his arm around Gorlak as the little goblin wept.

Melinor gazed out the window at the sunset. *Godspeed you to heaven.* He wiped his eyes.

A sound like the chorus of many fairy chimes filled the air. It took a moment for Melinor to realize that a swirling silver aura filled one side of the room.

He gaped.

The Nuncio's ring took on a life of its own, shining forth a coruscating field of luminance against the curtains. The light slowly formed an archway. Then, to his amazement, it snapped into a mirror-bright sheen and changed to glass.

Melinor gasped. Through the archway, he saw the interior of a massive cathedral, unlike any he had ever seen before. Statues of saints loomed in giant, exquisitely decorated sconces taller than a man. Two sets of steps made of red stone marched up on opposite sides of a round dais. At the top of the dais sat a marble altar with seven candles.

But what took his breath away was the structure towering above: four pillars of twisting, bronze-colored stone, surmounted by an elaborate roof with golden angel statues and a cross atop a curving peak.

"What is that place?" Carine breathed.

Melinor shook his head. "I don't know…"

As they watched, two men stepped into view by the altar. One was a stocky human dressed completely in white, with an ivory skullcap and a gold pectoral cross. He had dark, almond-shaped eyes and a golden, tawny complexion. Another dark-skinned human accompanied him, wearing a black cassock with a purple sash and a skullcap identical to Father Edward's.

Melinor couldn't believe his eyes. "Wait. That must be…" Eric began.

"I know…" whispered Dar.

The dark man knelt. The man in white blessed him, then embraced him as he stood. They both turned towards Melinor.

His heart skipped a beat.

"They can see us…" Connor breathed.

As they watched, the dark-skinned man took a deep breath, then strode directly at them. As he grew closer and closer, the archway's surface swirled silver and white, looking for all the world like sunlight on a lake. Then, just like a swimmer emerging from said lake, the man simply walked through the archway and into the room.

The light from Edward's ring snapped off and the archway vanished.

No one moved. The newcomer had eyes only for Edward. He advanced to the bedside, kneeling there with his hands folded in prayer.

Silence reigned, broken only by the ticking of Edward's clock.

The Grey Riders stood frozen.

Finally, the priest made the Sign of the Cross. He sighed, wiped his eyes and paused, motionless. After several heartbeats, he sighed and stood, turning to face them. He had a round, pleasant countenance with high cheekbones and lively green eyes. Melinor guessed his age to be between forty and fifty. He stood a little shorter than Buck.

He placed his hands behind his back and smiled. "I wish it could be under different circumstances," he said in a mellow baritone, "but this will have to do. From the descriptions I have been given, you must be Lord Melinor, Gorlak and the Grey Riders."

Melinor tried to think of something clever to say and his mind failed him.

The man bowed. "I am very pleased to meet you all. I am Thomas Williams, the new Papal Nuncio to Damora."

Chapter Twenty-One – Roll the Bones

"Careful with that!" Berek snapped. He glared at the Dark Elven warriors.

They inclined their heads respectfully, eyes glittering, but remained silent. Lifting a long, narrow box, they climbed up a set of stairs to a wide dais. Six flaming iron braziers surrounded the platform.

Supple arms encircled Berek's waist from behind. A familiar voice whispered in his ear. "Now, now, dear. Don't be mean to the servants."

He smirked. "Don't let them hear that. Queen Ildrisana wouldn't like it. It implies that she serves the Ja'al."

Adina peeked over his shoulder. "But she does!"

He gave her a look of mock disapproval.

She pouted. "I'll behave. We don't want dissension in the ranks."

He turned around and her arms looped over his shoulders, hands clasped behind his neck. He gazed into amused brown eyes. Adina's filmy long dress of bone-white fairly glowed in the light of Kaliri, the nearer moon. Green trim accentuated her curves in all the right places.

"You're feeling very adventurous tonight," he remarked. "I trust you've recovered from the loss of your favorite little vampire slave?"

Adina's jaw tightened. "You had to bring that up! Well, I'll admit it. You were right, Berek. She was more trouble than she was worth."

"Are we sure that she's destroyed?"

Adina gave him a languid smile. "Our spies in Eastridge saw the Grey

Riders returning with a body covered by a sheet. Based on what we now know, I am confident that she did not survive the battle at the cottage."

Berek eyed her critically. "You're sure this isn't going to bedevil you later?"

"More than sure. No matter what Brandawyn managed to do or not do, she is history. Now, it is a night of glory! We begin the march toward ultimate victory. The Dark Wave begins!"

He brushed the back of his hand along her cheek and the curve of her neck, resting his fingers on the back of her head. "Hmm. Such enthusiasm. Care to celebrate with me after this is over?"

Her eyes sparked. "I was counting on celebrating all night long," She gave him a long, deep kiss, caressing his tongue with hers.

Arm in arm, they ascended the steps. Two wizards wearing deep purple robes emblazoned with glowing red runes followed them. The summer wind murmured through the nearby trees. Through their branches, Berek glimpsed the lights of Eleth-Anor in the distance, brilliant against the sparkle of the Great Sea in the moonlight.

Berek savored a deep breath of night air, eyes roaming over the scene. Two platoons of Skullheads prowled the nearby forest and a squad of hobgoblin commandos guarded the base of the rocky hillock. The four Dark Elves stood at attention at the four points of the compass.

A fine night, he mused. *It is the beginning of the end for the followers of the King of Forests, the World-crafter, the Lord of Stone, the Thorn-crowned God, and all their incompetent allies.*

The wizards bowed. "All is in readiness, Lord Berek and Lady Adina. We can begin at your command."

Berek inclined his head. "Please, begin."

The mages raised their hands, chanting in dissonant chorus. Six flashes of pink light flared from the narrow box. The top flew off with a bang and landed at Berek's feet.

The wizards pulled on steel gauntlets and withdrew six black, oblong stones, then laid them carefully on a nearby table. Silvery, eldritch sigils writhed on their ebony surfaces.

The wizards bowed again to Berek and Adina and joined hands with theirs. Berek concentrated, focusing his magic power and feeding it to Adina.

She, in turn, added her own energy and passed it along to the mages. He then joined the wizards in a low, martial chant, full of promise of blood, looting, rape and death. Adina lent her high soprano voice in a paean of torment and despair.

Berek's vision became misty and dark, almost as if he stood in a tunnel of deep grey fog. The symbols on the stones flared as bright as day, then the rocks melted and warped into shimmering strips of blackness darker than any night. Berek, Adina and the wizards threw their hands up into the air and the tendrils shot off into the sky.

All his arcane power vanished and Berek saw spots before his eyes. He wavered on his feet.

"Careful," Adina whispered, gripped his hand. "We can't show any weakness."

She pressed a tiny vial into his hand. He uncorked it and downed the contents, feeling a wave of warmth and energy. His weariness receded and he shook his head.

He doubted if he could have conjured enough magic to light a candle now, but he didn't care. He envisioned the dark bands of evil soaring out into the night to carry out their glorious assignment. A sudden euphoria filled him and he pulled Adina close. She shivered with delight.

"It begins," he said.

***

Hannah Lervion reined in her pony at the top of the hill. The morning sunshine glowed in the mists of the forest far below, beyond the nearby city of Sentinel. Her eyes drifted past the woods, resting on the lowlands of Torosc and the town of Haleville, not five miles away.

She frowned. The Torosci town didn't concern her as much as the multitude of tents and pavilions near the walls. Smoke curled up into the warm, humid air. Metal glinted.

"Well," remarked a woman's voice to her left. "It looks like they're preparing for something."

Lady Cassandra Martin leaned her hands on her saddle pommel. Two wrist daggers gleamed on her forearms and a slim silver wand lay tucked in a velvet sash at her waist. Dark brown hair reminded Hannah of cherry wood.

Hannah bit her lip. "Agreed, Excellency. I'm just not sure why. It could be a training exercise or something else entirely."

"That doesn't look like a training force," remarked a deeper baritone on Hannah's other side. "Unless their training includes siege equipment. Believe me, I can tell."

Hannah smiled up at a dark-haired human astride a stallion next to her pony. He wore plate mail under a plain grey hauberk with the emblem of a falcon on the right breast. A longsword with an amethyst in the pommel hung at his hip. He rested a mailed hand on the crowned helm hanging from his saddle.

"Even from this distance, Lord Justin?" Hannah asked.

He looked down at her, eyes twinkling. "I am skilled in the arts of mass warfare, you know."

"If the warfare is against a turkey leg," Lady Cassandra retorted with a wink at her husband. Hannah grinned.

Justin Martin sat straighter in his saddle. "Ah. That reminds me: when is lunch?"

Cassandra rolled her eyes and turned back to the Torosci forces by the city. "I rest my case."

The trio sat on their steeds among the trees on the hilltop. They could observe without being seen, as long the Torosci didn't have some form of magical reconnaissance.

"You see how the darker structures are grouped near the city?" Justin noted in a more serious tone. "And the variety of larger forms moving near them? I'll bet those are draft animals, or maybe even ogres, to pull the siege equipment. There aren't any towers, so I'm thinking more along the lines of mangonels or scorpions, maybe medium ballistae. Nothing too heavy, but then, Sentinel is not very big."

"You think they're after Sentinel?" Hannah replied, peering at the area he mentioned. "I doubt it. That would be an act of open war. Besides, the twenty thousand people in Sentinel are nothing to sneeze at. And the city has stone walls."

"Yes," noted Cassandra, "but magical ammunition can make all the difference. Granted, Sentinel is not without its resources, but I see Justin's point. The formation is unusual."

Motion near the base of their hill caught Hannah's eye and she gripped the handle of Shriek. She relaxed when three light cavalry in mottled camouflage colors cantered up to her.

A blonde Elven woman saluted. "Lord Justin, Lady Cassandra, Captain Lervion, the scouts have reported back."

"What have they seen?" asked Cassandra.

The officer looked grim. "Another column rides from Carville to join the force at Haleville. They will arrive by tomorrow morning."

"How many?" Justin asked, stroking his chin.

"Estimates are about eight hundred."

Hannah frowned. "Two battalions." Added to the force already before them, it meant almost two thousand.

What are they up to?

"There is something else," the officer added. "Our dwarven rangers report underground activity in significant numbers."

"Underground?" The hairs on Hannah's neck prickled. "What kind of activity?"

The scout's lavender eyes met hers. "Dark Elves."

Hannah shot a look at Justin. His eyes grew hard and he nodded.

"We have to get back to Sentinel." Hannah gathered the reins and addressed the scout. "Replace the current scout team with a fresh one. We want someone watching, night and day. And make sure that at least one Dwarf and one Elf are in each team."

With another salute, the troops trotted their mounts back down the hill towards the forest.

"Dark elves," Cassandra murmured. "We all know they don't move unless they're confident in the odds of victory — and they don't send less than a regiment in any case. Add to that two thousand Torosci troops, with siege equipment, mustering at the border near a major Gorostoli town. They're not bothering to hide it. Why? They have to know we're tipped off by now."

"They're not worried," Justin said slowly, taking up his reins as well. "They don't think it matters."

Hannah took another look at the encampment and her heart clenched with a sudden, unnamed dread. She voiced her fear. "Could there be a Skull Gate in Haleville?"

Justin shook his head. "You would know better than I, Captain. From what you told us, all the destroyed Skull Gates are elsewhere. Besides, don't the Ja'al take great pains to conceal them? Three thousand troops isn't exactly subtle."

"Then let's pray there isn't." Hannah took up the reins. "We have to meet with Caridan and Caria and report back to the authorities in Sentinel, fast."

Hannah spurred her mount and rode back to Sentinel with the Martins. The unnamed dread followed close behind.

***

"Colonel Cintos has arrived my lord."

Zanilor, High Priest of the Ja'al, nodded to the orderly. "Show him in."

The servant returned with a slim human man in red and black livery of the Servants of Neralia. A mace and a handaxe hung from his belt and his boots were polished to a mirror shine.

Zanilor accepted his bow by inclining his head. "Colonel. You and your regiment are most welcome."

Kalar Cintos' black eyes glinted. "We are ready to take part in the great endeavor, Lord Zanilor."

"Excellent." Zanilor strode to a side table.

Morning sunlight streamed into the room through spired glass windows, shining on his throne and the pristine marble pillars. Zanilor gestured and a light flashed from a glass cube on the table. A listing of military units, support groups, and other assets sprang up in the air before him. He touched one of the lines and it flared golden.

With another wave of his hand, the listing vanished. "There now. With the addition of Ildrisana's division, three Skullhead Legions, the three Hobgoblin brigades, the Ogres, and the army of the Goblin King Furot, and the Bladefang Kaftu clan, that brings the total to... just about twenty-three thousand."

He watched as Cintos took in the hall with a mixture of trepidation and envy. "Something wrong, Colonel?"

Cintos' eyes drifted back to Zanilor. "The place looks very different."

Zanilor's eyebrows rose. "You mean from when Margoth owned it? Yes, it does look better, doesn't it? I cleared out all her moldy claptrap, spruced it up and added some enhancements."

Cintos smirked. "The atmosphere is a lot better. How did you get control of it?"

"Possession is nine-tenths of the law, Colonel. The old bitch didn't need it any more after Eleandir blew the shit out of her last summer at Hillton, so I just moved in."

Cintos slowly nodded. "I understand you were there at the battle."

Zanilor's mind flew back to that day on the hill near the lake, when he and the rest of Zhinia Margoth's Army of Liberation watched the duel between the lich princess and the Grey Riders. He remembered his elation when Margoth slew all but one of the Riders with some forgotten, hellish witchery, then his creeping apprehension as Andyn Eleandir had placed the hated Crown of Saint Alyssa on her head. He felt anew the disbelief when one simple half-elven Verian priestess had used that Christian relic to methodically take apart the Terror of the South, one of the most feared sorceresses of ancient times.

He suppressed a shudder. Verian and Christianity, working together. It turned his stomach.

"Yes," he said briskly. "Margoth, for all her power, was an arrogant idiot. She underestimated the power of the prophecy of the Song of the Grey Riders and took Eleandir too lightly. We will not make the same mistake."

He beckoned and they strode down the audience hall to another passage, then emerged through a side door into the forest. The filtered afternoon sunlight shone down through the trees onto teeming masses of soldiery in a variety of livery. Tents, lean-to's and pavilions clustered in orderly arrangements as far as he could see. The air rang with the sound of hammers on metal, voices in a dozen tongues, and the growls of fell-beasts.

Odors of roasting meat and nutty ale wafted in their direction as Zanilor and Cintos wandered down the makeshift boulevards, heading towards the center of the camp. A trio of priestesses of Gudarta clad in revealing leather outfits bowed to them as they passed. An iron box rested at their feet, throbbing with purple light.

Cintos grinned at the priestesses, who gave him alluring glances in return. He nodded at the box. "I see that the first installment is ready."

Zanilor smirked. "Only the finest for our guests."

They halted near the center of the camp. Zanilor allowed himself a contented sigh. "Beautiful, isn't it?"

Colonel Cintos hooked his thumbs in his sword belt. "Impressive, my lord, truly impressive."

A massive structure of bones and skulls arched overhead to a height of thirty feet, wide enough at its base to permit two carts side by side. At the apex of the arch, a fanged skull gaped at them.

"Our orders?" Cintos murmured.

"Link up with the Army of Death at the gap between Athor and North Corner. Then drive all the way to Hillton and Oakmoor."

"What about the garrisons in the local towns? They could slow us down. Don't forget Hanford in Forester, Sarith in Sun Plains and Jalek Dorn. They were quite the thorn in Margoth's side a year ago."

"Don't worry about the minor lordlings. The Kaftu are well-prepared to deal with them if they choose to sally forth. And we can always burn down Forester again, this time with the Hanfords and their brats inside it."

Cintos chuckled, clasping his hands behind his back to gaze up at the Skull Gate. "You are favored by the gods, Lord Zanilor. You managed to keep this one intact."

"Having decoys helps."

They stood without speaking. Zanilor basked in the martial splendor around him.

Kalar Cintos gave him a speculative look. "When?"

Zanilor smiled but didn't answer.

✳✳✳

Phillip, Sovereign King of Deran and Prince of the House of Kalar, stared at the polished disk of platinum set in the floor of the circular tower room. The fading daylight shone through the windows, glinting off seven silver pedestals arranged evenly around the perimeter of the disk. Each one looked like a slender candleholder, except that the top bore a small oblong ring of silver.

His eyes drifted to the view. From here, the tallest tower of the palace, he saw the whole of Oakmoor spread out below him. The day had been marvelously clear, with few clouds. On such a day, he could see all the way to Saint Martin's Town.

The thought of Father Edward filled him with sadness and he sighed.

"I'm sure Cardinal Williams will be a fine successor," he said to the empty chamber. He smoothed the front of his navy tabard, emblazoned with the arms of his House: a cross and crown under three stars.

Light footsteps behind him made him turn. A dark-haired woman in her middle-thirties with bright blue eyes smiled at him, lifting the hem of her gown to make it up the last step. Behind her, a young, dark-haired Royal Guard carried a box of dark wood with gold chasing.

"Just lay it there, please, Kimberley," she said to the young woman, who did as she was told.

"Will there be anything else, Highness?"

"No thank you, Lieutenant. I will ring for you when we're done. Please apply the locks and screening charms as you leave."

The soldier departed and Queen Ahlana glided to Phillip's side to kiss him soundly. "Stop fretting."

"Who says I'm fretting?"

"Your eyes say it."

Ahlana patted his shoulder and opened the box, handing him a small mirror with four blue gems around the frame. He inserted the mirror in the first of the holders.

"I have a few things to fret about," he added as they installed the other mirrors.

"I agree. But fretting never made things better," Ahlana said, snapping the last of them into place. "Let's see what the others say."

"Fair enough."

Ahlana pulled back her wide sleeves and raised her hands over her head. She closed her eyes and murmured soft words. A shimmering net of iridescent colors leaped up in a dome at the edge of the room and reached up to the ceiling. In an eyeblink, they were enshrouded in a hemisphere of colors.

Ahlana pointed at the first mirror. "King Marcus Delacroix of Astarel, I entreat you to answer."

The blue gems on the mirror flashed and she pointed at each of the mirrors in turn, naming a different person each time.

"Emperor Brion Aluin of Terenai…Duke Roger Kosorovsk of Rokon… High Matriarch Jolene Perez of Eldir… Prime Minister Henry Tiller of Evendale… King Jokadram Deoborin of Merdail."

With each name, the gemstones flashed. They waited.

"I'm not sure how they'll take the news from the Grey Riders," Phillip mused.

Now Ahlana's cheery demeanor turned more somber. "Neither am I."

Soft pinging sounds echoed in the room. Each mirror's surface flashed with an image of a different person. At a whispered word from the Queen, the images popped into life-size, translucent copies hovering above the platinum disk.

When all six images stood before him, Phillip bowed low. "Thank you for answering our request."

The images all bowed in return: young, blond Marcus of Astarel; Brion Aluin and his stunning Empress Beldryn; the aged Duke of Rokon; the small, slender, black-eyed Matriarch of Eldir; Henry Tiller of Evendale, smiling jovially as always and the Dwarven King of Merdail and his auburn-haired Queen Rikkeya.

"Thank you for hosting this time," said Brion.

"Glad to do it, Your Majesty," replied Ahlana with her trademark smile.

Jokadram lifted his chin. "Since this isn't our usual day for council, I'm assuming it isn't something routine."

Phillip shook his head. "No, it isn't. And you probably won't like what I have to tell you."

In as few words as possible, he related the story of Brandi and Megan Alenar and their discoveries while enslaved to the Ja'al. He finished with Melinor's conclusion that George Oxbridge had figured out a way to lock a Celestial Gate and then stood silent.

The faces of the other rulers were a study. Brion and Beldryn glanced at each other but said nothing. Rikkeya's jaw tightened and Jokadram's eyes were stormy. Duke Roger stroked his beard, eyes hooded. Henry Tiller blankly stared back at him, Jolene Perez stared down at something far away, eyes distant. King Marcus just looked shocked.

"Is this even feasible?" Marcus finally choked out. "I'm no wizard, but even I know that generating enough power to hold a space-time portal closed against all the protections the Elohir have to offer… well, it's mind-boggling."

"I agree," Roger Kosorovsk rumbled. "The treasuries of the Ja'al would have had to increase ten-fold just to manage a tithe of what you're describing."

Beldryn folded her hands at her waist. "On the surface, it would seem so, Your Grace, but don't forget how active the Jeredan Navy has been in recent years. And we all know that the Dark Lands have been recruiting free-lance mercenaries quite heavily for the last few years and sending them into the wilderness. They have been bringing in some costly prizes, from what our agents tell us. Couple that with the new taxes and they just might have the resources."

"But that's an unspeakable level of power," Jolene interjected. "They would have to have a huge amount of help to do that. I doubt if even all those realms working together could pull it off."

Ahlana met Phillip's eyes. "The new Papal Nuncio sent us a letter yesterday and he will be with us tomorrow. He thinks that the Ja'al had help. Infernal help."

Now all of the other rulers gaped at them.

"But, but that's a —" Rikkeya sputtered.

"Direct violation of the Ban!" Duke Roger thundered, striking a fist into his palm.

Brion Aluin nodded slowly. "Clearly. But based on the nature of the offense, it makes perfect sense."

The other rulers stared at him. He took a deep breath. "If you're planning on infiltrating daemon teams into our world to wreak havoc, then providing clandestine magical assistance in creating locking devices would be a small price to pay, wouldn't it? What can the Elohir do? Punish them for it? They'd have to break the chains holding their Gates closed, then help run down all the Infernal spies running around loose. They'd hardly have time to make new Gates or punish those responsible. I don't know if any of you have spoken to an Elohir about the War of Sundering, but it's not a pretty picture… and that's what they'd have to do to punish the Fallen."

Henry Tiller snapped his fingers. "Well, now this all falls into place! No wonder we've been seeing so much internal unrest and disruptive factions, so many arguments and intimidation. They've been trying to distract us from this very thing so that we couldn't interfere."

"But we have been interfering, Prime Minister," Ahlana noted. "All of us.

Our freelance teams have managed to destroy multiple Skull Gates and the materials for at least five more, plus ruin several decoys. The insurrectionist movements in our lands haven't resulted in popular uprisings – to the contrary, our information indicates that the common folk are getting fed up with all the agitators."

"With this new information, though," Jolene mused, "we will have to take steps. That much is certain."

Phillip straightened to his full height. "Are we agreed then, that the current situation is a clear and present danger to all our nations, as defined in the Northern Alliance Charter, and by extension, its treaty with the Kingdom of Merdail?"

A chorus of agreement arose.

"Then, as outlined in the charter," Phillip continued. "We will initiate a mutual exchange of military attaches with long-range Sending Mirrors. We will also take the following steps: all military branches on high alert, call-up of all militias, industries placed on war footing, academies and universities to divert their work in support of a war effort, and stockpiling of mundane and magical goods and resources. We will be coordinating with neighboring realms on joint task force composition and command structure."

The assembled rulers nodded.

"We should probably meet daily from now on," Roger suggested. "We can't let a day go by without tracking the Ja'al devilry."

Jokadram and Rikkeya volunteered to host the next meeting. Phillip and Ahlana bowed to the other sovereigns.

Before the images flickered out, Brion held up a hand. "Thank you, Phillip and Ahlana, for taking charge of the situation. We know that it has cost you."

Beldryn favored them with her luminous smile. "We should find time to meet when this is all over. I miss our visits."

Ahlana beamed. "I will look forward to it, Beldryn. I miss them too."

The images of the Emperor and Empress vanished, leaving the King and Queen of Deran alone in the twilight.

Ahlana gestured and the iridescent dome vanished.

Phillip stared absently out the window at the sunset. "We should protect the Riders' families. Now that the die is cast, they will likely send the Shrikes or Bloodswords after them."

Ahlana put an arm around his waist, nestling into his side. "Carine Del Rio wants to go to Astarel to be with Buck Bydecy's father and brother, so I sent her. We can ask King Marcus for some of his troops to assist."

Phillip nodded. "The Lomin and Eleandir families have ample protections but we should alert Colonel Eleandir and Matriarch Lomin anyway. I'm worried about the Cabots. The sons are in places where we can protect them, but the parents?"

"How about that young woman who helped Megan Alenar? And her beau? From what Andyn tells me, they are quite capable."

"Excellent idea. And we should send Gorlak down to Evendale."

She looked up at him. "Gorlak? Why? Connor's mother has ample resources."

His eyes narrowed. "Evendale is the smallest of the Alliance nations and a perfect target for an initial round of mischief. They are a tough nut to crack, but if the Ja'al loose daemon agents on them, it will be dicey for a while."

Ahlana rested her head on his shoulder. "Good. It will give him a purpose. I hear he's been quite despondent since Edward's death."

Phillip held her wordlessly.

"I know Edward is praying for us," she whispered.

"We can use everything he can give us," he replied.

Chapter Twenty-Two – Rumors of War

Melissa the Elohir ran a comb through her golden hair and inspected her reflection in the water. The rush and hiss of the nearby waterfall filled the glade and birds chirped in the nearby willows.

She spread her wings out behind her and regarded her reflection in the pond. Her tan-tipped white feathers fairly glowed. She smiled, satisfied.

A woman needs to look her best for her man.

Not that Coloman would really mind if her hair was a mess or her tunic wrinkled. He would probably grin at her and then put his own hair into a similar state of disarray and they would have a good laugh out of it.

"A few more days, Cole," she murmured, tucking her ivory comb into her shoulder bag. Thoughts of time with her husband made her heart beat faster and her smile softened. Her ten-year tour of duty on Damora — while a short time by Elohir standards — put a strain on their marriage. His twice-yearly visits helped. Now that she was going to get a year off, the wait was more bearable.

Best make sure the Gate is in working order. It won't do to have a glitch just before I come home.

With a little leap and beat of her wings, she drifted over the pond and alighted on a cluster of boulders next to the waterfall. She waved her hand. The curtain of water parted and she landed on a stone shelf beyond it. The waterfall resumed its normal flow behind her.

A passage behind the waterfall curved back into the rock. Barely perceptible symbols glittered on the floor, roof and walls, tracing a pattern of silvery letters along her way. She padded to the end of the passage and stopped at a solid rock wall.

A trio of bright orange beams traced over her body from tiny gems hidden in seams in the rock. The lights snapped off, to be replaced by twin blue shafts from the floor and a pair of green rays from the ceiling. She extended her Second Sight and mentally activated an entry code.

She sang a long phrase in Celestial and the wall melted away. She stepped into the massive cavern beyond. With a rippling sound, the wall grew back into place behind her. Three spheres of light glowed high above, near the ceiling, casting a pale glow. A rack with her armor and shield stood against the right-hand wall.

Melissa gazed at the towering, triangular frame of white metal that dominated the center of the chamber. The area inside the triangle showed a night sky and a spangled web of stars. A circle of Celestial runes sparkled on the uneven, rocky floor beneath her feet, surrounding the triangle. Melissa strolled around the structure, her fingers brushing symbols etched in gold on the frame struts. At her touch, a series of numbers and equations danced in her mind's eye. She knelt near the floor symbols, checking to make sure security measures remained intact.

She ran through calculations in her head and smiled. *Excellent. Ready for use.*

Then her senses prickled and she froze. Somewhere beyond time and space, *something* vibrated with a malevolent turbulence. The universe suddenly seemed wrong.

What in Heaven's name...?

The essence of space-time flexed and shuddered. The air vibrated in a clangor of disjointed gravitational waves. Nausea rushed through her. A spike of pain hit her in the temples and she staggered backwards, one hand on her head. Magical alarms went off, filling the chamber with a series of chirps and bells.

The wall behind her trembled and she spun, whipping out her blade. The blade flared blue light and she touched a hand to her chest. Three concentric spheres of gold, silver and copper light sprang up around her.

The rock wall vibrated, then parted. Six tendrils of inky blackness shot in through the gap and writhed into the cavern. Melissa's senses tingled wildly.

What is this?

She crouched, expecting attack, but the tendrils shot at the gate. Too late, Melissa sensed their intent. She sent a shattering wave of magical power at them. One of the tendrils burst into a shower of ashy dust but the others wrapped around the triangular structure. She leaped forward, slashing one tendril in half. The other four welded into place, forming dead-black undulating straps over the triangle. The starfield wavered and winked out.

To her horror, the structure's white metal surface became mottled and shot through with fingers of darkness, as if the Celestial Gate had become infected with some kind of disease. Then the three lights in the chamber winked out.

Melissa shifted to infra-red vision, then ultraviolet. The dark straps on the Gate shimmered in the latter spectrum.

Unable to believe what she had just seen, Melissa cast several detection and probing spells at the Gate. The Gate remained dead. Her heart sank.

Not possible!

She tried another set of spells designed to restart the Gate from an inert state. Nothing happened. She slashed the dark bands with her sword, but the severed ends simply reconnected to their nearest fellows.

Her nausea now twisted into fear — not fear for herself, but for the world of Damora.

She set her jaw, then sang a short phrase. A luminous sphere burst into being just below the ceiling. The scene looked even worse in the light.

Melissa flung off her clothes and marched to the armor rack. In seconds, she pulled on chainmail leggings and a byrnie. With a tap of her finger on each armor piece, the ties and straps automatically tightened to fit her body. She slipped on her boots, grabbed her shield and strapped her sword belt on.

She gave one last look at the cavern, her stomach in knots. The black bands remained locked onto the stricken Gate.

Melissa flew to the rock wall, dissolved it and raced through the passage beyond, bursting through the waterfall. Pushing herself to immense velocity, she raced over the treetops, heading towards the Dragonspine Mountains in the distance.

God, please let this be isolated to my Gate.

She flew at breakneck speed, not worrying about the birds and beasts she startled on the way, nor even the hobgoblin war party slinking through the forest. They lifted spears and raised astonished, terrified eyes. She flashed past without slowing. Swooping up, she soared past Whitehorse Peak, then farther into the Wilderness, finally stopping at a flat-topped mountain.

She glided down into a run, scrambling to a stop near a large boulder. An Elohir male alighted on the ground at almost the same time, armored in bronze plate mail, his halberd sizzling with amber fire. He raised garnet eyes to her.

"Simon!" she gasped.

"What happened?" her brother asked, putting a hand on the boulder.

She shook her head. "No time. We have to get to the Gate."

He sang a lilting song and the boulder faded away, revealing a circular hole in the ground. Both Elohir leaped up and floated down a shaft into a huge chamber hewn from the rock.

The pair stared at a curved, spired Gate in the middle of a large pond of water in the cavern. Straps of night coiled around it. Sickly green blotches speckled its blue metal surface. The space within it showed no starfield.

Melissa felt sick.

Simon's eyes blazed. "Does this have to do with the Ja'al and George Oxbridge?" he growled.

She nodded, stomach churning. "I'm afraid it does."

Simon stared at the Gate for a few heartbeats, eyes sparkling like diamonds in the shadows, then shook his head in frustration. "Nothing! No signal. I can think of only one reason someone would want to close the Gates: to prevent our people from entering Damora. And that means that someone wants to prevent us from interfering. Three guesses as to who is involved."

Melissa ground her teeth. "We have to make contact with the other Wardens and get to the armory. Let's check the Summoning Gate at Twinspire first."

He unfurled his wings and leapt upward. Melissa followed him up the entry shaft and out into the bright daylight. Brother and sister soared into the air and banked to the southwest, heading towards Shadow Lake.

Her mind spun through a myriad of scenarios as they shot through the clouds and sunny skies. *This has to be connected to the items recovered by the Riders and the other freelance parties. But they can't be this numerous! How would they have gotten so many into action?*

As they neared Twinspire Peak, she saw several figures flitting around near the Gate. Simon shot her a grim look. Her sword snapped out and her shield burned with silver radiance.

"Balris," she said as she alighted on the ground near the gazebo. "I might have known."

"Honored as always to see you, Lady Melissa. Lord Simon." The blond daemon smirked and bowed, his hands spread out at his sides. His white scale-mail armor glittered with a frosty sheen and he furled his dark purple bat wings.

Goat hooves crunched on pebbles and rocks as two hulking daemons took their places at Balris' side. Each stood at least eight feet tall. Dead-black, pig-like eyes glared at Melissa and Simon from fleshy, dark orange faces, fangs gleaming white against purple lips. Ruffs of white horns protruded from hairless skulls. They wore black brigandine with iron studs and carried two war hammers apiece. The pommels of their weapons were human skulls. Black and purple striped bat wings ruffled in the summer breeze.

Behind them, two other daemons prowled, sleek female figures encased entirely in blue-black chainmail. The wicked points of dark spines shone on vambraces and greaves. Glowing red eyes glittered from behind chainmail veils attached to black spired helmets. Each carried a pair of red-bladed scimitars. They flexed muscular shoulders and double bat wings of dark green unfurled. Dragon tails lashed the air.

Simon made a face. "Deathhammers and War Fiends? Your salary has increased of late, Balris."

Balris raised golden cat eyes to Simon. "I earned every copper, I assure you."

Melissa glanced at the Gate. Black straps entwined the gazebo. Blackened and withered foliage sagged nearby.

"So, this is your plan?" she asked. "Bind all the Gates? Don't think we won't figure out how to open them again. And then there will be hell to pay, literally."

Balris straightened, hands on his hips. "Will there? I don't think so. At least, no help will come in time to stop the Dark Wave."

Melissa felt a chill of fear. She shook her head, trying to keep her shock and disbelief hidden.

Balris took a couple of steps back, a sardonic smile on his face. "Yes, you realize it now, don't you? How does feel to be marooned on Damora with no help?"

Simon moved forward, but the other daemons blocked the way. The Deathhammers grumbled low in their throats.

Balris gave another mocking bow. "I leave you for the last time, Lord and Lady of the Elohir. Farewell… or, in this case, fare ill! This world will now be ruled by the Fallen and their servants, the Ja'al. The Dark Wave begins. The time of Light has ended!"

With that, he soared into the air, made an obscene gesture, and darted away.

Simon's hand flashed out and a whipcord of light snaked out after him, but one of the War Fiends slashed it in half.

Melissa took wing alongside her brother. The daemons followed suit in response.

"Just like old times," Simon said, waving a hand. Concentric spheres of silver and gold surrounded him. Melissa's shields flared to life.

The War Fiends laughed and clashed their blades together. Dark mist swirled around them and now four Fiends hovered in mid-air. Without even a pause, the Fallen Ones charged. Melissa and Simon split apart, heading in opposite directions.

Melissa shot up into the sky and called to her sword. A blinding flash of light dispelled the illusory Fiend chasing her.

That will make it a little easier…

She banked left and right, then looped over backwards. The War Fiend followed, casting bolts of purple fire at her. The plasma bolts detonated on her shields. The Deathhammer roared and a wave of sonic energy flung Melissa off course. She churned the air with her wings, righting herself.

The Deathhammer charged, swinging. She deflected one weapon with her shield and parried the other with her blade. She bit her lip. Blocking the hammers felt like she was trying to stop a charging ogre with one arm.

The War Fiend darted in, slashing. Melissa danced out of the way, kicking the Fiend in the side. The daemon lurched. Melissa dove.

Knowing the Fallen Ones pursued her, she banked down at the defiled Gate. When the structure was close enough to touch, she veered aside. The daemons cursed and she heard a loud thud.

She spared a glance over her shoulder. The War Fiend fluttered out of the way of the gazebo, missing it by a foot and careening off into the nearby shrubs. The slower Deathhammer lost its balance and rammed into the side of the gazebo, cracking a marble pillar. It shouted an obscenity at her and hurled a hammer.

The weapon shot out at her with an arrow's speed. She dodged, but it looped around back at her. She raised her shield.

The hammer hit like a catapult stone. She hurtled backward, her outer shield winking out. Her sword flared blue and a warning bell sounded. She dove again. The War Fiend's blades whistled through the air where she had been.

The Fiend screamed and hot gouts of flame hit Melissa's magic screens. She backed in mid-air, singing another enchantment to dispel the fire. The War Fiend thrust forth a hand and all the spikes on a vambrace lanced out at her. Melissa beat her wings and corkscrewed in flight. The spikes hummed past her, the air sizzling in their wake.

The Deathhammer now lumbered back up towards her, wings churning the air. The War Fiend charged, driving Melissa back with a flurry of blows, right into the Deathhammer's path.

Melissa gritted her teeth, then shouted a Word. A sphere of white light exploded, hurling the daemons back. They spun and swirled downwards, then righted themselves and surged upwards again.

She soared upward, heading towards her brother. To her relief, she saw him slash through the armor of his Deathhammer. The daemon gave a horrid bellow and faltered, spewing purple ichor. The War Fiend leaped in, raining blows at him. He parried methodically with his halberd. The clash of metal echoed off the canyons and mountainsides.

Simon's eyes flickered to meet hers. Melissa smiled and nodded.

Her opponents drew close. She loosed a pair of stinging bolts of electricity. The daemons dodged and she shot up into the sky. They pursued. She flashed past Simon as he hovered in midair, battling the War Fiend.

She focused a telepathic message to him and he nodded, gritting his teeth against the onslaught. His Deathhammer opponent surged at him, swinging lustily. He danced out of the way, kicking the War Fiend in mid-stroke.

Melissa banked and curved through the sky. The Fallen gave chase. With a burst of speed, she spun and turned back towards her brother. Rolling in mid-flight to her back, she cast five golden balls of flame with her shield-hand. The War Fiend slashed through two of them while the Deathhammer simply powered through the explosions with a roar of pain and fury.

Melissa shot down. Simon fought the daemons below and to her left.

She neared them. Two stinging pains hit her wings and she winced but kept her course.

"Now!" she shouted.

Melissa corkscrewed away and Simon shot up into the sky, his opponents in hot pursuit. The Elohir siblings flew towards each other.

Too late, the daemons realized their peril. They tried to slow as the two Elohir shot past. The daemons swirled away to avoid colliding with each other, cursing.

Melissa and Simon traded opponents and laid into them.

Melissa slashed Simon's War Fiend through the legs and bashed the wounded Deathhammer in the face with her shield. She banked into a tight turn. The Deathhammer reeled back and righted itself. It swung twice with its hammers. She deflected the blows, then swung her sword on top of the nightmare head. Her blade flashed blue and split the monstrosity's head in two.

Not waiting for the inevitable detonation, she whirled on the wounded War Fiend. The daemon hissed and raged, backpedaling in midair. It slashed and stabbed. Melissa blocked and parried, driving it back.

The Fiend shrieked. A cloud of red flame surrounded it. Melissa drew back.

She sang a short phrase and the cloud vanished. With an echoing shout, the Fiend pointed at Melissa. The spines on its armor vibrated and shot out like arrows.

This could hurt, Melissa thought, gritting her teeth. She threw her shield in front of her face. The spikes thumped into her shield and three transfixed her forearm. Searing pain lanced through her and she struggled to keep her arm up.

The daemon laughed in triumph and lashed out with its deadly red scimitars. Melissa spun and slashed. The fight rapidly devolved into a whirlwind of blades, bursts of magic, and ringing metal.

Melissa saw an opening. Gritting her teeth, she slammed her shield into the Fiend's face. The pain in her arm doubled, but the War Fiend reeled. She spun, her sword lashing out. The daemon's head and body parted ways. Both gracefully fell to earth.

Melissa panted, watching the remnants explode into flame and bones.

"You okay?" Simon hovered next to her.

She nodded. "Did you get the Fallen?"

"Beheaded one and cut the other into pieces."

Fragments of daemon burned in the tall grass near the gazebo.

"We'd better put that out," she managed, feeling dizzy. "No sense in causing a forest fire."

Her arm hurt unbearably. Simon guided her down to the ground, then yanked the spikes out.

She bit her lip to avoid screaming and spots swam before her eyes. Her arm looked like it had transformed into cracked, hot lava rock. She placed a hand on the injury and Simon did the same. Golden light glowed and her flesh slowly returned to normal. Her head spun from the effort, but at least now her arm merely felt sore.

She tossed aside her vambrace, which was a total loss.

Simon sat on a nearby boulder. He lowered his head and now she noticed that he bled from a dozen lacerations. His left arm hung slack at his side.

"Simon! Why didn't you say something?"

He waved a hand. "It was only a flesh wound."

She shook her head. "In three hundred years, you still haven't learned, have you?"

She laid her hands on his injuries, releasing healing power, watching the injuries fade and vanish.

"There now."

"Thanks, big sister."

"You owe me. Again."

"We'll see about that."

Brother and sister stamped out the small brush fires, conjuring water to extinguish the larger ones. As they watched the last vestiges of steam curl up into the air, Melissa put a hand on her hip and brushed the hair out of her eyes. The shimmering dark bands on the gazebo Gate mocked her.

"I'm sure some of the Gates are still open," she replied with a confidence she didn't feel. In her heart, she knew they were in dire straits. Balris wouldn't have dared to be so blunt unless he was certain of the outcome.

Simon shook his head. "We need to hold a War Council and try to contact Homeworld."

She nodded. "We're going to need help. *Damora* is going to need a lot of help."

He put his arm around her. She was suddenly, acutely aware that he also had a rotation home to Celestia. Thoughts of his Kelly probably weighed heavily on his mind.

"God will help us," she whispered.

Chapter Twenty-Three – To Rainbow Valley

Buck Bydecy capped his water skin and looped the strap over his saddle-bow. "How much farther to Marolpeth?"

A great golden dragon curled up on the hilltop raised his head. "A short ride, only an hour or so." He sniffed the air and frowned.

Buck didn't like the look of that. Anything that could worry Grandpa definitely worried him.

"Something wrong, Grandpa?" asked Dar, coming to his side.

Iron Thunder sniffed again and his eyes narrowed. He gently rested a massive claw against Dar's back.

"I am not sure, dear one," he replied, voice soft. "Something fell is in the air. I cannot tell what it is."

Buck shot a look at Andyn. She watched the dragon carefully.

"It's not anything you recognize?" she asked.

Grandpa shook his head. Andyn met Buck's eyes. She opened her mouth as if to speak, then closed it.

"We'd better get going then," suggested Khyron. "We should make the city just before twilight. Maybe Colonel Arkad will know something."

He swung into the saddle and Buck mounted Shadowbane.

"Wait." Grandpa sniffed the air and paced back and forth for a few seconds. Finally, he glared up at the blue sky and puffy clouds.

"The sky is too bright. We will be spotted easily," he said. "Fly low, just above the treetops."

"I don't like this," Connor whispered to Buck. "We won't be able to see very far ahead."

"Neither do I, but Grandpa is over six hundred years old," Buck reminded him. "We have to trust his instincts."

Eric activated Stealth and the hawk construct shot into the air, soaring high overhead.

"At least Eric can give us some advance warning," Connor said, spurring Phantom forward as Grandpa loped forward on the hilltop.

Buck urged Shadowbane to speed and the Riders lifted off with Iron Thunder in the center of their formation. He shot a glance at the golden dragon next to him.

So this is what it's like to fly with Dragon Riders? He mused. *I wish I could enjoy it more…*

They flew only a couple of dozen feet above the treetops with Eric in the lead and Dar right beside him. Buck kept his bow ready and eyes alert, seeking anything out of the ordinary.

He heard it before he saw anything: a sharp whistling sound far behind them followed by a bang. He twisted in the saddle. A glowing burst of pink fire rent the sky behind them — and then another. Eric's hand went up and Grandpa snarled.

Buck laid a magic arrow to his bowstring, the warhead sparkling with electricity. He heard another bang, then the blare of a horn up ahead. He raised his bow, heartbeat accelerating.

They soared through the air above the forest, yet nothing happened. Buck frowned, wondering if it were yet another Ja'al diversion.

Then more than two dozen flying creatures swarmed up from the forest below, just two hundred yards ahead. They appeared like a cross between a boar and an eagle. Wicked talons gripped spears, swords or axes. Dark grey wings tinged with red beat the air. Their hindquarters and legs were covered with dark leather armor. Fanged, pig-like snouts opened and they let out a chorus of squealing shrieks. Red eyes flared at the sight of the Riders.

Buck's heart leaped in his throat. *By the Earth Mother! What the hell are those things?*

He loosed two arrows in quick succession, hitting one beast in the leg and shoulder. The arrows sparked with miniature clouds of electricity when they hit. The creature screamed and fluttered down, crashing into the upper branches of a tree.

The Riders banked and split apart. Buck saw Andyn spray one of the creatures with a stream of fire darts. It lurched backward, then fluttered down towards the ground, lifeless. After about twenty yards, it exploded.

Buck growled a foul oath. *Daemons! Damn it!*

Two of the creatures swung towards him. He pulled up. A spearpoint pierced Shadowbane's barding and two sword blades pinged off Buck's armor. His pegasus let out a whinny of pain and Buck banked right. The creatures shot past.

He shoved his bow back in its case, sweeping out Khelios and swinging his shield up. The dwarven sword burned with golden fire, brighter than he had ever seen it.

Correction: he *had* seen it before, in a gully near a Skull Gate where he and the Riders almost lost their lives fighting the Fallen Ones.

"Come on, boy!" he shouted to his mount. He banked the other way.

The air above the trees looked like a maelstrom of windblown leaves, except the "leaves" were daemons, pegasus riders and one hopping-mad dragon. Buck dove straight towards Grandpa, then banked the other way. He cut an intercept course to a pair of daemons chasing Andyn. He slashed off one pig-head and shield-bashed the other daemon, sending it spinning into Grandpa's side. The dragon flicked his tail and slapped the daemon into the trees, where it exploded in a burst of flaming meat.

Two of the beasts dove down at Buck. He turned aside, only to find another pair charging him. Buck dove down again, then pulled up just above the trees. A daemon crunched into a treetop with a howl.

A sharp pain hit him in the back and Buck cried out in pain, turning Shadowbane. A daemon raced past under him, slashing the air with a hooked sword. Buck looped upside down, over and back, behind his pursuers. One of them spun in midair and hurled a javelin at him. The missile pinged off his shield.

Then all the daemons opened their mouths and hissed. Sheets of flame shot out from their snouts but Buck got his shield up in time. The fire curled around him.

Unfortunately, Shadowbane had no such shield. The pegasus screamed in pain as flames scorched his barding, setting his caparison aflame.

Buck hacked one daemon in two. Without missing a beat, he pulled Shadowbane right, then left. A luckless daemon didn't turn in time and he split its skull. It detonated as he shot past.

With his shield-hand, Buck undid the straps of Shadowbane's caparison and the flaming cloth fluttered down towards the forest. He pulled his mount up towards the cloud-mountains amid the bright blue sky.

He spared a glance behind him. His three pursuing daemons beat their wings and gave chase, snorting and shrieking. Then a great cloud of flame enveloped them. Three flaming corpses tumbled through the air and detonated. Grandpa blasted through their remnants.

Buck brought Shadowbane around again, swooping down towards his companions. Connor and a daemon raced along above the treetops in a running sword duel. His dancing sword fluttered in and out at the enemy like a deadly steel butterfly. As Buck watched, Connor's flaming sword and his animated blade found their mark. The daemon, floated down, trailing steaming ichor before bursting into flame.

Buck cast about all around him, up, down and to the sides, but no more daemons remained. Eric waved his hand again and pointed south. The Riders all followed him, accompanied by Grandpa.

They alighted in a meadow by a stream and Buck immediately hopped out of the saddle, reaching into his shoulder bag for a jar of healing ointment.

He drew in his breath sharply. Shadowbane bled from his side and his face and neck were scorched.

"It's okay, boy," he said in a soothing tone, popping the top off the jar. "I'm here. I'll take care of you."

The pegasus rolled his eyes and pawed the earth. Buck pulled up his mount's barding. A black, serrated spearhead had snapped off from the weapon shaft and remained embedded in the pegasus' side.

Buck marveled that Shadowbane could have taken him through the fight at all. He grasped the spearhead but a voice stopped him.

"Don't!" Andyn said. "He'll bleed to death. Let me help you."

He stopped short and she joined him.

"You stand ready with the ointment," she explained. "I'll pull it to the side little by little and you apply the medication. Then when we have most of it out, I'll give it a final tug."

He followed her directions and soon she yanked out the deadly point, dropping it in the grass. Shadowbane stood stock still until the end when he whinnied in protest and side-stepped. Buck brought him under control, speaking to him gently as Andyn applied ointment to his facial burns.

Andyn tapped Buck on the shoulder. "Now for you, sir," she said. "You're bleeding all over the forest."

He thought about protesting but knew from past experience that it was futile. He rested his arms on his saddle. Andyn unstrapped his backplate and moved it aside.

Now he felt the burn and sting of the wound.

"Good thing your armor is built the way it is," she remarked. "Your attacker got a sword point in between two bands, just under your shoulder blade. Didn't get a good thrust in."

Warmth flooded his back a second later and the pain receded. He moved his shoulder, wincing at the soreness.

"Thanks," he said, giving her a smile.

Andyn helped him with his straps. He gave her a quick kiss on the cheek. She bit her lip, eyes dancing, then slapped his shoulder armor and trotted off towards the others.

"No more of that for a while, eh, boy?" Buck stroked Shadowbane's nose. The pegasus nickered in response, tossing his head.

Grandpa stalked over to him. "Are you well?" he rumbled.

"Yes, Grandpa, we're fine thanks to Andyn and some medications."

"What were those things?" asked Connor, leading Phantom to join them. "I know they're daemons, but they're not like the ones we fought before. These things were fast, damned fast."

Khyron raised an eyebrow. "Pun intended?"

Connor grinned.

Dar shook his head. "Daemons of some kind. Beyond that?" he shrugged.

"There were so many of them," Eric noted.

No one said anything. Buck's stomach knotted.

"Which way now?" asked Andyn.

"Not up in the air, that's for sure," Khyron said. "Whoever was helping them had spotters on the ground with magical signaling devices. My guess is that they were a rapid-reaction force teamed up with another unit, maybe heavy infantry or something else requiring airborne support."

Grandpa nodded. "The highway is not far from here. It leads to Marolpeth."

Khyron nodded. "Good idea. Maybe we'll meet a road patrol and see if we can get a fast message back to the city. They need to be alerted."

"How far?" Buck asked. He peered into the sky beyond the trees.

"About twenty miles," Khyron answered. "The city is on the eastern side of a set of low hills with a sheer western face. You can't see it from here."

"Let's go," Connor said. "The sooner we alert them, the better."

They mounted up and rode northeast with Grandpa prowling alongside. No one talked and Buck kept his bow ready.

After about an hour, Grandpa halted. He raised his head and sniffed the air. "This is not good," he murmured.

"What isn't?" Khyron asked.

"Something burns. I smell death."

Without a word, they doubled the pace. Soon, they broke through the trees onto a highway on a ridge of cleared ground through the woods. Ahead of them, a massive throng of people and conveyances streamed in their direction. At the sight of them, the foremost members scrambled to a halt and gaped. An elven woman screamed.

Mounted elves lowered their lances and charged. Khyron cantered Zasural forwards, hands up and empty. "Hold! I am Lieutenant Colonel Demaris of the Imperial Army of Terenai. We come from the Northern Alliance."

The armored horsemen slowed and one of them trotted forward, lifting his visor. He inspected Khyron's badge.

"Welcome, Colonel. And in the company of a dragon! You are an excellent sight to behold."

"What's going on?" Buck demanded. His eyes roamed over the traffic. Composed mostly of elves, it seemed as if the population of a large city had suddenly decided to move to a different neighborhood.

A sudden thought hit him and he froze. "You're from Marolpeth!"

A deep voice rang out among the trees. "Yes, they were, though little is left of it."

A tall, dark-skinned winged man drifted out of the trees. His pinions were pure white with a black stripe down the center and he wore filigreed plate mail. A massive sword was strapped to his back and an odd-looking crossbow hung at his side. Bright emerald eyes swept over them as he landed on the road by the elven cavalry.

As one, the Riders bowed their heads and induced their pegasi to kneel.

"Hail, Heaven-sent," Grandpa said, gliding forward and inclining his own head. "I am Donnervassilianelikilandra of the Sunfire Clan."

The Elohir bowed low. "I am honored to meet you, Thunder-iron-first-tribe-wizard. Melissa has told me a lot about you."

"You know Melissa?" asked Andyn.

"We are colleagues. My name is Raymond."

"What happened, Excellency?" asked Eric.

Raymond glared back down the road towards Marolpeth. "Invasion. More than twenty-five thousand troops, mostly hobgoblins, ogres and trolls with some Ja'al Legionaries. They are assisted by over a hundred of the Fallen Ones."

Buck felt the blood leave his face. "What?"

"A hundred?" Grandpa asked in a weak voice. For the first time since Buck had known the dragon, Iron Thunder looked stunned.

Raymond nodded. "Yes. Skull Gate must have been opened some time ago, probably somewhere in the Wilderness."

Buck felt sick. He turned to his friends. Their eyes reflected horror, dismay and fear.

"We have noticed tribal movements along the border for some weeks now," the elven officer added. "It looked like they were getting ready to fight each other, just like they do every summer. Then, two days ago, they suddenly formed up into an army and marched on the city. Colonel Arkad sent out a regiment right away to guard refugees from the smaller towns, but they were outnumbered five to one. We retreated to Marolpeth. The enemy force kept growing. Yesterday he decided to evacuate to Tirevlan and is now fighting a rear-guard action to delay."

"How?" breathed Andyn. "I thought we had destroyed most of the Skull Gates."

Raymond gazed at her with emerald eyes. "Dear lady, that assumes we knew the total number constructed to begin with. Your tally may have only been for the Gates within the borders of the civilized nations."

"Marolpeth is lost," one of the other elves spat. "The daemons saw to that. We lost a lot of men to them."

"But why aren't there more Elohir?" Andyn asked in a plaintive voice. "Begging your pardon, Lord Raymond, but shouldn't your people be here to counteract the Fallen?"

Raymond opened his mouth, then closed it. He took in a deep breath. "Someone has found a way to bind our Gates shut and we haven't figured out how to open them back up again."

"Oxbridge!" Dar hissed.

"But how?" Connor growled. "Oxbridge had the formula and he died before he could give it to anyone."

"No."

They pivoted to Dar. "No," he repeated, eyes stormy. "We left with Megan's notes, but we don't know that his records were destroyed. As a matter of fact, the upper floor of his cottage was intact when we retreated."

Eric nodded slowly. "He was just paranoid enough to take his key materials with him to the cottage. I'm willing to bet the quick-reaction force from Carville went over the ruins with a fine-toothed comb. They've had a lot of time to sift through it all."

Raymond and Iron Thunder exchanged confused looks with the elves.

Buck sighed. This was getting them nowhere. "We'll go along with you to Tirevlan," he said. "If the Ja'al are after you, you have to keep moving."

The elven officer nodded and returned to his troops. The Grey Riders pulled off the road with Grandpa and Raymond. The refugees and their escorts filed past with many a fascinated look in their direction. Many of them were injured, and several carts hauled those too badly hurt to walk or ride.

"We were attacked on the way here," Connor said to Raymond. He described the battle.

"Those were Skreets," Raymond replied with a nod. "Mobile infantry escorts for heavier troops, sometimes used as pickets."

"They were almost as fast as the pegasi," Eric put in.

"Yes," Raymond added, "they are very fast. They resist many types of magic, but are susceptible to fire, including firedarts and, as you've seen, dragon breath."

"What other daemons are in the attacking force?" Buck asked. He was almost afraid of the answer.

Raymond's rested his hands on his belt buckle. "More Skreets, plus some Tigris Infernalis, War Fiends and Bone Knights."

Buck had no idea what War Fiends and Bone Knights were but he didn't want to be anywhere near them.

"We have to contact Father Thomas," Dar announced. "He has to know about this."

"We can't take the time," Khyron protested. He waved a hand at the traffic on the highway. "Not now. With the Ja'al this close, we risk discovery."

"Eric, can you see anything with Stealth?" Andyn asked.

Eric's eyes grew distant. "The Ja'al are less than five miles away. I can see them battling the Elven Army in the woods. The Elves have help from some other force – it looks like hill or forest sprites, harrying the enemy from the flanks. The Ja'al aren't moving fast, but they don't have to."

"We should help," Andyn said, clenching the handles of her maces. "All those people... and we've fought daemons before."

Khyron put his hand on her shoulder. "But that was only two, dear heart, and there are dozens with the Ja'al now."

"It won't help anyone if we don't find what we're looking for," Connor agreed. "We have to be somewhere else."

He shot a glance at Raymond.

The Elohir smiled. "I have been briefed by Melissa.."

"Well, one thing is for sure," Eric said, a faraway look still on his face. "Even if we head out immediately, it's going to be rough. The Ja'al have fanned out into line formations through the woods and the army stretches for miles. The Skreets are above, flying top-cover, along with some armored daemons with double-wings."

"War Fiends," Raymond mused.

Buck let out a deep breath. This mission was getting bogged down from the start.

"I have an idea," Grandpa said with a look at Raymond. The Elohir nodded.

"What?" asked Connor.

Neither spoke.

Andyn gritted her teeth. "Gentlemen?"

Raymond maintained eye contact with Grandpa. "The Ja'al won't notice you if they're preoccupied."

"With what?" demanded Andyn.

"Us."

Buck gaped at them. "You can't fight an entire army by yourselves!"

Raymond's eyes twinkled. "We won't have to. We'll just get them stirred up enough to focus on us. When they hesitate to figure out what's going on, we'll then retreat to help the elves in Tirevlan."

"Do you think it will be enough?" asked Eric.

Raymond exchanged a wicked grin with Grandpa. "Oh, I think we can arrange something."

***

"Well, they're doing a good job of it," Buck noted. Even from a mile away, he heard the shouts, screams, clangs of metal, sizzle of magic, and an occasional dragon roar. Flames leaped up from a section of the forest.

"Glad they're on our side," Dar answered, ducking under a tree branch.

Buck tore his gaze away and focused on riding as quickly and quietly as possible through the woods. The other Riders cantered alongside, their pegasi's hooves wrapped in cloth sacks.

Eric and Khyron led them. They followed as fast as they dared, wending between stands of oak, willow and elm, down hollows and past gurgling streams. Twice, they took wing to fly over narrow ravines. Always, Eric's construct soared overhead.

Buck kept his bow ready, though he wasn't sure he could hit anything in the dense growth.

Eric held up a fist and they stopped. He extended his arm and Stealth floated down and alighted. The construct vanished in a sparkle of light that wafted to the pin on Eric's cloak.

"We're clear," he announced, removing his helmet and mopping his brow. He sounded tired.

"Do you need to rest?" Khyron asked.

Eric shook his head and took a pull from his water skin. "They're about seven miles behind and to the north. Grandpa and Raymond have broken off and flown farther northwest and the Ja'al are regrouping. Let's keep going until nightfall."

Without any further discussion, they headed off again, stopping once to rest the pegasi and water them at a stream. They ate a quick and watchful supper of preserved rations, then climbed back into the saddle again. Finally, when the sun dipped low in the horizon behind them and the sky turned to orange-red, Eric called a halt.

"Dar and I will find a place to hole up," he said, cantering off.

The pair returned very quickly.

"There's a hollow behind a bank of elms upstream from here," Dar said.

Weary and wordless, they followed.

Buck stripped Shadowbane's saddle off and arranged his bedroll as the sky deepened into purple and black. They lit no fire, but Andyn produced a magic light for them.

Eric unwrapped the little Sending Mirror. "Now let's see about Dad's toy."

He held up the mirror. "*Servite Deo tantum. Sancta Maria, Mater Dei, ora pro nobis.*" The four aquamarines glowed and transformed into blue eyes that stared back at them.

Buck made a face. It looked like some odd, four-eyed creature and it was a bit creepy, to be honest. He expected a long time to pass, but a mild ping sounded not long afterwards.

Instead of seeing faces, they were surprised when an image of a room coalesced. Melissa stood next to Father Thomas and Melinor. The Riders crowded around.

Melissa sighed. "It's you! Thank the One God! Did you have any trouble?"

"Marolpeth is in ruins," Andyn said. "The refugees are on their way to Tirevlan. Grandpa joined forces with an Elohir named Raymond to divert the Ja'al. Raymond said that his Celestial Gate was locked by some evil magic. We think it was Oxbridge's devices."

If an Elohir was giving to swearing, Buck thought Melissa was just about there.

Father Thomas put a hand on her shoulder. "We don't have much time if a Ja'al army is nearby. This mirror has a very long range but it can be easily detected if someone is looking for it."

"Were you expecting trouble, Melissa?" Connor asked.

Melinor answered instead. "Yes. Because, my dear ones, the whole world is under attack."

Buck's heart stopped.

"What?" he breathed.

Father Thomas nodded. "Our information from Brandi and Megan was correct. The stones were made to lock the Elohir portals and they have done so. None of the Celestial Gates are open. Melissa, her brother Simon, Raymond and a few others are stranded here on Damora. A dark wave of evil is sweeping over the lands. The Ja'al and their allies are streaming in from the Wilderness, from Torosc and their allied nations: hundreds of thousands of goblins, dark elves, hobgoblins, Kaftu tribes, ogres, trolls, giants and evil dragons. Even the nations over the Great Sea are being invaded. They are supported by literally thousands of daemons loose on our world."

Buck's knees felt weak and he sat on a nearby boulder.

Oh no… Dad! Jack! And what about Carine? Oh great Earth Mother! She's in Tyler with them…

"How did this happen?" Dar whispered, joining Buck on the boulder.

Melissa sighed. She looked dejected. "We underestimated the perfidy of the Ja'al. Yes, they had Skull Gates in the known lands, and your heroism and that of our other freelance teams eliminated many of them. But there were additional ones in the Wilderness beyond the reach of our agents and others in Torosc, Morlan and Jered."

"The recent civil unrest has increased," Melinor added. "Riots have broken out in some major cities and several nobles in the Alliance have been assassinated, including Lord Dunston of Harlinsville."

Buck's jaw dropped. "Lord Dunston?"

Now Melinor twisted the end of his belt. "Yes, and I blame myself completely. Gorlak discovered that Lady Arlene was a Ja'al agent but we did nothing, hoping to draw her out and uncover her handlers. Before we could move, she killed her husband and disappeared. It was my fault."

Father Thomas put his arms around Melinor and Melissa's shoulders. "Now, none of that. The Ja'al had an extensive plan, but the efforts of our nations have removed many of the internal threats. This is significant. We do not have to deal with daemons boiling up from Skull Gates within our borders. The invasion is from without, and we can hold, for a time. And we think that the Ja'al are completely unaware of your location."

Melissa nodded. "Yes, that is our ultimate advantage. You have to find the Gate of Stars, and figure out how to open it to Celestia. Without it, we are doomed."

"What will you do?" Andyn asked.

"Organize our defenses and coordinate with the other Free Lands," Father Tom replied. "And Melinor has some ideas about the Alenar sisters."

Eric and Dar exchanged a look. "What about them?" Dar asked.

Melinor's lips set in a firm line. "Megan's notes indicated that George Oxbridge thought she had been magically contaminated before birth, and likely Brandi too. I'm not so sure. I intend to find out."

"In the meantime, stay the course," Melissa added. "Do not attempt to contact us until you reach the Titan's Crown. It is too risky. We are already tempting fate by talking this long."

Eric nodded. "Understood. We'll get it done."

In the mirror, even they could see Melinor's eyes had become shiny. "I know you will, son. Our prayers are with you."

The mirror pinged and went black.

For long minutes, they just sat without speaking. Buck took a good look at his friends. Their eyes dull with tiredness, expressions still shocked, they stared at nothing — all except Eric. Instead, he gazed at a tiny crucifix in his hand, the one he wore around his neck, the one Brandi had given him. Buck watched him run his fingers over it, almost like a caress.

Finally, he kissed it and stood. He held out his hand to Dar and pulled him up.

Dar stared at the crucifix in Eric's hand and his mouth set in a firm line. "You're right."

He addressed the other Riders. "I made a promise to Megan and I intend to see it through," he said. "I will find the Gate of Stars or die trying. I owe it to her, and to Brandi."

Eric's eyes glinted. "Thanks, Dar."

Buck rose as the other Riders joined them. He thought of his father, brother and sister… and Carine. He clenched the pommel of Khelios.

Above, bright stars spangled the firmament and the wind blew warm through the forests of Terenai.

"We'll see this through as we always have," Andyn said, taking Khyron's hand. "Together, as the Grey Riders."

"Together," they all whispered.

Chapter Twenty-Four – A Light in the Darkness

"This is quite a workshop."

Melinor Indidarc looked up from the table. "Courtesy of the Church, Father Tom."

The Papal Nuncio smiled back, ivory teeth bright against dark skin. "I'm glad we're putting the money to good use then."

The Nuncio clasped his hands behind his back and strolled around the perimeter of the workshop. He peered into some of the glass cases and inspected diagrams posted on corkboards on the wall.

Melinor watched him for a while, then turned his attention back to the tiny vials on the table. "I'm amazed that you can be so calm at a time like this."

Father Tom sounded amused. "Being agitated wouldn't help much, would it?"

"Aren't you worried?" Melinor opened one of the vials, swirling the blood sample within.

Father Tom sighed. "For the people of Damora's well-being, yes. For their spiritual safety, yes. For the ultimate ending, no. God wins."

Melinor paused and smiled. "You sound like Father Edward."

Father Tom chuckled. "Now that's a high compliment, and not one he would have given me in earlier years."

"You knew him well?"

The Nuncio smiled, touching one of the Heritage Stones on a shelf in its padded wooden case. "He was one of my university teachers. Taught me Theology and Mathematics."

Melinor drew a drop of blood from one of the vials and gently smeared it on a glass square. He placed the square on a flat wire mesh, conjured a light underneath it, then positioned four lenses at angles to the glass. With a whispered word, a three-dimensional image of the blood sprang up in the air before him.

There has to be something here… magical contamination is detectable, but you have to know what you're looking for.

He didn't realize he had spoken until Father Tom responded.

"How did you manage to get the blood?" the Nuncio asked.

Melinor gave a wry smile. "Preservation Nets were originally designed for logistics purposes, to keep food fresh for military units. They had to be able to check the materials periodically, so the creators designed in a tiny air pocket on one side of the Net. If you know how, you can use a needle or tiny bladed instrument to get a sample."

Father Tom nodded. "And Megan felt sure she was magically contaminated?"

"She felt it was a distinct possibility, for both her and Brandi. The Ja'al were certainly convinced."

"I see. Well, I'm glad you're looking into this," the Nuncio said.

Melinor sighed, the knot in his stomach tightening. Megan and Brandi's images floated in his mind's eye, resting peacefully on their biers under the ever-present glow of the Preservation Nets. His eyes stung.

I have lost my future daughter-in-law.

"I owe it to them," Melinor replied in a quiet voice, focusing on the image hovering in mid-air. Melinor moved his fingers and the image rotated slowly.

He bit his lip. He considered dozen different possibilities in his head but nothing obvious presented itself.

"What about one of these other devices?" Father Tom asked. "I don't know what most of them are, but maybe there's a different way to analyze Brandi and Megan's blood samples."

Melinor only grunted, lost in thought.

Father Tom brought him one of the Heritage Stones. "What does this do?" he asked.

Melinor spared it a glance. "Oh, that? Those were used in ancient times to prove inheritance, mostly for the great houses of the age," he explained. He rose and selected a different one himself. "You are correct in that they were used on blood samples, but they would just prove lineage."

Father Tom looked disappointed. "I see. Magical contamination wouldn't show up, then?"

Melinor shook his head, tossing the Heritage Stone in his hand. "No. But I can demonstrate, if you'd like."

Father Tom nodded and brought the other Heritage Stone with him. "How many Heritage Stones do you have here?"

"Dozens," Melinor replied. He dripped a drop of Brandawyn's blood into the Heritage Stone. The tiny channel at the top of the Stone glowed red and Melinor spun the Stone on its pointed end. A pattern of miniature symbols flashed as it spun, illuminating dozens of interlinked paths.

"Extraordinary," the Nuncio breathed. The top's momentum petered out and Melinor caught it before it fell over. The lighted symbols faded and darkened.

"It would flash repeatedly on the lineage line inside the stone if it detected a link," he explained. "Then I'd use a lens like this one here to see the script."

Father Tom's face took on an odd expression as he tossed another Stone in his hand. "Try this one."

Melinor's eyes narrowed. "Why?"

The priest gazed at the Stone as if seeing through it. "A hunch. A dream. Call it what you like."

Melinor stared at him for a second, then repeated the process.

A line winked in gold letters over and over again, like a firefly dancing in the woods.

Melinor's jaw dropped. "What?"

The Nuncio put his hand on his shoulder. "Which lineage is it?"

Melinor swiveled one of the lenses over and peered into it, jotting down a series of Dwarven runes. He snatched a volume from a nearby bookcase. Father Tom peered over his shoulder as he leafed through the pages.

Melinor touched the name on the page. "This one."

They stood in utter silence.

Melinor read down the page, leafing through the section, following a family tree. He pored over the text of several pages before setting the book aside.

"Would it explain things?" Father Tom whispered.

Melinor leaned his hands on the table, mind whirring. "Yes, yes it would explain a lot — and raise more questions besides."

Lost in thought, he stared at the page.

"What's the next step?" asked the Nuncio.

Melinor set his mouth in a firm line. "Record this, seal it with your signet ring, and hide it."

His eyes went to another tiny vial. "And then test Megan's blood…"

The End

(…for now…)

Appendix - Glossary

<u>Adina</u> – A female human priestess of the goddess Gudarta of the Ja'al cult, she is beautiful, shapely and blonde (though she changes her hair color on a whim). Intimately involved with the Skull Gates project, she hunted down and eventually captured Brandi and Megan Alenar, keeping Brandi for her own and transforming her through vile magic into a vampire slave. Adina is the mistress of Berek, though she is not above taking her pleasures wherever they present themselves.

<u>Agent</u> - A spy, bounty hunter or thief, depending on context and the particular agent's morals and ethics. Connor Lomin and Khyron Demaris are both agents who tend more towards the "spy" variety. Most agents provide a stealthy component to the groups they support. In military terms an agent would be part of a reconnaissance unit.

<u>Alenar, Brandawyn (Brandi)</u> - One of the original Grey Riders, a half-elven female, trained as a soldier and combat medic/corpsman. The older sister of Megan, she and her family were persecuted for their Christian faith and eventually fled their homeland of Torosc. During her time with the Riders, she fell in love with Eric Indidarc. Later, she was captured by the Ja'al and changed into a vampire thrall by evil magic.

Reserved but kind and devoutly religious, Brandi is quite pretty, with red-gold hair and violet eyes, but doesn't see herself as attractive. Brandawyn is also ambidextrous. Her pegasus is named Amicus (Lat. *"friend"*).

<u>Alenar, Daphne, OF</u> - Ranger Knight of the Falcon (*Orden Falconieri*, OF). The only sister of Megan and Brandi's human mother, she spirited her nieces northward away from Torosc to safety. Sometimes thought of as overly serious (like her niece, Brandawyn), she served as a devoted mother-figure to the sisters after the death of their parents. She perished in battle with Ja'al forces along with her brother, Stephen.

<u>Alenar, Megan</u> - Another of the original Grey Riders and younger sister of Brandawyn Alenar, she fled persecution in Torosc to arrive in Deran. After attending college in Terenai, she graduated as a wizard and scholar. She and Megan met the Grey Riders in Deran and helped them solve the mystery of *Whitehorse Peak*. When her aunt and uncle died fighting the Ja'al, she was sold into slavery to a Ja'al High Wizard to serve in his laboratory.

A strawberry blonde like her sibling, Megan is friendly and outgoing, somewhat vain and impetuous, yet fiercely loyal and brave. She is also very attractive, with amber eyes and a slender figure and is fond of baubles and fancy clothes. She loves Dar Cabot and rides a pegasus named Larinor (Elv. *"ranger"* or *"faithful guide"*).

Alenar, Stephen - Uncle of Brandawyn and Megan Alenar, he was the younger brother of Daphne Alenar. In addition to being a scholar, Stephen was also a skilled warrior and wielded potent magic in battle. Known for his teasing sense of humor, he died fighting alongside his sister against the Ja'al.

Aluin, Brion IV – Emperor of the Elven nation of Terenai, he is over two hundred years old, blond, slim, and a deadly combination of warrior, priest and mage. With a long Elven life span, he has seen much over the years and knew the grandparents of many current world leaders. He relies heavily on the advice of his wife, Beldryn, a skilled sorceress and priestess of Verian in her own right.

Alyssa of Tor Haldin, Saint – Powerful and holy queen of a petty kingdom during the late Paragon Age, Alyssa ruled over a domain located in present-day Torosc. Her battles against Zhinia Margoth were legendary and all the more remarkable since Margoth was Alyssa's first cousin. After Margoth was finally defeated at the Battle of Three-Nation Lake and disappeared, Alyssa returned to her kingdom. She and her husband and family died ten years later when a combination of wild tribes and opportunistic foreign powers overran her war-depleted nation.

Her Crown is a relic of jaw-dropping power, bestowing impressive magical abilities, healing capabilities and protections to someone of sufficiently pure heart, though it all comes with a price.

Astarel - Kingdom to the north of Deran, along the coast. The homeland of Buck Bydecy, it is a seafaring nation with a robust navy and an eclectic society comprised equally of elves, humans, dwarves and halflings. It is a member of the Northern Alliance.

Balris – A daemonic ambassador from Hades to the evil nation of Morlan on Damora. He is sly, calculating and sadistic but prudent, only exercising his skills when it will gain advantage for himself or his homeworld. About six feet, three inches tall, he has golden blond hair, black horns and wings, and amber cat-eyes. He is baffled by the origin of Megan Alenar's considerable magic skills.

Barnard – A human warrior sworn to the service of Kelani, he has a rather special talent that he uses to destroy foes of his mistress.

Berek – A blond Ja'al wizard of the Fourth Circle, he is assigned to work with Adina in tracking down the Alenar family, who are involved in interdicting various Ja'al plots. A smooth operator, he is more sensible and less fiery than his mistress and often sees the practical aspect of things. He detests Brandawyn Alenar but goes along with Adina's scheme to turn her into a vampire.

Blood Satyr – A type of daemon from Hades, it resembles a smooth-skinned satyr with red skin and stands over seven feet tall. Blood Satyrs have four arms and are formidable wizards, though they can mix it up in hand-to-hand combat as well. They do not have wings but can run very fast.

Blood Sign – An oath taken by dragons signifying that they have declared one or another group (such as a tribe, clan, religion or nation) as enemies. The Blood Sign amounts to a declaration of war, though it is taken by individuals or clans and not all dragons as a race.

Blue Mark – The code name for an agent of the Northern Alliance living in the Elven Empire of Terenai, charged with ferreting out plots and spies against the Empire or its allies.

Bull-satyr – Tall, heavy creatures that resemble a combination of satyr and minotaur, they have the lower bodies of goats, upper bodies of muscular humans, and heads of bulls. Not particularly intelligent, they are greedy and can be enticed into service with offers of treasure. Evil forces often use them as shock troops and they can carry large objects or pull heavy conveyances easily.

Bydecy ROA, Buckminster (Buck), Sir - Another of the original Grey Riders, Buck is a tall, rangy, sandy-haired human male warrior. He is a native of Tyler, Astarel and was made a Sword-Knight of the Royal Order of Astarel (ROA) after the Battle of Hillton. His easygoing nature is often mistaken for boredom. His father is named Alfred and he has a brother (Jack) and a sister (Summer). His pegasus is Shadowbane.

Cabot OSK, Darius (Dar), Sir - An original Grey Rider and native of the border town of Forester, Deran, Dar ran afoul of Ja'al goblin troops in the wilds and headed back to town for help, setting the events of *Whitehorse Peak* in motion. A young, dark-haired human male, he is a ranger/scout and adept in the woods. He grew to love Megan Alenar during their time together fighting the Ja'al near Forester. He rides a pegasus named Virasi (Elv. *"white star"*). After the defeat of Zhinia Margoth he was knighted into the Order of Saint Kira (*Orden Sancta Kiraensis, OSK*).

<u>Carville</u> – A large town (pop. ~ 12,000) in northern Torosc, Coastwatch Prefecture. It has a temple to Gudarta whose priestesses use "volunteers" from the local populace in their rituals. It is a hub for freelance adventurers. George Oxbridge (q.v.) owns a cottage near the place.

<u>Catrin</u> – A major city (pop. ~ 130,000) in the southern nation of Morlan. It is located in the jungle near the center of the country at an important cross-roads connecting other major cities. It is the home town of George Oxbridge.

<u>Chamber of Decision</u> – A mysterious place that the Riders (minus the Alenar sisters) encountered on the way to find the *Helm of Shadows*. Each Rider was separated from the others and shown two paths they could take in their lives— for good or ill. According to the Song of the Grey Riders, they had to choose.

<u>Changelings</u> – A set of magical blades forged on Celestia. With the use of a keyword, they transform into weapons of ice, fire, lightning, acid or holy power.

<u>Cintos, Kalar, Colonel</u> – A commander of episcopal troops of Neralia of the Ja'al pantheon, he was a liaison to Zhinia Margoth until her demise at the Battle of Hillton. He is later assigned to assist a Ja'al high priest named Za-nilor.

<u>Cla'Agik</u> – (Dw. *"That -Rotted"*) The name of the Church of the Diseased One comes from the Dwarven term for "that which is rotted". The faith is based on the premise that disease, corruption and illness are weapons that can be used to sow chaos and suffering. Perhaps surprisingly for their con-nection with rot and disease, the Cla'Agik are capable healers (due to the need to protect themselves from the contagions they attempt to unleash on their opponents). They flourish in Morlan, Jered, and wild places on the borders of civilized nations.

<u>Coastwatch</u> – Seaside metropolis (pop. 150,000) in Torosc where the Ale-nar sisters were born and raised.

Companion Pin – Enchanted pieces of jewelry, Companion Pins are keyed to a miniature golem resembling a small animal like a rat, hawk, ferret or cat. The constructs are summoned to serve the bearer of the Pin using a secret code word and share their special abilities (night vision, enhanced hearing, camouflage, etc.) with their masters. Stealth (a hawk Pin), owned by Eric Indidarc (q.v.), and Bloodflit (a bat/rat) owned by Ilyan Kalik (q.v.) are examples of Companion Pins.

Crossed Swords – A guild of assassins based in Deran and Terenai. Founded and ruled by the Hylar family, the Crossed Swords were used by evil forces to eliminate opposition. Eric Indidarc's real family name is Hylar and he is a son of the guild master; he escaped his former life and was adopted by Melinor Indidarc. In *Assassin Prince*, the Grey Riders joined him in destroying the Guild and bringing his parents to justice.

Culver, Arlene, Countess – Lady and ruler of Harlinsville. She is middle-aged, with brown hair and green eyes and is significantly younger than her husband. Her eyes indicate she thinks much but says little.

Culver, Dunston, Count – Lord and ruler of Harlinsville. He is over seventy but spry. He hired the Grey Riders to investigate a series of mysterious murders in his city in *Assassin Prince*. A retired judge, he spends his time helping the poorer citizenry with legal aid.

Daemon - Evil to the core, the otherworldly race of daemons spends most of its time trying to overthrow the Elohir or conquer various regions of Damora. They are known as the Fallen Ones because legend has it that they were originally Elohir who turned to the side of evil and worship of themselves (and the Dark One). While many Daemons look like nightmarish beasts, some are very attractive and almost human-like or elven in appearance. The overriding philosophy of the Daemons is that Damora is a free zone, ripe for the picking. Their home world, Hades, is the 4th planet orbiting the star Beta Hydri (G11 spectral class, 24.38 LY from Earth) and is a combination of stunning beauty and stomach-churning grotesqueness.

Damora - Imaginary world setting for the Grey Riders novels. The fourth planet orbiting the star 82 Eridani, it is roughly 1.15 times the size of Earth and possesses similar climate, regions and flora/fauna. The parent star is a G5V spectral class, main-sequence yellow star approximately 20 light years from Earth. It has two moons, Kaliri and Diometrius, which provide both tidal forces and substantial moonlight for the planet's surface. The technology level of Damora approximates the High Middle Ages of the real world, with significant differences due to the use of magic and scientific advancement.

<u>Darkhollow</u> – A haunted wood near Evonald, Terenai. Legends tell of a powerful wizard who dabbled in forbidden magic and destroyed himself, corrupting the forest in the process. The Hill Sprites who live near the Handor family keep a vigilant watch over it.

<u>Darkspawn</u> – Greater undead made from large creatures such as bull-satyrs or ogres. The process to create one is particularly awful in that the creature is still living during the ceremony (as opposed to zombies, which are already dead).

<u>Dark Reaver</u> – An eldritch horror crafted from fused animals and hellish magic, a dark reaver is a savage and powerful foe with a bad temper. It is a combination of frog, shark, boar, scorpion and alligator. Some sages speculate that they were created by one of the evil deities of the Ja'al pantheon. They are subterranean and can be captured if the right magic is used. They usually fight to the death because their limited intelligence doesn't allow the possibility of retreat.

<u>Darlon</u> - Major metropolis in northern Deran, pop ~ 170,000. Home to people of many races, creeds and professions, it is a trading center and university town. Ruled by a duke, it controls trade and access between Deran and the northernmost nations of Astarel, Eldir and Rokon.

<u>Deathhammer</u> – A type of daemon from Hades, a Deathhammer is a hulking brutish beast with pig-like features, fangs and white horns. They can use their great wings to fly but are not particularly maneuverable. As their name suggests, they are shock troops. They have a limited magical repertoire.

<u>Deathmist</u> – Daemons from Hades, Deathmists resemble a cloud of grey fog that floats low to the ground and extends silvery tendrils to attack. They radiate extreme cold and can drain the life-force out of someone by grappling them with their tentacles. They do not speak but can use telepathy.

<u>Delacroix, Marcus IV</u> – The young King of Astarel, he is twenty-three, blond and unused to rule, having been thrust into the position upon the untimely death of his father two years prior to the start of the *Grey Riders* series. Reputed to be a bit of a carouser before his father's death, he has surprised

his people by diligently working for their betterment. He is also a priest of Irial.

Delilah – Brandawyn Alenar's evil alter-ego created by vile magic when she was transformed into a vampire in the service of Adina. The polar opposite of Brandi, Delilah is lustful, greedy, cruel, and vain.

Del Rio, Carine – Druid and caretaker of one of the many groves near Oakmoor, Deran, she is a mentor and confidant of Buck Bydecy though she is only two years older. Dark-haired and green-eyed, she is a competent steward of the open lands near the city and can shape-change to the form of a black doe. Her mentorship of Buck promises to blossom into something more.

Demaris, Khyron, Major – A former beau of Andyn Eleandir who lost contact with her while on highly-classified missions for the Empire of Terenai, Khyron is blonde and has sea-green eyes. He is almost as stealthy as Connor Lomin, wields a bow with deadly precision, and is ambidextrous. He is also trained in airborne riding, one of the reasons he is asked by Melinor Indidarc to join the Grey Riders. His pegasus is named Zasural (Elv. *"wind-light"*).

DeMey, Saren, Lady - The half-sister of Eric Indidarc by adoption, Saren DeMey was found by Melinor Indidarc as an infant and raised by him and his wife, Anne. A devout Christian, Saren appears to be a complete contradiction in terms as she is half-daemon but fights for the forces of good. Dark-haired and dark-eyed, she transforms to a bat-winged, horned half-daemon at will. Saren continually guards against her daemonic background, as it is a permanent temptation to lust and savagery; however, to the common folk of Deran, she is known to be warm, generous, wise and gentle. As the wife of Terenil, the Earl of the Oakmoor suburb of Tallemar, she is a Countess of Deran.

DeMey, Terenil, Lord - The half-elven husband of Saren, he is an earl and the ruler of Tallemar, a suburb of Oakmoor, Deran. A skilled wizard and soldier in his own right, he is adaptable, thoughtful and unfailingly kind. His devotion to Saren is unquestioned. His personal guard is a platoon of magic-wielding armored knights. As part of the Foreign Ministry of Deran, he is privy to information about other nations and is rumored to have an extensive spy network.

<u>Deoborin, Jokadram</u> – (Dw. *"clever swordsman strong-fortress"*) Along with his wife, Queen Rikkeya (Dw. *"sparkling one"*) Jokadram rules the independent Dwarven kingdom of Merdail, located north of Torosc and east of Gorostol. Though he is keen for Merdail to be free of the constant maneuvering between the Northern Alliance and the Dark Lands of the south, he is nonetheless aware that his best allies are to the North. He and Rikkeya divide royal responsibilities between them; both are formidable warriors and seasoned field commanders. He and Rikkeya have five adult children and eleven grandchildren.

<u>Deorfast</u> - Large city in the mountains of northwestern Deran. It is a trading center and military installation and sits astride the Deor and Lonmar Rivers. It is ruled by a Count and Countess (at the time of *The Skull Gates*, Andareth Faldanor and his wife, Sidara).

<u>Deran</u> - Constitutional monarchy in the northern lands of the Western continent of Damora. A nation built from the remnants of the Esten Empire, Deran is also a meritocracy, where nobles are elected by their peers and the legislature is based on merit and ability more than noble connections. Deran has an advanced network of roads, potent military, and several universities. The seat of the Christian Church, Saint Martin's Town (St. Martin's) is in Deran.

<u>Dolmide</u> – Halfling hero-saint of the Irial religion. He was a scholar and monk who left a legacy of wisdom before taking up arms to defend his Paragon-era kingdom when the king was corrupted by evil magic. Despite the exclamation *"Dolmide's Beard!"* often used by Irial adherents, Dolmide himself had no beard.

<u>Dome of Glass</u> – A mysterious object or place from antiquity fashioned by the Ja'al and/or their allies to thwart attempts to find the Gate of Stars. Its location is unknown.

<u>Dwarf</u> - One of the major races of Damora. The term "Dwarf" comes from the ancient elvish word, *duarfaen* (Elv. *duar* = 'stone' + *fae/ fey/ fej* - = 'magic', literally "those of stone-magic"). A typical Dwarf male is about four feet six inches tall. Dwarves tend to be burly, sturdy or muscular for their size and can live for almost two hundred years. Males are often bearded (though not all are). They are generally honorable and appreciate strength and resolve in others. Their main talent, as indicated by the name bestowed on

them by the Elves, is in stonework and metallurgy.

Earth Mother – Nature-concept deification of the world of Damora as expounded by the Druids. Roughly equivalent to the concept of Gaia in the real world.

Eastridge – A major Deranese city (pop. ~120,000) in the south of the country.

Eleandir SMT, IO, Andyn, Lady - One of the Grey Riders, Andyn is a priestess of the Elven god Verian and a wizard. She has honey-blonde hair and amber eyes, a trim figure and a marvelous singing voice. Rather impatient and quick-tempered, she nonetheless displays unwavering faith, mercy, warmth and a nimble mind. Her husband was killed by Crossed Swords assassins. At the Battle of Hillton, she used a holy relic (the Crown of Saint Alyssa) to destroy Zhinia Margoth. For her exploits, she was knighted by the Elven Empire of Terenai and given the title of Light of Justice and Lichslayer. She is styled as Lady Andyn Eleandir, Servant of Mindra of Terenai, Imperial Order, Light of Justice. Her pegasus is named Medianox (Lat. *"midnight"*).

Eldir – A nation of the Northern Alliance, Eldir is a patriarchate and the seat of the faith of Verian. Possessing a climate similar to Germany in the real world, it used to be at odds with Rokon, a breakaway duchy, until the need for collaboration against the forces of evil caused them to bury the hatchet. It is ruled by the High Matriarch or Patriarch of Verian.

Eleison (Gr. *"have mercy"*) – A powerful magic horseman's mace found by the Grey Riders near Twinspire Mountain during the search for the Helm of Shadows. It strikes against evil with holy power and amplifies healing magic. Andyn Eleandir carries it and another, lesser magic mace; the smaller size of a horseman's mace (as opposed to the more massive footman's mace) permits her to wield them ambidextrously.

Eleth-Anor – (Elv. *"dolphin bluff/ cliff"*) – A major seaport city of the Elven Empire. Home to almost two hundred thousand souls, it commands a sheltered harbor in the Bay of Dolphins (Elethi-Rin). It is Andyn Eleandir's home town and her parents still live there.

Elethi-Rin – (Elv. "bay of dolphins") – A large gulf in the central coast of Terenai.

Elf - One of the major races of Damora. The term "Elf" comes from the ancient word for their race, *Ellfaen* (Elv. *ell* = 'life' + *fae/ fey/ fej* -= 'magic', literally "those of life-magic"). Elves are more slender than humans and possess intriguing eye colors, such as aqua, amber or violet; they also have a slight point to top of the ear, though this is not usually pronounced or even noted if the ears are concealed under hair, hat or helm. Elves tend to be a bit more reserved than the other races and have more of an affinity for magic of all kinds. They possess skills for getting along well with animals and have a remarkable talent for healing trees and plants.

Elohir - Denizen of the planet of Celestia (the 5th planet of the 61 Virginis star, a single G6 spectral class, main-sequence yellow star approximately 28 light years from Earth). Sometimes called "Celestials", they appear to be winged humans. Skin color covers the range of typical shades seen in humans (porcelain, tanned, brown, yellow, dark brown) and their eyes are the color of jewels. Their beauty is often described as 'unearthly'. All possess potent magical and martial skills but are usually reluctant to meddle in the affairs of Damorans. They are uniformly kind, wise, honest and just. Elohir live extremely long lives (~ 1000 years) if not killed in warfare with their evil kindred, the Fallen Ones (or daemons).

Esten Empire - An empire formed of various kingdoms controlling much of the known world during the second age of Damora (known as the Imperial Age and denoted in calendars by the letters IY (for Imperial Year)). It fell after over a thousand years of rule due to infighting, a breakdown in the social fabric and the influence of evil.

Ettin – A type of giant standing more than eleven feet tall and weighing over six hundred pounds, an ettin has two heads that can think independently. Each head controls one arm, though both communicate in concert to control the legs. They are sometimes used as guards by the forces of evil, but they are expensive — both heads often take part in negotiations for fees and they are clever as well as greedy. Unexpected events or surprises tend to confuse them, since both heads perceive the situation differently.

Evendale - Small halfling nation south east of Deran and northeast of Terenai. A republic, Evendale consists of seven districts or counties, each of which have a prescribed number of representatives (aldermen) and senators who draft laws that are approved by the Prime Minister, another elected position. A land with mild climate and productive farmland, Evendale borders on the Wilderness, which means the halflings are always on vigilant watch, having been invaded by evil tribes from the wild lands multiple times. Its capital city is Lakeview.

Evonald (Elv. *"water light"*) – An Elven town in Terenai of about 10,000 people located near the Bethyn River in northeastern Terenai.

Eye of Truth - A magical diamond, the Eye of Truth is actually a sort of lens that allows the owner to see the true nature of things and people. It can detect evil or good auras, see through illusion and discern truth from lies. It was crafted by an ancestor of Buck Bydecy and is owned by him. The Grey Riders helped him recover it during a quest in the novel *Eye of Truth*.

Faldanor ORD, Andareth, Lord - Half-elf healer and wizard, retired. He and his wife, Sidara, are Count and Countess of Deorfast, a mountain city in Deran and have helped the Grey Riders on occasion. Though not a member of the Order of the Three Magi he often assists them on behalf of his wife. He and Sidara are both Christian.

Faldanor OTM, ORD, Sidara, Lady – The wife of Lord Andareth Faldanor, Count of Deorfast, Sidara is an elven wizard, a member of the Order of the Three Magi and the Royal Order of Deran (*Orden Regnate Deraniensis*). She met Andareth when part of his free-lance adventuring group, the Four Silvers. She is very conservative, extremely pretty, and has a rascally sense of humor. She and Andareth have two children.

Fell-beast – A normal animal warped by vile magic and forbidden scientific knowledge into a servant of evil.

Fidelis – A magic spear that can contract to the size of a dagger or telescope to the length of a medium infantry spear, it was awarded to Eric Indidarc by Melissa of Celestia. It strikes with great power against evil things and, if thrown, returns unerringly to its wielder's hand via teleport when called. Though Melissa did not say it, there is some speculation that it is from the Paragon Age (q.v.).

Firedart - A magical attack spell used by wizards and sorcerers. It is essentially a small projectile of flame with a detonable core that looks rather like a tiny comet and has a limited range (about 100 feet or so). It produces the effect equivalent to a 9 mm pistol bullet and rarely misses.

Forester - Large town along the northern border highway of Deran. Forester is ruled by a baron and controls trade along the borderlands. Its defining feature is the central town proper, which is surrounded by a tall, well-built palisade with giant, living trees as its guard towers. It is the hometown of Dar Cabot.

Gariil – (Dw. "*random*") The god of chance and luck sometimes also associated with fertility, Gariil can take on male or female aspects. One of the original religions of Damora, it is still popular in urban areas. The religion is very loosely organized and clergy are often made simply by claiming the title and demonstrating priestly magic. Their temples are often nothing more than casinos or amusement centers. Due to their uncanny ability to turn a profit, they are tolerated in the evil realms of Torosc, Morlan and Jered.

Gate of Stars – A mysterious Gate of unknown nature that is feared by the Ja'al. Guarded by the Dome of Glass, its location has been lost in the mists of time.

Ghost Creeper – An evil, semi-intelligent plant that can detect the approach of non-evil creatures and set up a wailing sound. Their vines wrap around victims and insert a narcotic that makes them sleepy and clumsy. They are often set near Vampire Roses by servants of Darkness as sentries.

Gina – Andyn's alias while on a spy mission in Torosc.

Gnome - Half-breeds resulting from the marriage of halfling and Dwarf, gnomes possess features from each parent: natural affinity for stone and the underground from the dwarves and a cheerful disposition and natural talent with all things organic from the halflings. Somewhat taller than halflings but shorter than dwarves, gnomes are industrious and found in all the known lands. They usually have dark hair, tan-to-dark complexions, and brown, amber or grey eyes. A typical gnome lives about 180 years or so.

Goblin - Short, half-simian creatures who often serve as foot-soldiers for the forces of evil, goblins look somewhat like horned chimpanzees. Extremely agile and able to use any available weapon that is sized for them, they are also good at hiding in shadows. They dislike sunlight. Their social structure is usually in a hierarchical monarchy, with the chieftain or king of a particular tribe wielding absolute authority. Goblins particularly hate dwarves since the two races compete for underground areas and resources. They are capable miners and are about the size of a gnome or tall halfling (a few inches short of four feet tall).

Gorlak - A goblin formerly in the employ of the Ja'al, he switched sides after the Battle of Hillton when his life was spared by the Riders. Captured after the battle, he was asked to join the household of the Papal Nuncio. Under the Nuncio's tutelage and care, he flourished and now serves as a spy, with devastating success since few would ever entertain the idea of a Christian goblin. He admires the Grey Riders, adores Andyn and Saren, and soaks up new learning like a sponge.

<u>Gorostol</u> (Dw. *"friend alliance"*) – A large and somewhat eclectic nation south of Terenai and north of Torosc. Originally founded by dwarves, over the years it attracted folk of all races. It is now a buffer state between the oppressive Republic to the south and the Elven Empire to the north.

<u>Grey Riders</u> – The formerly free-lance mercenary group famous for defeating Zhinia Margoth at the Battle of Hillton. The original members were Buck Bydecy, Dar Cabot, Eric Indidarc, Connor Lomin, Andyn Eleandir and the Alenar sisters, Brandawyn and Megan. After the departure of the Alenars, they added Hlerv (Handor Lervion) to their team, but he perished while trying to rescue his sister from the Ja'al. Khyron Demaris, an old beau of Andyn's, later joined the group.

<u>Grey Riders, Song Of</u> – An ancient prophetic poem from the Church of Irial, it foretold the coming of riders on winged horses who would save a kingdom from a horrible evil. It came true when the real Grey Riders destroyed Zhinia Margoth, a lich princess, at the Battle of Hillton in *Helm of Shadows*.

<u>Grigor</u> – Connor Lomin's alter ego while in a spying mission in Torosc.

<u>Gudarta</u> - The evil goddess of torture and suffering, the seductive and sadistic Gudarta is a member of the Ja'al pantheon.

<u>Habakkuk</u> – A suit of magical chainmail with the ability to teleport its owner and one other person for short distances.

<u>Half-Elf</u> - The offspring of a union between an Elf and human, half-elves are a mix of their parents' heritage: magically talented, strong, adaptable and capable of learning new skills quickly. If it were not for the fact that they are noticeably taller than elves by a few inches, they would be indistinguishable from elves due to their predilection to inherit their elven parent's eye color, hair color and ear shape. Half-elves live to between 100 and 150 years.

<u>Halfling</u> - The smallest of the races, halflings (from the elven for "those

of hearth magic" - *haliv-fae*) prefer pastoral villages and countrysides to large cities, though they are at home in any setting. As adaptable as humans, halflings have a talent for craftsmanship (with things other than stone) and farming. They are known for their skill in the kitchen and the durability of their finished goods. Their hair color (blonde, brown or black), skin color (porcelain to dark brown) and eye color (blue, green, black or grey) remind the other races of miniature humans. They live about 100 years or so.

Handor, Rhonin, OF – A retired free-lance ranger who raises horses and lives with his family in central Terenai near Lake Colbethyn. His wife is Belinda and he has two children, Roger and Mary, who idolize the Grey Riders. A tall, burly man with a black beard, he is jovial and friendly yet perceptive. He has extensive experience battling both the Ja'al and the Vardish.

Harlan – The brother of Barnard, he serves Kelani in her duties as a Ja'al wizard. He has an unusual talent similar to his sibling.

Harlinsville – A mid-sized suburb of the Deranese capital of Oakmoor, Harlinsville has about 35,000 inhabitants. It is ruled by Lord Dunston and Lady Arlene, Count and Countess. A working-class town, it is relatively peaceful but has a shadowy underbelly.

Helm of Shadows – A magical helmet crafted by Zhinia Margoth, it allows its wielder to teleport great distances if the keywords are known. Since Margoth's destruction, it was claimed by Handor Lervion (q.v.), who realized its true nature as a relic of evil and ultimately hid it away. After Handor's death while trying to free his sister, Hannah, the Grey Riders recovered the Helm and it was ultimately destroyed by the Good Faiths.

Heritage Stone - A magical item, a Heritage Stone is used to prove paternity and lineage. It uses magical analysis of DNA from a blood sample to ascertain the relationship of the subject to a predetermined DNA pattern associated with a target family or person.

Hillton - Fortified Deranese city (pop ~ 27,000) perched on a hill along the shores of Sun Lake. It is ruled by a Count. Due to its position on the central plains, it is a major trading center and hub for nearby agricultural areas. It was the site of a siege and battle when Zhinia Margoth invaded Deran from the Wilderness in the novel *Helm of Shadows*. The battle ended when Andyn Eleandir used the Crown of Saint Alyssa to destroy Margoth. Her army disintegrated without her iron will to keep them from attacking one another.

Human - Humans on Damora are much like people in real-life, with the exception that they can use magic in the same manner as elves, dwarves, halflings and other creatures. Humans are energetic, adaptable, learn quickly and are endlessly curious about Damora and its people, flora and fauna. They live in all climates and places that will welcome them. The origin of the word "human" has no Damoran equivalent as it does not translate from any Elven or Dwarven syntax.

Humana - Language of the human race on Damora.

Ildrisana – A Dark Elven queen, she has often allied herself with other powerful evil forces, such as the Ja'al and Zhinia Margoth.

Indidarc SSM, Eric, Sir - One of the original Grey Riders, Eric is the adopted son of Melinor Indidarc, a famous wizard. Able to use magic and martial weapons with equal proficiency, Eric is cheerful, optimistic and friendly. He treats everyone he meets with the same courtesy and kindness, whether a beggar or noble. Eric has violet eyes and blond hair and is a half-elf. His pegasus is named Niveral (Elv. *"snow bright"*). For his role in the defeat of Zhinia Margoth, he was made a Knight of the Order of Saint Michael (*Servus Sancte Michael*). Later, in the novel *Assassin Prince*, he and the Riders brought down the Crossed Swords guild, run by his birth parents.

Indidarc OTM, Melinor, Lord - High Wizard of the northern kingdom of Deran, nobleman and confidante of royalty in the Kingdoms of the Northern Alliance. He adopted both Eric and Saren after his own children were grown. A formidable mage and genius with knowledge of magic, science, medicine, literature and history, Melinor is fluent in several languages. A kind but somewhat absent-minded man, he is singularly focused on thwarting evil plots in the known lands. He is a member of the Order of the Three Magi, a Christian religious organization composed chiefly of wizards and scholars. His wife, Anne, passed away prior to the start of the Grey Riders novels.

Inscrutable Globe – A magic spell of concealing that prevents auditory, visual or magical observation.

Irial - The halfling god of harvests, craftsmen and home, Irial is a benevolent deity who sometimes counts elves and humans among his adherents. The precepts of Irial are hospitality, kindness, courtesy, respect for people, animals and nature, and steadfastness in the face of hardship, whether caused by nature or evil designs.

Ja'al - Also known as the Manipulator Church (for their penchant for twisting words, lying and otherwise using others callously for their own ends) the Ja'al are one of the evil religions on Damora. The cult is a polytheistic religion worshiping a number of harsh and cruel deities. The precepts of the Ja'al are world domination, rule of the strong over the weak, eugenics, personal gain at the cost of others, and treachery.

Jeffries, William, Lord – A Baron of Morlan, he is one of the regents of the Catrin Magical Academy. He is urbane, charming, lecherous and greedy but a competent researcher with knowledge of ancient civilizations. He used to be married to Lady Ravida (q.v.) until he grew tired of her.

Jekka – A drink from Gorostol made from a dark brown bean that grows on vines, it is a cross between coffee and chicory and is highly prized for its invigorating qualities and smooth flavor.

Jered – A large nation south of Torosc, it is a confederacy of kingdoms originally established by pirates. Possessing miles of coastline, a multitude of islands, and a tropical climate, Jered is wealthy, powerful, and an ally of Torosc and Morlan in opposing the Northern Alliance.

Kalar, Ahlana II, PhD, OST – The Queen of Deran, she is twenty-nine years old, with a dusky complexion, brown hair and black eyes. A scholar and wizard by trade, she met Stephen at a religious retreat in her teens and never forgot him — nor he, her. She is sunny, optimistic, and resourceful and has an impressive arsenal of magic devices.

Kalar, Stephen IV, OSM – The King of Deran, Stephen is in his early thirties and has extensive experience in both the freelance sell-sword profession and military matters. Ahlana is his wife. A cautious and thoughtful man, he has learned the value of thinking before acting as well as the need to act swiftly if needed. He has black hair and blue eyes and tends to worry over possible outcomes. He is a paladin (a holy warrior dedicated to a religion — in this case, Christianity).

Kalik, Ilyan – Vardu priest of the Cult of the Red Moon. He is in charge of a secret Vardish project but has knowledge of a Skull Gate and Ja'al forces in his area. An average-looking man with a pleasant, inoffensive manner, his blue eyes betray a cold and uncaring soul.

<u>Kaljirre</u> (Dw. *"sky mirror"*) - Beautiful lake near the Gorostoli capital city of Meridian.

<u>Kantar</u> – An elven apprentice to George Oxbridge, he detests Megan Alenar and, together with his friend Olik, takes every opportunity to torment her.

<u>Kelani</u> – A half-daemon wizard charged with guarding special magic items related to the Skull Gates. Kelani is given guardianship of Brandawyn Alenar after Adina has trouble bringing Brandi to heel as a Ja'al seductress and agent. Kelani uses Brandi as a guard and servant while Adina goes off to the Ja'al Council to figure out how Brandi is able to resist her magical compulsions.

<u>Kentridge</u> – A city in Torosc from where Altus Volan (q.v.) hails.

<u>Khelios (Giantbane)</u> (Dw. *"sharpest"*)- A magical dwarven sword found by Buck Bydecy while on the quest for *Whitehorse Peak*, it bestows two abilities on its wielder: knowledge of the dwarven language and the ability to detect evil. It is particularly deadly to giants or any creature with giant blood (including cyclops). It has an unnerving tendency to suddenly launch itself at an enemy giant, dragging Buck along for the ride.

<u>Kortos</u> – An alliance of duchies on the great island of Derelia, northwest from Deran across the Great Sea.

<u>Kosorovsk, Roger IX</u> – Ruler of the Sovereign Duchy of Rokon, Roger is a canny, hard-bitten widower. He is gruff and practical but loyal and efficient. A Knight of the Order of the Falcon, he has fought many campaigns against savage goblin and ogre tribes from the northern wastes. He has six adult children and fifteen grandchildren.

<u>Lervion, Hannah</u> – The sister of Handor, Hannah was studying at a military academy at the time of the death of both her parents. She is forthright, honest, friendly and a fierce defender of her family with a high sense of justice. Temporarily reunited with her lost brother in *Assassin Prince*, she tragically lost him while trying to escape from the clutches of the Ja'al and her conniving uncle. A brown-eyed brunette, she is fit and very attractive but acts like the girl next door. She has a deep and abiding affection for Connor Lomin, who finds her irresistible.

<u>Lervion, Handor (Hlerv)</u> - A gnome wizard and spy, he joined the Grey Riders in *Eye of Truth* and helped them clear Buck Bydecy's name and avenge

the murder of Andyn Eleandir's husband. He was secretive and somewhat aloof in order to protect his secret identity as the heir of a shipping magnate's fortune. After stealing the Helm of Shadows, he escaped to his hometown of Meridian, Gorostol. He freed his sister from her Ja'al captors, but lost his life in the process. In the end, he regretted not appealing to the other Riders for help in his quest and is now celebrated as a hero.

<u>Lich</u> - An undead wizard. Liches are created when a wizard or sorcerer makes a pact with Dark Powers in order to forestall his/her own death, gaining immense magical power and undead status in the bargain. They exude an aura of terror but are greatly harmed by holy spells and items.

<u>Light of Justice</u> – Title given to honor someone who has destroyed a lich – a phenomenal feat considering the rarity and incredible power of that type of undead. Lights of Justice are rare to say the least. Andyn Eleandir was awarded the title for destroying Zhinia Margoth.

<u>Lomin, Connor</u> - Another of the original Grey Riders, Connor is a halfling who hails from Evendale. Serious, but with a somewhat ribald sense of humor, Connor appears stoic and sober most of the time. He is knowledgeable about traps, curious about ancient ruins and secrets, and wields a broadsword, a rather heavy weapon for a halfling. Dark-eyed and dark-haired, he has a muscular build but has an almost uncanny skill for moving unseen. His pegasus is named Phantom.

<u>Lomin, Janey</u> - Deceased wife of Connor Lomin. Along with her daughter, Rose, she perished in a plague known as the Whispering Death, which is thought to have been released into Evendale by Zhinia Margoth.

<u>Margoth, Zhinia</u> - A former Paragon Queen who used fell and evil magics to transform herself into a lich to avoid death near the end of the Paragon Age. She was a first cousin of Saint Alyssa of Tor Haldin (q.v.). Vicious, conniving, and cruel, Margoth appeared as a skeleton with pinpoint eyes of purple light, clothed in rotting royal robes and wielding a skull-headed staff. Her battle standard was a fanged skull with a crown of flame. She created a cursed magic helmet of teleportation named the Helm of Shadows. Andyn Eleandir destroyed her at the Battle of Hillton, Deran using a powerful holy relic.

<u>Marolpeth</u> – (Elv. *"blue grove"*) An elven city of about 25,000 people in the eastern part of Terenai.

<u>Martin, Cassandra, OST</u> – The Countess of Whitmark, Kortos, she is a

former freelance wizard. She and her family are friends of several famous retired freelance sellswords, including the Blue Mark and his wife, the Count and Countess of Deorfast, Caria and Caridan Meraloy, and the Lady and Lord of Sun Plains. A calm, no-nonsense woman, she is the perfect foil for her boisterous, energetic husband, Justin. She is a human woman of average height, with soft brown hair and grey eyes.

<u>Martin, Justin, OF</u> – The husband of Lady Cassandra, Justin is the fourth son of one of the Dukes of Kortos, a land ruled by a council of sovereign nobility. A human Knight of the Order of the Falcon with considerable military command experience, he and Cassandra are sent to Deran to help coordinate efforts to thwart the Ja'al worldwide. Of average height with dark brown hair and eyes, he is inquisitive and good-humored.

<u>Melissa</u> - An Elohir (q.v.) knight tasked with watching for the Grey Riders to arrive at Twinspire Mountain. She gave the Crown of Saint Alyssa to Andyn Eleandir to use in bringing down Zhinia Margoth. She also provided the angelic sword Rindara Starblade to Dar Cabot, the elven fire-blade Tiuz to Connor Lomin, and the magic spear Fidelis to Eric Indidarc. She is wise, kind, fierce in defending against evil and seems to be perpetually amused by the Grey Riders, whom she regards with great affection. She is stunningly gorgeous but acts like she doesn't know it. She is married to an Elohir named Coloman and her brother is named Simon.

<u>Meraloy, Caria, OST</u> – An elven mage of the Order of Saint Terenil (*Orden Sanctus Terenilensis*), she is sent from the Emperor of Terenai to assist Hannah Lervion. She is married to Caridan.

<u>Meraloy, Caridan, Colonel</u> – The husband of Caria, Caridan is a retired freelance warrior and Colonel in the Imperial Elven Army. He travels to Meridian to assist Hannah Lervion, an agent of the Northern Alliance.

<u>Mercato, Karen, MD, OP, OTM</u> – Edward Simpson's personal physician and a member of the Order of the Three Magi. She is also an elven Dominican nun.

<u>Meridian</u> – The capital city of Gorostol, it is a large metropolis in the foothills overlooking a beautiful lake known as the Kaljirre. It has over 200,000 inhabitants.

<u>Mikman, Kili</u> – A halfling spy in the service of the Ja'al High Command, Kili has a long history with the Grey Riders. He initially tried to recruit the

Alenar sisters to the service of the Ja'al, but the girls joined the Grey Riders instead in *Whitehorse Peak*. Later, in *Eye of Truth*, he kidnapped Buck's father in an attempt to slay the Riders but this also failed. He has an intense hatred for Connor Lomin. Kili carries an assortment of clever devices and disguises for spying and following targets. His cousin, Vidi Darkwater, is a notorious thug and assassin.

Mindra – A Verian hero from the Paragon Age. A soldier in the service of her king, she followed his orders without question until, in a vision from Verian, she realized that he was being manipulated by his councilors into oppressing those who disagreed with him. Taking up arms against the councilors, she was pursued but prevailed with the aid of the Church of Verian. She ultimately defeated her enemies, converting two of them and returning the king to the ways of justice. She is the epitome of the concepts of mercy, bravery, wisdom and discernment and is often invoked by those seeking to cut through the lies of the forces of evil. An order of knighthood was established in her honor in Terenai.

Morlan – A nation to the south of Torosc allied with the Dark Powers, Morlan is ruled by a Wizard King. It is a large nation with considerable natural resources and territorial ambitions. The climate is warm and humid much of the year and it contains vast tracts of verdant jungle. It is allied with Torosc and Jered.

Neralia - Evil goddess of child sacrifice, murder and domination, Neralia is one of the members of the Ja'al pantheon. Similarities between her church and the defunct worship of Garon-Zith have led many to speculate that the two goddesses are one and the same.

Northern Alliance - A multinational pact similar to NATO in the real world, the Alliance is composed of Deran, Astarel, Rokon, Eldir, Evendale and Terenai.

Northpoint – A large city (pop. ~70,000) on the northern coast of Torosc it is blessed with a commanding strategic location on a landmass that juts out into the Great Sea. It boasts natural harbors on its north and south flanks.

Oakmoor - The capital city of Deran, home to over a quarter of a million people. Oakmoor is based on three large hills at the confluence of the East River and Lonmar Rivers. It has several suburbs in addition to the main city proper.

<u>Octavio, Arless</u> – An extremely wealthy and arrogant young merchant in the Deranese city of Fenbluff, he has many connections throughout the Northern lands, of both the savory and unsavory varieties. The Ja'al have him on their short list of future allies, whether he likes it or not.

<u>Ogre</u> - Large, human-like creatures with fangs and odd-colored hair, ogres are brutish, violent, and not particularly bright. Their leaders are usually the more intelligent members of a particular tribe. Some of their number are smart enough to use magic. They are usually over seven feet tall and three hundred and fifty pounds. Used as shock troops by the forces of evil, Ogres are also greedy and fearless.

<u>Olik</u> – Elven apprentice to George Oxbridge. He secretly lusts after Megan Alenar but since Oxbridge has forbidden anyone to molest his most valuable slaves, he now hates her instead.

<u>Oxbridge, George</u> – A Wizard of the First Circle of the Ja'al High Council, George Oxbridge is almost ninety years old but looks forty years younger thanks to potions he brewed using forbidden magic. He is charged to carry out a special project that concerns the Skull Gates and purchases Megan Alenar from Adina. He is not a harsh master, but sees Megan and Varienne (q.v.) as simple tools rather than people. He has no attraction to women as such but a keen interest in anything that brings him magical power. He has a burning curiosity about anything mysterious, such as the source of Megan's increasing magical abilities.

<u>Paragon Age</u> – One of the major epochs of the history of Damora, it was ushered in by the event known as the Skyfire, when humans first appeared and brought Christianity with them. Records prior to this time are sketchy and incomplete. The age is so named because of the rise of rulers of petty kingdoms who were all superior practitioners of a particular branch of a freelance career (i.e. warrior, healer, mage, etc.). It ended when some of the Paragon rulers succumbed to evil influences and tried to expand their nations at the expense of their neighbors. Alyssa of Tor Aldin and Zhinia Margoth were two Paragon rulers.

<u>Pegasus</u> – A winged horse. In the Grey Riders novels, they are omnivores due to their part-raptor heritage and can be domesticated. They are wildly expensive to acquire and maintain and are the fastest flying mounts alive.

<u>Perez, Jolene</u> – Standing only as tall as a female Elf, the black-haired, dark-

eyed Matriarch of Verian rules both the nation of Eldir and her church. Just thirty-four years old, she was elected to the position upon the death of her mentor. Due to her small size and youth, she is often underestimated, a factor that she plays to her advantage over and over again. She is unmarried.

Preservation Bead – A small bead of amber imbued with a mighty spell affecting spacetime. If broken over an object, it releases a Preservation Net, a magical effect that reduces the flow of time to one ten-millionth of normal for anything it covers. Preservation Beads are extremely expensive and lose their potency after a time period measured in weeks.

Puup - Buck Bydecy's pet pigeon who somehow manages to avoid getting killed despite being in or near several battles. By the time of *The Skull Gates*, he has retired to the gardens of the Papal Nuncio's residence in Saint Martin's, Deran.

Quartermaster's Bag – A magic bag that can contain many times its volume in items. Highly prized by military units, they are not the most glamorous of magic items, but are extremely useful and difficult to make.

Ravida (Kaldasa), Lady - A colleague of George Oxbridge, she is a Ja'al wizard and member of the cult leadership. She was formerly married to William Jeffries, a Baron of Morlan, but divorced him when his womanizing became an Achilles heel in her quest for advancement in the cult. She is arrogant and dismissive of those she perceives as beneath her station.

Red Moon, Cult of – An offshoot of the Vardu religion, the Red Moon is a secretive group known for human sacrifice, violence, treachery and territorial ambitions. Its origin is unknown but it uses the image of a bloody Kaliri (q.v.) in its symbology.

Rindara Starblade – A magic bastard sword given to Dar Cabot by Melissa of Celestia. It has a night-black blade that glitters with the light of a thousand stars and is especially potent against daemons and the undead. It was crafted on Melissa's home world.

Roadwardens – The state police/highway patrol of Gorostol.

Rokon – A member of the Northern Alliance, Rokon is one of the smaller nations. Originally a duchy of the Patriarchate of Eldir, Rokon broke away prior to the forming of the Alliance. The two countries have since resolved their differences, attributable to the need for teamwork as required by the

Alliance charter. Rokon has a climate much like Norway in the real world.

Saint Kira, Order of – Christian order of military scouts, guides, mages and agents operating worldwide. They are often members of elite strike teams.

Saint Martin's (Town) - Major port city in Deran (pop ~ 80,000). It is the seat of the Christian church and the base of the Curia, the ruling council of Christianity on Damora. The Papal Nuncio makes his residence there.

Saint Michael, Order of - Christian military order of knights and warriors dedicated to protecting the innocent against evil. They are often used as heavy assault infantry or cavalry but include mages and clerics among their numbers.

Sending Mirror – The Damoran equivalent of a cell phone, it can be used to communicate over distances by showing an image of another person who has a similarly designed mirror. Many are useful for short range communications and some can transmit and receive over vast distances. The signals can be tracked, however, and the more powerful the mirror, the easier it is to track.

Shadow Lake - Medium sized freshwater lake in the wilderness east of Evendale. It lies in the shadow of the local mountains, one of which is Twin-spire. It is near the location of a ruined fortress where the Grey Riders found the Helm of Shadows and were given powerful magic items, such as Tiuz.

Shriek - A magical infantry sword found by the Grey Riders near Twin-spire Mountain. It makes its wielder stealthier and does great harm to undead. It was owned by Handor Lervion and his sister, Hannah, now carries it in his name.

Shrikes – Another assassins guild on Damora, it often competes with the Crossed Swords and the Whiteclaw for business. Its emblem is a small black bird sitting atop a white skull.

Simpson OTM, O.Praem, Edward Cardinal – The official representative of Christianity to Damora, the Papal Nuncio. Edward Simpson is a spare human man who appears to be about seventy years old but is rumored to be much older. His nation of origin is unknown. Though he has great knowledge and is alleged to have awesome, otherworldly powers, he rarely takes part in any action and is content to lead the Order of the Three Magi and

Christendom on Damora. His demeanor is humble, thoughtful, and kind, yet demanding. He is known for asking probing questions. To those he knows well, he insists they call him "Father Edward".

<u>Skyfire</u> - A mysterious event from antiquity that changed the face of Damora. Legends say that visitors from another place arrived on disks or globes of fire and brought with them the Christian faith. The location of the actual arrival and the details of the event are lost in history. As a point of reference, it is rumored to have taken place more than 5000 years before the events of *Whitehorse Peak* (the first of the Grey Riders novels).

<u>Skreet</u> – Small daemons from Hades, Skreets look like a cross between an eagle and a boar. Used primarily as skirmishers, light infantry or air patrol, they tend to swarm opponents. Able to use a variety of weapons, they also have limited magical abilities.

<u>Skullhead Legion</u> - Paramilitary guard force in the service of the Ja'al cult leadership. Known for their brutality, greed and utter disregard for life, they are often used as shock troops. They are fanatical and fight to the death.

<u>Skull Gate</u> – Horrid structures made of iron bars and the bones of sacrifices, the Gates are the brainchild of the Ja'al cult. Fully thirty feet tall and twenty wide, they are spacetime portals to Hades, the homeland of the daemons (Fallen Ones).

<u>Spectral Sword / Sword of the Devoted Defender</u> – A magical blade, it is actually contained in a small silver brooch. Connor Lomin owns one as a reward for his part in the victory over Zhinia Margoth. It is individually keyed to one person only. At the command word, a misty, ethereal sword leaps into being in front of the owner of the brooch. The spectral blade defends its owner and attacks any other opponents on command. It can harm apparitions such as ghosts, specters and wraiths.

<u>Star-steel</u> - A light and strong metal similar to high carbon spring steel with some additional alloying. It is very expensive and is often used in the fashioning of weapons. Its metallurgical cousin, Star-silver, is used for armor.

<u>Stealth</u> - Eric Indidarc's enchanted familiar. Summoned from a magic item called a Companion Pin, it transforms to a realistic hawk upon command. When active, it gives Eric the ability to see through its eyes as it flies high above.

<u>Sun Lake</u> - Body of fresh water near the Deranese city of Hillton.

<u>Sword-Knight</u> – One of the orders of knighthood of Astarel, bestowed by the royal house or nobility. All are hereditary (can be passed along to successors). Sword-knights are the lowest order, followed by Shield-Knights, Helm-Knights and Crown-Knights (Royal Guard). Buck Bydecy is a Sword-Knight.

<u>Tallemar</u> – A major suburb of Oakmoor, Deran, it is home to more than 30,000 souls. It is ruled by the DeMeys, Earl Terenil and Countess Saren.

<u>Targanon</u> – A nation across the Great Sea from Morlan, its terrain and ecology are as varied as its people. Vast jungles, verdant plains, towering mountains and scorching deserts can all be found within its borders. Though some areas are very civilized, others are nothing short of barbaric.

<u>Terenai</u> (Elv. *"Realm of the Elves"*) - The hereditary homeland of the Elven people, Terenai lies due south of Deran and also shares borders with Evendale, Gorostol and Merdail. A verdant and fruitful land, it is heavily forested in places. It is ruled by an Emperor (or Empress) and is the oldest of the nations on Damora. Its capital city is Mil-Tereth (Elv. *"King's Palace"*).

<u>Thivin's Wort</u> – An herb used in making designer (coded) poisons and their antidotes.

<u>Three Magi, Order of the</u> - Secretive order of Christian mages and scholars in service of the Papal Nuncio. Composed of extremely skilled practitioners, it counts Melinor Indidarc as one of its number (and he is one of the few publicly acknowledged members).

<u>Tigris Infernales</u> – (Lat. *"Tiger Hellish"*) A breed of half-tiger, half-human daemon from Hades. Winged and capable of using magic, they are also a deadly sword fighters.

<u>Tiller, Henry</u> – The Prime Minister of Evendale, Tiller is the consummate politician: affable and optimistic on the outside but clever, resourceful and somewhat underhanded behind closed doors. He enjoys the support of the halfling nation because of his ability to anticipate situations and be proactive. He is three and a half feet tall with black hair, brown eyes and an easy smile. He is married and has six children. Unknown to most of the world, he is also an accomplished agent and a deadly shot with a crossbow.

<u>Tiuz</u> – (Elv. *"fire/ flame"*) An infantry sword resembling a gladius, it is a

magic blade of ancient origin wielded by Connor Lomin. At a command word, it blazes to life with a fiery edge.

Torosc – (Dw. *"kingdoms"*) An oppressive land south of Gorostol ruled by a council of five Archons, it is an amalgamation of several petty kingdoms welded together during a time of upheaval. One of its provinces, Coastwatch, was the home of the Alenar sisters prior to the death of their parents. It is the center of activity for evil forces with designs on the lands of the Northern Alliance.

Troll - Large, brutish bipedal creatures similar to ogres but taller and heavier. Trolls are hairless and can have four arms rather than two. Somewhat related to giants, they are considerably less sophisticated. They prefer mountains and forests and will kill and eat anything edible. Cruel, greedy and selfish, they can be outwitted by smarter creatures. Some more intelligent of their species can learn to use rudimentary magic. Trolls have the unnerving talent of being able to blend in with trees and rocks by merely holding still; they use this ability to ambush the unwary.

Twinspire Peak - A mountain in the wilderness east of Evendale near Shadow Lake, it held secrets related to the Helm of Shadows.

Tyler - A major city of Astarel (pop. ~ 100,000) located on the coast just north of the border with Deran It is known for its large harbor, excellent fishing fleet and naval base. It is the hometown of Buck Bydecy.

Vampire Rose – An evil, semi-intelligent plant with blood-red blossoms and black leaves, vampire roses mesmerize the unwary with their flowers and then slice their victims to ribbons with long thorns, feeding on the blood of the dying.

Vardu – The religion of the god of death, Vardu close second to the Ja'al as the most feared of the Dark Faiths on Damara. Adherents are known as the Vardish. The religious symbol is a skull and crossed swords. Priestly vestments are usually dead black, a deathly grey or bone-white. Due to their connection to the undead, they are in competition with the Cla'Agik, who claim the sphere of corruption and rot. They also compete with Arachnia of the Ja'al for rule of the sphere of assassination and Torvu for rule over the undead. The church is highly organized.

Varienne (Walker) – A young blonde human woman from Deran kidnapped by Viper slavers, she befriended Altus Volan, the son of her captors, and captured his heart. George Oxbridge purchased her for her healing talents. She became a helper and confidante of Megan Alenar.

<u>Varon</u> – Hill sprite captain who works with the Handor family.

<u>Verian (Elv. "*Lord-Highest*")</u>- Elven god of forests and nature. Followers of Verian worship in open structures usually in groves or copses of trees. The organizational structure is somewhat loose, with a council of high priests and priestesses making decisions of doctrine and teachings every year. Verian teaches that liberty, love, kindness, right living, charity and respect for creation are paramount. Andyn Eleandir is a priestess of Verian. The prayer "*Verian, ald-adani!*" ("Lord-Highest, Heaven's Light!"), is used by Andyn to destroy or repel undead.

<u>Vipers</u> (slavers) - An organized criminal group hailing from Jered specializing in human trafficking and drugs.

<u>Volan, Altus</u> – The son of Viper slavers, Altus began to have second thoughts about the family business when his parents captured Varienne Walker. After trying unsuccessfully to purchase Varienne's freedom himself, he left home and joined the Skullhead Legion and became an officer. Further disillusioned by his life, he had a turning point when he and his band captured Megan Alenar. When she was freed by her relatives, they set him free and offered him a new chance at life – which he took in hopes of finding Varienne.

<u>War Fiend</u> – Slender, human-sized daemons from Hades with double bat wings and a dragon tail, War Fiends are savage, intelligent and versatile. They are used as anything from combat wizards to medium infantry. They have access to a deadly array of battle magic and are swift, agile fliers.

<u>Whiteclaw</u> – An assassin's guild on Damora that often competes with the Crossed Swords and the Shrikes for customers. Their emblem is a white, clawed hand. They have, in the past, targeted the Grey Riders.

<u>Whitehorse Peak</u> - A large mountain north of Forester, Deran, so named because its geology and snow-fall pattern reminded the people nearby of a white-maned horse. It is the site of the recovery of the pegasi (as described in *Whitehorse Peak*) that the Grey Riders own at the time of *The Skull Gates*. Its dwarven name is Kelematris (Dw. "*Mountain -Horse*").

<u>Zanilor</u> – A high priest of the Ja'al, he was the church's representative to

Zhinia Margoth and brought a sizable number of Ja'al troops to the Battle of Hillton. When Andyn Eleandir destroyed Margoth, he saw the army disintegrate and withdrew his force as quickly as he could. He is a clever and resourceful survivor.

ABOUT THE AUTHOR

A route to fantasy fiction through the aerospace industry may seem an odd one to take, but PG Badzey has been writing stories since grammar school and has never stopped, even though his path took an unconventional turn for someone interesting in writing. A trained systems engineer, he kept up with creative writing and coursework throughout a career working on the C-17 airlifter, the International Space Station, the Delta IV Rocket and the James Webb Space Telescope. He has enjoyed and been influenced by JRR Tolkien, C.S. Lewis, Katherine Kurtz, Christopher Stasheff, Terry Brooks and C. Dale Brittain, to name a few. He is the author of the first four novels in the *Grey Riders* series, *Whitehorse Peak, Eye of Truth, Helm of Shadows,* and *Assassin Prince*, all of which received 5-star ratings from Readers' Favorite. Other publications include short stories published in *Dragonlaugh*, an online fantasy humor magazine, and *Brevity in Paradise* (the Orange County Writers Guild (OCWG) anthology). PG Badzey has studied martial arts for many years, helps mentor a world-class high school robotics team, and is active in his parish community. He lives in California, is a member of the OCWG and has taught seminars on fantasy writing in Orange County Libraries.

Find out more about the World of the Grey Riders at
https://pgbadzey.wordpress.com!